The Vintage Dress Shop in Primrose Hill

Also by Annie Darling

ANNIE DARLING

The Vintage Dress Shop in Primrose Hill

HODDER

First published in Great Britain in 2023 by Hodder & Stoughton
An Hachette UK company

2

Copyright © Annie Darling 2023

A CIP catalogue record for this title is available from the British Library

Paperback ISBN 978 1 399 71532 4
eBook ISBN 978 1 399 71530 0

Typeset in Plantin light by Manipal Technologies Limited

Printed and bound in Great Britain by Clays Ltd, Elcograf S.p.A.

Hodder & Stoughton policy is to use papers that are natural, renewable
and recyclable products and made from wood grown in sustainable forests.
The logging and manufacturing processes are expected to conform to the
environmental regulations of the country of origin.

Hodder & Stoughton Ltd
Carmelite House
50 Victoria Embankment
London EC4Y 0DZ

www.hodder.co.uk

'Vain trifles as they seem, clothes have, they say, more important offices than to merely keep us warm. They change our view of the world and the world's view of us.'

Virginia Woolf, *Orlando*

Dedicated to anyone who's ever known the transformative power of a really, really good dress.

PART ONE

Chapter One

Sophy Stevens was having a bad day.

Correction. A bad week.

Make that a bad month.

Maybe even a bad year. In fact, she might even have been born during a bad moment in the cosmoverse when none of the constellations were aligned, Mercury was well and truly in retrograde and it was a full moon.

It would explain a hell of a lot.

But right now she could only focus on one bad day at a time and, as bad days went, this particular Thursday was fair to middling.

As Sophy came out of Chalk Farm station, the February sky was a perfect blue. Not a cloud in sight, which was odd when she felt so downcast.

It was really too cold to eat ice cream, and Sophy would have much preferred a large white wine, but she'd been meeting Johnno at Marine Ices for years. The tradition was long-running enough that she could remember the ice cream parlour when it was in its original spot, just opposite the tube station. Run by an Italian family, Marine Ices was a London institution, and one that Sophy hoped would never fall out of favour because a large bowl of their hazelnut ice cream would be her Death Row meal.

It was also a tradition that sometimes Johnno would turn up and sometimes he wouldn't. Sophy took her phone out of her bag to check if there was an apologetic message heavy with emojis. Though sometimes, when he was a no-show, he didn't even message. Not for a few days.

Just to make sure, though it was a case of hope over experience, Sophy messaged him.

There in five.

But when Sophy reached the ice cream parlour in three, she was amazed to see Johnno already waiting for her with a knickerbocker glory in front of him, two spoons, because he still thought she was eight.

'Kiddo! I swear you get more beautiful by the day,' he greeted her, with the broad Australian accent that even thirty years in London couldn't wither.

'I have a huge spot on my chin,' Sophy said as Johnno stood up so he could hug her. He wasn't much taller than Sophy and she was only five foot four in her socks. But what Johnno lacked in height, he made up for in sheer charisma.

It wasn't just that he was wearing a pink and white cowboy shirt tucked into leather trousers or that what little hair he had, close-cropped, was the same shade of neon pink as his shirt; it was Johnno's presence.

He could charm the birds right out of the trees. He could make the starchiest, stiffest people break out into sunny smiles (a skill that came in particularly useful when dealing with traffic wardens). He could walk into a room and within five minutes he was everyone's best friend. Johnno was a chancer. A ducker and diver. A wheeler-dealer. A cowboy. A wide boy. A bad boy. Or as Sophy's mum had said gently to six-year-old Sophy when they'd waited in vain for an hour at Marine Ices one Saturday afternoon for Johnno, 'I know that he can be tremendous fun but the thing is, Soph, you shouldn't really expect too much from your dad.'

It was a lesson that Sophy had learned the hard way. Though she couldn't even remember a time when the three of them had been a family because Johnno had left, or rather Caroline had thrown him and all his stuff out onto the street, when Sophy was still a baby.

Sophy was ten when Caroline had got married (Johnno had promised to marry her when she first got pregnant but never got round to it) and she always thought of Mike as her proper dad. A dad who'd done PTA evenings and school plays and ferried her around north London to dance classes and competitions, sleepovers and trips to Brent Cross shopping centre to hang out with her friends.

But biologically Johnno was still her dad. He might have been a somewhat absent, unreliable presence in Sophy's life but, when they did manage to meet up, he was very good at imparting useful life advice. ('Never trust a bloke who doesn't tip well.' 'Anyone you meet after midnight is up to no good.' 'Always make sure that you've got a spare pair of pants and a tenner on you.') He was also quite handy when Sophy needed backup. Like the time she'd been working as a waitress in a French restaurant in Soho and her boss had put his hand up her skirt, then sacked her when she'd objected. Johnno had rolled up, fixed her ex-boss (who was a good head taller than him) with a flint-eyed look and then threatened to break every bone in his body and pluck out his internal organs for the pigeons in Leicester Square to feast on. Even Sophy had believed him. Her lecherous ex-boss had taken three hundred quid out of the till, given it to Sophy and begged her forgiveness.

You had to take the rough with the smooth when it came to Johnno, so Sophy sat down, picked up her spoon and asked him how he'd been.

'Can't complain, Soph,' Johnno said, because he wasn't a moaner and couldn't stand whingers. Especially whinging Poms. 'The sun's shining, birds are singing, I'm eating ice cream with my beautiful daughter, what more could a bloke ask for?'

'Right, yeah, when you put it like that.' Sophy took another mouthful of ice cream and wondered how best to lead in to her news. 'You don't miss Australia at all? It's been ages since you visited.'

Johnno steepled his hands, so Sophy could see the words 'love' and 'hate' tattooed on his knuckles. Johnno's life motto was that it was better to regret something that you had done rather than something you hadn't done, but he'd once told Sophy that the only thing that he really regretted was having the word 'hate' tattooed on his body. 'I went back for Mum's sixtieth,' he calculated. 'That was what? A couple of years ago?'

'She's going to be seventy-three this year,' Sophy said gently.

'That so? Bloody hell.' Johnno widened his faded-denim-blue eyes in disbelief. 'So, you're in regular contact then with your grandparents? I know your other lot want me horsewhipped.'

Not horsewhipped, but it was true that Caroline's parents didn't have a good word to say about Johnno, and as for his own parents, Bob and Jean just sighed a lot when his name came up during the regular FaceTime chats Sophy had with them.

'I speak to them, occasionally,' she explained now. 'Well, once a month. Sometimes twice a month.'

'Well, why shouldn't you? I must give them a ring,' Johnno said vaguely, which meant that he might remember this urge at some point in the future but who could even guess if he'd act on it.

'In fact, I'll be talking to them a lot more quite soon,' Sophy said, because now she had the perfect lead-in to her news. She smiled brightly at Johnno, who stared back at her unmoved (another piece of his life advice: 'Never trust someone who smiles with all their teeth'). 'You see, I've decided, it's just as well you're sitting down, I've decided that … I'm …'

6

'Spit it out, Soph. Neither of us are getting any younger.'

Sophy put down her spoon, so she could clasp her hands together. 'I'm emigrating. To Australia.'

'Say bloody what now?' Johnno was usually so laid-back that it was a wonder he didn't fall over but now he reared back in his seat, face turned to the heavens so that, for one horrible moment, Sophy feared that he was having a stroke. 'Are you out of your bloody mind?'

No, not a stroke. Just processing her big news.

'I've never explored the Australian part of my heritage ...'

'That's because the Australian part of your heritage is a sheep station in the middle of bloody nowhere.'

'It's practically on the coast and Grandad says that I can borrow the truck whenever I want to.'

'So you're going to live with them?'

'To start with. It's their golden wedding anniversary at the end of August, which you should know about because they're your par—'

'And can you even drive?'

'Technically I can. Mike and Mum gave me lessons for my eighteenth and I passed my test on the fourth go, but who drives in London? I mean, there's nowhere to park and it's super-expensive and—'

'You're going off-topic, love,' Johnno advised, leaning forward now so he could stare at Sophy like he was seeing her for the first time. 'What does your mum say about this?'

'She's getting used to the idea.' Sophy decided to gloss over Caroline's reaction, which had mostly involved shouting, 'Have you taken complete leave of your senses?' very loudly. 'I know that it all seems like this has come out of the blue but it hasn't. Not really. I need this. I've been wanting to change things up for ages. I just needed a push...'

Her voice was wobbling like washing on the line on a windy day and she could feel the tears begin to stream down her face and plop into the half-melted ice cream.

'What gave you the push, kiddo?' Johnno asked. Sophy knew that Johnno didn't like whingers and that really their relationship, such as it was, was all surface. Neither of them went too deep. So she'd planned to be very positive about her news; but now she was crying and it all came spilling out.

'I got made redundant,' she choked out. 'Not even redundant. I turned up for work, like I have done every day for the last ten years, and the shop was boarded up and there was a note on the door from the official receivers that the company had gone into administration. So, no redundancy pay; in fact, I'm still owed for December's wages, all my Christmas overtime, which I'm probably never going to get.'

'Soph, sweetheart, I can give you the money...'

'You don't have to do that,' Sophy protested. 'I can find another job. I have ten years' retail experience. I've been an exemplary employee. Except now I can't even get the area manager to answer my messages on LinkedIn and give me a reference.'

'They'd better give you a reference,' Johnno growled, but this wasn't something he could fix by turning up at the company's shuttered headquarters and threatening violence.

That wasn't even the worst of it. 'Then when I got home, I was pretty upset and, when I told Egan, he didn't even say he was sorry. He just asked me how I was going to pay the rent.'

'I never liked him,' Johnno said of Sophy's boyfriend of the last five years, though they'd only met once. Johnno had all but crushed Egan's fingers to pulp when they'd shaken hands. 'Anyway, doesn't he own that flat?'

'How do you remember that?' He didn't even know how old his actual mother was and yet Johnno had squirreled away the information that Egan owned his own flat. Or rather his parents had bought it for him. 'I didn't want to leech off him, so we split the bills and I paid rent—'

'You were paying him rent *and* bills. OK, me and that Egan are going to be having words...'

'You won't be having words because me and that Egan have broken up and so now I'm thirty, *thirty*, and I'm unemployed and I'm single and I'm homeless,' Sophy summed up, then she couldn't speak any more but sat there hiccupping and sobbing and trying to dry her eyes with a napkin, which scoured her face raw because it was better suited to mopping up ice cream spills.

Johnno let out a shaky breath. 'Homeless? Caroline and Mike won't let you move back in?'

'Well, not technically homeless. They're happy to have me but I have to sleep on the sofa because Mum's turned my old bedroom into a *home spa*.' Sophy finished on a wail.

'So, hate to rag on you when you're down, but is this why you're set on moving to Oz? Because it's a bloody stupid idea.'

'No, it's not. It's a great idea.' But Sophy didn't even have a chance to list the reasons why it was a great idea because Johnno had launched into the story she'd already heard many times about how he couldn't wait to leave Australia and had followed his mates over, who were in a punk band called The Birthday Party. 'Nick Cave, you heard of him? He's done all right for himself. And so have I, because I'm not up to my elbows in sheep dung. You're not going, Soph. I forbid it.'

Sophy stopped crying in favour of laughing. 'You forbid it? Right! I'm an actual adult person. You can't forbid me to do anything and you're the person who always tells me that I should try everything at least once. Well. I'm trying Australia and you can't stop me!'

'But emigrating…' Johnno spluttered.

'Yes, emigrating, because have I mentioned that I'm thirty and I'm stuck and I lost my job of ten years that I didn't even like that much and London is the most expensive city in the world after Tokyo and there isn't a single eligible man on the dating apps, it's dick pics as far as the eye can see, and I just need something to be different.' Sophy banged her fist on the table. '*I* need to be different.'

'You can be different without haring off halfway across the bloody world—'

'Not another word,' Sophy snapped, and she knew she must be channelling her mother because Johnno mimed zipping his lips shut and sat back with arms folded and a cowed expression.

They sat in silence. It wasn't at all how Sophy had thought this conversation would go. She and Johnno never argued. They kept things light. It was what they did. It was how they functioned.

Of course Johnno, being Johnno, couldn't keep quiet for longer than one minute and fifteen seconds, though that had to be a personal best. 'Anyway,' he said. 'You can't just go to Australia. They're fussy about who they let in. You'll need a visa and they don't come cheap either…'

'I don't need a visa,' Sophy said but Johnno shook his head.

'You will, Soph. A mate of mine fell in love with a girl from Canberra and flew out to marry her and they still wouldn't let him in without a visa and a few thousand quid in savings—'

'I don't need a visa,' Sophy repeated, and if she'd inherited a certain tone of voice from her mother, the way that she was currently lifting her chin all ready for an argument was pure Johnno. 'I don't need savings either, though of course I'm not going to turn up empty-handed.'

Johnno was on his phone. He lifted up a warning hand at Sophy for daring to interrupt his scrolling time. 'Yeah, see? You need a visa,' he said, showing her his phone screen and the website of the Australian Home Affairs department. A website that Sophy knew very well. 'You might be on the skilled occupation list.'

'I'm not because I don't have any extraordinary skills, apart from cashing up and dealing with customers that are getting arsey,' Sophy said. Her lack of extraordinary skills did sting but that was one of the reasons why she wanted to emigrate: to learn new skills, extraordinary or not.

'No need to look so fed up, kiddo,' Johnno said brightly, stabbing at his phone with his index finger. 'There's this sponsored family stream lark and that only costs $145 and you can stay up to twelve months. Much better than emigrating.'

'But I want to emigrate.' It was quite hard to get the words out through gritted teeth. 'My best friend, we were at school together, Radha, lives out there now. I was going to go with her back then but Egan asked me to move in with him and I thought that was the better option.' Sophy sighed. She really was the poster girl for the road not taken. 'Anyway, she's getting married in October, I'm one of her bridesmaids, so with that and Bob and Jean's golden wedding ... they both feel like signs, you know?'

'Signs that you stay there for a few months and then come home,' Johnno insisted.

Sophy shook her head. 'Radha was only going out for a gap year but she fell in love with Australia.' And also a software designer called Patrick. 'She says that she finishes work and then she's straight onto Bondi Beach ten minutes later. She's even learned to surf.'

'Well, you're not going to learn to surf in Queensville,' Johnno said flatly. 'Might be near the coast but there are no decent waves.'

'Surfing was just a for-instance …'

'And you'll still need a visa and thousands of pounds…'

'But I won't.' The only way to get Johnno to listen was to raise her voice so that the two girls on the next table, clearly bunking off because they had their school blazers on, turned to look at her. 'I can claim Australian citizenship by descent. Because I have dual nationality.'

Johnno frowned. He wasn't usually so slow on the uptake. 'Come again?'

'You were Australian at the time of my birth—'

'Still am, love,' he said proudly, even though apparently the last time he'd been back to his motherland was thirteen years ago.

'So, I just have to fill in some forms, provide written references that I'm of good character, pay around three hundred dollars and I'm good to go,' Sophy explained. She opened her bag and pulled out the plastic folder where she kept her ever-increasing collection of documentation. 'I just need a couple of bits and bobs from you. I made a list.'

Johnno didn't even hold out his hand for the piece of paper that Sophy offered. 'It looks like a long list.'

'It has *three* things I need you to do: give me a copy of your passport, a copy of your birth certificate, and first have them verified by a solicitor…' Sophy felt inevitable doom descending on her. 'You do have a copy of your birth certificate, don't you?'

'Well, not to hand.' Johnno shrugged in a way that absolutely did not inspire confidence. 'It'll probably turn up. Anyway, when are you planning to go?'

Sophy fixed Johnno with another look, even steelier than the last one. 'It's Bob and Jean's fiftieth anniversary on August fifteenth and I want to be there by then. To surprise them. It's the end of February now and I need that paperwork from you within the next month to get my application processed ASAP.'

'A month isn't a lot of time,' Johnno said, somewhat predictably, though most people knew exactly where their birth certificates and passports were. Then again, Johnno's unpredictability was the most predictable thing about him.

'One month,' Sophy repeated and hoped that the message had sunk in. 'Also, the airfares go shooting up after June because of the school holidays. In the meantime I'm going to find a job, any lousy job, so I can save for my airfare and some spending money, then I'm out of here. I just need you to sort out the stuff on that list as soon as—'

'A job,' Johnno echoed. 'You need a job. Well, I can help you with that. Though I still think this is a crazy idea.'

That was rich coming from Johnno, the king of crazy ideas, but Sophy did really need a job so she decided that now wasn't the time to point that out.

'You know someone who's looking for staff?' she asked hopefully, though she was sure that whatever job it might be, it wouldn't be a regular nine to five. One of his mates worked in the reptile house at London Zoo.

'Me, I'll give you a job. At the shop,' Johnno said. He waved a stubby hand. 'I'll talk to Freddy. He sorts out all that stuff for me. Yeah, you can come and work for me in the old family business. How does that sound?'

Sophy didn't want to be churlish, but the thought of working in Johnno's shop didn't fill her heart with gladness. On the contrary, it made her heart sink like a ship's anchor.

Johnno's Junk. Ugh!

She'd only been there once when she was little but Sophy could still remember the fusty, dusty smell that had caught at the back of her throat. The old, limp clothes. Yellowing paperbacks with garish covers. The stuffed fox head, its fangs bared, in a glass display case.

'Maybe it's not such a good idea me working for you. You shouldn't mix business and pleasure and all that,' Sophy said, gently, because she really did appreciate the offer but already she was *itching* at the mere thought of all that creepy old tat in Johnno's Junk.

It was a source of much mystery to Sophy and her mother as to why Johnno had never been declared bankrupt. Or how he always managed to be flush with cash. Like now, as he opened his wallet and started thumbing through a sizeable wad of notes.

'Let me give you some cash to help you out until you're back on your feet,' he said, because he was generous to a fault.

'Oh no, you mustn't,' Sophy protested, holding up her hands to ward off the bundle of twenties that Johnno was trying to thrust at her. 'I have a bit saved up.'

'Now come on, love. Let your old man spoil you a bit.'

'No, your money's no good round here,' Sophy said firmly.

'If you won't let me give you money, then at least let me give you a job,' Johnno wheedled, fluttering his lashes at her, which looked ridiculous but somehow she was smiling. He was impossible. 'Come on! You and me working together. It will be fun.'

Despite ten years' retail experience, finding another job was proving to be very difficult. Sophy had no references, as the HR department at her old job had also been locked out of the company HQ. And she hadn't really climbed up the career ladder either, shunning any opportunities for promotion or advancement as too much responsibility for not that much more money. Also, despite what she'd just told Johnno, she had hardly any savings left.

She would have to fumigate herself at the end of each day, but she did need a job and it would be nice, or a distraction at least, to spend some time with Johnno. 'All right,' she agreed. 'But only until I find something be— I mean something else.'

'Something better?' Johnno asked with a grin because he knew exactly what she'd been going to say. 'What could be better than working in my shop?'

Quite a lot of things, but by the time Sophy was on the tube heading back to her mum's house in Hendon, she was feeling nostalgic for all the good times she'd had with Johnno. When he'd actually turned up for them, that was.

She was also feeling better about the future. That was the other thing that she always forgot about Johnno: he'd missed his true calling. He could make a fortune as a motivational speaker.

'You're smart, you're funny, you're a straight talker and, luckily, you take after your mother when it comes to looks,' he'd said as he'd walked her back to the station. 'There's nothing you can't do, Soph. I reckon you'll be all right. Better than all right. You're going to do wonders, kiddo, but there ain't any wonders to be had on a flaming sheep station. Now, I'll be in touch about the job soon.'

And that was that. It might even be the last time that Sophy ever saw him before she left for Australia, but at least she'd be able to tell Bob and Jean that their wayward son had a heart of gold.

Chapter Two

A week later, on a Tuesday morning, Sophy was back at Chalk Farm station. No one, not even her mum, had been more surprised than Sophy when she got a message from Johnno to say that he'd sorted out a job for her and would meet her at the station to 'get you started. Introduce you to everyone and all that jazz.'

Sophy wasn't sure why they were meeting in Chalk Farm again when the shop was in Holloway. But she'd learned a long time ago that it was best not to wonder too hard why Johnno did anything.

Even though it was a grotty junk shop next to a chicken shop and she was used to working in a large fashion store on Oxford Street, Sophy still had first-day nerves. She didn't know how many staff Johnno had – though it couldn't be very many – and whether they'd resent her for coming in and think that she meant to lord it over them. She also hadn't known what to wear. She didn't want to wear anything too nice. In her old job they'd worn all black, bought at a staff discount from the latest drop, but you couldn't wear all black in a junk shop. It would show up all the dust and cobwebs and, oh God, mildew. There was bound to be mildew.

Sophy had settled for a navy blue and white polka dot jumpsuit and her second nicest trainers because she was going to be on her feet all day. Not her Vejas but her Veja dupes. As she waited for Johnno, she pulled out her pocket mirror and scrutinised her face. Her eyes were the same blue as Johnno's but her poker-straight red hair and pale skin came from her mother's side of the family, who all hailed from County Cork in Ireland. Sophy wiped away a smudge of mascara and was just thinking about reapplying her lipgloss when someone tapped her on the shoulder.

She whirled round. 'Oh my God, this is twice now that you've actually turned up when you said you would! Is this an all-time record?'

But it wasn't Johnno. Standing there was a tall man in jeans, a black polo shirt and Harrington jacket and with artfully messy hair. He looked like he was a member of one of the indie bands that littered this part of north London. Maybe he was lost and needed directions back to Camden?

'Are you Sophy?' he asked in a voice that had clearly had most of its cockney edge smoothed out.

Not a member of a minor indie band then. And also … 'You're not Johnno.' Sophy pointed out the obvious.

'I'm Freddy,' he explained, holding out a hand for Sophy to shake. 'Johnno asked me to meet you.'

Johnno had mentioned something about a Freddy. 'You sort things out for Johnno?'

'I'm actually a solicitor by trade but I hate wearing a suit,' Freddy said with a shrug and a twinkle in his dark eyes. He had olive skin, that riotous mop of curly chocolate-brown hair and a cheeky, conspiratorial grin. Sophy could see why Johnno liked him. She felt automatically disposed to like him too. 'Johnno sends his apologies. Said he had to go and see a man about a dog.'

When she'd been little, Sophy had always been excited and hopeful on the numerous occasions that Johnno went to see a man about a dog. Until she realised that there wasn't going to be a dog. It was just Johnno being completely unreliable yet again. 'Does he really have a job for me?'

Freddy nodded. 'That's why I'm here. Don't worry, you're in safe hands. Shall we walk and talk?'

There was a lot to talk about. 'I don't have my P45 yet. Did Johnno tell you about my last job? That the company went into administration? Everything's in the hands of some official bankruptcy people, so I'm not sure how it's all going to work with a temporary job. I'll probably have to go on an emergency tax code. Can Johnno even afford for me to go on the books or will it be cash in hand? Not that I'm saying I want it to be cash in hand but they take all your money when they put you on an emergency tax code…'

'Why don't we go to the shop?' Freddy suggested. 'Everyone's there and they're dying to meet you.'

Sophy nodded. 'Are we going to get a bus? We could walk up to Camden and get the 29.'

'A bus?'

'To the shop. Or an Uber?'

'But it's just round the corner.'

'Freddy, the Holloway Road is not just round the corner.'

'The Holloway Road?' Freddy shook his head. 'We're not going to Holloway.'

He took Sophy's elbow and guided her round the corner so they could walk over the bridge that led to Primrose Hill. Nestling next to the slightly down-at-heel and achingly cool Camden Town, Primrose Hill was one of those villages that London did so well. Full of large stucco white Victorian villas and Regency terraces painted in pretty sherbet colours and a main shopping thoroughfare thronged with chichi boutiques, artisanal eateries and thriving independent shops.

Primrose Hill was for the seriously wealthy; who else would be able to afford its multimillion-pound houses? It was the perfect place to take their designer pooches for a stroll on Primrose Hill itself, with its views stretching over nearby Regent's Park and, beyond that, the church spires

18

and skyscrapers of London. To jog along the towpath of the Regent's Canal. Or watch the world go by from the window of a café where there wouldn't be much change from a ten-pound note after purchasing a Peruvian-blend latte made with Fairtrade newly activated almond milk.

Primrose Hill was not a place where the tat that Johnno sold would go down very well. No wonder Sophy was confused. 'Has the junk shop moved then?'

It seemed like Freddy was equally confused. 'The junk shop? What junk shop?'

Sophy frowned. 'It doesn't make any sense. Why would Johnno move the shop to Primrose Hill? Primrose Hill is *so* posh and Johnno's Junk is not posh. It's like the absolute opposite of posh.'

'I don't know what Johnno's Junk is and, quite frankly, I don't want to. Here we are.'

Here was a terrace of shops. The fanciest of merchants. A yoga studio. An interiors shop. A dry-cleaner's that looked more minimalist than any dry-cleaner's that Sophy had ever seen.

The last shop in the little terrace had its exterior painted the most perfect Wedgwood blue. In the window was one dress. But what a dress! It was black and strapless, with a tight bodice, sweetheart neckline and a skirt that consisted of layers and layers and layers of tulle shot through with something to make them sparkle. It was one of the most beautiful dresses that Sophy had ever seen. It was the kind of dress that you had adventures in. She could picture a woman, an impossibly beautiful and willowy woman, wearing that dress in a nightclub. She'd be drinking champagne from a slender flute while a jazz band played and a coterie of debonair men hung on her every word. It was that kind of a dress.

Sophy finally tore her eyes away from the dress to look at the signage. *The Vintage Dress Shop*, it said, in an elegant, understated script, like the shop sign had been rolled through an old-fashioned typewriter.

'This isn't Johnno's Junk,' Sophy pointed out.

Freddy gave her an even stare, though a muscle in his cheek was pounding away. Maybe this was what Egan had meant during their vicious, final argument when he'd said that she was the most annoying woman he'd ever met. 'No, it's not. Johnno did mention another shop he used to have but that closed down at least twenty years ago.'

A pang of guilt speared Sophy's insides. She hadn't known that. She knew the barest of facts about Johnno's day-to-day doings. But then for her to know all the ins and outs and latest developments in Johnno's life, he'd have had to have been in her life too.

'He never said,' she muttered, as Freddy opened the door and gestured for her to step through it.

It might have fancy signage and a fancy font and a beautiful dress in the window, but Sophy steeled herself for the fusty, musty smell of old clothes that people had probably died in.

She actually put a hand over her nose to ward off the stench – until she realised that the interior of the shop didn't smell of mothballs and wet wool but something expensive and exclusive. Clean, very clean, and with the faintest scent of perfume. Like the times that Sophy had dared to set foot in some swanky Bond Street boutique, then promptly walked out again when the snooty sales assistant had given her the evil eye.

Sophy did a slow three-hundred-and-sixty-degree turn as she tried to take it all in. There was so much that her eyes wanted to linger on. Rather than being dark and poky with racks of garish clothes and cubbyholes and baskets full of tacky accessories like the vintage shops that Sophy had been in before, usually dragged there by her stepsister Cress, the shop was light and airy.

The walls and floorboards were painted a soft, chalky white: a perfect backdrop for the dresses. So many dresses. They were arranged by colour. There was an entire wall of green dresses: from the lightest softest seafoam to a bright emerald and a dark, mossy bottle green. The yellow rail spanned lemon sherbet to the most vibrant egg yolk. There were blue dresses, purple dresses, red dresses. An entire section devoted to little black dresses.

It was a lot like the frock equivalent of the perfectly curated and colour-coded bookshelves that Sophy had seen on Pinterest and Instagram.

Everywhere that she turned, she was met with another delight to feast her eyes on. There were the display cabinets (that looked like they belonged on a 1930s ocean-liner) full of costume jewellery, all bright colours like sweeties.

In the centre of the room were two shocking-pink velvet sofas (though they were more chaise longue than settee) and at the back of the room there was a 1930s ocean liner sort of desk, sleek and curvy, and beyond that a series of curtained-off cubicles – the changing rooms.

Immediately, Sophy felt out of place in her on-trend jumpsuit, which had seemed like a perfectly appropriate and easy-wash outfit for her first day in a temporary job, rooting about in an old junk shop. Now it seemed really garish and out of place. Especially when there was a woman standing behind the desk who looked like the very last word in chic. She had a razor-sharp jet-black bob, its edges so straight you could take a ruler to them. She was tall and slim, her figure shown to perfection in the fitted black dress she was wearing, and, when she came out from behind the desk, she glided across the floor in the kind of heels that Sophy had only had nightmares about. Of course, she had the most perfect arched eyebrows and Cupid's-bow lips outlined in a bright red that Sophy would never have the courage to wear. The lips were currently stretched in a thin sort of smile, which wasn't even a little bit welcoming.

'Freddy,' the woman said in a thin voice to match. Her eyes briefly skimmed over Sophy and then, as if Sophy wasn't worthy of her attention, her gaze fixed on a point beyond Sophy's shoulder.

'Phoebe,' Freddy said, the tone of his voice not quite as friendly as it had been before. 'This is Sophy. Johnno's Sophy. Sophy, this is Phoebe, who practically runs this place single-handedly.'

'It's lovely,' Sophy said with what she hoped was a friendly smile and not a smile that said *I only got this job because of my dad and I'm going to be a constant thorn in your side*. 'I've never seen so many gorgeous clothes all in one place. Do you only sell dresses or do you sell separates too because—'

'Everyone's waiting upstairs,' Phoebe said, cutting through Sophy's perfectly reasonable question. 'I'll get Beatrice to cover the shop floor.'

She turned, so Sophy could see that she was wearing seamed stockings, walked past the changing rooms to a door marked *Private* and disappeared.

'Takes a while to warm up to people,' Freddy said, gently steering Sophy through the shop, past the cubicles, to a wrought-iron spiral staircase painted gold. 'We'll go up to the atelier.'

The atally whaty?

Sophy felt her cheeks flame as she realised that she'd said it out loud, but, to his credit, Freddy didn't laugh at her gaucheness but gave her a kind, comforting sort of smile. 'The atelier. It's where they do the fittings and keep the wedding dresses and expensive gowns,' he explained.

Sophy wound her way up the stairs, which opened out onto a beautiful room. No, it wasn't anything as mundane as a room. It was a salon. A gilt-edged salon. Her feet in her knock-off trainers sank into the softest, plushest cream carpet. Up here, closer to heaven, it smelled even more glorious: of roses and geraniums and sheer, understated luxury.

Of course there were more dresses. Wedding dresses, Freddy had said. Their colours ranged from the delicate white of snowdrops to the buttery richness of clotted cream and the dull gold of the old one-pound coins. They were made from lace and satin and silk and fabrics that Sophy could only guess at: organza, shantung, georgette, taffeta ... Then she was sidetracked by a glimpse of an anteroom full of the most elegant gowns; hanging there was a pale blue Grecian-inspired dress, intricate bead-work dancing across the fabric.

She turned her attention back to the main room, then wished she hadn't. There was a raised circular platform where she supposed brides and the sort of women who bought beautiful vintage gowns could admire their own reflection, because they were surrounded on all sides by mirrors. Sophy kept catching glimpses of herself, and she looked as flustered and disconcerted as she felt.

Sophy was realistic about her own utter ordinariness. If it weren't for her red hair, nobody would ever be able to pick her out of a police line-up; not even if they'd witnessed her committing all sorts of horrific crimes. She was average height, average build; like every other woman she knew she fought a near-daily battle between her dream of dropping a dress size and her love of carbs; and she had all the usual features, which sat in the right place on her face. She liked her blue eyes, courtesy of Johnno, and her full lips, courtesy of her mother. She didn't like the anxious little furrow between her eyes, which seemed to be a permanent feature these days. Everything else was quite indistinguishable, literally. If Sophy didn't use mascara and an eyebrow pencil, it was impossible to tell that she had actual eyelashes and eyebrows.

23

She really didn't belong in this place with these people.

Because, like downstairs, there were sofas in the centre of the room; these were cream and gold, and sitting on one of them were two more women in chic black dresses who looked like Hollywood goddesses imported straight from the silver screen. Across from them was a ridiculously handsome man, long of limb, floppy of hair, jutting of cheekbone, wearing an exquisitely cut light grey tweed suit with a perfect pink pocket square. He was tapping away at his phone. Sitting next to him on a powder blue satin cushion was a very grumpy-looking, black French bulldog.

'Oh my God,' Sophy muttered under her breath. She wasn't just miles out of her comfort zone. She was continents away from her comfort zone. The ridiculously handsome man raised his head, as if he'd heard her anguished aside. He was even more ridiculously handsome face-on. Then he very slowly and deliberately winked at Sophy and her nerves were momentarily swept away by a fluttering feel of a very different kind.

'You're fine,' Freddy assured Sophy in a low voice, which was very sweet of him – but absolutely untrue. Phoebe had appeared at the top of the stairs, all ready to give Sophy another flinty look. Her bewitching green eyes (of *course* she would have bewitching green eyes) lingered on the patch of jumpsuit where Sophy had managed to spill a tiny drop of coffee earlier. 'Let me introduce you to everyone.'

'Everyone' turned out to be Chloe and Anita, the other sales associates. Chloe was tiny and blonde and Anita was tiny and dark and, though both of them were unfailingly polite, neither of them were exactly friendly.

'And you've met Phoebe,' Freddy reminded Sophy. Not like Sophy was likely to forget it when Phoebe's gaze kept resting on her with an expression that flickered from disbelief to faint amusement. Someone should tell Phoebe that she had the worst poker face ever.

'But you haven't met Charles,' said Phoebe, and she actually cracked a genuine, warm smile as she glanced at him. 'He sources all our jewellery and some of our high-end pieces.'

It was Charles's turn to look Sophy up and down. Not in an unfriendly way – there was something warm and welcoming about his gaze – but more as if he were assessing the raw material, seeing right down to her bones. Sophy wasn't sure how she felt about that. If possible, it made her even more flustered than she'd already been. Then he stood up, unfolding his long length from the sofa so Sophy had to look up at him – he was well over six foot – and took the few steps to where she was cowering. She held out her hand, expecting that he probably wanted to shake it, but instead he raised it to his mouth so he could kiss it. It was a very suave, very practised move, but it still made Sophy feel a little swoony. '*Enchantée*,' he murmured against her skin. Then her hand was back in her custody and Charles gave her one brief but charming smile before he sat down again.

Obviously gay, Sophy thought with a pang of regret. No man wore a suit that exquisitely tailored, had cheekbones sharp enough to cut glass and murmured something in French instead of 'pleased to meet you', and was straight. Sadly.

'Last, but not at all least, is Coco Chanel,' Freddy said, and the French bulldog gave Sophy the most withering look of all. She had huge ears and, instead of a collar, a pearl necklace circled her thick neck. 'She's the brains of the operation. And of course, everyone – this is Sophy, Johnno's daughter. Our new sales associate.'

'Oh no! There's no need for… I mean, I'm just helping out in a temporary way to save up money to go to Australia,' Sophy explained. She made a wringing motion with her hands. 'I'm happy to muck in.'

'Johnno says Sophy has got over ten years' experience in retail fashion and we're very lucky to have her,' Freddy said, digging a none-too-gentle finger between Sophy's shoulder-blades. 'I know she'll be an asset.'

Nobody else seemed sure about that, including Sophy herself.

The rest of the day passed in a haze of unpleasantness. They all trooped back downstairs, Freddy left and, when Sophy asked Phoebe what she could help with, she was directed down to a windowless basement, where she spent the rest of the day packing up inferior vintage garments, including several boxes of boiled-wool cardigans that smelled of wet dog, to be sent off for recycling.

These clothes were absolutely nothing like the dresses being sold in the shop and Sophy was pretty sure, even odds, that – just as she had feared – someone had died in one of the garments she was gingerly picking through. Maybe up to four or five someones.

She took a measly half-hour for lunch at one, though Phoebe acted as if she couldn't believe Sophy's audacity at wanting to take thirty minutes to grab a sandwich and think hard about her recent life decisions. Mind you, that was nothing compared to Phoebe's incredulity when Sophy offered to take over in the shop when she went on her own lunch.

'You can't do that,' Phoebe said coldly. 'You don't know anything about vintage or our customers or… No. Back to the basement with you.'

Sophy spent the rest of the afternoon sorting through more dead people's clothes (some of them were really, really whiffy) and it wasn't until six o'clock that she was released from her pongy purgatory by Phoebe. 'Oh, you're still here?' she said, feigning surprise, as she appeared at the top of the basement stairs. 'I'd completely forgotten about you. We're closing now, unless you wanted to put in some overtime.'

'I really don't,' Sophy said, gathering up her bag and jacket.

She was still fuming about Phoebe and her snotty, snooty attitude when she got off the tube at Hendon Central. Her misery was compounded when she reached into her bag for her phone and saw she had a message from Egan, her ex.

Loads of your stuff is still here and you owe me £323 for your outstanding share of the bills. He was obviously not missing her, Sophy thought as she walked the short distance back to her mum's and the little three-bed house that Sophy at twenty-one had been so pleased to leave for a houseshare in Manor House with a couple of friends. Now Anjula and Kate were both married, had a child apiece and had gone from London to green and leafy places where it was possible to buy a small house without having to sell both kidneys.

Whereas Sophy was right back where she started: living with her mum and feeling that she really hadn't achieved anything since the days when she was a sulky teenager skulking in her room and dreaming about all the adventures she'd have when she was a proper grown-up.

Now she was the big three-oh and it felt like, apart from the odd mini-break, she hadn't had a single adventure. No wonder it was hard to put a smile on her face as she opened the front door.

Caroline and Mike were in the kitchen and there was something lovely and garlicky and herby cooking. They were standing over the hob with their heads together, laughing about something, but both looked round when Sophy dropped her keys on the hall table and padded down the hall towards them.

'How did it go, love?' Caroline asked, her pretty, pale face flushed from slaving over a hot stove.

'Yes, hard day at the office?' Mike added.

Despite the whole thing about her childhood bedroom being turned into a home spa, they'd welcomed Sophy back, though they'd got used to having the place to themselves.

27

Maybe that was why Sophy felt as if she was intruding. She also mourned her independence. She'd spent five years living in various houseshares with various friends. Then she'd lived with Egan for four years and now she was back in Hendon. Though she tried to be cheerful and put a brave face on it, there were times, like right now, when all Sophy wanted to do was lie on the beige tufted-wool carpet, hug Lollipop, her mother's cat, to her chest and cry and cry and cry.

Instead she tried to make her smile look convincing. Also, Lollipop wasn't much of a hugger. 'Yeah, it was great,' Sophy said with as much enthusiasm as she could muster, which wasn't very much. 'I'm quite tired.'

'Well, you would be, being on your feet all day again.' Caroline nodded, scanning her daughter and seeming to miss nothing, from the shadows under Sophy's eyes to the way she shuffled from side to side because her feet were throbbing in her knock-off designer trainers. 'Dinner will be ready in ten minutes. Why don't you go into the lounge and I'll do you a tray. Special treat.'

It *was* a very special treat. Caroline had a very dim view of people eating in the lounge. If Sophy wanted a bowl of microwave popcorn as they watched a movie, her mother would moan about getting popcorn kernels down the side of the sofa and how it would attract mice.

'Actually, Mum, I really need a bath. I'm covered in the stench of dead people. Can I take a raincheck on dinner?'

It wasn't until Sophy was in the bathroom, door locked and taps running, that she let herself do what she'd wanted to do since approximately ten o'clock that morning. She burst into tears.

She only stopped crying when she was finally submerged in rose-scented bubbles and realised that she could stop a good third of her current agony by simply not turning up at The Vintage Dress Shop the next day.

Chapter Three

It wasn't that anything looked brighter the next day. On the contrary, the sky was as grey and overcast as Sophy's mood when she walked to the tube station for another eight hours toiling at the coalface of retro fashion. It also hadn't helped that she'd woken up to a WhatsApp message from her old schoolfriend Radha, now living the sunny expat life in Sydney. 'Hurry up and get here soon, Soph! Surf's waiting!' It was accompanied by a photo of Radha on a sandy beach, her tan and eyes glowing, as the sun set spectacularly in the background.

Sophy wanted the glowing tan (though she wasn't sure that her milk-white skin possessed even trace amounts of melanin) and the spectacular sunsets. Although she was going to start her new Australian life at her grandparents' sheep station in Southern Australia, Sophy was definitely considering relocating to Sydney after that. She'd have Radha to show her the ropes and she couldn't wait to sign up for surf lessons from some chiselled, tousle-haired surfie who looked like one of the Hemsworth brothers. Then she'd remembered that she couldn't pay the airfare to Australia in chocolate buttons. She needed money. And that was why she *was* going to turn up for her second day at The Vintage Dress Shop, and not let the horrible Phoebe scare her away. She was also going to turn up because she wasn't a quitter – but oh, how Sophy longed to be a quitter!

To cheer herself up when she got to Primrose Hill half an hour later, Sophy stopped at a charming little bakery for a coffee to go and a flaky pastry. The astronomical price of these two items made her feel a lot like crying again. Then, her feet dragging with every step, she made her way to the shop.

Sophy took a deep breath, pulled back her shoulders and opened the door with a bright smile on her face. 'Good morning, everyone!'

'Everyone' was Anita, who mumbled something that might have been 'Good morning' back, and Phoebe, who was sitting behind the ocean-liner desk, like she was sitting on a throne, and not bothering to dial down her furious expression.

'What on earth do you think you're doing?' she demanded.

'I'm here to work, just like you,' Sophy said evenly, though she felt pretty bloody far from even. 'Do you have a problem with that?'

'Do I have a problem?' Phoebe echoed incredulously. She rose gracefully to her feet, so she could stand there with her hands on her hips. 'Yes, I have a problem. Can't you read?'

As accusations went that was pretty out there. Of course Sophy could read. Then she realised that Phoebe was pointing at a sign with one perfectly manicured red nail.

Food and drink are forbidden on these premises by express order of The Management.

'What? I can't even have a cup of tea every couple of hours? There is a thing called workers' rights, Phoe—'

'No food or drink anywhere near the dresses,' Phoebe clarified sharply. 'If you *must* eat or drink, then you'll have to do it in the back.'

Sophy scurried past Phoebe to get to the office at the back of the shop. She couldn't remember the last time she'd been made to feel no bigger or better than a … a … a dung beetle. It was probably the time when she'd been hauled in front of her headmistress, aged twelve, after she'd been caught red-handed sticking a wad of discarded chewing gum under her desk in a biology lesson.

She wasn't twelve now, she was a grown woman; but Phoebe had a way of looking at Sophy like she wasn't fit to share the same air.

Beatrice was in the back office. She was a slightly less intimidating version of Chloe and Anita. She had the same uniform of a little black dress and heels, but at least she knew how to smile and whisper, 'Don't worry about Phoebe. She's just very protective of the dresses. We have a little table and chairs outside; do you want to have your coffee there?'

Through a set of French doors there was a tiny little terrace with a wrought-iron table and chairs that overlooked the Regent's Canal with its brightly painted moored barges. It must be lovely to sit out there when it was sunny. It was still lovely, though somewhat cold, to sit out there on a grey March morning and wolf down her croissant and gulp the coffee, even if they tasted like ashes and dishwater now.

As days went, it wasn't as bad as her first day had been. There was no more sorting through the clothes of the recently deceased. Sophy spent most of the day in the back office with Beatrice, who explained their inventory system, which felt like slightly familiar territory.

When Beatrice took an early lunch Sophy did try to venture out onto the shop floor, just so she could start familiarising herself with the stock. Everything was arranged by colour; but where did sizing come into it? What were the price points? How was she meant to know which decade a dress was from?

As if she'd surreptitiously put a tracking device on her, as soon as Sophy approached the rails of blue dresses, Anita watching warily from the wings, Phoebe was suddenly beetling down the spiral staircase. Sophy didn't know how

31

anyone could negotiate a spiral staircase so quickly and in such high heels.

'It all right,' Sophy assured her. 'I washed my hands. Twice!'

'Have you really?' Phoebe's voice fairly dripped with scepticism and, though she was a proper grown-up, Sophy found herself holding out her hands for the other woman's inspection. Then she realised what she was doing and snatched them back.

'I appreciate that whole world of vintage fashion might be new to me but I do have many years of retail experience,' Sophy said hotly. It was her turn to stand there with her hands on her hips, to the consternation of two women who had suddenly entered the shop. Sophy turned to them with a smile that was very slightly manic. 'Hello! Welcome to The Vintage Dress Shop. Do have a look around, and give me a yell if you need any assistance.'

Sophy wasn't sure but she thought she heard Phoebe growl with irritation at her jaunty greeting; though the growl could also have come from Coco Chanel, who'd come lumbering down the stairs to see what all the fuss was about. Even the shop dog had some serious attitude.

'As you said, you have absolutely *no* experience of vintage fashion.' Phoebe sucked in an angry breath. 'I even heard you say to Beatrice that you thought people might have *died* in our dresses…'

The two women who'd entered swiftly exited at that.

'It was a joke,' Sophy said, but she was determined not to get sidetracked from what she wanted to say. Or rather to give Phoebe The Terrible some home truths. 'Anyway, I worked at Belle Girl for the last ten years and for the last five I was a *senior* sales associate at the Oxford Street store.'

'Senior just means that you'd been there longer than anyone else,' Phoebe pointed out, like that was nothing to be impressed about. It was also perilously close to the truth.

'It was a very big store. It was the flagship store!'

'Hasn't Belle Girl just gone into administration?' Phoebe arched one already perfectly arched eyebrow, as if she suspected that Sophy was personally responsible for the entire chain of two hundred shops going bust.

'It's a very challenging retail landscape and we were taken over by a venture capitalist who was more interested in stripping back our costs than investing in—'

'And it was a fast fashion chain. T-shirts for a fiver, dresses for ten pounds made by workers in the developing world who toiled away in appalling conditions and barely earned enough money to feed their families. Plus, I'm sure a large percentage of your stock probably ended up as landfill,' Phoebe continued, and she had a good point. Several very good points that Sophy herself had agonised over, especially after seeing a documentary on BBC2 shortly after they'd had to dump an entire range because the design department had plagiarised the work of an up-and-coming designer who'd put them on blast on social media.

'We were in discussions about doing a range of sustainable clothing,' she said weakly because none of the bad things about high street fashion were in Sophy's control. So it wasn't really her fault that she'd been part of the problem rather than part of the situation, whereas…

'Vintage fashion is the ultimate sustainable clothing,' Anita piped up from behind the desk, where she'd been all but cowering until now. 'A lot of our stock is over seventy, eighty years old and still wearable. It blows my mind sometimes. Although, you have to be careful when you wear some vintage pieces because modern antiperspirants can rot the armholes like nobody's business.'

'We are getting way off-track here,' Sophy gritted. 'I'm here to work, not to tread on anyone's toes, so let me work.

Give me a crash course in vintage fashion. At least let me have a look at the stock.'

She moved towards the stairs, because she loved a pretty dress as much as the next person and she was dying to have a good rummage through all the wedding dresses and posh, posh frocks upstairs. Alas, she didn't even make it up the first step, because suddenly both Phoebe and Coco Chanel were physically blocking her from heading up to the atelier.

'I'm sorry,' Phoebe said in a tone that suggested that she wasn't even a little bit sorry, 'but there are hundreds of thousands of pounds of stock in the atelier and we don't have any appointments booked, so there's no need for you to be up there. If you want to be helpful, you can make some coffee – as long as you don't bring it out on the shop floor.'

Sophy retired to the tiny kitchen and tried to ignore the pinprick tingle of her eyes. She wasn't going to let Phoebe reduce her to tears. God, two months ago she wouldn't even have let the Belle Girl area manager, who was a terrific bully, talk to her like that. But it had been an awful two months and she was off her game, out of her depth and now making coffee like she was the Saturday girl.

For the rest of the day, Sophy kept out of Phoebe's way. Anita let her pack away some costume jewellery, but even that simple task was explained to her like she was incapable of independent thought.

'So, one more time, once you've wrapped the piece in tissue paper, then you put it in a seal-top bag, then write a description of it on a sticker, put the sticker on the bag and then if it's a brooch you put it in the drawer marked brooches and if it's—'

'If it's a bracelet, then I put it in the drawer marked bracelets. Yes, thanks Anita, if I'm not sure about anything, I'll ask you,' Sophy said. It was just as well that she had all those years of retail experience because it meant that she was an expert at hiding her frustration, anger and sheer, teeth-grinding irritation behind a perky smile.

Actually, it was quite nice to sit at the ocean-liner desk and get to handle some merchandise. Especially such pretty, sparkly merchandise. Sophy even tried on some of the big, gaudy cocktail rings, after first checking that no one was about to rush over and tell her off.

It was also quite fascinating to watch Phoebe and Chloe with the customers. Only one rail-thin, expensively dressed woman with a Chanel bag slung nonchalantly over her shoulder was granted admittance to the atelier; everyone else was happy to look through the second-tier downstairs dresses.

Sophy would have asked them, if she'd been allowed to even make eye contact, if they were shopping with a special occasion in mind or if they had some idea of what they were looking for, but Anita and Phoebe didn't do any of that.

Anita was keen to impart fashion facts about any frocks the women (and they were all women) lingered over. 'Forties rayon with a kick-pleat,' she'd announce. Or, 'Sixties minidress heavily influenced by Paco Rabanne.'

Whereas Phoebe might know a lot about vintage fashion but she knew sweet FA about making the customer feel like a queen. 'Oh, that's a very petite cut,' she cooed doubtfully when a young woman took a gorgeous emerald green sheath off the rail. She might just as well have said, 'It's never going to fit you, fatso.'

'Hmmm, that's really more of a sitting-down sort of dress. You want to wear it to a wedding? And there'll be a lot of dancing? Well, it's your decision, but that dress is eighty years old and I always think that when people buy a vintage dress it's more that they become the caretaker of it rather than the owner,' Phoebe mused, and another woman, cheeks aflame, hurriedly put the pretty pink fifties wiggle dress she'd been sighing over back on the rail.

Then her cheeks got even redder when Phoebe gently tutted and put the dress where it had been originally, between a sherbet pink and a candyfloss pink frock, not at the more shocking pink end of the rail.

'I'm so sorry,' the woman trilled nervously.

'It's all right, no harm done,' Phoebe said with a smile that reminded Sophy of a shark wearing lipstick.

Did the shop even make a profit? Sophy wondered, and then she asked herself again how the *hell* Johnno's Junk had transitioned into this fancy, fussy vintage emporium that was even more intimidating than the time Sophy had gone into the Louis Vuitton shop on Bond Street to buy Caroline something really special for her fiftieth birthday. (Which had turned out to be a coin purse, because it was all Sophy could afford.)

The day dragged on, slower than a slug on crutches. It was just gone five and Sophy was staring at the clock on the wall, willing the minute hand to creep closer to the six so that it would be going-home time, when the door was suddenly flung open so violently that it crashed back on its hinges.

A small, old women in a bright red raincoat appeared in the doorway. 'Can someone get the stuff out the taxi and pay the driver?' she demanded in a hoarse cockney accent.

'Oh my God,' Phoebe muttered, and was out of the door with the petty cash tin in seconds, while the woman collapsed on one of the sofas.

'Make me a cuppa, Neet, I'm gasping,' she groaned, listing to one side like a scuppered ship.

'Milk, two sugars?' Anita asked timidly.

'No milk, four sugars,' the woman snapped with more ferocity than Phoebe would ever be able to muster.

Sophy was pleased, and also fascinated, by this distraction. The woman had full make-up on, though one of her false eyelashes had come adrift and looked like a sooty-legged spider clinging to her lower lash and her bright red lipstick had bled. Her hair, though, was impeccable: a blue-rinsed helmet that looked as if it would remain intact no matter the elements. In fact, it looked as if it might withstand a nuclear attack.

'Who's this when she's at home?' the woman asked as she caught sight of Sophy sitting bewitched behind the desk.

'Oh, don't worry about her, it's only Johnno's daughter,' Phoebe said as she hurried back in to the shop with her arms full of garment bags. 'Reenie. You *promised* you wouldn't smoke but these bags positively reek of Benson & Hedges. Oh no, and you're not lighting up in here. The dresses!'

'Also, it's against the law,' Anita added as she hovered in the no-man's-land between shop floor and office. 'Where did you want your tea?'

'Right here,' Reenie said implacably, though she'd tucked her cigarettes and lighter back in her voluminous black patent handbag.

Phoebe raised her eyes to the ormolu-adorned ceiling. It looked to Sophy as if she were saying a silent prayer. 'You try the patience of a saint.'

'The saints wouldn't have me, darling,' Reenie cackled. Sophy was warming to her. 'Anyhoo, I did all the alterations, but I could only let that charmeuse wedding dress out by a quarter of an inch, if that. She'll have to lose at least another five pounds. And the seams on that Jaeger were gone, darling. I did my best but it might be time to give it a decent burial.'

Phoebe did cross herself then. 'Oh God.'

'Even him upstairs wouldn't have been able to do anything with it,' Reenie said.

Phoebe winced as Anita brought the tea in on a tray and Reenie grabbed the mug with no regard for the pink velvet she was sitting on. Then, once Reenie had taken a few enthusiastic slurps of tea, Phoebe handed the garment bags

37

over to Anita, who received them with much reverence. Phoebe took a seat beside Reenie.

'Now, we're coming up to wedding season and we're going to be so busy and there's a perfectly lovely room upstairs with everything you need—'

'Oh, I couldn't do those stairs. They'd be the death of me.'

'But we really need you on site,' Phoebe persisted in the softest, sweetest voice. She even fluttered her eyelashes, which, unlike Reenie's, were firmly in place. 'It would make life so much easier for fittings.'

'Life isn't easy, pet,' Reenie said and took hold of Phoebe's hand. 'And your life's about to get much harder, I'm afraid.'

Phoebe glanced in Sophy's direction, almost as if she was looking for sympathy or reassurance. Sophy shrugged helplessly. 'Hard?'

'I matched five numbers and the bonus ball a couple of weeks ago, didn't I?' Reenie patted her handbag as if her Lotto winnings were safely tucked inside. Even though they'd only been acquainted for fifteen minutes, Sophy wouldn't have been surprised if there was a million quid in there. 'About time I retired. I'm not getting any younger.'

'Nonsense. You always say that you've got the energy of a woman half your age,' Phoebe said, panic rising in her voice. 'You, retire? Don't be silly.'

'Already put a deposit down on a new-build bungalow in Bournemouth. Lovely sandy beaches,' Reenie said, finishing the last of her tea with a gulp and a delicate burp. 'So, can you tell Freddy to put my cheque in the post? I'll be in Paddington for another week or so and can one of you get me a cab or one of those Ooobers?'

Anita ordered Reenie an Uber while Phoebe begged her to reconsider the Bournemouth bungalow. 'Or we could even courier the clothes down to Bournemouth. I mean, what are you going to do with yourself?'

Phoebe sounded like she was about to get down on her knees and beg. But Reenie was not for turning. When her Uber turned up, Phoebe escorted her out of the door, still extolling the virtues of how important it was to keep your mind and your sewing fingers active.

'Wow,' Sophy said to Anita once Reenie and Phoebe were out of the door. 'That was... I don't even know what that was.'

'That was Reenie, our repairs and alterations lady. She used to work for Hardy Amies,' Anita breathed in hushed tones. 'We have three brides coming in for fittings next week. What are we going to do, Pheebs?'

Phoebe was back in the shop, ashen-faced and wringing her elegant hands like she was wringing someone's neck. 'I don't know,' she said quietly, seemingly one syllable away from losing it completely. 'We'll have to tell Johnno. Has anyone even seen Johnno this week? Sophy?'

They both looked at Sophy, who shook her head. 'Johnno and I don't have the sort of father–daughter relationship where we keep track of the other's whereabouts.'

'I'll talk to Freddy,' Phoebe said with a sigh. 'Though will he be able to source a fitter with Reenie's knowledge and expertise? Highly unlikely.'

'What are we going to do about our brides?' Anita asked. She sat down heavily on the nearest sofa. 'There's no way that Judith Tavernier can wear that ivory dress with the gold trim as is. It needs a good eight centimetres off the hem.'

'And the beadwork on that Ronald Paterson is a hot mess,' Phoebe said, coming to sit next to Anita.

Sophy thought they both might cry. She knew nothing of the dresses or the brides, and she still hadn't even been allowed upstairs, but she felt a bit hysterical herself. Still, it wasn't like she was responsible for sorting this out. She wasn't a senior sales associate any more. She was just a girl on a temporary tax code who could only be trusted with the most menial tasks while she saved up the money for her ticket to Australia.

But then again, saving up would take weeks, and Sophy was meant for more than menial tasks. It would be good to get a tiny bit of respect round here. Also, as one of the senior sales associates of a flagship Oxford Street store, she was used to having to put out fires. Once quite literally, when a bin of returns started smouldering.

'We cannot be responsible for sending brides down the aisle in substandard vintage,' Phoebe exclaimed. She sounded even closer to tears. 'Our reputation would be ruined!'

'Guys! Guys!' Sophy said excitedly, daring to venture out from behind the desk to the forbidden land of the shop floor.

'Can you even imagine, a bride on her most very special day, realising that there's a hook and eye missing?' Anita gasped as if she'd experienced something similar.

'Don't, Anita! It doesn't bear thinking about.'

'Guys! There's no need to worry. I know the perfect person to replace Reenie,' Sophy butted in. 'You'll love her.'

'You know a perfect, lovable alteration person who's as talented and skilful as Reenie who worked at Hardy Amies for thirty years?' Phoebe's voice was back to its usual setting: dripping with disdain.

But, for once, Sophy was undaunted. 'I do, I really do. I've got this!'

Chapter Four

Phoebe had still been very doubtful about Sophy's ability to rustle up a Reenie replacement but, after much umming and ah-ing, she magnanimously granted permission for Sophy to come in late after she'd spoken to the candidate.

'Somehow I suppose we'll manage without you,' she'd sniffed. She really was a colossal cow.

Of course, Sophy could have arranged things over the phone, but that would have needed the person to actually answer their phone rather than shy away from it when it started ringing. And if Sophy had tried messaging or email, then they'd definitely try to wiggle out of it.

No, the best way was face to face, which was why the next morning Sophy travelled to one of her least favourite places in London.

The Museum of Religious Relics was situated down a back street in Chelsea. The turretty, red-brick house had been bequeathed to the museum by someone very rich and very religious. Certainly, the museum would never have been able to afford such vast premises in such an expensive postcode otherwise.

Sophy slipped through the door, already anticipating the smell of church and mice droppings that permeated the air. She hurried past a display of plaster-cast saints experiencing various kinds of torture, then slipped through a door marked *Private*.

No one challenged her because the museum was chronically understaffed. They didn't even have a security guard. Then again, who would want to steal a plaster-cast effigy of Saint Sebastian with a gazillion arrows piercing his narrow chest? No one, that's who.

Behind the scenes at the museum was a rabbit warren of passageways and storerooms. Sophy eventually found what had originally been the servants' stairs back in the day when it was a private residence, and hurried down them to the shadowy, airless basement. In a tiny windowless room, hunched over a sewing machine, with a not-fit-for-the-purpose lamp trained on what she was doing, was the person Sophy had come to see.

'Well, hello there, sister-friend!' she chirped and Cressida Collins raised her head and promptly brained herself on the lamp.

'Ow! And also, hello sister-friend, what are you even doing here?' she asked.

Sophy spread her arms wide in the manner of a magician about to pluck a rabbit from a hat. 'I've come to take you away from all this!'

Cress didn't look too thrilled at the prospect. 'It's far too early for lunch, Soph, and these robes aren't going to mend themselves,' she said, bending her head to focus again on the yellowing, heavy brocade cloth she was working on. 'I don't know why but it's always the archbishops that are very hard on their capes.'

Strictly speaking, they weren't sisters, but rather stepsisters. One of the reasons why Sophy had been so happy to welcome Mike into their little family when she was ten was because she'd gained a stepsister, like a bonus gift with a purchase. She'd always wanted a sister.

Thinking back now, Sophy realised how nervous Mike and Caroline must have been when they introduced the girls, as Mike had weekend custody and if she and Cress had hated each other then their parents' future together would have been tricky.

Sophy could still remember how nervous and excited she'd been that Saturday morning over twenty years ago. She'd barely eaten any breakfast and had spent the morning kneeling on the sofa, staring out of the window as she waited for Mike's Ford Mondeo to pull up. But when it had, the enormity of the situation suddenly dawned on Sophy (what if Mike's daughter hated her?) and she'd fled to the sanctuary of her bedroom until Caroline had knocked gently on the door.

'I know you're scared, darling, but poor Cress is even more scared. She's won't even get out of the car,' Caroline had said, coming to sit on the bed and stroke the hair back from Sophy's pale face. 'Could you be really brave and come out to say hello to her?'

'Why do I have to be the brave one?' Sophy had wanted to know, but she got her answer when she was finally coaxed out with the promise of fish and chips and her choice of a DVD from Blockbuster later, and saw Cress cowering in the back seat of the car.

She was far more frightened of Sophy than Sophy was of her. Even though Cress was maybe the prettiest girl that Sophy had ever seen in real life. She had masses of curly brown hair and soft features that now Sophy thought of as ethereal. Back then she'd thought that Cress looked like the kind of girl who always got picked to play Mary in the Nativity, whereas Sophy was always relegated to playing a sheep. Not even one of the backup angels.

Sophy had poked her head into the back of the car and looked around the vehicle, avoiding Cress's pinched and terrified face, for inspiration. Her gaze had finally come to rest on Cress's Spice Girls backpack and suddenly she had something she could work with.

43

'Who's your favourite Spice Girl?' she asked. 'Mine's Geri because we both have red hair and believe in girl power.'

'Posh!' Cress squeaked, which was a bit disappointing because Posh Spice was easily Sophy's least favourite Spice Girl (all Posh seemed to do was pout and point at things), but the ice had been broken and Cress had got out of the car and they'd spent the afternoon in Sophy's bedroom practising the dance routine to 'Spice Up Your Life' and comparing their favourite boarding-school set books. It was a foregone conclusion that Cress would stay for fish and chips and a DVD from Blockbuster.

It had been a lot like falling in love at first sight.

Cress was still the prettiest person Sophy had ever seen in real life. She was also still painfully shy, hating confrontation and change as much as she hated mustard and wasps. She was someone who always took the path of least resistance. Even though she'd gone to Central Saint Martins and done a degree in fashion conservation, she'd taken the first job she was offered at the Museum for Boring Old Religious Stuff, and was still there ten years later. She still lived with her mum, Diane, who had never turned Cress's room into a home spa, and she was still dating Colin, who'd asked her out when she was sixteen and, as far as Sophy was concerned, wasn't fit to kiss the hem of Cress's fetching, handmade work smock.

But Sophy rarely voiced her concerns about Colin, even though he took Cress for granted and was a mansplainer from way back. Whenever Sophy did bring up the subject of how Cress could do a lot better, Cress would squirm. 'Oh, he means well,' she'd say, which was a pretty weak endorsement of her boyfriend of fourteen years.

Now, Sophy came further into the room so she could perch her behind on the edge of Cress's work desk. 'You remember when we talked about me emigrating to Australia...'

'No!' Cress put the archbishop's robes down so she could stick her fingers in her ears. 'We're not talking about you emigrating to Australia because it's the most awful idea in the world. La la la, I can't hear you!'

'But the bit about *carpe diem*,' Sophy said loudly. 'That bit. I'm here to get you to seize this very day by the scruff of its neck and give it a good shake. Then you're going to come with me...'

'I can't. I have some cassocks that need mending.'

'I'm offering you a job, Cress. Working with high-end vintage fashion all day and every day.'

Cress tightened her beautiful rosebud mouth as she continued to make tiny, almost invisible stiches, but she did look up just the once, her eyes full of longing. 'I already have a job.'

'We have a dress in the shop that is almost identical to the dress that Audrey Hepburn wears in the opening scene of *Breakfast at Tiffany's*: black, sleeveless, floor-length...'

'Givenchy,' Cress breathed reverently like she was saying a prayer. 'Hubert de Givenchy designed all her dresses for *Breakfast at Tiffany's* and you know that bit where she sings "Moon River"?'

'I know it well,' Sophy said, because *Breakfast at Tiffany's* was one of Cress's favourite films, which meant that Sophy had had to sit through it at least a hundred times. At least. So she knew exactly what Cress's next words were going to be.

'It's why when she died, Tiffany took out an ad in the *New York Times* dedicated to their huckleberry friend,' Cress said, her voice catching as she took the tissue that Sophy had all ready to go. This wasn't either of their first times at the huckleberry friend rodeo.

'We have another dress in the shop that's a lot like the dress Audrey wears in *Funny Face*, when they're doing the fashion shoot...'

'Oh, stop it,' Cress tried to say sternly but failed miserably. 'Which dress? Is it the white strapless one or the one with the black embroidery and the double skirt?'

'There's only one way for you to find out,' Sophy told her, and she launched into the pitch that she'd been working on all of the night before and quite a lot of this morning. It was a very fashion-heavy pitch, extolling the virtues of getting to handle lovely dresses all day rather than the ceremonial robes of doughty clergy. Sophy knew for a fact that at least one cardinal had actually died in his fancy frock – keeled right over while they were choosing a new pope – because it was easily the most interesting artefact in the whole museum.

'You'd have your own lovely space just off the wedding dress and posh gown atally... atelia... um, salon?'

'Are you trying to say atelier? It's French for both shop and workroom.'

'Yes, that. It has a skylight so no more ruining your eyes in this dark, dank basement – where, by the way, I can see three mousetraps without even having to look for them.'

'We do have a terrible problem with mice,' Cress said mildly, but Sophy could see even the talk of vintage frocks was yet to put a fire in her belly. Sophy would settle for even a low flame.

'It's in Primrose Hill, right by the canal, which is much easier to get to from your place,' she went on. Cress lived in Finchley. 'Just a few stops on the Northern line and of course you'll be working with me, your favourite stepsister and, quite frankly, Cress, I really need a friend in that place.'

'Why? Are they mean? Are all the people that work there really intimidating and know everything about fashion and will mock me terribly if I mispronounce Balenciaga or Lucien Lelong?'

Sophy immediately realised her mistake and frantically backtracked. 'Well, I don't know who either of those people are but the women in the shop are really nice. Really nice. But they're all very obsessed with vintage fashion. It's all they ever talk about.' Sophy crossed her fingers behind her back, even as she knew a moment of doubt. Was it fair to put Cress in close proximity to Phoebe? God, Phoebe would eat her alive. 'Look, Cress, you would love the actual job. You're wasted here. You know you are. You're always saying how much you hate it.'

Cress looked around anxiously in case anyone had heard that last bit, but she was as usual stuck down in the basement on her own. She'd once said to Sophy that there were times when she felt like the Radio Four *Woman's Hour* presenters were her only work friends. 'I have very specific skills,' she said. 'I don't mean to be big-headed but I don't think you could afford me, and I really can't manage on any less than I get here.'

'How much do you get here?' Sophy asked. It was something she'd often wondered and had decided that maybe the fusty old benefactor who'd donated the premises had also left the museum enough money that Cress was paid a pretty hefty wage.

With a put-upon air, Cress wrote something down on a Post-it note and pushed it at Sophy, who read the figure with disbelief. Sophy used to think that she was poorly paid considering she was senior sales associate of an Oxford Street flagship store, but...

'I know it's a lot...'

'Oh my God, Cress! That isn't even minimum wage. Freddy, he's Johnno's business guy, says he can pay you this much.' It was Sophy's turn to write a number on the Post-it note and push it back.

Cress gasped like she'd just pricked her finger. 'This... this is beyond the dreams of avarice.'

'So, you'll come and work with me then?'

Cress still wouldn't seal the deal, even though it then turned out that she was on a zero-hours contract and that she was pretty sure the mice had fleas because she had some unexplained bites on her ankle. Eventually she agreed to visit the shop the next day, though even that was a battle.

'I can't say I have a dentist's appointment if I don't have a dentist's appointment. That would be wrong. And have I mentioned the cassocks…?'

'If you don't, I'm going to get that black dress that looks like the one Audrey Hepburn wore in the opening scenes of *Breakfast at Tiffany's* and I'm going to unpick the hem with my nail scissors,' Sophy threatened.

'You wouldn't,' Cress said, aghast, and of course Sophy wouldn't. Phoebe would then kill her, painfully and slowly, with said nail scissors – but Cress didn't know that, and reluctantly she agreed to fake an emergency dentist's appointment.

'Though it's tempting fate. I bet I get toothache before the day's out,' she said mournfully as Sophy sent a location pin to her phone.

Chapter Five

Cress's introduction to The Vintage Dress Shop didn't get off to the best start. Sophy met her at Chalk Farm station and she could see from her stepsister's face, as grey as the leaden March skies, that Cress was regretting her decision to scope out another job.

'I've been at the museum for nearly ten years. It's not very loyal to just up and leave, is it?' she asked Sophy fretfully as they crossed over the bridge.

'It's not very loyal after nearly ten years to have you on a zero-hours contract, either.' Sophy could have said a lot more but she didn't. In times of turmoil and potential change, Cress needed very gentle handling. Still, there was one thing she needed to mention. 'Just so you know, Phoebe, the manageress, she can be a little bit prickly. Just a little bit.'

Which was a lie; Phoebe was as prickly as a whole desert full of cacti. Cress's face went from grey to bedsheet white.

'Oh God, why do I let you talk me into these things?' she murmured. 'This is like the time you persuaded me to get a day ticket to that festival and it rained and was so cold that the Red Cross had to hand out those silver foil blankets. And we got food poisoning from the falafels.'

'This is *nothing* like that time,' Sophy said. Even though the skies were still overcast, Primrose Hill was looking pretty. She pointed out the fancy interiors shop and her favourite café for getting exorbitantly priced coffee, 'and if you go down there, then you hit the canal. Did I mention that there's a little patio at the shop with canalside views? Lovely in summertime.'

Cress made a non-committal 'hmm' and then they got to the shop and when she saw that perfect black strapless tulle dress in the window, her face stopped looking quite so pinched. Though Sophy could feel her own face tightening up as she opened the door and gestured to Cress to step inside.

Cress took a few tentative steps towards the door so Sophy had to give her a good shove to get her properly over the threshold, where they were met by Phoebe and that Charles in a *lilac* tweed suit. Lilac tweed! It looked good on him, making his blue eyes and thick blond hair really pop. He was sitting on one of the sofas drinking tea from one of the fine bone-china cups that Sophy never used because they were only big enough for a thimbleful of liquid, if that, and she was terrified of breaking one.

'...there are quite a few estate sales coming up. Always good for wedding dresses,' Charles was saying while Phoebe nodded eagerly.

'You know I adore a thirties silhouette and of course anything with that fifties nipped-in waist. Hides a multitude of sins on some of the more... metabolically challenged of our brides,' Phoebe added.

Charles nudged her with his elbow. 'That's almost tactful for you, Pheebs. Has Freddy finally sent you to a sensitivity training workshop?' he asked. Sophy would never have dared to tease Phoebe, but Phoebe just rolled her eyes and nudged him back. Then her lighter mood disappeared as she saw Sophy standing there with Cress cowering behind her.

'Oh, it's you,' she said, as she did every morning, as if she hoped that Sophy might just stop turning up. 'And is that... who is that?'

'Obviously the sensitivity training workshop wasn't that successful,' Charles murmured over the rim of his teacup, which made Phoebe glare at him, then turn her glare back to Sophy and...

'This is Cress, my stepsister and a clothing restoration genius,' Sophy said in a voice that was almost a growl and which she hoped implied that if Phoebe was mean to Cress then Sophy would end her. 'She's got a degree from Central Saint Martins and she's spent nearly ten years working at a museum restoring very important ecclesiastical garments—'

'Well, that sounds far too niche for us. We don't get a lot of popes popping in,' Phoebe said, but subsided when Sophy narrowed her eyes so much it was a wonder that she could still see out of them.

'*As I was saying*, Cress has tons of experience and she knows *everything* about vintage fashion and she makes the most amazing clothes and she can repair and alter things that were fit only for the bonfire. You should have seen what she did with my aunt's wedding dress, which had fag burns on the bodice and a rip in the skirt, so my cousin—'

'Yes, yes, we get the idea,' Phoebe said and Sophy stopped. Not because of Phoebe but because Cress was looking as if she wanted to burst into tears and flee for the hills. Not necessarily in that order.

'Sounds like a very impressive CV,' Charles said kindly and Sophy threw him a grateful look, but then her attention turned back to Cress, who was staring at the rails of dresses with trepidation.

When Cress got really freaked out, she tended to shut down, and now it really didn't seem like a good idea to have dragged her out of her comfort zone, away from her musty cardinals' robes, and put her in front of Phoebe.

'You all right?' Sophy asked softly.

Cress didn't answer but started delving in her black tote bag, which she'd made herself and had embroidered the words 'Cross-stitching is my superpower' on it in pink thread.

Was she after her phone so she could request an urgent exit? Or tissues because she was about to start crying? Neither. Cress fished out a pair of white gloves, the gloves she wore when she was handling religious cloth and which always made Sophy imagine that Cress was about to perform a mime.

Cress pulled on the gloves, Phoebe and Charles staring at her in bemusement, then approached the blue rail. 'This… This…' She carefully gathered up the skirt of a jaunty white dress adorned with blowsy blue cabbage roses. 'This is a Horrockses!'

'It's not horrid,' Sophy hissed. 'What are you like?'

'I said Horrockses, not horrid,' Cress said with a little tinge of exasperation. 'Oh my goodness, I've never seen one in the flesh. I went to the Horrockses exhibition at the Harris Museum in Preston, and there is that range they're doing for ASOS, but this, *this*, is something else.'

'It is a Horrockses,' Phoebe confirmed as Cress nodded, vaguely, because she hadn't needed confirmation. 'They are really hard to come by.'

'I'm not surprised,' Cress said, running a reverent hand along the dresses hanging up. She stopped when she got to a bright blue number. 'And of course, this is Biba. Unmistakeable.'

'Isn't it fantastic? Practically in mint condition.' Phoebe smiled as she stood up. She was pretty even when she was glaring, sniping and generally being thoroughly unpleasant, but when she smiled she was unmistakeably beautiful.

'How exciting,' Cress decided, looking around the room again at the many rails. Sophy was surprised that her eyes weren't flickering rapidly as she cross-referenced the dresses with the encyclopaedic knowledge of vintage clothes that she had stored in her head. 'I know that you only have Sophy's word for it, but I really do love vintage.'

'That's clearly obvious,' Phoebe said, warmly, because by now she'd melted like ice cream spilled on a hot pavement.

'I should have brought some examples of my work but I just thought— I only came because I knew you wouldn't let it go if I didn't, Sophy…' Cress tailed off with an apologetic smile. 'But now I'm so glad I came just to be in the same room as a Horrockses.'

'Prepare to be amazed because I haven't even shown you the atelier yet,' Phoebe said eagerly, rushing over to the stairs and unclipping the velvet rope. 'We have a Courrèges up there.'

'Stop it!' Cress was beaming, all teeth and gums, as she practically ran to the stairs.

'And two 1950s Jacques Griffes,' Phoebe said, as she led the way, Cress hot on her heels.

Sophy was left with Charles, who was cucumber cool as he finished his tea, while she felt like she usually did when she was in this shop with these people: flustered and out of place.

'That went better than I expected,' she muttered, more to fill the silence, which felt a little awkward.

Charles gave her another of those kind smiles and gazed up at her. She was suddenly painfully aware that she still hadn't figured out a suitable work outfit for the shop. There was no way she could spend all day in the fitted dresses that Phoebe (and Chloe and Anita whenever they were rostered) wore and she couldn't spend all day in heels either. Phoebe could trip up and down the stairs in her five-inch heels without even breaking a sweat but until about five minutes ago, Sophy had suspected that Phoebe wasn't even human.

Sartorially speaking, Sophy had had to branch out on her own. She stuck to all black but, one day she'd trialled black trousers and shirt and Phoebe and Chloe had looked at her like she'd sprouted two heads overnight. She needed clothes that she could move around in, so she'd resorted to what

Egan used to refer to as her 'sack dresses'. Today she was wearing a loose-fitting black trapeze dress with her knock-off Veja trainers. Not that it mattered what she wore as she still wasn't really allowed on the shop floor anyway.

Charles didn't seem that perturbed by Sophy's non-vintage outfit. He unfolded himself from the pink velvet sofa and gestured at the stairs. 'Shall we?'

'I'm not meant to go up there,' Sophy admitted, flushing because somehow, along with her job, her boyfriend, her home, she'd also lost her backbone in the last couple of months. 'Not without fumigating myself and putting on a hazmat suit first.'

'Her bark really is much worse than her bite,' Charles said, taking Sophy's elbow so he could guide her firmly to the stairs. 'But let's make sure that she hasn't barked or bitten your stepsister. After you.'

Even though Charles quite clearly wasn't interested in her – or in women generally – Sophy felt very self-conscious of the fullness of her skirt as she led the way. She clutched the material to her so she wouldn't flash Charles anything as she hurried up the stairs, still concerned that Phoebe might have reverted to type and started being vile to poor Cress.

Nothing could have been further from the truth. The two women were gushing over the hand-sewn beadwork on a fondant pink... 'Hardy Amies gown. I know people say that Britain has never produced a decent couturier, but I always remind them about Hardy Amies.'

'And what about Charles Creed? Lachasse? Digby Morton? Even Norman Hartnell.'

'Exactly! Though Christian Dior was in another league.'

'He was. He really was,' Cress sighed rapturously.

Phoebe took a deep breath. 'One time Charles unearthed a 1947 New Look dress, black velvet, it was exquisite.

Destined straight for a museum, though he let me touch it first.'

'Oh my God... I would never wash my hands again if I got to touch a New Look dress, though actually I'd be wearing my gloves before I even dared to touch it so I suppose that really wouldn't be an issue.'

'What have I done?' Sophy hissed under her breath, because she'd been worried, very worried, that Phoebe might be horrible to Cress, but this was much worse than anything she could have contemplated.

The two of them having nerdgasms about dresses. A shared passion. A language that Sophy couldn't speak. They might even become best friends.

'Let me show you the sewing room. You don't mind working on site?' Phoebe threw over her shoulder as she led the way to the little workroom tucked under the eaves. 'I'm always up here, so you won't be on your own all day. If there's anything you need in the way of threads and findings, just let me know.'

Sophy looked at Coco Chanel, who was ensconced on her favourite blue satin cushion. Coco Chanel evil-eyed her back. She had a lot of sass for a tiny dog that looked like a gremlin and farted all day. She was also a tougher nut to crack than Phoebe and wouldn't even take treats from Sophy, which was one of the reasons why Sophy was a cat person. You expected a bit of backchat from a cat.

'What's that face for?' Charles asked, though he wasn't looking at Sophy but at the cream silk dress that he'd pulled from a rail even though he hadn't washed his hands after his cup of tea.

'This hasn't gone quite like I expected,' Sophy admitted. 'I mean, it's gone well, but...'

'You were hoping Cress might be backup and instead she's been welcomed into the fold?'

'You're very perceptive.' Sophy folded her arms. 'I don't like it.'

Charles smiled. 'I was the middle one of seven and the other six were all girls. I learned a lot. Mostly by keeping quiet.'

'So the mysteries of the female psyche are like an open book to you?' As Phoebe was otherwise engaged – Sophy could hear her trilling about Cress's prowess with invisible stitching – Sophy dared to park her bottom on one of the gilt and cream brocade sofas.

'I could live to be a thousand and have a hundred sisters and the mysteries of the female psyche would still continue to elude me,' Charles said. He was standing just under one of the ceiling spotlights, which showed off his exquisite bone structure to its best advantage. He was elegant, Sophy decided. Egan hadn't been at all elegant. Especially not after his Friday-night curry, when he'd stick out his bloated belly and belch and expect Sophy to find it amusing. 'But then, where would the fun be if everyone was an open book?'

'I'm an open book,' Sophy said a little glumly. 'I have zero mystery.'

'Nonsense. You're about to go to Australia to work on a sheep station, like an old-fashioned adventuress. Following in the footsteps of trailblazers like Gertrude Bell and Freya Stark.'

Right now, The Vintage Dress Shop on a quiet March morning seemed a world, a lifetime, away from an Australian sheep station. Besides…

'I don't plan on actually handling the sheep.' She grimaced at the thought. 'And the sheep station is very near the coast. Very, very near, so it's not like I'm going to be in the middle of the outback where there are snakes and other things that might kill you if you step on them. I'm only going to spend a few weeks at the sheep station, then I'm heading to Sydney for a friend's wedding.' Sophy glanced at one of the rails of wedding dresses and wished, not for the first time, that she'd been able to be with Radha and her other bridesmaids when she tried on dresses and hadn't had to just make do with a highlights reel on the group chat instead. 'I don't think you get any snakes on lovely sandy beaches, do you?'

It was Charles's turn to grimace. 'I love living in a country where when I wake up in the morning, I know there's going to be zero chance of finding a lizard on my forehead.'

'Lizards! I can't cope with lizards.' Sophy would have to ask Bob and Jean about possible lizard encounters, but for now she heard the door open and had to hurry downstairs so the shop wouldn't be unattended, as Beatrice had a meeting with their website people, Chloe wasn't rostered for the day and Anita wasn't due in until the afternoon. And of course Phoebe was still busy fangirling Cress's intimate knowledge of embroidery technique.

The customer was quickly despatched – she needed a pirate costume for her son for school tomorrow. Sophy directed her to the fancy dress shop on Camden High Street, by which time Charles was back in the shop too and sorting through a cardboard box that Sophy hadn't noticed before.

'This has all been very entertaining and it's been lovely to talk to you properly, but I actually popped over because I have some deadstock pieces for you.'

The warm glow from Charles's words (because lately Sophy needed all the validation she could get) was replaced by icy dread.

'Deadstock?' she echoed, all her worst fears confirmed. 'I *knew* people had died in this stuff. I knew it!'

Charles looked up from his box of dead people's accessories, his eyes glinting with amusement, his mouth curved in a now wicked smile. 'I have an understanding with several of the local undertakers.'

Sophy collapsed on one of the pink sofas. 'Please tell me you're joking.'

'And shatter all your illusions about the nefarious side of the vintage business?'

'This is one of those rare occasions when I'm really happy for all my illusions to be shattered,' Sophy said with a plaintive look at Charles, who was crouched at her feet. He even looked elegant on his haunches. And amused. Still very very amused.

'Deadstock just means dead inventory; items that were never sold,' Charles explained. 'You must have encountered deadstock in your last job. Johnno mentioned that you'd worked for Belle Girl.'

It seemed as if Johnno and Charles had had quite the chat about Sophy, taking in not just the last chapter of her illustrious career but her plans for the future, lizards, snakes and spiders notwithstanding.

'We didn't have deadstock. We sold everything. Even returns that, quite frankly, weren't fit for anything other than burning. Shop policy was that if you marked it down enough, then someone would always end up buying it,' Sophy recalled as she peered down at the contents of this mystery box. There were about fifty or so small boxes in there, which Charles was rifling through with his long fingers that looked like he should be playing fiddly piano concertos or performing delicate, life-saving surgery on someone's heart. 'What have you got in there, then?'

'Seventy 1950s Bakelite brooches.' Charles took out one of the boxes and prised off the lid to reveal a small black cat, its back arched, tail twitched, its eyes picked out in green. 'Quite fun, no?'

'It's very cute,' Sophy agreed as Charles placed the brooch on her upturned palm, the tips of his fingers brushing her skin, which for some strange reason made her want to shiver. But in a good way. A very good way. She tried to ignore it, push it away with whatever she could think of to say next. 'And you also source all those posh frocks upstairs? '

'That's just the side-hustle.' Charles opened another box. Inside was nestled a brooch in the shape of a little white Westie. 'The day job is vintage jewellery. If you were in the market for a tiara, then I'm your man.'

'It's funny you should mention it, I was thinking only the other day that I didn't have enough tiaras.' It was one of only three occasions in her life when Sophy could actually think of the right thing to say at exactly the right moment.

Charles gifted her another of those smiles that made Sophy feel like she wasn't just funny but clever and beautiful and even sexy, because it was a warm, appreciative smile and his eyes were fixed on her face, like Sophy's face was very pleasing to him.

She had to stop it. Stop *this*. Stop developing a massive crush on a man who so obviously didn't fancy women, and would have been completely out of her league anyway. She just wished that he wasn't so handsome or so tactile or so beautifully dressed and that he would stop looking at her like that, because it made her feel all hot and bothered in a way that she couldn't remember ever feeling with Egan. Not even in the heady, early days when they couldn't keep their hands off each other.

Sophy realised that she was staring at Charles and he was looking right back at her, the smile gone but the warm look in his eyes still there.

Were they having a moment? It felt like they were having a moment—

'Sophy, what are you doing touching the merchandise? I hope you've washed your hands!' The moment was abruptly gone, murdered by Phoebe, who must have crept down the stairs because Sophy had never heard her approach.

She turned her head away from Charles and blinked uncertainly and, when she opened her eyes, there was Cress, beaming from ear to ear.

'It's all decided,' she said happily. 'Friday is the end of the month, when my salary gets paid in, so I'm going to start here on Monday.'

'That's brilliant!' Sophy said, levering herself off the sofa so she could give Cress a celebratory hug. 'I knew you'd be perfect for the job.'

'It is brilliant,' Cress agreed. When Cress was happy, she gave the best hugs. But then she was freeing herself from Sophy's arms to throw her stepsister an anguished look, brow furrowed, lips quivering. 'So, will you phone up the museum for me on Monday and say that I've suddenly had to leave the country and you don't know when I'll be back?'

Chapter Six

It was much better to be in Phoebe's good books than it was to feel like she was shooting tiny daggers into you whenever she glanced your way.

Phoebe was delighted about Cress, though Sophy did hear her murmur to Beatrice, 'So weird that they're friends. I mean, Sophy doesn't even know who Mary Quant is.'

Sophy did actually know who Mary Quant was but, even if she hadn't, Phoebe would have filled her in, because she'd clearly decided that Sophy had passed some kind of arbitrary probation period. Or else Phoebe had realised that Sophy was going to keep turning up every day, whether she liked it or not, so they might just as well make the most of it.

The next morning, after washing her hands – and not even the sternest hospital matron was as exacting on the subject of hand hygiene as Phoebe – Sophy was allowed on the shop floor.

'I'm going to train you up,' Phoebe promised ominously. Sophy was all ready to bristle because she'd forgotten more about customer service than Phoebe even knew, but it turned out that Phoebe wanted to impart the mysteries of selling vintage fashion.

By lunchtime, Sophy was reeling from all the new knowledge that had been stuffed into her head. The dropped hems of the twenties. Nineteen thirties bias cut. The utility clothing of the forties and the New Look silhouette and wiggle dresses of the fifties before they moved on to the minidresses and Pop Art of the sixties.

Phoebe had all sorts of fascinating facts at her fingertips. That clothes rationing hadn't ended as soon as the Second World War was over but carried on until 1949. British women had been rightly furious that there were French ladies swishing about in their ginormous New Look skirts while they were still having to replace the gussets of their knickers with stockinette. 'When the queen got married in 1947, she bought the material for her dress with her ration coupons. Lots of people tried to donate their coupons to her, but the Palace sent them all back.'

'I would have absolutely kept my clothing coupons for myself,' Sophy said and Phoebe nodded.

'I know, me too!'

It was a beautiful moment of solidarity. It didn't last but also it didn't dissipate into the open hostility that had been the theme up until then.

'So, pricing? How does that work?' Sophy asked, which was a reasonable question so there was no need for Phoebe to close her eyes and pinch the bridge of her nose like she had a headache coming on.

'I can't… there is no… You are *not* to price anything yourself,' Phoebe said sternly. 'It's very complicated. It depends entirely on the dress: the era, its condition, who was the designer? Is it deadstock? What's it made from?'

'That does sound complicated,' Sophy muttered. She was happy to leave that to Phoebe rather than to be punished for selling a two-hundred-pound dress for a tenner. Even downstairs, some of the price points had made Sophy's eyebrows shoot up. You'd be hard pressed to find anything for less than fifty quid, and most of their dresses were priced between a hundred and fifty and two hundred and fifty pounds.

'It's getting harder and harder to source decent vintage,' Phoebe explained as she gave Sophy a low-down on the yellow rail. 'It makes me so sad to think of all those poor dresses that weren't looked after properly, then got thrown out through no fault of their own. Or worse, they languished in the back of a wardrobe for decades and when their owner died some heavy-handed oaf who didn't know what they were doing got rid of them.'

'Yeah, that is terrible.'

Colin, Cress's lesser half, was fricking obsessed with music in a boring, trainspottery way. He refused to listen to his favourite albums on anything but vinyl and he would spout facts, figures and opinions for hours if you'd let him. From the evils of Spotify to how George Harrison was the best Beatle and that really there'd been no truly new or groundbreaking developments in music since 1979. Sophy dreaded getting stuck next to Colin on the rare occasions they were graced with his presence. But Colin and his boring, encyclopaedic knowledge of obscure bands from yesteryear had nothing on Phoebe. Sophy liked fashion. She liked the transformative power of a new dress. But Phoebe and her old frocks took it to a whole other level.

'Anyway, there's a label in every dress.' Phoebe removed a bottle green woollen shift that Sophy was now about seventy per cent certain was early sixties to point out the handwritten label inside. 'Not pinned, Sophy. We *never* pin. Look, it's looped through on a ribbon and there's the size, the price, the era and designer if we know it.'

'About sizing...'

'We use modern sizing. Ignore the size on the manufacturer's label because vintage sizing is much smaller. A vintage size ten would be equivalent to a size six now.'

'That's just mean,' Sophy said, putting the dress back on the rail under Phoebe's supervision.

'People were much smaller back then. They didn't have access to such good nutrition as we do, or family-sized bags of kettle chips,' Phoebe pointed out.

'Because I always wondered... I've read in loads of places that Marilyn Monroe was actually a size sixteen—'

'Fake news!' Phoebe gasped. 'She was tiny. I saw some of her dresses in an exhibition when I went to LA and I doubt I could even have got one of them over my head.'

'But *you're* tiny,' Sophy said. Not that she really wanted to get into a discussion on body size, but it was too late; Phoebe was already looking unbearably self-satisfied at Sophy's comment.

'It's a trade-off. If I want to fit into the good vintage then I don't allow myself to eat carbs or chocolate. Ever,' she said.

'No dress is worth no chocolate ever,' Sophy insisted, but she didn't want things to get frosty again when they'd been getting on so well. 'Did you ever think of organising the dresses according to size?' At her old shop, they'd had detailed diagrams from the merchandising team every time new stock dropped.

'We did when we first opened but it wasn't very aesthetically pleasing, everything jumbled together.' Phoebe winced at the memory. 'Then I decided to arrange everything by era but that looked messy too, so in the end I went for colour-theming. It looks *amazing* on Instagram.'

'It looks amazing in real life too, but how do you even remember that you have a size twelve gold lace dress that would be perfect for a wedding if it's all arranged by colour?'

'Because I have every piece of stock memorised,' Phoebe explained, because of course she did. 'So do Chloe and Anita. Beatrice sticks everything up on the website anyway and you can set the search function to size or colour or era, but I think that's cheating.' Of course she did. 'Don't worry, you'll soon get the hang of it. Now, shall we approach the thorny topic of accessories?'

'Maybe we should quit while we're ahead and leave that for another day?' Sophy said pleadingly. She had so much new knowledge in her head that she was pretty sure it had knocked out quite a few neurons devoted to Spice Girls lyrics and the dates of all of her friends' birthdays.

'You're probably right,' Phoebe said. Clearly, the Friday feeling agreed with her. 'But actually, there was one thing I wanted to say to you...'

Sophy tensed every muscle in her body. 'Really? What was that?'

'You are going to have to start wearing vintage, you know, even if it is only in work hours. Although once you start wearing vintage, you'll never want to go back to civilian clothes,' Phoebe said smugly. 'I could pick out some black dresses for you, like we all wear.'

'But I'm not going to be here for very long and also, like Britain before we Brexited, I need freedom of movement,' Sophy said, pleased that her backbone wasn't completely missing. 'Those dresses are so form-fitting.'

'Why wouldn't you want to fit your form though?' Phoebe asked, eyes like a barcode scanner as she stared at Sophy's figure. 'Don't take this the wrong way, but that dress is doing nothing for you. It looks like a sack.'

'Which other way would you like me to take it? It's a trapeze dress, they're very on-trend actually.'

Phoebe waved one perfectly manicured hand dismissively. 'Pfffttt. Trends never stick around but style is timeless.' Then she must have realised that she'd reverted to beastly type because she gave Sophy a winsome smile. 'Just try a few things on. For me.'

Sophy really didn't want to do Phoebe any favours, but they had been getting on so well and what harm could it do to try on a couple of dresses? Phoebe was already pulling a fifties black broderie anglaise dress from the rail. It wasn't tight. Or rather the bodice with its boatneck and cap sleeves was, but the skirt was very full and swishy.

'I think this would look great on you. Oh, and there's a lovely white dress with sailboats on it, that might be fun,' Phoebe said, eyes raking up and down Sophy's body more thoroughly than any man ever had. 'My God, are you *smelling* the dress?'

More of a surreptitious sniff, Sophy had thought. 'No!'

'You should know by now that we launder everything that comes in – and if you ask me if anyone has died in either dress, I *will* smack you,' Phoebe threatened, thrusting the white dress at Sophy.

'And if you do, I will take you to an industrial tribunal,' Sophy countered, but Phoebe just scoffed and then with her hand at the small of Sophy's back frogmarched her to one of the cubicles at the back of the shop.

Once the chintzy curtain was shielding her from view, Sophy *did* smell the black dress. It smelled all right. Clean. Not like it was going to give her a bad case of scabies. Cress had once bought a sixties coat that smelled so badly of BO that nothing could get rid of the stench. Not Febreeze, or a fresh breeze (she'd hung it on the washing line for a week), not even several delicate cycles in the washing machine; in the end, she'd had to bin it.

Sophy pulled off her very on-trend and also directional black trapeze dress and, without much enthusiasm, wiggled into the black fifties dress. The bodice was very tight. So tight that she couldn't even pull it down over her boobs – and it wasn't like she had that much in the boob department that it had ever been an issue before.

'How are you getting on in there?' came Phoebe's querulous cry and then, to Sophy's horror, she was yanking back the curtain to reveal Sophy half in and half out of the black dress.

'Get out!' Sophy shrieked. 'Do you do this to your customers?'

Phoebe didn't get out. 'Side zip,' she said obliquely.

'*What?*'

'Must I do everything myself?' Then Phoebe wasn't getting out but approaching Sophy so she could take a firm hold of her in one hand and a firm hold of the dress in the other. 'Side zip.'

Suddenly the bodice was loose enough that Phoebe could tug it into place and then zip it back up.

'Oh! Weird.' Sophy turned to look at herself in the mirror and, though her face was pink and her hair was escaping from her ponytail, it pained her to admit that the dress fitted perfectly. As if it had been made for her.

'I knew you had a waist,' Phoebe announced with great satisfaction. 'But FYI, you're definitely wearing the wrong-size bra. That one is too big for you in the cup. It's not supporting you properly and you'd find that—'

'Shut up!' Sophy gritted, because she was a 34C and had been since she was fifteen.

'I'm being *helpful*.'

'No wonder we don't have that many customers,' Sophy replied and, as soon as she said it, they heard the bell above the door tinkle and then a familiar voice...

'Where is everybody? It's second Friday, kids. Johnno's here to take you to the pub!'

67

Chapter Seven

Phoebe left the changing cubicle without a backward glance, Beatrice bustled out of the office, Chloe and Coco Chanel came tripping down the stairs so they could all greet Johnno like he was just back from an expedition to the Antarctic.

'We were about to officially declare you a missing person!' Phoebe told him, leaning in as Johnno wrapped an arm round her shoulders.

'Had to go and see a man about a dog, didn't I?' was the very predictable reply.

'But you were gone weeks!'

'Had to see several men about several dogs,' Johnno improvised. What hair he had left wasn't pink any more but a bright orange, which clashed with his ruddy complexion.

'You know Coco Chanel prefers to be an only dog,' Beatrice giggled and then Johnno let Phoebe go so he could scoop up the stand-offish pooch and press enthusiastic kisses to her grumpy face, while she struggled and squirmed. He finally let her go so she could jump up on one of the pink sofas and glare at the assembled company reproachfully.

'So, you sold lots of dresses then? Freddy said that Reenie quit. That's a bugger.'

'We've got a Reenie replacement starting on Monday,' Phoebe said, as she walked over to the desk. 'Cressida. I think she's going to be amazing. Somehow Sophy managed to find her.' She shrugged to convey that she still wasn't over the fact that Sophy had been their saviour in their hour of need, and that if Sophy was related to Cress then maybe Sophy wasn't as bad as she'd previously thought.

'Sophy?' Johnno queried and Sophy, who was peering round the side of the changing room curtain because she hadn't been able to get herself out of the black dress, felt her insides plummet. Had Johnno, her actual biological father, forgotten who she was? 'You mean my Sophy? I hope you've been treating my girl nicely, Pheebs.'

Both Phoebe and Sophy humph'ed at that, then Johnno caught sight of her. 'Ah, Soph, there you are!'

'Yes, remember when you offered me a job? I mean, I've been working here for the last two weeks, so...'

'Yeah, yeah, of course,' Johnno hurriedly assured her, which didn't make Sophy feel any better. 'Saving up so you can go back to my ancestral homelands. God, that dress looks beaut on you, darling.'

Sophy had ventured out of the changing room but now she wanted to retreat as Chloe and Beatrice, and even Coco Chanel, turned to stare at her.

'That dress *does* look amazing on you,' Chloe gasped. She sounded quite surprised.

'So chic with your trainers,' Beatrice added and, before Sophy could protest that she already had lots of black dresses and all her wages were meant to be going towards her airfare, the hefty staff discount was applied and Beatrice said that it was all right, she'd just deduct the money out of Sophy's wages.

Then the cashing up and the vacuuming and the count-less other tasks that needed to be done to close the shop were accomplished in record time, while Johnno sat on the sofa with Coco Chanel perched on his lap like she was the prow of a ship.

'Watching you all run round like headless chickens has made me work up a thirst,' Johnno said, as they all trooped out of the door so Phoebe could set the alarm. 'Where shall we go? The White Swan?'

'Pheebs is banned for life from The White Swan,' Chloe said sweetly. She seemed a lot more chippy now she'd clocked off.

'I am not banned. I said that I would never go back there because they don't give you a bottle of tonic. They give you soda water from the tap but they try to charge you for a bottle of tonic,' Phoebe snapped as she locked up. 'So I threatened them with the Trading Standards...'

'... and then they banned you for life,' Chloe reminded her with a smile.

'Well, I wouldn't go back there if they paid me.'

'The Hat and Fan it is then!' Johnno said quickly, and he led the way, or rather Coco Chanel, sporting a very fetching pink diamanté lead and collar, surged ahead, her bottom and stump of a tail wiggling furiously.

The Hat and Fan was down a side street that led to the Regent's Canal. It was one of those Victorian pubs that London excelled at. A proper old-fashioned boozer with intricate patterns etched into its lead glass windows, ornate vine leaves carved into the mahogany wood of the bar and red velvet banquettes as far as the eye could see. As it was late Friday afternoon, it was full up with workers happy to have downed tools for the weekend, though being Primrose Hill none of them had downed actual tools. But they'd switched off their computers and put their email on Out of Office until Monday morning and were starting the weekend with a drink and a bowl of mixed nuts.

Once they'd taken everyone's orders ('and make sure the tonic is in a bottle, not from the tap. Slimline tonic and a slice of lime, not lemon') Sophy went to the bar with Johnno.

He still seemed surprised to see her. He'd *begged* her to come and work for him, she thought, then sorted things

70

out with Freddy and discussed her with Charles. So she wasn't sure why it was such a shock to him that she was on the payroll.

It was also a shock to see the easy, breezy relationship that Johnno had with the rest of the staff, including Phoebe. Especially Phoebe. They were all big with the banter and the in-jokes and surely Sophy should have banter and in-jokes with Johnno. She was his flesh and blood, but she felt like an add-on.

Sophy needed to remember that working in his shop didn't change the fact that she and Johnno had always led very separate lives. She'd be gone in a couple of months anyway. Which reminded her, she really needed to gently nudge him about the documentation he was meant to be digging out for her dual citizenship application.

'By the way, have you had any luck finding your passport or your birth certificate?' she asked, but he'd just caught the attention of the man behind the bar and didn't hear her.

'Ah, Henry, mine host,' he said warmly, because he was clearly more pleased to see the barman than Sophy. 'Can I introduce you to Sophy, my beautiful daughter?'

'Lovely to meet you,' Henry said. He looked almost as Victorian as the fittings in his pub, with huge mutton-chop whiskers and waistcoat and pocket watch. He reached across the bar to shake Sophy's hand. 'You clearly take after your mother rather than this ugly mug.'

'She does,' Johnno agreed. 'But you're still fond of your old man, aren't you?'

'You have your moments,' Sophy decided because, as was so often the case with Johnno, she went from being hurt and disappointed in him to suddenly getting the warm fuzzies when he showed the sweet, thoughtful side of his character.

It was a very slow procession back to their table in the snug. Not just because they each had a heavy tray groaning

71

with drinks and mixers and bowls of nuts and crisps but because Johnno was greeted on all sides and, every time, he introduced Sophy, as his 'lovely daughter'. And 'Have you met my girl, Sophy, she's joined the family firm?' And even, 'This is Sophy, yes, my daughter, the one I told you about. Said she had brains and beauty, didn't I?'

'You've told people about me?' Sophy asked once they were seated and she had her hands clutched round a very welcome gin and tonic.

'Why wouldn't I?' Johnny asked, his weatherbeaten face creased in confusion.

'Well, because—'

'Ah, Freddy! My main man!' Johnno called out as Freddy came through the door. He saw them, waved and headed their way. 'I've put my card behind the bar. Get yourself a drink. Pheebs, Freddy is here.'

Phoebe, who was sitting across the table from Sophy with her gin and tonic, not soda water, and with a slice of lime, not lemon, raised her eyebrows a fraction of a centimetre. 'Yes, I did notice, thank you very much.'

Sophy decided that she'd park the awkward topic of why Johnno had been singing her praises when they hardly ever saw each other. Not important. Not when there was a whiff of scandal to be had.

'What's the story with Phoebe and Freddy?' she whispered to Chloe, who was sitting on her other side, surreptitiously hand-feeding crisps to Coco Chanel. 'Is there a story there?'

'Can't stand each other,' Chloe whispered back.

'Really? What gives?'

Chloe shrugged. 'I don't know. I've only worked at the shop for the last year and a bit and they already hated each other.'

It was comforting to know that she wasn't the only target for Phoebe's wrath, but also very annoying that Chloe had no dirt to dish.

When Freddy arrived at their table with a bottle of fancy imported lager, rather than sitting next to Phoebe, who had plenty of room on the banquette next to her, he grabbed a low stool and sat down in between Johnno and Sophy, his knees almost touching his ears.

'Do you want to swap?' Sophy asked. 'I don't think that stool is designed for anyone taller than a small child.'

'No, you're all right,' Freddy said with a smile. Except his smile was more of a cheeky grin and, when he shrugged off his jacket, she could see that his arms were covered in tattoos. Not even the regulation-issue tribal armband favoured by Egan and all of his friends but full-colour sleeves featuring a pirate ship, birds of paradise and an exotic sea creature. 'So, how has it been in the shop?' He shot a pointed look towards Phoebe's end of the table. 'Everyone been treating you all right?'

Sophy wasn't one to tell tales out of school. Apart from when she got back home each night and would regale her mum and Mike with examples of Phoebe's extreme beastliness. 'Oh, everyone's been great,' she told Freddy.

Then Chloe pointed out two members of a band who'd been pretty famous a few years ago. Then it was time for another round and by the time she was on her third gin and tonic and they'd decided to order some bowls of chips to mop up the alcohol, Sophy was feeling pleasantly buzzed as she texted Caroline to tell her to put her dinner in the fridge.

It was then that Charles walked in.

He was in another one of his impeccably cut suits. Charcoal grey but paired with a pink floral Liberty print shirt, and he was smiling straight at Sophy. Her stomach did a delicious tip and turn. Or rather he was smiling at the table en masse, because he greeted them all with a cheery, 'I might have known I'd find you reprobates in here. Who's ready for another drink?'

Sophy tried not to stare at the long lean line of Charles while he was at the bar. She'd have thought he'd be more comfortable in some exclusive members' club in the West End, but, like Johnno, he shook Henry's hand, then stayed to have a chat as if he were a regular too.

As Charles headed to their table Sophy averted her gaze, but there was no one really to talk to except Phoebe, who was staring down at her phone, and Coco Chanel, because everyone else had decamped to the pool table in the lounge bar.

'Sophy!' Charles put his drink down, a bottle of the same lager that Freddy was drinking, though Charles didn't seem like the sort of man who drank lager, especially out of the bottle. Then he was leaning down to brush a kiss on her cheek – and ooh, the other cheek.

He smelled amazing. Of some expensive cologne that was woody and a little bit exotic. Then he sat down next to Sophy so that their knees bumped together.

'Hi,' she said, inexplicably shy because there was nothing like drinking three gin and tonics in ninety minutes to really bring out a girl's crush.

'You look lovely,' Charles said. Sophy's foolish heart leapt. 'Is that a dress from the shop? Vintage? God, it could have been made for you.' Her foolish heart sank. He meant that the dress, which she was still wearing because there hadn't been time to change, looked lovely, rather than the person who was wearing it. Or did he? 'So, hard day at the office?'

'Phoebe's been teaching me about vintage fashion. I'm ninety per cent certain that I know what a bias cut is now,' Sophy said. At the mention of her name, Phoebe looked up, smiled vaguely, then went back to staring at her phone screen, so it was almost as if Sophy and Charles were alone. Albeit alone in a very busy pub.

74

'I know the bias cut is meant to be flattering, but I think it's very unforgiving,' Charles said because, of course, he'd know all about bias cuts and dropped hems and kick-pleats.

'Unless you are whippet thin, it's going to show up every lump and bump,' Sophy decided with a shudder. 'Especially as every bias-cut dress we stock seems to be made of crêpe or satin or some other very clingy fabric.'

She shot a fearful look at Phoebe in case her bias-cut bitching had been overheard, but Phoebe was tucking her phone into her old-fashioned handbag and picking up Coco Chanel's lead. 'Right, time to get this young lady home,' she announced. 'She needs her beauty sleep.'

It would take many decades of sleep to smooth out Coco Chanel's crumpled, cross little face, Sophy thought as Phoebe slid out from the banquette and hurried to the door. 'See you tomorrow,' she called out, in an uncharacteristically friendly manner, then disappeared into the night.

Phoebe's exit was the cue for something of an exodus. She hadn't even been gone two minutes when Freddy, who had been playing pool, rushed out of the door with a hurried wave. Then Chloe and Beatrice came over to say that they were heading to a bar in Soho, a band was playing, and did Sophy want to come too?

Sophy was flattered to be asked but a strange development had taken hold once she'd reached thirty. Now she couldn't hit bars at gone ten and expect to be home in the wee small hours then get up bright and early for work the next day. Or anyway, she couldn't do it without industrial amounts of caffeine and a pounding headache. Also, even though she was thirty, she was living back at home and though she didn't have a curfew like she'd had as a teenager, Caroline intimated very heavily that she couldn't really settle until Sophy was home so it would be great if she could be in by eleven. 'But earlier would be good too. Even better, in fact.'

'I think I'll pass,' she said lightly, noting that neither Chloe nor Beatrice looked that devastated. 'In fact, I should probably be getting home.'

'Oh, don't go,' Charles said with the tiniest of pouts. 'I've only just got here and you'll be condemning me to tracking down Johnno and having to talk abut boring things like football and welding.'

'I don't think Johnno's that interested in welding,' Sophy said with a giggle. (There was something about Charles and his pout and now the batting of his annoyingly long eyelashes that made her giggle.)

'But you'll stay? I'll even throw in another bowl of chips,' Charles said, as Chloe and Beatrice disappeared.

'One more drink but it's my round,' Sophy said firmly, but when she got back from the bar their table had been annexed by a group of quite shouty young men in suits and so she had to sit next to Charles on the small patch of banquette that was left. So close that their thighs were pressed together, and even their elbows were touching when they leaned forward to pick up their glasses or take another chip.

It felt very intimate. Charles was telling her about an engagement ring he was sourcing for a prospective groom. But every time he argued with his soon-to-be-fiancée, the money he wanted to spend on the ring went up or down depending on whose fault the argument was.

'Do you have a shop then?' Sophy asked. She could just imagine Charles having a tiny shop crammed full of brilliant jewels somewhere very exclusive but very old-fashioned. Like the Burlington Arcade off Piccadilly, which didn't seem to have changed much since the days of the Regency. Or maybe a little showroom in one of the mews around Notting Hill and Ladbroke Grove. Or even…

'A little office above a bookie's in Hatton Garden,' Charles said, which rather killed the picture that Sophy had of a fancy shop with bow windows and lots of rings and tiaras and bracelets arranged on satin cushions.

'Hatton Garden?' Sophy asked, because she'd only vaguely heard of it.

'London's jewellery district. Basically one long road, which stretches from Farringdon down to High Holborn. It's no Bond Street but if you want a princess cut solitaire diamond on a claw setting, then it's the best place for it.'

'What's a princess cut?' It felt like Sophy knew nothing about anything. A couple of months ago, her life was settled, safe, absolutely surprise-free. She knew her Oxford Street store better than she knew her own face. She knew where every single item of clothing was, either on display or in the stockroom. And if she didn't, there'd be a schematic from Merchandising appearing on the Webex imminently.

She also knew everything there was to know about Egan, good and bad. And if it seemed that often the bad outweighed the good, then that was just the way it was when you'd been in a relationship for so long. They might not have been love's young dream any more but they rubbed along all right. So it had been quite the revelation when Sophy had realised Egan regarded her more as a lodger with benefits than the person he wanted to share the rest of his life with.

Now, she was floating on uncharted waters in a dinghy that listed to one side. Or that was how it felt. The future hadn't been exciting and full of possibilities; it had felt uncertain and unknown. Even the house where she'd spent her teen years, after Caroline and Mike had married, didn't seem like a safe place to lick her wounds and plan her next move. Especially when her bedroom now had a sunbed, foot spa and Caroline's back-stock beauty products in it.

Maybe that was why Sophy had decided that instead of floating aimlessly, she was going to take a deep dive. The dive didn't get much deeper than emigrating to Australia, half a world away.

It was all right to feel uncertain in a new place, a different country on a different continent. Scary but the good kind of scary. Every day would feel like an adventure: full of new sights and experiences. It would be weird if Sophy didn't feel unsettled being in a new place, but that was better than feeling unsettled in the place she'd grown up. That felt like a failure.

'My description of a princess cut must be sadly boring, because I can tell you haven't been listening to a single word I've said.'

Sophy's unhappy train of thought was derailed by Charles's words puncturing her cloud of self-pity. 'Oh God, I'm so sorry...'

'Nothing to apologise for. I am quite dull when I get on the subject of princess versus emerald cut,' Charles insisted. He didn't look cross. If anything he looked rather concerned. 'Are you all right? You seemed deep in thought and as if not all of them were happy ones.'

'I'm fine,' Sophy said automatically because that was what she always said. 'Just... what with the new job and well, my living situation has changed and this year has turned out very differently to how I thought it would. I'm not sure I do well with changes but then I'm moving to Australia and changes don't get much bigger than that, do they?'

'But you can't make an omelette without breaking a few eggs,' Charles said. 'At least that's what I tell myself.'

'I do like omelettes,' Sophy mused. 'Omelettes aren't scary. They're actually quite comforting.'

'Depends on the filling though. Look, are you sure that you're...'

'It's the gin,' Sophy said, because there had to be something she could blame her mood on rather than her current life situation. 'I shouldn't have drunk gin tonight. They say that gin makes you maudlin, right? Gin tears, mother's ruin and all that.'

'I could get you something else,' Charles suggested because he really was the sweetest man. So kind and perceptive. Maybe a little *too* perceptive. 'Though maybe you shouldn't start mixing your drinks so late in the evening.'

'Yeah, things could get ugly.' Sophy picked up her glass of gin and tonic and gently tapped it against Charles's lager. 'Cheers.'

'Now I have to cheers you back or else we'll really be in trouble,' he said as Sophy finished what was in her glass and decided that it was time to call it a night. Johnno had disappeared, no doubt to see yet another man about yet another dog, and if she continued drinking gin and Charles continued to be kind and perceptive she'd probably end up crying on his shoulder.

'Right, I'm cutting myself off and ordering an Uber. Otherwise I'll ruin your suit by getting tear stains and mascara all over it,' she said.

'Nothing that my dry-cleaner couldn't sort out,' Charles assured her, but Sophy shook her head. She didn't want him to think that she was one of those sad, clichéd women who automatically assumed that every gay man she met was her new best friend.

That was the other thing about drinking too much. Instead of getting the tube home in an economical fashion, it always seemed like a good idea to get a car door to door just as late-night price surging kicked in. Between this and Phoebe forcing her to buy expensive second-hand dresses, it would be this time next year before she saved up her airfare.

'Oh no, you're looking all sad again,' Charles said, lifting his hand so he could brush his thumb against the downturned corner of Sophy's mouth. It was a gentle, friendly touch (though Sophy couldn't remember the last time that any of her friends had felt the need to touch her face), but it seemed to ignite a thousand delicious tingles not just on Sophy's face but all the way through her body and right down to her toes. She had to concentrate very hard on not quivering.

'I'm not sad,' she said, though certainly she wasn't happy. 'I think I must have Resting Sad Face like some people have Resting Bitch Face'. One of those people being Phoebe.

'Even though you're not sad, I'm going to treat you to lunch next week,' Charles said as Sophy gathered up her bag and coat. Sophy felt a small but delicious frisson at his words. Clearly, Charles had decided that they were going to be friends, and it wasn't as if she was going to be having him in any other way.

'Lunch would be nice, but we'll go halves.' Her phone said that her driver was three minutes away, so she stood up. Charles stood up with her.

'No, I insist. My treat. Do you get a day off in the week?' He held the heavy pub door open for her and now Sophy allowed herself to shiver as she was greeted by a rush of cold, damp air.

'Wednesdays.' Sophy had started to dread her days off. Previously she'd loved having a lie-in, then maybe heading out for a yoga class with a friend or a swim at the gym round the corner, but now most of her friends still lived on the other side of London, she'd cancelled her gym membership and Mike referred to their local pool as 'a verruca soup'. This week on her day off, Caroline had asked her to clean out the kitchen cupboards, so lunch with Charles had to be more fun than that. In fact, it would be approximately a thousand times more fun than that because she'd be spending an hour or so with Charles. An unpleasant thought occurred. 'Not anywhere too fancy. I'm not really a fancy kind of person.'

'Oh, I think you could be any kind of person that you wanted to be,' Charles said obliquely. He was looking hard at Sophy and, though his face was clearly illuminated by the lights from the pub, it was impossible to know what he was thinking. 'Why don't you come to the office first and I'll let you try on a tiara and then we'll go for lunch. How does that sound?'

'Really? A real tiara?' Sophy had never been one of those girls who liked to pretend that she was a princess, but apparently she was one of those women who had been harbouring a secret wish to try on a tiara.

Ten minutes ago she'd been teetering on the edge of the pit of despair and now she was laughing as Iban in a Toyota Prius came slowly down the road. Sophy waved manically so he wouldn't drive past her.

'So, I'll see you Wednesday then,' Charles said.

Sophy nodded. 'You will. I'll be thinking about how to wear my hair so it really suits a tiara.'

'It's such lovely hair. The colour...' Charles murmured thoughtfully, and then he caught the end of Sophy's ponytail so he could gaze at the ends of her hair. God, she really needed a trim. 'You couldn't even bottle this colour. It's extraordinary.'

'Ginger,' Sophy said, though if anyone ever dared to call her a ginger, she'd snap that she was a redhead.

'Nothing that prosaic,' Charles said, and she couldn't open the car door when he was holding her ponytail hostage, but then he freed her, only to tuck a stray lock of hair behind her ear, and the tingles started all over again.

'It's just as well you're gay, Charles, otherwise I'd totally be falling in love with you,' Sophy blurted out. 'Head over bloody heels.'

'Gay?'

'Yes, gay. Or do you prefer to identify as LGBTQ or just simply queer? Though my cousin Shay identifies as non-bin—'

'But I'm not gay,' Charles said, with a frown, so Sophy was suddenly quite sure she knew what he was thinking and it wasn't anything good.

'Oh God, I'm so sorry…'

'Please don't mention it.'

Was that don't mention it as in it was no big deal? Or was it don't mention it as in never, ever talk to me again?

'I really have to go,' Sophy said a little desperately because she felt… She didn't even know how she felt. Embarrassed. Idiotic. Ashamed. Definitely not all that drunk any more. 'Look, shall we just cancel Wednesday?'

'Absolutely not. I'm looking forward to Wednesday,' Charles confirmed, but he was still frowning.

Sophy clambered into the car, with very little grace and cheeks on fire. Charles was still standing there with a considered look on his face as Iban pulled away from the kerb and asked her if she'd had a good night.

Sophy put hot hands on her burning cheeks. 'It was bloody awful, but thanks for asking.'

Chapter Eight

Cress started work at The Vintage Dress Shop on the Monday. Right away, Sophy's suspicions were confirmed that her stepsister wasn't going to be the backup that she had hoped for.

They'd met at Chalk Farm station so they could walk to the shop together. Cress had had a light in her eyes and a spring in her step that she hadn't had for a while.

'After all those years of handling ecclesiastical bits and bobs, I finally get to work with beautiful dresses, every one with a story behind it.' She put a hand on her heart, eyes misty with emotion. 'It will be an honour and a privilege to restore them to their former glory. And get paid for it!'

'All right, steady on,' Sophy muttered. She'd never known anyone so excited at the prospect of a full day's work ahead.

As soon as they got to the shop, Cress took off her coat, hung it up on the coat stand in the back office, then pulled on one of the handmade work smocks she always wore over plain black trousers and a jumper. This one was...

'Is that a forties novelty print?' Phoebe asked, eyes wide at the sight of many many poodles cavorting over the navy blue background.

'It is.' Cress held out the corners of the smock. 'I hope Coco Chanel won't mind being in close proximity to so many poodles.'

'I'll have to give you some treats to put in the pockets.' Phoebe beamed even though it wasn't even ten on a

Monday morning. Far too early for her to be in a good mood. 'I *love* pockets.'

'I love pockets too!' Cress stuck her hand in the deep pockets that she sewed into all her smocks so she'd have somewhere to stash her thimbles and boxes of pins and measuring tape. 'Did you know that in olden times they tried to ban women from having pockets in their dresses, because they didn't want them to have anywhere to store seditious material?'

'Seditious material?' Sophy queried.

'Pamphlets complaining about the king or the government and telling the workers to rise up,' Cress explained. 'Pockets are *literally* a feminist issue.'

Sophy had never really thought about pockets in that way before. She wasn't sure that Phoebe had either, because there was a moment's silence, which Sophy punctured with the thought that had tormented her all weekend.

'Here's a funny thing, I thought Charles was gay...'

Phoebe rolled her eyes. 'Charles, *gay*? Don't be ridiculous,' she scoffed. 'His last girlfriend was the accessories editor at *Vogue* and the one before that, Odette, she was French. So chic, so elegant, although it turned out that she was also so married.'

'He's definitely straight then?' Sophy clarified despondently, because she'd really put her foot in it with Charles. He probably thought she was some kind of horrible homophobe or was so unsophisticated and narrow-minded that she assumed that any man who worked in fashion and wore a lilac suit had to be gay.

'I'm bored of talking about this,' Phoebe said with a sniff. 'Anyway, that is *exquisite* top-stitching, Cress.'

Then she tucked her arm into Cress's and led her away. 'I'm so glad you're here. We have a bride coming in today and I can already tell that she's going to be very high-maintenance and will want loads of alterations to whatever

84

dress she eventually picks. You'll have to come and rescue me, Cressy, if you can hear her giving me a hard time.'

Sophy shared an incredulous look with Beatrice at the notion that Phoebe might need rescuing from a customer. More like the other way round. And yes, it was official; Cress was going to be of absolutely no use.

As Cress and Phoebe had decamped to the atelier and Beatrice was busy updating the website with pictures of new stock and Anita was going to be late because she had a dentist's appointment, Sophy was left on her own to relive the torment of those two minutes on Friday night when she'd told Charles that he was gay and then, oh God, intimated that she might be falling in love with him. She really wasn't sure which was worse. It was probably a photo finish. Sophy had to stop thinking about it while also coming up with a bulletproof excuse to get her out of lunch on Wednesday because she could never face Charles ever again.

If he came into the shop, she'd have to lock herself in the back office and not come out until he'd gone. In fact, it might be a good idea to find some other employment alto-gether. It wasn't like working in a vintage dress shop was Sophy's vocation in life. Not like it was for Cress or Phoebe.

Sophy was vocation-free. Always had been. She'd drifted into working for Belle Girl after Johnno had extricated her from her bar job. They were taking on extra staff for Christmas and Sophy had just never left. Now she tried to contemplate what sort of job would make her happy. What was her passion in life? What was she truly good at?

These weren't hard questions, but Sophy couldn't find an answer to a single one. It was another reason why she was going to Australia: so she could have an opportunity to reinvent herself. Maybe it would turn out that she'd be really good at surfing or discover a passion for sheep farm-ing. Stranger things had happened.

The door opened and a young woman with a clenched jaw and an older woman with a harried expression entered the shop. It was Phoebe's high-maintenance bride and her mother, so Sophy directed them upstairs. Then, having worked in retail for such a long time, she deployed her impeccable skills at looking busy even when she wasn't. She pretended to rearrange the dresses, because God help her if she mucked up the colour coding. She gave the jewellery display cases a quick wipe down and when, finally, some browsers arrived, she helped them pull some clothes to try on for a fancy golden wedding anniversary.

'Because they've been married fifty years, our grandparents have gone with a fifties theme. Where are your fifties dresses?'

'They're actually arranged by colour,' Sophy said. 'Why don't you tell me if you want fifties foofy dresses with the big skirts or something tighter and sexier.'

She asked them their sizes and their preferred shades and didn't mind fetching and carrying frocks to and from the changing rooms, though Anita, who'd eventually turned up, whispered that they weren't there to wait on the clients hand and foot. But the busier Sophy was, the quicker time went, and an hour later she'd made three successful sales. For the first time in the two weeks since she'd started working in The Vintage Dress Shop, and actually even before that, Sophy felt the warm glow of a job well done.

If there was one thing she was good at, it was customer service. It wasn't even about the sales, though the sales were nice. It was about someone leaving the shop having bought a dress that made them happy. All three women had looked gorgeous in their chosen dresses and who didn't feel better about themselves when they actually liked the reflection staring back at them in a mirror?

Maybe it wasn't the passion that Phoebe and Cress had for vintage clothes, but if Sophy was looking for her own niche at

The Vintage Dress Shop, then it would be providing a positive customer experience, because goodness knows none of the other staff were. It was also worth remembering that when she got to Australia, Sophy would have no trouble finding a job with her superior retail skills and the glowing reference that she was sure Freddy would write for her if the Belle Girl HR department were still locked out of their computers.

In Australia, Sophy could work to live rather than live to work and hope she could afford the rent on a London shoebox. After a day charming customers and giving them a good retail experience, Sophy would be straight down to Bondi to feel the sand beneath her toes; her hair would settle into permanently tousled beachy waves, her skin flushed an attractive colour by the sun. It would be easy to drop a dress size if she was swimming all the time. Radha said that she lived in shorts and strappy little tops and flip-flops and maybe Sophy would too.

Flip-flopping back to the little house with sea views that she'd share with some laid-back Australians to fire up the barbie...

Sophy's Bondi reverie was interrupted by the harried-looking woman who'd accompanied the difficult bride coming listlessly down the stairs.

'Everything all right up there?' Sophy asked in her perkiest voice. She'd missed her perkiest voice!

'Not really. I'm just making things worse. Apparently, I'm not allowed to have any opinions on a dress that I'm paying for,' the woman said glumly. She was a statuesque blonde with the kind of bone structure that Sophy longed for, but she looked close to tears. 'I thought we were going to have a lovely day together, we've booked in for afternoon tea after this, but now she says she won't be able to fit into anything if she keeps scoffing cakes.'

It was a problem. Phoebe's problem, thankfully, but Sophy could teach Phoebe a thing or two about how to interface with customers. 'I was just about to put the kettle on, if you fancy a cuppa?'

The drizzly greyness of the weeks before had given way to blue skies and the sun glinting off the water of the canal. Sophy and Hege (she was originally from Norway) sat on the little patio at the back and Sophy made soothing noises as Hege went into some detail about how her previously delightful daughter, Ingrid, had become increasingly impossible since she got engaged.

'I'm sure she doesn't mean to. But getting married is a lot, isn't it? Not just having to make decisions about table settings but you're deciding to spend the rest of your life with one person.'

Sophy sighed. Had she made a conscious decision to spend the rest of her life with Egan or had they just drifted into togetherness in the same way that they then drifted apart? At least emigrating to Australia was Sophy grabbing life by the throat, instead of just drifting through it. 'That would make anyone a little bit challenging.'

'When I married Ingrid's father, it was a quick trip to the registry office with our best friends as witnesses, then we went down the pub,' Hege remembered with a wistful smile. 'Yesterday we had a heated debate about whether to swathe the chairs at the reception in tulle with a big bow at the back.'

'I suppose times have changed,' Sophy murmured. 'But it's nice that you and your daughter get to plan the wedding together. My friend is getting married but she's emigrated to Sydney, so her mum can only help with the wedding planning via FaceTime.'

Sophy was saved from having to think up any more platitudes by the chime of Hege's phone. 'I've been summoned back upstairs.' She sighed. 'Will you come with me? You have a very calming presence.'

Phoebe clearly didn't think so because she glared at Sophy when she saw her trailing Hege up the spiral stairs.

'I'm only here under duress,' Sophy wanted to say, but she didn't get a chance because within a minute Ingrid and Hege had launched into an argument about the merits of an oyster satin dress versus a blush pink one.

'Why? Why do you want me to look so hideous on the most special day of my entire life?' Ingrid demanded.

'Of course I don't want you to look hideous. You're being absolutely ridiculous, Inge. I've a good mind to make you pay for the wedding yourself and then maybe you'd remember that you're not actually one of those Kardashians.'

'I will pay for it myself and then you'll have it on your conscience when I have to feed our guests fish fingers and oven chips!'

'Well, at least that would force you to make some decisions!' Hege snapped, collapsing back on one of the sofas. 'I have lost the will to live. Officially!'

Phoebe wasn't much help. Her usually impeccable façade was looking a bit frayed. Her fringe wasn't its usual millpond smoothness, almost as if she'd been tugging at her hair, and she had a furrow between her eyebrows, which looked painful.

'Brides are the worst,' she hissed at Sophy. 'And Ingrid is the worst of the worst.'

Sophy was brilliant at customer service but she also liked not being shouted at by a red-faced, rather than blushing, bride-to-be. Still, God loved a trier.

She hesitantly approached the unpredictable Ingrid, whose face was as scrunched up as Coco Chanel's, who was sat on her favourite blue cushion and snoring loudly as World War Three raged around her. 'Hi Ingrid, I'm Sophy, a colleague of Phoebe's. I was just wondering what your vision was for your wedding day?'

The glare that Ingrid shot her was positively demonic. Sophy wilted a little. 'Not fish fingers and oven chips!'

'Obviously,' Sophy said in a soft, modulated voice because Ingrid might bolt at any loud noises. 'Have you got a Pinterest we could have a look at?'

'I just want to look beautiful,' Ingrid all but wailed and, when she wasn't the colour of a Belisha beacon, eyes puffy from crying, it was obvious that she was an absolute raving beauty. She had delicate features, glossy dark wavy hair, and skin the colour of caramel when it hit the sweet spot in the saucepan.

'You're lucky because you have the kind of complexion where you can wear anything,' Sophy pointed out. 'Not like me. Put me anywhere near something yellow and small children start crying.'

'Promise me you'll never wear yellow,' Phoebe muttered from somewhere behind Sophy. 'That pink dress is going to swamp her, get her in the oyster.'

'Not many brides can wear oyster satin, but I just know that you'll look stunning in it,' Sophy said with a lot more conviction than she actually felt. 'It would wash me out completely.'

'Stunning?' Ingrid asked doubtfully. She looked at the dress she was clutching, then looked at herself in the mirrors that lined far too much of the walls of the atelier. 'I suppose I might as well try something on while we're here.'

Phoebe took her into the changing room while Sophy poured Hege a glass of champagne, which apparently they offered to all the atelier customers. She quite fancied having a medicinal swig herself.

There was no need. Ten minutes later, Ingrid emerged with an ear-to-ear grin on her face, wearing the oyster satin gown, which was cut on the bias and, because she was tiny with no lumps or bumps, clung to her lovingly. 'Mum, I've got the feeling!' she gasped, as Phoebe gave her a hand so she could step up onto the little platform and admire herself from a multitude of different angles. She was glorious in every one.

'Oh, Inge. You look so beautiful,' Hege said, her eyes tearing up again. Sophy quickly seized a box of tissues, which were encased in a gold and cream enamel box.

'But this is the only dress I've tried on.' Ingrid turned this way and that.

'When you know, you know,' Phoebe murmured.

'Maybe you should try the pink just to make sure,' Sophy suggested, because there was no way that the pink could even begin to compete with the exquisite, elegant vision of Ingrid in bias-cut oyster satin.

Phoebe's furious face made her wish she'd kept her big mouth shut.

Still, Ingrid tried on the blush pink dress. Its skirt consisted of layer upon layer of delicate tulle. It was basically a meringue, a very tasteful meringue, and Ingrid was drowning in it. Death by meringue.

'No,' she said firmly, after taking just one look at herself. 'Definitely the oyster. Right, Mum?'

'Definitely,' Hege said just as firmly. She was on her second glass of champagne and looked utterly serene now. 'Now, don't shout at me. But the oyster satin is a little too big.'

'Nothing we can't sort out. We have the most wonderful alterations lady. We poached her from Matches Brides,' Phoebe added, in a low voice because that was a complete lie.

But Cress *was* a wonderful alterations lady and, once Ingrid had changed back into her soul dress, Cress scurried out from her skylit little eyrie where Sophy knew she'd been cowering while things had got heated and started measuring and pinning and tucking.

Sophy probably should have gone downstairs now she was no longer needed, but it was quite the treat to be

91

upstairs in the atelier. Besides, Phoebe was busy making suggestions about accessories so Sophy was free to wander about and touch the dresses, even though she hadn't washed her hands after she'd had her cup of tea.

The dresses up here didn't just look more luxurious, more special, than even the prettiest dresses downstairs. They felt the same way too. Sophy rubbed her thumb appreciatively over a heavy ivory silk, which felt slippery and gorgeous. Then her attention was caught by a beautiful soft grey coat and dress that she thought might be crepe de Chine and was definitely from the 1930s like the oyster satin.

'Hege? Have you thought about your outfit because I think this would look amazing on you,' Sophy said, lifting it off the rail. 'Do you want to try it on?'

'Oh my God, that would be perfect,' Ingrid breathed. 'It has sort of the same vibe as my dress and you *do* look good in grey, Mum.'

Mother and daughter left an hour later, all ready for their afternoon tea, having left a hefty deposit for the oyster satin gown and the grey crepe de Chine coat and dress, which just needed a little dart here and there.

Sophy hoped that her smile wasn't too smug as she waved Ingrid and Hege off. 'Have an éclair for me!'

Yes, she really was a people person. It was like her superpower, Sophy decided with satisfaction as she shut the door, turned round – then couldn't help but squeak.

Phoebe was standing right behind her. Or rather looming. Her fringe was back to its usual poker-straight precision and her face was wearing its habitual enraged scowl.

'What?' Sophy asked tremulously. No, she wasn't going to let herself be intimidated by Phoebe. She tried again, this time without her voice shaking. 'What's up?'

'How dare you?' Phoebe could hardly get the words out. If she'd been a cat, her back would have been arched, tail twitching. As it was, her eyes promised Sophy untold pain. 'I had everything under control.'

'You didn't have anything under control. In fact, you begged me to steer her into the oyster satin.'

'That's not how I remember it,' Phoebe said icily. 'You're not even allowed *in* the atelier, much less running amok, pulling dresses off their hangers…'

'I was hardly running amok. I was *assisting*.'

Phoebe snorted like an angry little dragon. Sophy wouldn't have been surprised to see plumes of smoke emerging from her flared nostrils. 'Taking over, more like.'

It was typical that just when Sophy thought she might have realised what her low-key passion in life was, just when she'd started to maybe perhaps get her groove back, along would come someone to ruin it.

She was so over it.

'Just what is your problem?' she asked with a snarl that made Phoebe back away. 'I'm trying really hard not to step on your toes. You're the manageress. You know more about the shop and the stock than I ever could. You're amazing at that. So again, what the *hell* is your problem?'

Phoebe drew herself up to her full height. In her vertiginous heels she towered over Sophy. The effect was impressive. Also, kind of intimidating. 'Just stay down here,' she bit out. 'You're not to go upstairs without my express permission. And remember to wash your hands before you go near the dresses.'

'I'm fed up with you treating me like a child,' Sophy snapped, squaring her shoulders, because why was it that everyone thought she was a pushover?

Egan.

Her mum who was still expecting her to sleep on the sofa though she'd promised to get rid of the sunbed because she never ever used it.

Her line manager at Belle Girl who'd always browbeaten Sophy into working extra hours.

The official receiver who didn't seem at all bothered that Sophy was still waiting to be paid her last month of salary and overtime.

Then there was Johnno, who might have given her a job, which meant he was responsible for Sophy's current hell, but for her whole life he'd just turned up when he felt like it. He'd cared nothing for Sophy's emotional needs and also, how long did it take a fully grown man to find his bloody birth certificate and passport?

Finally, there was Phoebe, who wasn't scowling any more but regarding Sophy with a lofty expression.

'If you don't like it here then no one's forcing you to stay,' she said. It was half challenge, half taunt.

And Sophy might be a pushover but she never backed down from a dare. 'Maybe I *will* leave,' she said. 'Loads of companies would love to have me.'

Phoebe arched one exquisite brow. 'Really?'

'Yes, really!' Sophy insisted.

Phoebe allowed herself a triumphant smile. 'Well, in that case don't let the door hit you on the arse on your way out.'

PART TWO

PART TWO

Chapter Nine

Sophy had rarely been more pleased to have a day off, especially as the atmosphere in the shop the next day had been icy with a chance of snow.

A huge part of Sophy, at least seventy-seven per cent, hadn't wanted to go crawling back to The Vintage Dress Shop at all. But though she'd updated her profile on LinkedIn and looked to see if Selfridges (no harm in aiming high) were taking on new staff (they weren't), she wasn't going to walk away from paid unemployment no matter how much she wanted to.

Thankfully, Phoebe hadn't reminded Sophy that she'd kind of quit the day before; instead she'd stalked about like a villain in a Bond movie. Though it was Sophy she couldn't stand, Chloe had also suffered the full force of her wrath when she'd been caught feeding Coco Chanel a piece of apple.

'Her digestive system is very delicate,' Phoebe had hissed, cradling Coco Chanel like she was a little baby and not the most ungracious gremlin to ever waddle on the Earth. 'If she has an accident on the carpet, oh my goodness, it doesn't even bear thinking about.'

'But Phoebe's lovely, so welcoming,' Cress had insisted when Sophy had prised her away from some beadwork repairs to go and get lunch. 'We have such a laugh. She made this really funny joke about Elsa Schiaparelli...'

'Elsa who? Do I know her?' Sophy had asked and Cress shook her head and patted her arm gently.

'Never mind. You had to be there.'

And although Sophy knew that a few in-jokes about some obscure fashion designers couldn't compete with the close friendship, the *sisterhood*, she had with Cress, it still stung.

It was still stinging the next day when Sophy got out of the tube at King's Cross and walked up the Grays Inn Road, but, as she took a left towards Clerkenwell, she was also consumed by a feeling of utter dread. She'd have done anything to get out of seeing Charles. She'd been steeling herself to ask Freddy for Charles's number so she could call him and regretfully decline the lunch invitation. But Charles had sourced her number first, probably from Freddy, and sent her a text.

Looking forward to seeing you on Wednesday, he'd written, following up with detailed directions and a location pin.

Sophy could still have regretfully declined, but she had to face Charles sooner or later. So it might as well be sooner, for what was going to be probably the most excruciating hour of her life. She tried to tell herself that it was no big deal. She'd say sorry and then she and Charles, who was nothing more than a colleague really, would have a slightly awkward lunch together.

It was obvious now to Sophy that the reason why she'd thought Charles was gay wasn't just because of his daring dress sense or his encyclopaedic knowledge of fashion, it was because not once had he ever even momentarily looked in the direction of her boobs. Or her legs. And clearly the real reason was that he was used to a much higher calibre of woman than Sophy. The kind of women who worked for *Vogue* or were so French, so elegant, that Sophy was like a lumbering oaf by comparison. No wonder Charles was always far more interested in the clothes she wore than in her body. Probably because he wanted to make sure that the sight of Sophy didn't offend his eyes.

Which had made dressing for their lunch date (no! not a date) quite problematic. Sophy had left the floor of Caroline's home spa strewn with clothes. She had so many sack-like dresses in a muted colour palette, mostly black. She'd even been tempted to buy another dress yesterday with her staff discount. Yes, it had been black, but it was adorned with red poppies that Cress had promised didn't clash with her hair. But then Sophy decided that she was being silly. Even with the discount, the dress was over a hundred quid. That was like one hour of the flight to Australia.

In the end she'd waited until Caroline had gone to work and then rifled through her mother's wardrobe until she found a blue check dress with bracelet sleeves and, although it was semi-sack-like (the apple really hadn't rolled far from the tree), it did have a waist and a swingy skirt. Sophy paired it with trainers and then hastily arranged her hair in a messy bun, the emphasis being on messy.

It had been much easier in her old job, when she'd worn a black shirt and black trousers every day and pulled her hair back into a ponytail so it wasn't in her face. Then some tinted moisturiser, mascara, lipgloss and she'd been good to go. Sophy was never going to be one of those pulled-together women, but today she'd taken great care with her make-up. She'd even put on lipstick instead of some barely-there gloss.

Sophy turned right into Hatton Garden. She wasn't sure what she'd expected from London's jewellery district but it was something a bit more flashy, a bit more showy than just an ordinary London street with quite boring-looking shops. It was also very quiet. There weren't hordes of wealthy-looking people parading up and down, hoping to throw down wads of cash on some serious stones. Hatton Garden wasn't boho like Primrose Hill, or as bougie as Bond Street. It was kind of dull, even if most of the shops were jewellers.

Some of them even had distinctly unglamorous signs proclaiming that they bought any kind of gold or diamonds.

There *was* a lot of bling in the windows, but mostly understated bling, Sophy thought as she eyed up a ring that was marked as a baguette cut. So many different cuts.

As she walked in the direction of Holborn, Sophy was sure that the street would get more *sophisticated*. Charles wouldn't work anywhere that wasn't, surely? But when her blue dot met the arrow on Google Maps, she found herself standing outside a bookie's. Not a sophisticated or glamorous bookie's either.

Her stomach plummeted to her feet as she pulled out her phone. Charles had instructed her to call him when she arrived. Sophy took a deep breath. She had to stop acting like she was a teenage girl about to go on her first date (no! not a date!).

What if he'd completely forgotten that they'd arranged lunch? What if he'd been called away on some jewellery emergency? What if he was about to give her such a telling-off for what she'd said that...

'Hi! Sophy!' Charles sounded very pleased to hear from her when he answered promptly on the third ring. 'Are you outside? I'll come down to let you in.'

He hung up before Sophy could say a word. There was just time to check her make-up in her pocket mirror, deal with a stray glob of mascara and button up her denim jacket then decide to unbutton it again, before a small side door to the left of the bookie's entrance opened. There was Charles, looking splendid in a periwinkle blue suit that matched his eyes and a shirt so crisp and snowy white that it had to be box-fresh.

'Hello! Hello! Hello!' he called out, as if he was nervous too.

'Hey,' Sophy said, waggling her fingers in greeting.

'Going to have to hurry you, I'm afraid,' Charles said, gesturing for Sophy to come inside.

'Oh, sorry!' She brushed past Charles, who closed the door behind her. They were in a tiny lobby. Lobby was probably too grand a word. A tiny space between the street door and a steel inner door.

'I'm trusting you not to look,' Charles said as he tapped a code into a security pad. 'Unless you have a photographic memory and you're actually a very heavily disguised international diamond thief.'

He was being nice to her, which made it easier but also harder. Sophy summoned up a shrug. 'You've found me out. I've been working a long con this whole time.' Her voice was rusty like she'd forgotten how to use it.

'I knew it,' Charles said, ushering her through the inner door to a corridor with several doors off it. 'No lift, I'm afraid, and I'm on the top floor.'

He tapped on another security panel, then pushed open a door that led to a stairwell. 'How many floors?'

'Four. Sorry.'

'I think I'm going to save my energy for climbing and not talking.' It was the last thing Sophy said until she was standing, legs trembling slightly, outside a fourth-floor door, which Charles unlocked, with just an old-fashioned key this time. There was a discreet gold nameplate on the door.

Charles Radley, vintage gems.

'There is where the magic happens,' Charles said. He wasn't even a little bit out of breath, whereas Sophy could feel her heart thumping hard. She was really unfit. She was going to have to stop taking the lift at Chalk Farm station and take the stairs instead.

'Come in.'

Charles's office was absolutely, perfectly Charles.

It was less an office and more of an inviting but elegant space. The walls were a deep, smoky grey, almost black, as were the floorboards, which were mostly obscured by a

Persian rug that looked old, which probably meant it was an antique; its intricate pattern was picked out in soft blues and faded pinks. One wall was lined with books, their spines adding to the *mélange* of colours in the room.

There was a leather Chesterfield couch the colour of butterscotch and two wing-backed armchairs, one of them upholstered in a vivid peacock blue and the other – Sophy blinked her eyes because she had to be seeing things – in a moquette that she recognised because it also adorned the seats of the Victoria Line tube trains.

There was a desk and a leather chair, and a MacBook, looking quite incongruous and out of place in this room that seemed to hark back to another age.

'This is lovely, Charles,' Sophy said, slowly turning a circle as she tried to take it all in. There was always something new to look at: a collection of three black jet art deco figurines on a shelf; a Chinese vase of vivid pink peonies on a little brass end table; a stack of vintage editions of *Vogue* on Charles's desk. 'It doesn't feel at all like an office, it's as if I'd wandered into your living room.'

Charles didn't smile, but he ducked his head and looked pleased as if Sophy's opinion on his workspace was very important to him. 'Well, I like it,' he said. 'And I do want people to feel comfortable. It's a very intimate business when you're buying a piece of jewellery. It should feel special when you choose your engagement ring or a pair of cuff-links or a necklace to mark a birthday or an anniversary.'

When Sophy and Cress had turned sixteen, only three weeks apart, Mike and Caroline and Cress's mother Diane and her new partner Aaron had taken them to Tiffany on Bond Street. *The* famous Tiffany (Cress had been so overcome that she'd burst into tears as soon as they'd got through the door). Though their matching silver keychains had been the least expensive items in the store – and they still hadn't come cheap – Sophy had felt so special just standing in that gorgeous shop with its walls painted the unmistakeable Tiffany blue. Even the staff had recognised the significance of the occasion and treated them like they were royalty.

'I know exactly what you mean,' Sophy said, and she was glad that she and Charles were on the same page, despite what had happened and the crass thing she'd said.

If it hadn't been for that awkward moment, then Sophy wondered if she and Charles might even have moved from being acquaintances and sort-of colleagues towards being friends. He was still looking at her so warmly like he didn't hate the sight of her, and oh, actually now it was starting to feel a little awkward.

'Why don't you sit down?' Charles suggested as if he too had sensed that the moment had got a bit weird. 'Are you ready to play dress-up?'

'Yes, but… look, what I said on Friday night, I'm so sorry. It's just that you're so beautifully dressed all the time. Also, you know so much about fashion,' Sophy gabbled. 'But I'd hate you to think that I think that there's anything wrong in being gay or non-binary or identifying any way that you want to. I really didn't mean it like that…'

'You just jumped to conclusions,' Charles reminded her gently, not that she really needed the reminder. 'Oh, it's OK. I'm teasing you. Stop looking so stricken. I get this all the time.'

Sophy let out a tiny sigh of relief that Charles didn't think she was an awful, homophobic person. 'It's also… when I'm talking to you, you listen. Like, you *really* listen as if you're actually interested in what I have to say. Is it any wonder that I thought you were not into, um… women?'

Charles shook his head, face despairing, eyes dancing. 'Is the straight man bar really that low that you think because a man is a good listener and knows his Balenciaga from his Balmain that he's gay?'

'The bar isn't low so much as on the floor,' Sophy said sadly, thinking, as ever, of Egan, who would make a winding-up motion with his hands when she'd been talking for longer than a couple of minutes. And who never noticed what Sophy was wearing, unless it was to complain that she either wasn't showing enough flesh or she was showing too much.

'I do hope you haven't been torturing yourself over this,' Charles mused. 'It's cool, we're cool. Now, are you ready to be showered in semi-precious gems?'

'Oh, yes please!' Being showered in semi-precious gems instead sounded like a splendid way to kill some time.

She perched on the edge of the Chesterfield as Charles disappeared through a door hidden in the panelling behind his desk. She could hear him shuffling about, the sound of drawers being opened and closed. At one point – she strained her ears – he seemed to be muttering.

Finally he emerged, laden down with intriguingly shaped boxes. He sat down next to Sophy on the couch and placed the boxes in the space between them. Then he began to open them all. The little ones had rings nestled inside them. Small flat boxes for bracelets, larger ones for necklaces.

Sophy didn't think she'd ever seen such colours. She touched the tip of one finger to a large oblong-shaped pink stone on a delicate silver chain. 'Is that a pink diamond?' she asked reverently.

'Sadly, not. Far too rich for my tastes,' Charles said, gently lifting it from its satin-covered resting place. 'This is tourmaline. It comes in all different colours but the pink and the green are the most popular. Do you want to try this on?'

Sophy didn't even have to think about it. 'Go on then.'

She expected Charles to hand the necklace over but instead he leaned forward to place it round her neck, his fingers brushing against her skin as he fastened the clasp without even having to look at what he was doing. He'd be similarly skilled when it came to getting a bra on and off, Sophy bet – except *why* had she just thought that? She could feel her cheeks heating up. Or maybe that was because Charles was adjusting the position of the necklace, one finger dipping into the hollow of her collarbone, and he hadn't taken his eyes off her. It occurred to her that though they might have cleared up the whole issue of his preferred sexual orientation, they'd yet to discuss the second part of her damning statement on Friday night. That if he wasn't gay then Sophy would most likely fall in love with him.

And here was Charles pretty much doing everything he could to make Sophy do exactly that.

'Perfect,' he announced, reaching for a small hand mirror on the end table next to him. 'That looks perfect on you, Sophy.'

Of course, it wasn't Sophy who was perfect. It was the necklace. But she took the mirror from Charles and sighed a little because the necklace was so beautiful and there was something about it that made her sit with her back a little straighter, her demeanour more poised than usual. She also had a hectic glitter to her eyes that matched the gleam of the necklace, and she didn't want to be big-headed or sound like Keira Knightley simpering in *Love Actually*, but she thought that she looked quite pretty.

'Perfect,' Charles said again.

'This is really gorgeous.' Sophy couldn't stop touching the stone. 'So, when you say it's semi-precious, does that mean it's not very expensive?'

'Not very expensive.' Charles pressed his lips together but failed to hide his mischievous smile. 'I mean, you've only got about ten grand worth of semi-precious stones round your neck.'

'Bloody hell! Take it off!' Sophy reached up to fumble with the clasp but Charles gently pulled her hands down, his fingers encircling her wrists more delightfully than any bracelet ever could.

'Oh, sweetheart, we haven't even got started,' he drawled, threading his fingers through hers for one fleeting second before setting her free.

Then Charles proceeded to load Sophy up with semi-precious stones. Sliding the most extravagant rings onto her fingers. His thumb pressing against the pulse at her wrists, which was fairly thundering away, as he put bracelet after bracelet on her, like they were made of candy and not the gemstones whose names he recited like poetry.

Aquamarine. Aventurine. Ametrine. Amethyst. Carnelian. Citrine. Garnet. Heliodor. Jade. Jasper. Lapis lazuli. Malachite. Moonstone. Onyx. Obsidian. Opaline. Pearl. Peridot. Quartz. Seraphinite. Serpentine. Sunstone. Tanzanite. Tiger eye. Tanzanite. Tourmaline. Turquoise. Verdite. Zircon.

It was the single most sensual experience of Sophy's thirty years. For eight of those years she'd been with Egan and he'd never come close to making her tremble like this, her heart thumping, her breath catching, limbs heavy and languid, by just saying words at her. Though to be fair, Egan was more likely to recite the names of the clubs in the Premier League or his preferred items from the menu of his favourite Chinese takeaway, Golden Valley.

There'd also been absolutely no lavishing her with semi-precious stones. Just a silver ring ('that absolutely doesn't mean anything so don't be getting any ideas, Soph') for her twenty-fifth birthday from a high street chain of jewellers.

So no wonder that, as Charles opened the last box, which was bigger than all of the others, Sophy was all but swooning.

'Finally, the *pièce de résistance*,' he said as he removed an actual blooming tiara from its resting place. 'Pearls, opals and alexandrite.'

Sophy didn't know what alexandrite was but it sparkled in the light as Charles placed the tiara on her head with as much reverence as if he were crowning a new monarch. She held her breath as he adjusted the surprisingly heavy coronet, then stroked back a few errant strands of hair that had escaped her bun.

'Exquisite,' he said with great satisfaction. 'Oh, Sophy, you have the most ideally shaped head for a tiara.'

As compliments went, it was one of the most random ones Sophy had ever received. But the real compliment was the look in Charles's eyes, as if the sight of Sophy with her ideally shaped head afforded him so much pleasure. Although she was weighted down with jewels, she also felt so light that she could easily float off the sofa.

To break the gaze, to stop looking at Charles, who had ideally shaped everything, Sophy picked up the hand mirror and looked at herself. The tiara did look good – she was ready for a ball at Downton Abbey – but the necklaces, the brooches, the bracelets... She bit her lip but one stray breathy giggle leaked out of her mouth. Then another one caught her unawares and another and another until she had to lean back on the sofa because she was laughing so hard.

'Charles... I look... like a Christmas tree,' she spluttered. 'They could stick me up in Trafalgar Square this December and job done!'

Charles looked affronted. He sucked in a breath and furrowed his brow in such an exaggerated way that Sophy was sure he was doing it for comic effect. 'Too much?'

She held up a hand, which was quite the feat when she was wearing so many rings and bracelets. 'Just a bit.'

Then Charles was laughing too. He laughed so hard that he wheezed and had to wipe the tears from his eyes. 'Phoebe would be the first to tell you that Coco Chanel said that before leaving the house, you should look in the mirror and take one thing off.'

Sophy nudged Charles with her elbow. 'Coco Chanel said that? But Coco Chanel is a dog!'

It set Charles off again. He laughed so hard that he listed to one side so he was leaning against Sophy, his forehead on her shoulder, which was the only part of her upper body that was semi-precious-stone-free.

'Please... tell me you're joking and... You do know who the original Coco Chanel is, don't you?' he begged plaintively once he could form words again.

Sophy was tempted to draw the moment out but instead she rolled her eyes and poked him in the ribs with her elbow again. 'I couldn't resist. I do know a few things about fashion designers from yesteryear.'

'Of course you do,' Charles soothed. He was still pressed against her, shoulder to shoulder, thigh to thigh, but then he sat up straight. 'Though I'm sure the canine Coco Chanel shares her namesake's view that women should always be a little underdressed.' He eyed Sophy speculatively, which had her all giddy and fighting for breath again. 'You, my dear, need to take off quite a few things.'

He meant the jewellery, but Sophy knew that she'd be reliving the husky way he'd said that last sentence for quite a few weeks. She really needed to get a grip on herself and, actually, talking of Coco Chanel, the pooch edition, reminded her of... 'Phoebe. I'm finding it quite hard to um, establish, any kind of, you know, rapport with her. Any tips?'

'Phoebe's a lovely woman...'

'I'm not saying she isn't...'

'Prefers dresses and that malodorous dog to people, but you just have to... It is an awkward situation,' Charles allowed. Sophy knew all about awkward situations. 'Have you talked to Johnno about it?'

'We don't really see each other that often.' Sophy frowned. 'Or really talk to each other that much.'

'He's very fond of you,' Charles said, and objectively Sophy knew that, or hoped it was true, but also there'd never been much concrete evidence of that fondness. 'Anyway, I wouldn't worry about Phoebe.'

'You wouldn't?'

'Not when you're disappearing off to Australia soon,' Charles reminded her. 'Not much call for knowing about vintage designers of yesteryear when you're working on a sheep station.'

He actually shuddered a little as if even the concept of a sheep station was horrifying, even though it was very near the coast.

'Yes, Australia.' Sophy nodded. 'Can't wait.' being with Charles was thrilling but so were the pictures that her grandmother Jean had emailed overnight of the imaginatively named Lamby, a lamb that they'd had to hand-rear last year. 'We always get a couple of lambs each year who need to be bottle-fed for whatever reason. Reckon you'd be up for it?'

Sophy had planned to steer clear of the sheep but bottle-feeding a cute lamb was an entirely different matter. 'It's going to be challenging but lots of fun too. So many different experiences, whereas every day here feels the same.'

'I'm sure communing with the sheep will be very exciting, very fulfilling,' Charles said in a deadpan voice, as if he were sure of no such thing and it wasn't as if all Sophy would be doing in Australia was sheep wrangling.

'I'm starting off at the sheep station but then I'm going to Sydney to see my friend Radha. I'm probably going to settle in Sydney. She lives right by Bondi Beach. Spends half her time there. But I also want to go to Melbourne to stay with one of my aunts. Melbourne's meant to be very cool, very arty,' Sophy said, a little wistfully because she was neither of those things. 'There are so many places I want to visit. And I've always wanted to live by the sea.'

'But first, the sheep station,' Charles pointed out.

'Well yes, but that's because it will be my grandparents' fiftieth wedding anniversary.' With some effort because her hands were still weighted down with rings and bracelets, Sophy pulled out her phone. 'I've set up a countdown and everything!'

She had no one willing to share her excitement and anticipation of her new Antipodean life. Caroline seemed to think it was a phase that Sophy was going through, much like the time she'd gone vegetarian for all of two days when she was fourteen. Cress refused to talk about it, even going so far as to clamp her hands over her ears, and Egan, when Sophy had informed him of the news, had sneered, 'Yeah, like that's really going to happen.'

Of course, she might have gone travelling and ended up in Australia years before if Egan hadn't asked her to move in with him. At the time, Sophy had thought it was because he couldn't bear to be without her. That it might not be a declaration of love, but it was a sign of Egan's commitment to their relationship. She'd never imagined that it was really because he was hoping to make some extra money by charging her rent.

But even when times were good with Egan, and especially when they were bad, Sophy often wondered what would have happened if she had gone to Australia with Radha back then. How her life would be different. How *she* would be different.

It was her big 'what if' moment and Sophy was fed up with 'what ifs', but, when she tried to explain that to people, to Cress, or her mum, they immediately countered with all the reasons why she shouldn't go to Australia.

But Charles was an impartial third party. It was no skin off his exquisitely aquiline nose if Sophy was heading halfway round the world for the foreseeable. And given her excruciating comment the other night, it would do no harm to remind Charles that she was going to Australia and that she was very, very enthusiastic about going to Australia. So clearly she wasn't in love with him. A medium-sized crush wasn't the same thing at all.

'Do you want to see the countdown?' she asked him a little desperately.

He shook his head, his face impassive. 'I think we'd better get all this frippery off you.'

The removing of the jewels was brisk and businesslike, the strange and lovely intimacy of earlier gone. Charles even explained about the difference between princess cut, emerald cut and baguette cut stones as he packed away his spoils, though Sophy barely took in what he was saying. She just liked the shapes his mouth made as he talked, how his passion for his job was written all over his face.

It was just as well that it was a medium-sized, unrequited crush and nothing more, because there was no way a man like Charles would ever be interested in someone like Sophy. Not when his tastes ran to *Vogue* editors and impossibly elegant Frenchwomen.

'Don't look so sad,' Charles said when he emerged from his little cubbyhole after locking away all those pretty pieces. 'I'm sure one day you'll find someone who'll buy you a tiara. Or better yet, you could buy one for yourself.'

'From my wages from the sheep station,' Sophy said dryly.

Charles shuddered again. 'Don't.' Then he visibly brightened. 'I promised you lunch, didn't I? Are you hungry?'

Sophy could always eat. Even when she'd been absolutely in despair a few weeks before, her appetite had remained the one constant in her life.

She expected Charles to take her somewhere chic. Probably Japanese. Definitely minimalist. But once they'd descended the hundreds of stairs and were out on the street, he steered her round the corner to a shabby-looking café.

Not Japanese then. And definitely not minimalist.

'I know it looks rough but this place does the best bagels in London. Even better than Brick Lane,' he said, as he held the door open for Sophy and a rush of homely cooking smells rose up to greet her.

When Sophy had lived in her Manor House houseshare, there had been many times that she'd stopped off at Brick Lane on the way home from a Saturday night out to buy bagels for Sunday brunch. 'That's a bold claim.'

'One that I'm more than happy to stand by,' Charles said and Sophy was pleased that they were back to their jokey banter as he worked his way through a salt beef bagel with all the trimmings and she happily munched on a bagel with smoked salmon and cream cheese that was larger than her head.

They kept the conversation light but, when Charles mentioned popping into the shop on Friday, she couldn't help but sigh a little.

'Do you really not like working there?' he asked softly.

Sophy sighed again. 'It's not that. And like you say, it's only going to be for a little while and also, Johnno's doing me a favour and I don't want to be ungrateful. But they don't really need me.'

'I'm sure they do. You wouldn't believe how busy it's going to be once the unholy trifecta of wedding season and prom season and garden party season starts.'

'I don't fit in there,' Sophy admitted, not just to Charles but to herself as well. 'I'm a people person. I actually like dealing with the public as long as the public aren't being rude, but that shop... I just don't get it.'

'Don't get what?' Charles paused with one half of his bagel held aloft.

Sophy put her own bagel down. 'I don't understand why anyone would want to fork out serious money on an old dress when you could have a lovely brand new one. And yes, I still believe that chances are someone's died in at least one of them. There! I've said it.'

Charles gasped like he'd just stubbed his toe. 'Blasphemy!'

'I'm just saying.' Sophy shrugged, then picked up her bagel again. 'Some of those dresses come in with *stains* on them and I know they all get sent out to be laundered, supposedly, but—'

'No! I've heard enough!' Charles actually dared to cover Sophy's blasphemous mouth with his hand. 'You don't find the dresses even a little bit soul-stirring?'

There was no denying that some of the dresses were beautiful. But they also felt a lot like school. Each one came with a long lecture full of terminology that Sophy didn't really understand, especially when Phoebe was wanging on about voided velvet chiffon or foliate motifs. Then there were bishop sleeves and Bermuda collars and chemical lace.

'It's just a lot to take in and what's the point when I'm going to Australia in a few months,' Sophy said firmly. Just the thought of having to go to work tomorrow was giving her a leaden feeling in the pit of her stomach, which had nothing to do with the quantity of carbs she was in the process of consuming. 'In fact, I've already told Phoebe that I'm going to leave.'

Charles raised his eyebrows. 'Oh. Have you lined up another job?'

Sophy shook her head and couldn't help but sigh. 'No, but I will.'

'Because I saw on the news last night that unemployment figures are at a five-year high,' Charles said not at all helpfully. 'Have you told Johnno you're leaving the shop?'

Sophy sighed again. Deeper. Much deeper this time. 'No,' she admitted. She hadn't thought about Johnno's feelings but then, it wasn't as if Sophy was one of his number-one priorities. Though he had given her the job in the first place and apparently spent quite a lot of time talking her up to his friends and acquaintances. Added to that, Sophy needed to chivvy Johnno into handing over his birth certificate and passport and that would be much easier to do if she saw him regularly enough to remind him. It was the seeing Phoebe regularly that was the real problem. 'I don't want to tell tales or moan but me and Phoebe, we just rub each other up the wrong way. For some bizarre reason she seems to be threatened by me, which is ridiculous because we both have very different skill sets. I'm very good with the customers...'

'And Phoebe's very good with the vintage dresses as long as none of those customers want to go near them,' Charles finished for her. 'Or, heaven forfend, actually take them off the rails and try them on.'

Sophy wanted to nod and sigh again but she settled for shrugging her shoulders instead. 'Though, weirdly, the one time that we did seem to get on was when she spent an afternoon teaching me about vintage fashion. I can hardly remember any of it now though.'

It was true; apart from the bit about the poor old wartime ladies having to replace their knicker gussets with stockinette, Sophy couldn't remember the difference between a box pleat and a kick-pleat or tell her Hardy Amies from her Norman Hartnell.

'It does seem rather silly to look for another job when you already have one,' Charles pointed out gently.

'I know but I don't want to work in a place where my line manager hates me because...'

'She doesn't hate you. Phoebe just has a very… unfortunate manner,' Charles said, because for someone who happily wore a lilac suit in public he was the king of understatement. 'And you get to work with your stepsister, so that's a plus point too.'

'I suppose,' Sophy grudgingly agreed, and she knew that despite her best intentions to find a new job the fire in her belly after that argument with Phoebe had all but fizzled out and she'd end up doing what she always did: taking the path of least resistance. 'It is convenient too. Only a few stops on the tube, and I don't have to work Sundays.'

'Phoebe will warm up eventually,' Charles said and, though Sophy was being her most Eeyore-like, there was nothing but kindness and concern in his expression. 'Luckily for you, I've just enrolled you in an immersive course on vintage fashion.'

Sophy narrowed her eyes. 'You have? When did you do that? While I was in the bathroom? It's very kind of you, Charles, but you should have asked first. I haven't got the money to—'

'Not another word!' Charles held up one elegant hand. 'It just so happens you've been awarded a scholarship to the Charles Radley Institute of Vintage Fashion. It's a very exclusive establishment.'

'It sounds like it.' Sophy couldn't help but smile. And she couldn't help that her crush on Charles was threatening to upgrade to full-on unrequited love. 'You really don't have to do this.'

'It's my pleasure,' Charles said smoothly. 'Now, what are you doing next Wednesday? Actually, I don't care what you're doing. Cancel all your plans, school will be in session.'

Chapter Ten

There were no more major blow-ups with Phoebe over the next few days, as if they'd both agreed, without actually speaking about it, to keep to their respective patches.

Charles had been right about the start of wedding season. They'd also had three different but all very well-heeled women come into the shop wanting a show-stopping frock because 'I've actually been invited to one of the garden parties at Buckingham Palace. For my charity work, you know,' so they were suddenly very busy. Thankfully, it was only March and far too soon for teenage girls needing prom dresses to descend on them as well.

'So much busier than I ever was at the museum,' Cress marvelled when they all decamped to the pub on Friday night. There was no Johnno, but apparently he put money behind the bar for them every week, and there was no Charles, though every time the door opened Sophy sat up like Coco Chanel (the dog) did whenever anyone opened a bag of pork scratchings.

It seemed to take an age for next Wednesday to arrive but finally it did, along with a text message from Charles asking her to meet him at South Kensington tube station at two that afternoon.

The station was rammed, mostly with children of all shapes and sizes and nationalities, there to visit the Natural History Museum or the Science Museum. Every single one of those children was wearing a cumbersome backpack, all the better for bumping into people. By the time Sophy got through the ticket barriers, she felt like a skittle in a tenpin bowling alley.

Charles was already waiting, leaning against a poster advertising oat milk. He was wearing his lilac tweed suit with a black shirt, which even in central London made people look twice as he caught sight of Sophy and waved at her.

She'd also stayed true to type and was wearing another sack dress, although, again, this was one of Caroline's because they had slightly more of a waistline than her own sack dresses. This one was black with tiny green polka dots, but she'd managed to forsake her trainers in favour of black tights and black ankle boots because it had been raining on and off all day.

'You look lovely,' Charles said, bending down to kiss Sophy's heated cheek, then the other one.

'You look as if you haven't had to do battle with a lot of small children,' Sophy said, allowing herself a brief, admiring glance at the impeccable crease in Charles's trousers. Then she averted her gaze before her eyes could travel upwards. 'One of them kept bashing me with their lunchbox all the way up the escalators.'

'Poor Sophy.' Charles took her elbow to steer her out of the tube station. 'Much quicker to come out here and nip across the road instead of walking along that subway that never ends.'

'We're going to a museum,' Sophy stated, not very enthusiastically, because there was nothing much to do at South Kensington unless it was to go to a museum. She was already reliving the memory of several very boring school trips to the Natural History Museum to stare slack-jawed at dinosaur bones or to the Science Museum to gaze glassy-eyed at a working model of the solar system.

'Not just any museum,' Charles corrected her. 'The V&A.'

The V&A was the Victoria & Albert Museum; Sophy knew that much. Even the thought of an afternoon in Charles's company couldn't put a spring in her step as they crossed over the very busy Exhibition Road towards the imposing Victorian building that rose up like an ornate wedding cake; all turrets and fiddly, frilly bits.

When Charles had mooted the idea of a crash course in vintage fashion, Sophy had envisaged cosy days cocooned in his lovely office, sitting side by side on his Chesterfield as they leafed through books full of beautiful pictures of beautiful women in beautiful dresses. Charles would speak and Sophy would surreptitiously watch the shapes his mouth made as he talked and let his voice drift over her. Because he was one of those people who could read the phone book out loud and make it sound like poetry.

She hadn't imagined that they'd go to museums. Museums were boring. They just were. Full of old, dusty things or dioramas of scientific stuff that nobody would really want to visit unless they had to because they were at school.

'I'm a member,' Charles said as they entered the cavernous entrance hall, which was marble and tourists as far as the eye could see. 'And none of the current exhibitions are relevant to our interests...'

'They're not?' Sophy asked, a little more brightly as she'd just seen a poster advertising an exhibition on Medieval Middle Eastern Art and she really didn't fancy that or could see how it was anything to do with vintage fashion.

'Not today.' His hand was at Sophy's elbow so he could gently guide her in the right direction. This time it was across the entrance hall, striding straight past the shop, though Sophy perked up because who didn't love a gift shop? Then through a long gallery devoted to South-East Asia until Charles stopped. They'd reached their destination.

'Fashion. You've brought me here to look at clothes and then quiz me on the difference between Lanvin and Lagerfeld?' Sophy asked aghast. 'I might just as well be back at the shop!'

'Excellent pronunciation,' Charles said with a broad smile because he was an unfeeling brute. 'It will be fun, I promise you.'

It wasn't fun to start with. Though there were some interesting things to look at: kimonos, a pair of papyrus sandals maybe dating back to 30 BC and a huge dress called a mantua from the 1750s, with such an enormous skirt, like a crinoline on steroids, that Sophy decided that its poor owner would only have been able to get through doors sideways.

'As for sitting down, forget about it!'

Then they came to a display of wedding dresses. Sophy had quite enough of them at the shop, thank you very much. She ran her eyes over the spotlit mannequins without much interest, until her attention was caught by something that Phoebe would never have allowed in the atelier. It was a white gabardine and silver PVC minidress and coat designed by John Bates.

'A very important sixties designer,' Charles said. 'Arguably overlooked though he was doing miniskirts before Quant and Courrèges.'

Sophy squinted at the information card. The dress had been designed for and worn by a *Vogue* fashion writer called Marit Allen when she married a film producer, Sandy Lieberson, in the summer of 1966.

Instantly Sophy was transported to the very groovy Swinging Sixties. She could imagine the wedding party all decked out; the men like the Beatles on the cover of *Sgt. Pepper's Lonely Hearts Club Band* and the women in miniskirts and maxidresses in psychedelic patterns and clashing colours.

'I bet her mother was furious that she wore a dress so short that everyone could see her pants,' she said to Charles, who shot her an amused look before they moved on.

Predictably, there were a lot of voluminous dresses in various shades from white to cream, including a 1930s embroidered satin silk dress with a huge train designed by Norman Hartnell, which would have made Phoebe crack a smile.

Hopefully they'd be done soon and then Sophy could explore the gift shop because this was deathly dull – although…

'Ha! They've put this dress in the wrong part of the fashion exhibit,' she said as they came to a beautiful ruby-red sheer shirt dress with a slip underneath in the same rich colour. It was delicately draped and gathered, the sleeves ending at the elbow in a cuff. 'I would absolutely wear that if it wouldn't clash with my hair.'

'I disagree. Lots of redheads look good in red,' Charles said, staring not at the dress but at Sophy's hair, which she'd gathered up in her usual ponytail.

'Unfortunately I'm not one of them.' Sophy leaned forward to read the information provided. 'Turns out it *is* a wedding dress. From 1938.'

The red silk gauze dress had been worn by a woman called Monica Maurice, who was a trailblazer in so many ways, not just in her daring sartorial choice of a wedding gown. She was an industrialist, known as the 'Lady of the Lamp' in the Yorkshire coalfields, and had a love of racing cars and flying. In 1938 she'd become the first women member of the Association of Mining Electrical Engineers. Monica was clearly a woman of many layers.

'I love Monica,' Sophy said with a wistful sigh as she peered intently at the black and white photograph of Monica on her wedding day, a tiny birdlike woman with a huge smile. 'I feel like I know her. I can just picture her wearing this red dress and not caring what people thought of her for not wearing a long white frock.'

'As Virginia Woolf wrote, "we are what we wear",' Charles quoted.

Sophy looked down at her slightly waisted sack dress and wondered what it said about her. Nothing that good. That she valued comfort, convenience and conventionality over being someone like Monica who laughed in the face of all those things. 'Bloody hell, I hope not.'

'The thing about clothes though is that you can decide who you want to be every morning when you get dressed,' Charles said as they moved away from the wedding dresses and further into the permanent fashion exhibition. 'Clothes have the power to change our mood. They're a way of expressing ourselves, of being creative, of announcing who we are without having to say a word.'

'Is that why you wear your suits?' She pulled a face. 'I mean, I love your suits, but they're not the usual grey suits that most men wear.'

'If you look at nature then the male of the species has always gone full technicolour dreamcoat in order to attract a mate. Think of peacocks or mandrill monkeys or the wattle cup caterpillar.'

'You just invented that caterpillar, didn't you?'

'I did not!' Charles had already pulled out his phone and within seconds was showing Sophy a photo of a caterpillar that looked like it had been coated in fondant icing. 'It wasn't until the end of the eighteenth century, the great masculine renunciation, that men stopped wearing flamboyant clothes that indicated how wealthy they were, and adopted a sartorial style that reflected the new way of thinking of rationality and practicality. I think I was born in the wrong century,' he added mournfully.

Sophy was very glad that Charles had been born when he was, but she still wasn't completely happy about being dragged around a museum on her day off. Afterwards there was a trip to the gift shop, then Sophy treated Charles to coffee and cake in the V&A's main café, which was like sitting in the centre of an ornate, extravagantly decorated Fabergé egg, and where, in between forkfuls of carrot cake, Charles explained that he hadn't always had the courage to wear a beautifully cut lilac tweed suit.

'I began my career in a very stuffy, very starchy gentleman's outfitters on Savile Row that had been there since God was a boy. Some of the staff had been there even longer than that. It was grey wool as far as the eye could see.' He took a ruminative sip of coffee. 'Every morning Mr Frobisher, the manager, would check our nails to make sure they were spotless, and woe betide you if your hair was anything other than an inch above your shirt collar.'

'It sounds horrible. Like something out of Dickens.' Not that Sophy had ever read any Dickens, but she'd seen an adaptation of *Bleak House* on the telly a few months ago.

'It was quite grim, although I did get a really good education in gentlemen's tailoring. Then I left to work at a more contemporary, cutting-edge establishment a few doors down and my old colleagues would cut me if they saw me in the sandwich shop.' Charles put a hand to his chest, like he'd been mortally wounded. 'I'm not going to lie, it hurt.'

'So how did you get from gentlemen's tailoring to tiaras?'

'By way of cuff-links, would you believe?' Charles put down his fork to look at Sophy, who was listening with her chin resting on her palm. 'Started hunting down vintage cuff-links at car boot sales and junk shops, spiffing them up and selling them on as a sideline, and realised that was much more fun and much more profitable than asking if sir dressed to the left or to the right.'

'Dressed to the left?' Sophy echoed with a frown. Charles arched an eyebrow and held her gaze until light dawned and Sophy knew from the sudden heat to her face and Charles's smirk that she'd gone red.

They parted ways outside the museum, Sophy to battle through the rush hour crowds to go home and Charles saying that he was going to walk along to Knightsbridge to 'pick up a few bits in Harvey Nichols for dinner'.

Sophy thought she was pushing the boat out if she picked up a few bits in M&S for dinner, usually when it was after hours and she could descend on the heavily reduced, yellow-stickered items. Charles's life, his world, it was so far removed from her own.

'So, we'll do this again next week? Further your fashion education?' Charles asked, derailing Sophy's unhappy train of thought. 'Another museum I'm afraid, but I promise we'll go out for cake afterwards.'

The very last thing Sophy wanted to do was trudge around another museum looking at old things. But it didn't seem like such a bad way to spend an afternoon if she was with Charles.

'I don't think you're ever going to turn me into a vintage fashion fangirl,' she warned him.

'Stranger things have happened!' Charles tucked that one strand of Sophy's hair that would never behave itself behind her ear and then, as if he couldn't help himself, his fingers were threading through her ponytail so he could gently tug the end of it. 'So, it's a date then.'

Chapter Eleven

Despite the rush hour crowds and the hordes of small children with their backpacks and even the fact that she couldn't get a seat until Golders Green, Sophy floated back to Hendon.

She could still feel the phantom tug of Charles pulling her ponytail as she put her key in the lock. She had tried not to read too much into it – just a friendly gesture from a man who probably thought her hair colour resembled some semi-precious stone that she wouldn't even be able to pronounce. But she'd entertained quite a rude fantasy about Charles pulling more than her hair the whole time she'd been straphanging from South Kensington to Leicester Square then had to change lines.

'I'm home,' she shouted because of the time she'd let herself in unannounced and had caught Caroline and Mike snogging on the sofa. All three of them were still traumatised. 'What's for dinner? Shall we get a takeaway? I could really fancy a curry.'

'Ah, there you are.' Caroline appeared in the living room doorway, her face tight and tense. 'I texted you ages ago.'

'Sorry, I'm trying not to stare at my phone at all hours ever since I read a piece online that too much screentime can give you—'

'Yes, well, never mind that.'

Sophy paused from hanging up her jacket on the coat-stand because Caroline's voice was tight and tense as well. 'Is everything all right?'

Caroline jerked her head in the direction from which she'd come. 'There's someone here to see you.'

'To see me? Oh my God, it's not someone from the official receivers, is it?' Sophy asked, an ice cube of dread trickling down her spine. Sometimes, only very occasionally, at her old job, the till hadn't tallied at the end of the day. They'd been allowed a certain amount of discrepancy, but what if since the bankruptcy the administrators wanted to recoup every last pound and penny?

'No, don't be silly. It's *him*,' Caroline added on a hiss.

'Charles?'

'Who's Charles?' Caroline dropped her voice to a whisper. 'It's Egan.'

'What the…?'

Egan didn't deserve his voice to be announced in a stagy whisper, like his presence was a big deal. Even if Sophy hadn't seen him since that day six weeks before when she'd left her door keys on the hall table that she'd actually paid for. Then, apart from a couple of terse messages about picking up the rest of her stuff and the outstanding utilities bills, they'd gone from eight years of being together to silence.

Now the thought of taking the ten steps into the living room filled Sophy with nothing but an irritable kind of gloom as she brushed past Caroline, but not before sharing an exasperated glance with her mother.

Egan was sitting in Mike's chair, his leather recliner with cup holder and a holster on the other side for the remote control, though Caroline and Sophy loved to wind him up by changing the channels using the app on their phones. He smiled at the sight of Sophy, though she didn't smile back but just folded her arms and looked down at him. In much the same way that Lollipop was looking at Mike from his perch on the back of the sofa. Disapproving. Very, very disapproving. Not even Coco Chanel could look as judgemental as Lollipop when he really put his mind to it.

Not that there was anything particularly offensive about the way Egan looked. He was handsome in an everyday kind of way that you didn't have to think too hard about. Dark hair, dark eyes, an olive complexion, which complemented the expensive veneers he'd had done for his thirtieth birthday. He was wearing his second favourite shirt, a blue Ralph Lauren number, his Sunday casual chinos, his second favourite pair of trainers, his second favourite aftershave and an ingratiating expression.

'Hey, Soph! Surprise!' he said in a jaunty, jovial voice like he didn't realise that Sophy low-key kind of hated him now.

'What do you want, Egan?' She rolled her eyes because she knew exactly what he wanted. 'I'm not paying the cable bill when most of it is for your premium sports channels that I never even watched. And I'm not paying the outstanding amount on the utilities bills either. Not when I bought most of the furniture in your flat, *as well as paying rent.*'

'Come on, don't be like that,' Egan said, doing that thing he did with his eyebrows where he kind of knitted them together so they almost touched in the middle. 'I can't believe you're still mad at me.'

Sophy flung herself down on the sofa. She couldn't believe she was still mad at Egan either. It was so weird to see him sitting there. It felt a lot like he was a stranger. Which was crazy because, apart from Cress, Egan was the person whom Sophy knew better than anyone. She knew everything about him; and yet every year he'd needed reminding of the exact date of her birthday.

Usually this unhappy fact about Egan made Sophy clench her fists, but her hands were in her lap and that was when she realised that she wasn't mad at Egan any more. She was just over him. Had been over him almost as soon as they'd called it quits.

She hadn't been pining for him. Neither had she been nostalgic for the good times that they'd had, because the good times had become so rare and mostly their relationship had been routine, apart from the times when they sniped at each other. Or rather Sophy had sniped at Egan, constantly. His crimes had ranged from leaving his used teabags on the draining board and expecting Sophy to speak to his mother every Sunday afternoon while he went down the pub, to eyeing up other women when they were out. No big crimes of passion. No huge rows. A constant low-level bickering had been the soundtrack of their relationship.

So Sophy could say with all honesty, 'I'm not mad at you. Not any more. We were going nowhere, weren't we?'

'I wouldn't say that.' Egan gave her a considered look. 'I've missed you, Soph.'

'You sound quite surprised about that. You sure you're not missing the five hundred quid a month I was paying you in rent, even though you didn't even have a mort-gage?' Sophy finished on a huff because maybe she was still a little bit mad with Egan. 'Didn't even show me one bit of sympathy about losing my job and not getting my last month's wages and all the Christmas overtime I was owed… No! I am not doing this. I don't want to fight with you any more.'

'Could have fooled me,' Egan muttered. Five minutes and they'd already slipped back into their usual bickering ways.

Sophy attempted a smile that felt more like a teeth-baring grimace. 'See? I'm calm. So, what's up with you?'

There was nothing up with Egan. Apart from the absence of Sophy, his life was following its usual pattern. Work, gym, beers and bantz with the lads. Lather, rinse, repeat.

But then Sophy's life, before it had quietly imploded, had meant working nine hours a day, longer during their frequent sales and in the run-up to Christmas, clear up after Egan, drinks with the girls on Saturday night if she wasn't already dead on her feet. Lather, rinse, repeat.

After a lengthy monologue on how he was now experimenting with macro counting in his eternal quest to bulk up, Egan suddenly remembered how conversations were meant to work.

'And you? What's new? Your mum said you're *still* talking about going to Australia. Wish I could take some time off for a long holiday,' he said, because he definitely was still a little mad at Sophy too.

'It's not a holiday, I'm emigrating. And I'm not just talking about it, it's really happening. Going to stay with my grandparents on their farm to start with; it's their golden wedding anniversary in August.' Sophy got that scrunched-up feeling in her tummy that she always did when she manifested an image of herself being at one with the sheep, half excitement and half nerves. She also allowed herself to revel in the stupefied look on Egan's face. She wasn't completely predictable. 'And I did tell you that Radha was getting married in October and asked me to be one of her bridesm—'

'Yeah, but emigrating. To Australia. That's a bit extreme.' Egan grinned. 'You're gonna be crap on a farm, Soph. Do you remember that time we went to that festival and we were driving through the countryside, got a whiff of some manure and you started retching?'

'I didn't retch.' It had actually been more of a dry-heave. 'I was hungover!'

'We did have it large the night before. It was Paulie's birthday, right?'

Sophy nodded. 'I haven't drunk tequila since.'

'Or danced on any bars?' Egan had that easy smile that Sophy hadn't seen in ages. It was quite nice to remember that it hadn't been all bad.

'I was lucky not to have broken every bone in my body,' she said with a smile of her own and it was so much better to be civil, amiable instead of trying to score points off each other.

'So, I was thinking...' Egan struck a pensive pose, which didn't really suit him. 'It was kind of a dick move to charge you rent and I can manage without that five hundred quid a month, but...' He leaned forward to put his hand on Sophy's knee and she tried not to tense up at the strangely unfamiliar yet familiar touch. From the sofa, Lollipop hissed out a warning, like Caroline had planted him there as a chaperone. 'I can't manage without you. Don't suppose you fancy moving back in?'

'Oh, Egan...' Sophy patted his hand. It was lovely to be asked, to know that on some level she mattered to him. Being back with Egan would be *easy*. But she didn't want any more 'what if' moments. She didn't want to miss out on really living in favour of just plodding through each day as it came.

Nothing in her life was easy right now. Not the job at The Vintage Dress Shop. Or the logistics of her new life in the Antipodes – which reminded Sophy that she still hadn't got the documents she needed from Johnno. The delightful interludes with Charles were charged because Sophy had feelings for him that she had no business to, not when he was just being kind. Even being back at home was hard when she was *still* sleeping on the sofa.

Sophy's eyes narrowed. 'Have you been talking to my mum?'

Egan immediately looked shifty. 'Well, I did phone to find out if you were going to be home and we got talking. She did say that maybe we were being hasty throwing away eight years like they didn't even mean anything. That it couldn't do any harm to, you know, chat things out.'

'Right, I see.' Sophy removed Egan's hand so she could stand up. 'I'll just be a minute.'

'I'd love a coffee if you're going anywhere near a cafetière…'

Sophy wasn't. When she opened the living room door she saw Caroline beetling back to the kitchen, almost as if she'd been earwigging.

'Mum!'

'What?' Caroline asked, making a great show of turning round from her shelf of cookery books, which she'd been pretending to peruse. 'Everything all right in there?'

This wasn't easy either. 'Do you want me to move out?' Sophy asked, the threat of tears making her voice throb a little. 'Is that why Egan's here? Is that why I'm still on the sofa even though you said that you didn't even use the sunbed and you'd put it on Gumtree although that was weeks ago.'

'Of course not, we love having you here,' Caroline insisted, a flush edging up from her neck to her hairline, in the exact same way that Sophy got when she was feeling flustered.

'You and Mike are used to having your own space, I know that, but I won't be here for long. I'll be going to Australia soon. Soonish, anyway.'

'You don't *have* to go to Australia.' Caroline caught Sophy's hand so she could tug her closer and envelop her in the sort of hug that would always make Sophy feel safe. 'We all do strange things when relationships end. When me and Johnno split up, I had a fringe cut in and it took two years to grow it out, so I just thought there was no harm in you talking to Egan, seeing if you couldn't work things out.'

'I don't want to work things out,' Sophy mumbled. 'Is that OK?'

'Of course it's OK.'

'And I really am going to Australia. I want to go to Australia. I'm *excited* about going to Australia.'

'Well, don't blame me if you get bitten by a tarantula.'

Sophy decided that she might as well go for broke. 'I'm grateful to be here but that sofa is giving me backache and some nights I wake up with Lollipop sitting on my head.'

'Fine!' Caroline pushed her daughter away so she could snatch up her phone, which was on the worktop in front of her. 'I'm putting that bloody sunbed on Facebook Marketplace right now!'

Chapter Twelve

The sunbed was still in situ when Sophy left for work on Friday morning, though Caroline swore that someone was coming to pick it up that lunchtime.

'Me and my lower spine thank you,' Sophy said, although she wasn't convinced that the sunbed's days were numbered. But she was preoccupied by the thick cream envelope that had arrived in the morning post.

Radha Bhati and Patrick Hall
request the pleasure of the company of
Ms Sophy Stevens
On the occasion of their wedding...

All morning Sophy couldn't help but think of Radha. How different her friend's life would have been if she'd decided to stay behind in England when Sophy had moved in with Egan rather than go travelling.

Radha didn't have to torment herself over her 'what if' moments because she'd chosen adventure rather than stagnation.

Thankfully the shop was busy that afternoon, so Sophy couldn't spend much time wallowing in 'what if'. Especially as the busyness was something that Phoebe got quite cross about when she came down from the atelier to find the shop full of browsers.

'Who are these people?' she demanded when she tracked Sophy down to the basement storeroom. 'Don't they have jobs? I wish they'd stop touching my dresses with their sticky hands.'

Sophy was trying to find a dress that had been put up on the website but wasn't on the rails or listed in the shop inventory on the computer. 'Maybe you should have a little table by the front door with bottles of hand sanitiser on it for when people come in,' she suggested facetiously, as Beatrice, who was helping her look for the stray dress, buried her face in a leopard faux fur coat to hide her giggles.

Phoebe gave Sophy a long hard look that would have had Paddington Bear suing for copyright. 'You know what? That's not actually a bad idea,' she said slowly. 'I bet you can get quite fancy hand sanitiser. I wonder if Diptyque do a range.'

Then she was gone and by the time Sophy had tracked down the dress, which had been packed away with the heavier winter dresses, and sold it to a grateful customer, it was almost five o'clock. No matter how busy the shop was, the last hour on a Friday afternoon always crawled by.

'Time for the pub soon,' Anita said, as she waited outside one of the changing cubicles for a woman who seemed hell-bent on trying on every dress in the shop. 'Unless this one kills me first,' she mouthed.

The browsers were thinning out by half past five when the door swung open hard enough to crash back on its hinges, which made everyone jump, and there was Johnno, almost entirely obscured by the mountain of clothes he was clutching to him.

'Ladies! Help a fella out, will you?'

Sophy rushed to relieve Johnno of some of his burden. The clothes had been packed in slippery plastic garment bags so it was quite hard to get purchase on them.

'I'll take them downstairs,' she said.

'Just dump them on the sofas,' Johnno insisted, though one of Phoebe's favourite diktats was about how the sofas in the shop weren't a dumping ground for anything other than customers' bottoms. ('And only if they're actually planning on buying something.')

'I've got a vanload of these outside.'

Almost as if she could sense that skulduggery was afoot, Phoebe appeared at the top of the spiral stairs to see off a prospective bride who'd been trying on prospective wedding dresses for the last three hours. No wonder Phoebe looked very tight of lip. 'Well, why don't you have a think about the cream silk,' she was saying. 'And let me know either way tomorrow.'

'It was a mushroom silk,' the woman said. She had a very pugnacious look to her face, like she enjoyed having a good bit of argy-bargy just for the sake of it.

'Definitely cream,' Phoebe said. Her jaw was clenched so hard that it looked painful, until she glanced down and her whole face transformed into a huge, happy grin that Sophy would never get used to. 'Dresses! New dresses!' She managed to clasp her hands together in ecstasy as she came careering down the stairs.

'Johnno's gone out to get some more,' Sophy explained. 'Apparently, he's got a whole van full of them.'

'Be still, my heart!' Phoebe plonked her bottom down on one of the sofas, though she wasn't a customer, and began to rifle through them. 'Oh my God! These are Biba with the labels still on them!'

'Original Biba or Biba revival?' Anita asked as she saw off the woman who'd tried on every dress in the shop and was now leaving with just a silk scarf that had been reduced to a tenner.

'Original Biba,' Phoebe said in a croaky voice like she was about to start hyperventilating.

'Beatrice! Original Biba!' Anita yelled in a good impersonation of a foghorn, so that Beatrice came beetling out of
the back office.

'Sixties Biba or Seventies Biba?' she asked. To Sophy it
was like they were talking in tongues. Then Cress stuck her
face over the curved banister of the spiral staircase.

'Did someone say original Biba?' she called out.

Phoebe lifted her radiant face. 'Cress, you have to
come down and see this stock. I think I can see some
black silk with beading and if it is what I think it is, I'm
going to wet myself.'

It was what Phoebe thought it was. 'A 1960s black silk
shantung sequinned bell-shape evening gown,' she said rapturously once she'd pulled it from the pile. 'I've been looking for this dress for years.'

Sophy didn't know why because it was just a very creased
sleeveless silk dress with a sparkly bodice. It was verging on
the sack-like.

'This is seventies Biba, but a Barbara Hulanicki design
and quite Ossie Clark, no?' Cress asked as she held a lairy,
flowery cotton maxidress to her, even though she never
wore anything but jeans and a plain top outside of work.
In work, her handmade smocks were as daring as she got.

Phoebe had more conniptions when she came to a sheer
black lace dress, but mostly she worked steadily to divide
the clothes into two piles. The door crashed back on its
hinges again as Johnno, with Freddy bringing up the rear,
staggered in with more clothes.

'It's like Christmas,' Beatrice exclaimed, rushing forward
to grab some of the garment bags.

'Oh, Sophy, there you are!' Johnno said in wonder like
he'd forgotten once again that she was working in his shop
just as he'd asked her to. 'And who's this vision of loveli-
ness? Is this the famous Cress?'

'Not famous,' Cress muttered, eyes not on Johnno but on a tapestry coat with three-quarter-length sleeves. 'And you're Sophy's dad.'

'One and the same,' Johnno agreed and Sophy cringed slightly from her position behind the counter where she was attempting to cash up. They were both her family – her blood family and her chosen family – but it felt horribly awkward.

Cress ducked her head the way she always did when she was embarrassed, though Johnno winked at Sophy as if to say that everything was all right, because he was truly terrible at reading a room.

Meanwhile, Freddy flung his dresses onto the sofa, which earned him a glare from Phoebe. 'Don't manhandle the stock, please,' she said tartly, which made Freddy glare back and mutter something under his breath.

Then Phoebe went back to sorting through Johnno's spoils, which he said he'd got from 'a man who knows a man who does house clearances', but he said it with a shifty look, which made Sophy suspect that their provenance might not be strictly kosher.

Phoebe and Cress, who was granted permission to rifle by Phoebe with the same graciousness as if she were being handed the freedom of the city, soon had a pile of dresses for the shop and a much larger pile of dresses and assorted other garments that they wanted nothing to do with.

'What do you want me to do with them then?' Johnno protested. 'Can't you do a bargain bin and sell them for a fiver a pop?'

'A bargain bin?' Phoebe echoed like Lady Bracknell having an attack of the vapours over a handbag. 'We don't do bargain bins. This is a quality establishment and I don't care if that purple velvet jacket is Biba, it's just not the right aesthetic.'

Johnno dropped to his knees and clasped his hands in prayer. 'But, Pheebs...'

The lady in question tossed her head like a horse refusing to jump. 'But, Pheebs, nothing.'

With much grumbling, Johnno and Freddy took Phoebe's rejected items back to the van and promised to meet them in the pub. As Sophy went back to her cashing up, one of her few responsibilities as all the other women hated doing it, she couldn't help but marvel at the way Phoebe had handled Johnno.

Apart from a little passive-aggressive moaning via text message when Johnno proved himself to be completely unreliable, Sophy never dared to confront him head on about anything. Their relationship was so infrequent, so casual, that she never wanted to do anything that might fracture it completely.

Later, when they were in The Hat and Fan and Sophy found herself sitting next to Johnno, whose hair still bore the faint traces of the vibrant orange he'd sported a few weeks before, she also marvelled at the fact that she'd seen more of her dad in the last few weeks than she had in the last few years.

'And how is my beautiful daughter?' he asked, as if reading her mind. Sophy noticed now that when they were together he treated her quite carefully, not with the same backchat that he gave Phoebe.

'Which beautiful daughter is that?' Sophy asked and pretended to look around.

'Uh-uh, no doing yourself down.' Johnno wagged a finger at her. 'Everything all right? You settled in now?'

'I think so.' Selling vintage fashion might not be the one true calling that Sophy was looking for but she felt as if she had some purpose at the shop now, whether it was cashing up or treating the customers as valued guests rather than as annoying distractions who only came in to put their grubby hands on the clothes. 'Charles is giving me a crash course in fashion.'

Even saying his name out loud felt very daring, but Johnno didn't seem to realise that his beautiful daughter had a stupid, ridiculous crush on the man who supplied his costume jewellery.

'You're in good hands with Charlie,' he said.

'He lets you call him Charlie?' Charlie didn't really go with the bespoke suits in fantastic colours and those elegant, patrician features.

'Not to his face.' Johnno grinned. 'Said he'd never darken my doorstep again if I did. So it will have to be our little secret.'

'How did you two meet anyway?' Sophy was curious to know how Johnno and Charles, who were as different as chalk and cheese, oil and water, polka dots and stripes, had ever met, let alone forged a close working relationship.

'You probably don't remember my old shop. I had this place on Holloway Road…'

'Oh my God! Are you kidding? Johnno's Junk, of course I remember it!' Sophy giggled over the rim of her glass. 'When you offered me a job, I thought that was where I was going to be working.'

'No!' Johnno rolled his eyes.

'Yes! I even asked Freddy if we were going to walk up to Camden and catch the 29 to get there.'

'But, Soph, I closed down Johnno's Junk… oooh, well over twenty years ago now.' Johnno wasn't grinning any more and looked quite pensive as he took a sip of his lager.

'You never mentioned it. I just assumed it was because the last time I went there – first and last time – I had a scream-ing fit about this mangy stuffed fox in a glass case. I've had nightmares about it ever since,' Sophy said with a theatrical shudder, but even that didn't make Johnno find his grin again.

'But the shop, the new shop, it's been a huge part of my life for a couple of decades…' Johnno shook his head but didn't have to finish the rest of the sentence; didn't have to say that Sophy hadn't been a huge part of his life during that time.

But Sophy didn't want to start picking at old wounds and she was pretty sure, from the discomfited look on his face, that Johnno didn't want to either. It was Friday afternoon, Sophy was nursing a large gin and tonic, and Charles might put in an appearance at any moment. She felt pretty content.

'You still haven't told me how you went from selling mangy fox taxidermy to a swank vintage dress shop in the nice part of town,' she reminded him with a little nudge. Johnno shot her a small, hesitant smile, which was very unlike him.

However, his long, convoluted story about how The Vintage Dress Shop came into being was pure Johnno. Apparently, once a month a rich, elderly woman dripping in jewellery and wearing a fur coat, no matter what the weather, would swoop into Johnno's Junk and buy pretty much everything on his vintage dress rail.

'I had a Saturday girl who'd do the rounds of the chazzas for me and buy up old dresses – that was when you could still find decent vintage in the chazzas – then I'd sell them for a fiver.' He shrugged expansively and raised his eyes to the heavens. 'I didn't know how much they were worth. Talk about where there's muck, there's brass.

'Turns out this old dear, she had a place in bloody Mayfair, was putting a two hundred per cent mark-up on some of these frocks and I thought to myself, mate, you need to get in on the action and the rest is history.'

Johnno had then hired fashion students to go round the charity shops, car boot sales and church fetes because they had a better eye, got rid of the more junky bits of his inventory and, within a couple of years, gave up the lease in N7 to move to the more rarefied climes of NW1. 'It was during Britpop. You couldn't move round Primrose Hill without falling over a member of Oasis or Blur and they all had girlfriends and wives who'd spend a few hundred quid on a boho seventies dress without blinking an eye.'

They'd ticked along for a few years and just when Johnno had decided that vintage clothes was done because it was getting harder to source decent stock and maybe he should go back to the junk business, Phoebe had come on board and persuaded him that they needed to go more upmarket than back downmarket.

'So, how did you meet Phoebe?' Sophy suspected that Phoebe had entered Johnno's life in a puff of sulphurous smoke. She also wanted to know if Johnno had even started to look for his birth certificate and passport; but then two things happened that made her not really care about either of those things.

The first thing was that Coco Chanel, who shunned all human touch unless it was Phoebe's (doing nothing to disprove Sophy's theory that maybe Phoebe was a witch and Coco Chanel was her familiar), suddenly plonked herself down on Freddy's lap, contorted herself onto her back with some difficulty because she really wasn't very ergonomically shaped, then allowed him to rub her belly. That was definitely something out of the ordinary.

'Not that out of the ordinary,' Phoebe insisted. 'Coco Chanel can be very personable and, anyway, it's probably because Freddy's been eating pork scratchings.'

'I haven't been eating pork scratchings. Maybe it's because I'm a lovely bloke. They say that about dogs, don't they? That they're good judges of character.'

'Do they?' Phoebe was pure ice queen, but Freddy just smirked and raised his bottle of lager in salute, which made Phoebe look even more cross.

The second thing was that, just when she'd given up on him, Charles suddenly appeared. He stood in the doorway surveying the packed bar and, when his eyes lit on Sophy, he shot her a smile, which made her heart lift. So different to how she'd felt when she'd come home to find Egan sitting there.

It was another late one. Another evening when she and Charles were the last ones standing and, as he waited with her outside the pub for her Uber to appear, it felt like they were the last two people left in the world.

'You'll text me when you get home so I know you're in one piece,' Charles said, lifting up the ends of Sophy's ponytail so her hair was shot through with the LED glare from the lamppost they were standing under.

It was a long time since a man had cared that Sophy got home in one piece. Egan never even waited up for her and, when she made it back from a long sesh, would often complain that she'd woken him up. Even though it seemed to Sophy she was always walking on eggshells around him.

'And we're still good for Wednesday?' Sophy asked hopefully. 'London Bridge station, you said. I am going to google museums in the area, unless you're taking me to the London Dungeons.'

'I'm not taking you to the London Dungeons and please don't google, it will ruin the surprise.' Charles gave her a stern look (even his stern look was thrilling), then the moment was shattered by the triumphant beep of the horn as Steve in a Honda Insight let Sophy know he'd arrived.

She was still floating on a little cloud of contentment as she unlocked the door of her mum's house. It didn't really feel like home, but it was the closest she had right now.

Mindful that she'd drunk quite a few gin and tonics, Sophy forced herself to drink two glasses of water in the vague hope that it might head off tomorrow's hangover. Then she tiptoed up the stairs so she could brush her teeth and take off her make-up in the bathroom before heading back down the stairs to sleep on the sofa.

'That you, love?' her mother called out. She and Mike always slept with their bedroom door ajar to stop Lollipop from scratching at the paintwork and demanding entry.

'Yes, sorry, didn't mean to wake you. Go back to sleep,' Sophy whispered back, opening the door to the spare bedroom/home spa so she could retrieve her pyjamas.

She stood there blinking. How much had she had to drink tonight – surely she was seeing things? Or rather *not* seeing things.

The sunbed was no longer there. Neither was the hood dryer, the foot spa, the wheeled IKEA trolley full of lotions, potions and unguents. The gigantic cat tree that Lollipop wanted nothing to do with. Even the boxes containing Mike's prized collection of Spurs programmes had been cleared out.

In their place was a bed. A double bed too, already made up with fresh linen and pillows plumped to perfection. There was a bedside table, chest of drawers – she opened the top drawer to find all her knickers had been neatly folded and put away – and a hanging rail for her dresses.

Sophy felt a lump lodge itself in her throat. Eyes smarted as if the tears were about to put in an appearance. It wasn't just that she had a proper room to call her own now so that her mum's house would feel like home; it was the thought of Caroline and Mike taking the time to make Sophy feel like she was home.

And the finishing touch? Even though Sophy had long given up on cuddly toys and had, quite unsentimentally, chucked out her childhood teddy bear, nestling on the pillow was a plush koala with its stumpy arms outstretched.

142

Chapter Thirteen

On Wednesday, for Sophy's next lesson Charles took her to the Fashion and Textile Museum in Bermondsey, a bright orange building with neon pink flourishes, which was a world away from the Victorian splendour of the V&A.

It was a small space with no permanent collection, but its current exhibition, *Night And Day*, was a celebration of 1930s fashion.

Unlike the V&A, where all the clothes were behind glass and there'd been too many people blocking Sophy's view, there were no such hindrances this time. The clothes, arranged in themes, were just *there*, maybe behind a velvet rope or on a dais, but Sophy could get close enough to see the slightly uneven stitches on a brown crêpe dress.

'The economy had crashed in 1929, so the women of the thirties had to be quite thrifty,' Charles explained when Sophy expressed surprise that so many of the clothes on display were home-made. 'That's why lamé was so popular as a fabric. Much cheaper than the sequins on all those twenties flapper gowns.'

'And so many different colours,' Sophy noted as she scrutinised a peach lamé evening gown with chiffon sleeves and an extravagantly plunging back. 'People really got dressed up back then.'

'That's the thing, isn't it? When you feel like it's the end of the world, then you want to go out with a bang,' Charles mused and Sophy would have said that she was a practical, pragmatic sort of person but she found it very easy to imagine the fizz of excitement for a 1930s woman as she got ready for a night on the town. Maybe a cocktail party at a swank London hotel. Or a supper dance at a louche Soho nightclub. The feel of cool satin against her heated skin as she slipped on a floor-length red and cream art deco-inspired dress.

Charles would look splendid in top hat and tails, Sophy thought as they passed a mannequin wearing just such an outfit. There was something a little bit Fred Astaire about him. Sophy wouldn't be at all surprised if he suddenly broke into a soft-shoe shuffle and danced with her cheek to cheek around the exhibition.

'Do you dance?' she asked without thinking, and couldn't blame Charles for looking surprised at her question.

'Very badly. Why do you ask?' He arched his eyebrow in the manner that Sophy always found quite delicious. It was such a quintessentially Charles mannerism. 'No, don't tell me. You're actually a very successful ballroom dancer, twice national champion, but your partner Pablo, real name Paul, has slipped on a tube of greasepaint and you need someone to tango with as a matter of urgency.'

Charles's vivid imagination was something else that Sophy found quite irresistible. And she could play along. Especially as Charles was nearer to the truth than he could ever know. 'If I can't find someone to dance a tango with at nationals, my dreams, my ambition to be an international champion, will be crushed.'

'Like Pablo's ankle?'

'Exactly.'

They wandered through the exhibition, which finished up in a little side gallery full of black and white portraits of debutantes taken by Cecil Beaton, and continued to discuss how Pablo and Sophy's rumba in Blackpool had taken the dance world by storm.

Occasionally Charles would throw out a snippet of information about one of the dresses they were meant to be studying ('Look, Sophy! These two dresses are made from Liberty prints. I adore a Liberty print') but mostly they were silly. Sophy missed being silly.

At her old job, she might have reached the giddy heights of assistant manager but she was too fond of mucking about and having a laugh, so she'd remained senior sales associate. She could be silly with Cress, of course, but Sophy hardly saw her, even though they were working together. Cress would disappear up to her skylit eyrie each morning and had to be coaxed down for lunch break. Egan, despite his faults, had had some good qualities but a sense of humour hadn't really been one of them. So many of Sophy's other friends were married, with kids, which meant that they'd moved out of London because it was too expensive and too polluted and too crime-y once babies entered the picture. The ones that were still around were in Deptford. So, technically in the same city, but it would be easier and quicker to go from London to Manchester than from Hendon in north London to the wilds of south London.

No wonder Australia seemed like a good idea.

But for now there was London, and Charles. When they finally left the museum after a rummage around the gift shop, Sophy realised that they were just round the corner from Borough Market: a foodie mecca of stalls selling everything from gourmet cookies and locally produced honey to exotic meats and organic vegetables.

'I promised you cake and I promised that I was buying,' Sophy said as they headed in the direction of the Thames.

It wasn't a part of town that Sophy knew well but it was steeped in history. There was Tower Bridge of course and Guy's Hospital, still retaining some of its original buildings from when it was first built in the 1720s, and the Gothic splendour of Southwark Cathedral, which had stood on the banks of the River Thames, in one incarnation or another, for over a thousand years.

Butting right up to the cathedral was the modern monolith of the Shard, its glass tiles gleaming in the April sunshine.

London was such a mixture of the old and the new. It was something that Sophy had always taken for granted. Where she'd lived in Deptford, there'd been chicken shops and betting shops and all the detritus of modern life on a high street where buildings from the late seventeenth century still proudly stood. Even in Hendon, which wasn't the most happening of London suburbs, Sophy always thrilled to the sight of the blue plaque on a block of flats commemorating Amy Johnson, the famous aviatrix. Famous, in part, for being the first woman to fly alone to Australia. That had to be a good omen.

'Penny for them,' Charles said as they crossed over Borough High Street towards the market. 'You were deep in thought there.'

'I was just thinking about Amy Johnson.' Sophy smiled sheepishly. 'Random, I know.'

'Well, you will be following in her illustrious footsteps,' Charles reminded her.

'Hopefully I won't have to fly the plane myself.' Sophy shook her head as a way of physically shaking off any doubts she might momentarily be having of leaving all that London had to offer. Australia was new and exciting; it was Sophy's shiny, bright future, and, in her present, there was cake. So much cake.

'I'm very serious when it comes to purchasing cake,' she told Charles, which was really a warning that she'd want to do a complete circuit of the market, all three of its sites, before she made any decisions about pastries.

'Can I confess something?' Charles asked in such a grim voice that it made Sophy pause in her admiration of a delicious display of German cakes positively oozing creamy custard, honey and flaked almonds.

'Is it something awful?' Immediately her mind was racing with possibilities of what Charles was about to unload on her. But mostly it was the same variation on a theme: that he'd noticed that she had a crush on him and, while he thought she was a lovely girl, he just wasn't into her that way.

God! She'd made it so obvious.

'It's just that…'

'I'm so sorry, Charles…'

They both came to an awkward halt and gestured for the other one to continue.

'Sorry,' Sophy said again. 'You were saying…'

'I didn't mean to interrupt you.' Charles took hold of Sophy's arm to pull her to one side because they were creating a bottleneck next to the very popular aforementioned German cake stall.

'No, you go first,' Sophy insisted, because maybe the hard truth coming from Charles's lips – that she wasn't sophisticated enough or pretty enough or worldly enough to tempt him – would be what she needed to stop with this ridiculous, one-sided crush. It wouldn't be pleasant but it would be good for her. 'Please…'

'I was just about to admit that… well, don't take this the wrong way, because I know you have very strong feelings but I don't feel the same.'

'Oh God, I'm *mortified…*' Sophy put her hands on her burning cheeks.

'It's not your fault. One could say that I lead you on…'

'You were just being friendly and I read too much into it…' By now, one of the nearby artisanal traders could have fried a free-range, organic duck's egg on Sophy's face.

Charles tilted his head in concern. 'Well, I did have a slice of carrot cake when we went to the V&A last week, so no one would blame you for thinking I had a sweet tooth.'

'No it's my—What?'

'But really I prefer savoury so if you are determined to treat me, then I'd much rather have some cheese,' Charles finished with a conciliatory smile. 'You've been so excited about the cake all afternoon and I hate disappointing you.'

'Oh no, no, no. It's fine!' Relief made Sophy quite giddy, which might have been why she gave Charles a friendly, strictly platonic, thump on the shoulder, which was so enthusiastic that he staggered slightly. 'Cheese. Yes, you absolutely can have cheese. Stinky, sweaty, smelly cheese, it's yours!'

'OK, glad we've got all that cleared up,' Charles said, rubbing his shoulder. 'Shall we get your cake first then?'

Even though she was meant to be saving up airfare, by the time she and Charles were sitting on a bench overlooking the River Thames as tugboats and pleasure cruisers bobbed past them Sophy was one hundred English pounds lighter. At least.

She hadn't bought just one cake but a box of babka buns, eclairs, canelés, shortbreads and a whole selection of viennoiseries, including a pear and almond Danish that she was calling first dibs on, which she'd take in to work tomorrow. Then she'd bought a sourdough loaf, several jars of gourmet nut butters, two packs of Ginger Pig sausages and a selection box of cheese for Charles.

Now, she warded off his attempts to feed her a cube of cheese by gripping his wrist in a vice-like hold. 'Just how stinky, sweaty and smelly is it?'

'It's none of those things,' he protested, trying to make another foray towards her face. 'It's an oak-smoked cheddar. You'll love it.'

It turned out that Sophy did love it, but not as much as she loved Charles popping it in her mouth, the tips of his fingers grazing her lips, so that she was still floating on a little cloud of lust when they retraced their steps back to London Bridge station.

'The shop's not open on Sunday, is it?' Charles asked suddenly, as Sophy relived the moment when he fed her cheese for the fiftieth time. 'Do you think you could swap your Wednesday off for a Monday?'

Sophy had been slightly dreading the possibility that this might be the last of their educational forays and that Charles considered her either graduated with a working knowledge of vintage fashion or an absolute hopeless case. Even the thought of two consecutive days tramping around museums would be worth it if it meant spending two consecutive days with Charles because yes, she really was that desperate for the crumbs of friendship he kept throwing her.

Except… 'I'm sure Anita wouldn't mind but Phoebe gets a bit mardy when people try to swap their days off.'

Now that wedding season was well and truly upon them, Phoebe had even mooted the idea that no one should have any days off at all. She couldn't seem to fathom that, for the rest of them, The Vintage Dress Shop wasn't the centre of the universe.

'I love vintage as much as the next person…'

'You love it a lot more than the next person,' Sophy pointed out and Charles gently cuffed her chin, so she could relive that moment too for the entire journey home.

'I do, but Phoebe is going to be carted off to vintage rehab if she's not too careful,' Charles said, as they joined the rush hour crowds pouring into the station. 'You know what? I'll clear it with Johnno or Freddy. Just pack an overnight bag.'

'Overnight? Where are we going?'

And although Charles travelled with her all the way to Euston before he needed to change lines, he refused to fill Sophy in on his plans.

'It's a surprise,' he said with a teasing smile. 'And it wouldn't be a surprise if I told you, would it?'

Chapter Fourteen

When Sophy arrived at The Vintage Dress Shop the next morning, everyone was delighted that she came bearing a box of flaky pastries.

Everyone except Phoebe. As she was always telling them, she didn't do carbs. Not that she didn't do carbs before Marbs. Or she didn't do carbs after six. She just didn't do carbs full stop.

'It actually explains a hell of a lot,' Beatrice whispered as they took their flaky pastries out onto the little canalside terrace even though it was a cold morning with the threat of rain in the air. 'She'd be a completely different person if she started off the morning with a round of toast.'

'I couldn't function without bread,' Cress said, her mouth full of a mixed berry brioche. 'Or rice. Or pasta. Or potatoes. Carbs are life.'

When they filed back into the shop, Phoebe made them go outside again to brush themselves down in case they shed crumbs near the dresses.

'I dread to think how much butter was in those croissants,' she lamented because she really was a pastry buzz-kill. 'The thought of grease stains on my lovely frocks! No, it's too awful to contemplate.'

She stood over them while they washed their hands to her exacting specifications and then, and only then, were they allowed to go about their business: Beatrice to the back office, Chloe and Sophy to the shop floor and Phoebe and Cress up to the atelier, where they were expecting the return of Hege and Ingrid for their second fittings.

'I'm not anticipating any problems,' Phoebe said, fixing Sophy with a beady eye. 'So your presence absolutely won't be required.'

Sophy was quite pleased to keep out of Phoebe's way. The shop was always quiet first thing in the morning and so, as she and Chloe desultorily straightened dresses, they talked about the *Night And Day* exhibition, which Chloe had visited on her day off.

'I'm still having visions of that white crêpe gown with the rhinestones and the cowl neckline,' Chloe said dreamily. 'I'm not being big-headed when I say I have the collarbones for a cowl neckline. What was your favourite dress?'

Sophy could hardly remember what any of the dresses looked like. Her memories of the exhibition had been completely obliterated by the touch of Charles's long fingers touching her face, brushing against her mouth. The amused but tender way that he'd looked at her—

'Soph! What was your favourite dress?' Chloe asked again as Sophy came to with a start.

'Um, oh… I liked the black evening gown,' she said at last because there definitely had been at least one black evening gown.

'Yes! Good choice. The black cloque bias cut or the black crêpe with the embellished neck and cutaway—'

'Chloe, is that a crumb on the floor?' There wasn't a crumb on the floor, but anything to make Chloe stop giving Sophy a run-down on every single black dress there'd been in the museum.

'What? No! I don't think so,' Chloe yelped, but she'd already dropped to her knees to scrutinise the painted white floorboards for any rogue flakes of pastry.

The day seemed to pass extra slowly. It started raining before lunch, which meant there wasn't much footfall, and so Sophy went downstairs to help Beatrice pack up some orders from the website. Even though it was raining, she still took her full hour lunch break, though she couldn't persuade Cress to come out as she hadn't quite finished the alterations to Ingrid's wedding gown.

'It has to be perfect,' she said, when Sophy tried to persuade her to at least come downstairs to eat some lunch. 'If it were my wedding dress, then I'd want it to be impeccable.'

The idea that Colin might actually stir himself to propose to Cress was one that Sophy couldn't imagine would ever come to pass. Colin was not the stuff that dreams were made from. He was quite content to live with his parents even though he and Cress had been dating since they were teenagers. Though Cress was also content to live with her mother Diane and stepfather Aaron.

'Sometimes Colin stays over or I stay with him,' Cress said whenever Sophy gently introduced the subject of how weird it was that she and Colin hardly ever got any alone time. 'Besides, we're saving up for a deposit on a flat. Colin says it's silly to waste money renting and filling a landlord's pocket and that it makes sense to live with our parents until we can afford our own place.'

Maybe Cress had so much passion for her career – she was still sparkling every day when she came into work – that she didn't have any passion left for relationships, Sophy decided as she slumped against the sales desk after lunch. She pulled out her phone and stared longingly at the photographs of the Bondi Beach sunsets that Radha frequently sent her, which Sophy had turned into a slide-show of spectacular pink and orange skies, streaked with blue and melting into the sea.

Might be edging into autumn now, but it's still warm enough to swim. And eye up surfer dudes! Radha had said in her last message.

Chloe was helping their one customer wriggle into a very tight silver lamé dress. The woman had come prepared in double Spanx but there was still a lot of grunting and groaning and 'Just breathe in,' 'But I *am* breathing in,' coming from behind the be-swagged curtain.

Sophy didn't even have the energy to look busy as the door opened and a troop of women entered the shop. They'd probably only come in to shelter from the rain that was now so horizontal it made a noise as it hit the windows.

'Sophy?'

She lifted her head from her phone screen with great effort, then quickly straightened up.

'Hege! So lovely to see you again,' she said enthusiastically as she came out from behind the desk. 'And Ingrid. Your dresses are looking amazing. I think you'll be very pleased.'

Ingrid didn't look at all convinced; neither did the three other young women with them.

'I still think you should have gone to Browns Bridal,' one of them, a shorter, maybe even more beautiful version of Beyoncé with a British accent, said in a stage whisper. 'Why would you want a second-hand wedding dress?'

'I know, right?!' said another one, a perky-looking posh girl whose ponytail swung jauntily with every step she took

It was quite all right for Sophy to be dubious about the origins of some of their dresses, even to still think that someone had to have died in at least one of them, but she wasn't going to let three posh girls (they all spoke with braying voices and had that gleaming, glossy, self-satisfied look that only comes from attending a top public school and never having to check the price tag before buying something) come in *her* shop and chat shit about the frocks.

'Every single one of our dresses is a unique, heirloom piece with its own story to tell,' Sophy informed them, her hands on her hips. 'Then you get to be part of that story. Plus, those old-time designers really knew their way around a woman's body.'

It was true. The cunning little bust darts on the black dress Phoebe had forced Sophy to buy did amazing things to Sophy's breasts, even though Phoebe kept reminding her that she was *still* wearing the wrong-size bra.

'These are Ingrid's bridesmaids,' Hege said with a slightly manic smile like she couldn't wait for Phoebe to crack open a bottle of champagne. 'We even suggested that they might buy their dresses here.'

'Or we could just look on Net-a-Porter once you've decided on your colours, Inge,' Jaunty Ponytail admonished.

Ingrid scowled, which didn't bode well for her fitting. 'I have decided on my colours.' She took a deep breath and Sophy was sure she was slowly counting to ten. 'Grey to match Mum's dress and ashes of roses...'

'It's a grey-toned pink,' Hege added quickly, like she'd been explaining what ashes of roses was quite a lot. 'Very flattering.'

'We found the perfect dress in the perfect colour,' Ingrid said a little desperately. 'But...'

'I don't do cleavage,' the third member of the wedding party, a strapping blonde Valkyrie, all but wailed.

'And I don't do sleeveless.'

'And no one should do cleavage *and* legs. We've been through this, Ingrid,' British Beyoncé said sternly.

Dealing with Inge and her bridesmaids was way above Sophy's pay grade. 'Well, why don't you go up to the atelier where Phoebe, our manageress, is waiting for you?' Sophy rubbed her hands in glee, then immediately felt guilty. But not that guilty. 'I'm sure she'll have lots of opinions about what you should wear.'

They trooped up the stairs as Chloe, pink-cheeked and panting, emerged from the cubicle with the customer who was finally zipped up in the silver wiggle dress but didn't seem very happy about it.

'You look gorgeous,' Sophy said, though the customer was even more pink and panting than Chloe. 'Shall I ring that up for you?'

'You're going to have to because I can't get out of it,' came the mournful reply. 'I'm going to spend the rest of my life in this dress, even though I can't even get the skirt hitched up so I can go to the loo. What am I going to do?'

'Zip won't budge,' Chloe groaned, hurling herself down on one of the sofas. 'We might have to cut her out of it.'

'But…' Sophy cringed.

'Yes, and then Phoebe will cut me. Probably use Cress's sharpest pinking shears to do it.' Chloe flung her arms over her face. It was clear that she was all about the problem rather than the solution.

'Let me have a look,' Sophy said, ushering the customer back into the cubicle, although she could only walk by taking tiny mincing steps. The woman braced herself with forearms against the wall.

'I know I shouldn't have had a curry on Saturday night,' she sighed. 'I'm a lardy lady who's going to have to be cut out of a dress.'

'We'll have no talk like that,' Sophy said as she peered at the long back zipper. 'It's the dress's fault, not yours. It's a pretty unforgiving fit and who knows how old this zip is? It's older than both of us, that's for sure.'

'That's really nice of you to say but I didn't just order a tandoori chicken and rice, there was lamb bhuna and peshwari naan and a mango lassi…'

'You're actually making me really hungry.' Sophy took hold of the tag on the zip and gave it an experimental tug. 'Ah! It's moving— Oh...'

It got halfway down, right where the woman's hips flared out, and stuck fast.

'Double Spanx-ed and my arse is still enormous.'

'What's your name?' Sophy asked, because this was a very intimate situation. It was a first-name kind of situation.

'Louise; pleased to meet you.'

'Hi Louise, I'm Sophy. I would shake your hand but I don't want you to make any sudden movements.' She patted Louise on the back in what she hoped was a comforting manner. 'Just wait here. I'll be back in a tick.'

'I'm not going anywhere. You're going to have to start charging me rent.'

Chloe was still lolling about on the sofa in defeat. 'Are you going to get the scissors?' she asked fearfully.

'Scissors and Phoebe is an absolute last resort, right?'

'Yes! I'm too young to die.'

Sophy glanced around the shop for inspiration. 'Is there something we could put on the zip to lubricate it? It's not caught on any material; it's just really stiff.'

'If we stain the dress with something greasy, then Phoebe will still cut us,' Chloe hissed with a terrified look at the stairs as if she expected Phoebe to suddenly appear, like she had some kind of bat sonar that instantly alerted her when someone was about to violate one of her precious frocks.

'We might not stain it,' Sophy said weakly. 'Not if we were really careful.'

They both pondered the situation until Chloe looked up with a faint glimmer of hope on her face.

'I have this stuff I put on my eyebrows. It's like this clear gel; maybe we could try that?'

Sophy thought that all three of them must have stopped breathing as Chloe lubed up the teeth of the stuck zipper with her brow gel.

'Right, Louise, you need to suck in everything you've got.' Sophy took hold of the tag with a tissue between her thumb and finger so she had a good grip, and sent up a swift but heartfelt prayer to the gods of retail.

It must have worked, because slowly Sophy was able to inch the zip down. It did get stuck just before she reached the bottom, but Chloe was there to apply more gel and finally Louise was released from her silver lamé bondage.

'Oh my days!' she gasped, doing a victory dance in her beige double Spanx. 'I can't wait to go home and put my comfies on.'

'That dress definitely needs a new zipper,' Chloe said, as she folded it up. 'I'll have a word with Cress and see—'

'No, but I'm taking the dress,' Louise interrupted, like the last very stressful half-hour hadn't happened. 'Apart from the whole getting stuck in it thing, it looked amazing on me.'

'It did look amazing,' Sophy agreed, but she couldn't in good conscience allow Louise to walk out of the shop with a dress that she probably would have to be cut out of at a later date.

'This is just the incentive I need to lay off the lamb bhuna and the peshwari naan,' Louise continued as Sophy and Chloe shared a look of helplessness.

In the end, Louise was made to see reason and conceded that she would let them put in a new zipper at no extra charge and return in a week. 'Honestly, I'm a curry-free zone now,' she said as she paid the deposit on the dress.

'This makes me feel so guilty about selling dresses that are sized much smaller than civilian dresses,' Chloe mused. Then, with another look to the stairs and the muffled sound of raised voices, she added, 'Phoebe flat-out refuses to let a customer try on a dress if she thinks that it might be too small.'

'It's a wonder that Phoebe actually allows any dress to leave the shop,' Sophy said and she and Chloe both grinned, until Sophy's phone beeped and she pulled it out of her dress pocket to find a message from Phoebe, who really did seem to have a spider sense for when someone was bad-mouthing her – or, worse, one of her frock children.

COME UPSTAIRS NOW!!!!!!

Chapter Fifteen

With stomach-churning dread, Sophy mounted the stairs, already rehearsing the passionate speech she'd give in her own defence. Maybe Phoebe had installed cameras in the changing rooms so she could see what they got up to when she was otherwise engaged. Though wasn't that against the law?

Then Sophy turned the corner, climbed the last few steps – and put a hand to her mouth at the absolute scenes in front of her.

'What the...?'

Hege was in her grey coat and dress and looked beautifully elegant, not at all matronly. Ingrid was half in and half out of her dress as she stood on the dais; Cress crouched at her feet. Not to do anything useful like pin the hem but to avoid the chaos that reigned all around her. Now, for the first time, Sophy was grateful that she'd missed out on shopping for wedding and bridesmaid dresses with Radha and the other bridesmaids if this is what they'd got up to.

British Beyoncé and Valkyrie were stripped down to their undies and trying on dresses, which they were yanking from their satin padded hangers with absolutely no respect for the fact that they were unique heirloom pieces that cost more than Sophy earned in a month. Heaped on one of the sofas was a crumpled pile of dresses that had obviously been discarded.

'Everyone tries on the wedding dresses,' Beyoncé was insisting gaily as she tugged down the skirt of a delicate, paper-thin ivory silk charmeuse. 'It's all part of the fun, isn't it?'

Meanwhile Valkyrie was dropping it like it was hot in a 1930s crêpe and lace dress, which had survived the Second World War but seemed far too fragile to survive being twerked in.

Only Jaunty Ponytail wasn't partaking. Instead she was sitting on one of the gilt and brocade cream sofas *munching her way through a packet of crisps* and saying earnestly, 'I'll pass. I bet someone has died in one of those dresses.'

Now Sophy knew what it meant to be hoist by her own petard. No wonder Coco Chanel wasn't lolling on her blue satin cushion but was cowering under one of the sofas, and Phoebe... Phoebe...

Was Phoebe actually crying? If she was, they were tears of utter rage.

'You *have* to make them stop,' she was growling at Hege, who might have looked elegant but was also looking like she was wishing for a swift and pain-free death. 'Those dresses are antiques. If they get damaged, they'll have to be paid for.'

Sophy wondered if she could just quietly disappear back down the stairs, but it was too late; Phoebe had seen her.

'Sophy!' she barked. 'Can I have a word? In the work-room!'

'Uh, yeah, sure thing.' Sophy's legs, which were working entirely independently from Sophy's brain, carried her further into the ninth circle.

'I think I'm having a heart attack,' Phoebe said, as she shut the door behind Sophy. 'Seriously, my heart is doing this weird fluttery thing.'

'Please don't have a heart attack. What is going on up here?' Sophy collapsed onto Cress's swivel chair. 'I can't believe that you let them put their hands and God knows what else on the dresses.'

'They're monsters. They wouldn't listen to a single word I said. They laughed at me. You don't even want to know how much champagne they've necked.' Phoebe clutched at her heart. 'Hanging's too good for them.'

'What are you going to do?' Sophy asked because, again, this was beyond her pay grade.

'You're a people person,' Phoebe said slowly, giving Sophy a considered look, which Sophy didn't like one little bit.

'Well, I am a person…'

'Yes! You're very good at customer service.' Phoebe nodded her head as if she'd come to a decision. 'I need you to go out there and make them, just, like, *stop*.'

'But how am I meant to do that? There was actual slut-dropping going on, Pheebs. Once the slut-dropping starts no weapon forged can defeat it.'

'We need to create a diversion.' Phoebe gave a little moan as she clutched her chest tighter, so Sophy wondered if she really was having a cardiac incident. 'Or at least steer them away from the really expensive, most beloved of all the dresses.'

'They did say that they hadn't bought their dresses yet. Ingrid said her wedding colours were grey…'

'But Hege's already wearing grey…'

'And ashes of roses…'

Phoebe perked up a little at that. 'Oh, I love ashes of roses!' Then she slumped again. 'Not a wedding colour though. We don't have a single dress of that shade in the shop.'

'Is there another colour that would go with oyster satin and grey?' Sophy wondered out loud, then flinched as Phoebe seized her hands.

'That's it! Yes! You are a bloody genius, Sophy,' Phoebe said, straightening up, pinning her shoulders back and baring her teeth as she reassumed her fight face. 'Right, we're going back out there. Follow my lead.'

Sophy didn't know what lead she was meant to be following, but at least Phoebe was looking her usual terrifying self again.

'OK, that's quite enough,' Phoebe said crisply. She turned her phasers towards Valkyrie. 'Put that dress down *now!*'

Valkyrie let the cream silk dress slide from her nerveless fingers to the floor. 'Sorry,' she said, crouching down to pick it up.

'That dress was worn by a bride who, in 1946, married a man who'd spent three years in a prisoner of war camp and you're treating it like it's a ten-pound piece of fluff from Primark,' Phoebe continued, assessing the three women with her laser-like eyes, then landing on Jaunty Ponytail and her crispcrumb fingers. 'And you're about to get grease stains on a dress that was made from a piece of lace woven by blind nuns in *the nineteenth century.* Please go and wash your hands!'

'Crap! I'm sorry,' Jaunty Ponytail said.

'And also you're ruining what should be a really beautiful experience for me,' Ingrid proclaimed tearfully from her dais. 'It's my wedding dress fitting and you've done nothing but diss my dress and behave like we're on my hen do, when actually I told you I wanted a classy hen do. Why? Why do you hate me?'

'We absolutely don't hate you.' Beyoncé sounded close to tears herself. 'We were just bringing the fun.'

'Honestly, what would your mothers say?' Hege shook her head. 'There's a time and a place for fun and this isn't it!'

Phoebe shot Sophy a look that was imploring but also promised certain death if she didn't deploy her legendary people-person skills.

'There's no reason it shouldn't be fun. But, like, low-key fun,' Sophy said hesitantly.

'I really don't mind you trying dresses on if you're careful with them,' Phoebe insisted, though one of her eyelids was twitching with the strain of lying. 'I was thinking about the wedding colours. Going to be very hard to find dresses in ashes of roses, but it would make a beautiful accent colour, if you three wore black dresses.'

There was a moment's silence. A welcome relief. Coco Chanel even crawled out from underneath the sofa so Phoebe could scoop her up and start stroking behind her enormous bat ears.

'Black?' Ingrid queried doubtfully.

Hege didn't look impressed either. 'Isn't black unlucky for a wedding? "Married in black, you'll wish you were back?"'

'I think that's only for the bride,' Sophy said, as Phoebe nodded approvingly.

'It's a bit boring, isn't it?' was Jaunty Ponytail's contribution.

'Black is very refined,' Sophy said a little desperately because she was fast running out of positive things to say about black bridesmaid dresses. Though compared to the pastel yellow meringue she'd been forced into when Caroline married Mike, she'd have much preferred black.

'It's so chic,' Cress piped up, even though her mouth was full of pins, something that always freaked Sophy out when she saw it. Somehow, during the furore Cress had managed to get Ingrid all the way into her dress, and was now making adjustments. 'What is more chic than a little black dress?'

'Everyone looks good in black,' Phoebe said firmly. 'I've got some lovely dresses you could try on and because they'll all be in the same colour, it's a great way to express your own individual styles.' She gave Valkyrie a swift up-and-down. 'You have the perfect figure for a Grecian-style column dress I have downstairs. The drape on it! Perfection!'

'What do you think I'd look good in?' Beyoncé stared at herself side-on in the mirror, sucking in her stomach. 'I haven't been to the gym in weeks.'

'I have a fitted sheath dress that would look wonderful with your curves.' Phoebe had already moved on to Jaunty Ponytail, who was tall and willowy. 'And you can pretty much wear anything. Let's pull some things.'

Sophy sidled over to Phoebe. 'Shall I take them downstairs?' she asked out of the corner of her mouth.

Phoebe shook her head. 'Best to keep them contained. I'll go and get some dresses and you are to stay here and don't let them *touch* anything.'

Sophy did think about putting back all the dresses that had been tried on and dumped, but the colour coding in the atelier was very subtle. What was the difference between cream and oyster? Mushroom and taupe? Ivory and white?

Instead she kept up a steady stream of inconsequential chatter about the hen do, the centrepieces, the honeymoon and whether Chinese lanterns were bad for the environment, until Phoebe returned with a swathe of black dresses over her arm.

Then, while Sophy watched in amazement, the three bridesmaids each tried on only one dress, then declared that they'd found their wedding outfit.

Phoebe had many faults. Many, many, *many* faults; but oh boy, did she know how to make the perfect match between dress and wearer. She was like a dress whisperer.

There also seemed to be something about slipping into an elegant black dress and being pleased with the results that calmed the three women down. After choosing their wedding wear, they sat decorously on the sofas and lavished praise on Ingrid for finding a beautiful wedding dress, which was going to 'look simply amazing on Instagram'.

By the time they all left, it was almost closing time and Sophy was physically and emotionally drained. 'I feel like

I just ran a marathon. Not even an ordinary marathon but one of those extreme marathons where they run for a week.'

'When in reality, you had to walk half of the five-kilometre fun run we did for charity,' Cress reminded her as she put all the discarded wedding dresses back where they belonged, because of course Cress knew the difference between oyster and cream.

'I don't do running,' Phoebe said, which didn't come as any surprise. She'd been downstairs to check that Chloe and Beatrice had shut up the shop to her exacting specifications and was now back with a smile on her face, which was very disconcerting. 'Sophy…'

Sophy's stomach dropped. *Now what?*

'I don't know what I'd have done without you.' Phoebe wasn't just smiling but smiling warmly. 'You really do have great people skills.'

'I didn't do anything,' Sophy demurred, and she had to give credit where credit was due. 'You're the one with serious skills. First you terrified them into submission and then you put each of them into the perfect dress on the first go. How do you do that?'

'I don't know. It just happens.' Phoebe walked over to the little alcove just before Cress's workroom. 'And of course, Cress, you're always wonderful so no surprises there.'

She emerged with a bottle of champagne. 'I think we bloody deserve this. Just don't tell Freddy, right?'

'Oh, do you think we should…?'

'Our lips are sealed.' Sophy shut Cress down with a very pointed look. 'Apart from when we're drinking the champagne, that is.'

It was lovely and unexpected; Phoebe even praised Sophy for her crisis management over the stuck zip on the silver wiggle dress. Apparently Chloe had confessed everything as

165

soon as Phoebe asked why there was a pink repair tag on the dress, which was hanging up outside the changing room.

'Of course, I'd have been furious if you'd got eyebrow gel on the dress itself, but you didn't,' Phoebe said, because she could only be nice if it came with a disclaimer.

Sophy was starting to realise that, so she said nothing but continued to sip champagne and turn over the events of what had been a very hectic afternoon, until she suddenly frowned. 'Hang on a second! You said that one of the dresses that got manhandled was made in 1946 for a woman who married some bloke who'd been a prisoner of war…'

'And your point is?' Phoebe raised her eyebrows and allowed herself a superior little smile.

'My point is that clothes were rationed until 1949, so how did they have enough clothing coupons for a cream silk dress with an absolutely enormous train?' Sophy's frown grew more ferocious. 'Also, wasn't that a thirties design with the graduated stitched stripes? You made that story up, didn't you?'

'I don't know why you'd say such a thing.' Phoebe shared a sorrowful look with Coco Chanel. 'Every dress has a story.'

'I just didn't realise that some of the stories were completely made up,' Sophy grumbled but, before she could grouse any further, Cress grabbed her hand and squeezed it tightly.

'You recognised a 1930s wedding dress by its graduated stitched stripes?' She gave a happy little sigh. 'I am so proud of you, Sophy. Four weeks ago you didn't know your Mainbocher from your Molyneux.'

'Sorry to break it to you but I still don't, but I do know when someone's spinning me a yarn.' She prodded Phoebe's foot, which she'd never have dared do if she wasn't on her second glass of champagne. 'Blind, lacemaking nuns?'

'Stranger things have happened.' Phoebe lifted up Coco Chanel, which was no mean feat as she was denser than a breeze-block, so she could nuzzle her face. 'As if I would make up stories about the provenance of our dresses. I'm shocked that you'd even think such a thing.'

'I'm so on to you,' Sophy said and now they weren't just bonding but actually exchanging banter. Or they were until Phoebe's phone beeped with an incoming message. She glanced down at the screen and whatever she saw there made her scowl.

'It's from Freddy,' she bit out.

'Oh my God, how does he know about the champagne?' Cress yelped, looking around fearfully. 'Is there CCTV in here?'

'He informs me that he's swapped your day off with Chloe's day off, so you're not coming in on Monday,' Phoebe told Sophy icily as if she'd had her vocal cords imported from some frozen tundra. 'Apparently, it's Johnno's express orders so you can go gallivanting around with Charles.'

'Not gallivanting,' Sophy said, then she realised it was completely up to her what she did on her days off. 'I would have cleared it with you but Charles said there was no need.'

Phoebe stood up and brushed down her dress. She never seemed to mind that there might be dog hair on her clothes or on her precious sofas and carpet. 'I knew this would happen,' she said crossly. 'Special treatment that undermines my authority.'

'It's a day off,' Cress pointed out courageously. 'What difference does it make whether it's Monday or Wednesday?'

'It's the principle of the thing.' In Sophy's experience, people always started banging on about the principle of the thing when they didn't have a leg to stand on in an argument.

But she wasn't going to tell Phoebe that. She wasn't stupid. Also, she only had to put up with Phoebe for however long it took her to get her airfare together.

Even braving snakes and lizards in between shearing sheep on a remote, dusty farm had to be better than putting up with Phoebe.

Chapter Sixteen

Phoebe was still tight of lip and flared of nostril when they closed the shop on Saturday afternoon.

Charles had messaged Sophy to say that he'd pick her up after work, they'd be away for two nights and she'd need one fancy daytime outfit. Annoyingly, he was still unforthcoming on any other details.

Sophy had spent the last two days on a very detailed fantasy, which involved them rocking up to a posh hotel to find there'd been a problem with the booking. There was only one remaining room. With one bed in it! She'd read enough romance novels to know that that kind of thing happened all the time.

But before she could move on to imagining them in bed together, trying desperately to keep apart, Sophy would then remember that should she have to share a bed with Charles, her honour would remain intact, goddamn it, because Charles didn't have designs on her. And never bloody would. He saw her as many things. The daughter of a good friend of his. The newest member of staff at a shop where he offloaded some of his cheaper costume jewellery finds. But mostly he saw Sophy as a project. A protégée. Someone he'd taken pity on. She was the Eliza Doolittle to his Henry Higgins.

Then Sophy would remember that Henry Higgins had realised that he couldn't live without Eliza Doolittle and her foolish little heart would think about skipping a beat. Then she'd go back to agonising over what she had to wear that could possibly be described as fancy. Even, dare she think it, *sexy*. None of her sack dresses had one solitary sequin between them.

'I packed a jumpsuit. The navy blue one that feels like silk jersey but isn't,' she'd said to Cress on Saturday afternoon as they took advantage of a rare sunny day in a very soggy April to eat their sandwiches outside on the patio.

'I don't know Charles very well but if he wants you to bring something fancy to wear then I don't think a navy blue viscose jumpsuit is going to cut it,' Cress said gently.

'What am I going to do then? Where am I going to find Charles's idea of formal wear when I have twenty minutes left of my lunch hour and there is no way I can afford to buy clothes in very expensive Primrose Hill boutiques?'

Cress put her finger to her chin as she considered Sophy's plight. 'I don't know. How are you going to find something to wear at such short notice when you only have twenty minutes left of your lunch break in the vintage shop where you work that gives you access to hundreds of dresses and a thirty-five per cent staff discount? It's got me stumped!'

'You're not even a little bit funny,' Sophy said and she wasn't laughing either when Cress frogmarched her back into the shop, stood over her while she washed her hands (Phoebe was definitely a bad influence on Cress), then made her try on dresses.

Eventually they settled on a 1960s forest green metallic brocade dress with a leaf pattern in a lighter shade. It had cap sleeves and was tailored to give Sophy 'a classic hourglass silhouette', according to Cress. Though when you were used solely to sack dresses and jumpsuits, anything even a little bit fitted felt like it was a bandage.

'You can wear the silver wedge heels that you were going to wear with that jumpsuit,' Cress said with satisfaction. 'You'll have to go bare-legged.'

'But it's too cold for bare legs in April and I haven't shaved in weeks.' It was one of the advantages of being single. Sophy had to nip out to the chemist while Phoebe was tucked away in the atelier to buy some razors, then shave her legs over the sink in the tiny loo between the changing rooms and the office.

No wonder Sophy had a feeling of impending doom as she hefted up her overnight bag and followed Cress through the empty shop on the dot of five thirty.

'Mum and Aaron are out out, so Colin's coming round and we're going to order dim sum and watch a film called *In the Mood for Love;* it's set in Hong Kong in 1962 and has *the* most exquisite dresses in it,' Cress was saying.

'Shouldn't you be out out too?' Sophy asked because it was Saturday night and, just like most other Saturday nights, Cress was planning to spend it in in. 'Unless you're going to take advantage of having the place to yourselves to get up to no good?'

'Says the woman going away for a dirty weekend,' Cress said, slapping Sophy on the bottom as she shooed her out of the door.

'How can it be a dirty weekend when Charles doesn't— Wow!'

There was a sleek, silver vintage car parked outside, its roof down, and Charles, in a staid black suit made a lot less staid by his pink floral Liberty print shirt, was holding the passenger door open.

'Your chariot awaits,' he said, as Sophy stepped out into the road.

'Happy travels,' Cress called out with a wave of her hand. 'Don't do anything I wouldn't do.'

Sophy rolled her eyes. 'But you don't do anything, Cress!'

'Whatever. See you on the flipside.'

Sophy turned back to Charles, who ushered her into the car with one hand and took her overnight bag with the other.

'Do you mind having the top down?' he asked. 'Will you be too chilly?'

Probably, but Sophy wasn't going to miss the experience of leaving London on a Saturday evening in a convertible with a handsome man at the wheel, her hair blowing gently in the breeze. Also, she was quite toasty in the black jumpsuit she'd worn for work and a thick cardigan.

'I'm good,' she said, running a hand over the petrol blue trim of the dashboard. 'Nice wheels.'

'It's a 1960 Mercedes-Benz,' Charles said, as he climbed into the car then shut the door. 'Sadly not mine, but borrowed from a friend. We won't be doing a hundred in the fast lane but she still goes at a fair old clip.'

'Doing a hundred in the fast lane is illegal anyway.' Sophy fastened her seatbelt. 'So, we're going on a motorway, then? Any other clues?'

''Fraid not. It's a surprise,' Charles said maddeningly, as he indicated they were pulling out from the kerb by turning the inner ring of the steering wheel. 'Do you like surprises?'

'Love them when I'm organising them for other people, hate them when I'm not in on it,' Sophy replied, and Charles laughed.

This was what he was born to do; driving a vintage sports car, the soft evening sun making his hair blonder, his cheekbones a little sharper. When he slipped on a pair of vintage Ray-Bans, Sophy thought that she might actually have swooned.

When she was in the car with Mike, Sophy usually hooked up her phone so she could control the playlist – she'd been listening to *a lot* of Taylor Swift in recent months – but the Mercedes didn't have a USB port, so they had to make do with the push-button period radio and jazz. It was mellow jazz and not noodly, plinky-plonky jazz so that was something.

But mostly they talked. Charles had finally sold the tiara to a very rich woman in Texas who didn't seem undaunted that opals were meant to signify bad luck. 'I did tell her that I couldn't offer a refund if she got partially eaten by a buzzard but she said that they didn't have a lot of buzzards in the part of Texas where she lives so she'd probably be all right.'

Then Sophy hit him with the highlights of her week, from the travails of Louise being stuck in the silver wiggle dress to the utter carnage that had unfolded in the atelier. And how annoying it was that Johnno hadn't replied to any of her texts asking if he'd found his birth certificate or passport yet. Sophy was now averaging a text to Johnno every other day and trying not to panic about how few months there were until her grandparents' golden wedding anniversary.

Charles was a brilliant talker but he was also a great listener. So many men didn't know how to do that. Egan had had selective hearing at best. Never hearing Sophy when she was asking him to put a wash on or take his dirty plates to the kitchen. Or, indeed, when she was talking about her feelings. But he could have been in another room in the middle of a thunderstorm and he'd still be able to hear her open the fridge door and would yell, 'I'll have a bottle of lager, ta!'

But Charles listened attentively to everything Sophy had to say, nudging her commentary along with appreciative comments, engaged questions and lots of laughing at the funny bits.

By now, they'd left London behind and were on the motorway with all signs pointing to the west.

'Bristol?' Sophy asked but Charles shook his head. 'Further than Bristol, then? Somerset?'

'Sophy, darling, don't spoil the surprise,' he said gently as Sophy's stomach dipped deliciously at the endearment.

'What's after Somerset? Devon? Cornwall?'

'I'll never tell.' Charles shook his head.

It was dark and Charles had put the top back up after they left the motorway and began to follow the signs to...

'Bath! We're going to Bath, aren't we?' Sophy exclaimed excitedly.

'Well, I suppose there's no harm in you knowing as we're going to reach our destination in about fifteen minutes,' Charles said. He looked pleased that he'd managed to keep up the subterfuge for as long as he had.

Sophy and Cress and their respective mums had done a mini-break to Bath a few years before. They'd stayed in an Airbnb on an impossibly grand crescent and had spent the two days shopping (Cress had spent *hours* in VV Rouleaux, a shop that sold all manner of ribbons and trims and gew-gaws) and eating cake and...

'Oh my God, you brought me all this way to drag me around the Bath Fashion Museum!' Sophy said like the ingrate she truly was. 'I mean, hurrah, Bath!'

'We're not going to the Fashion Museum, although if you really wanted to go then I guess we could find a spare afternoon...'

'No, it's all right. I'll be good, I promise.' Sophy pouted a little until Charles shook his head and laughed again.

'No museums then.'

Because it was dark, it was hard to make out the beautiful and quite rugged scenery that surrounded Bath, which Sophy recalled sat in a basin with hills on all sides. But as they got nearer and nearer to the town centre, the old buildings made of Bath Stone looked gloriously buttery in the glow of the streetlights. Even though it was the twenty-first century and there were roads and cars and takeaways and all the accoutre-ments of modern living, there was always something a bit magical about coming to a place so steeped in history as Bath.

Charles stopped talking as he navigated up a very, very steep hill and then parked. 'This is us.'

Sophy peered out of the window at a row of terrace houses all crammed together, but she couldn't make out much more than that until they got out of the car. While Charles retrieved their bags, she looked up at the yellow stone houses, each one of them with a gaily painted front door.

Charles unlatched the gate of number twenty-three, which had a mint green door and matching hanging baskets.

'A friend of mine works in Bath, at the Fashion Museum that you so cruelly maligned, but spends the weekends in London, and is very generous about lending his house out to passing pals,' Charles said as he adroitly retrieved a set of keys from one of the hanging baskets.

'You have very useful friends,' Sophy noted with a pang, because so many of her friends had actually been couple friends and, since she and Egan had split up, she was very much the odd one out. She'd even been unceremoniously removed from a couple of WhatsApp groups.

Thank goodness for Cress and thank goodness for Charles, her newest friend, Sophy thought as she followed him into the narrow little house. The interior was charming, with more mint green wood panelling in the hall, the floor-boards painted white. Charles took her down some stairs into a kitchen-cum-reception room with a scrubbed farmhouse pine kitchen table and an old-fashioned dresser painted cream and crammed full of vintage china, bunting pinned to the floating shelves, which were home to jars of brightly coloured ingredients and a set of lilac Le Creuset pans. The whole effect was charming and colourful and eclectic.

'This is lovely,' Sophy said. It was so different to the flat she'd shared with Egan, which had been a symphony of greys and creams and, Sophy now suspected, had absolute zero personality.

'There are two guest rooms upstairs,' Charles said casually, which put paid to Sophy's fevered fantasies about there only being one bed and possibly a freak snowstorm that would strand them for days. 'But we should probably have something to eat first. Are you hungry?'

There was no point being coy about it. It was nearly nine o'clock and a long, long time since her lunchtime tuna baguette. Sophy was already pulling out her phone to fire up Deliveroo. 'We'll get a takeaway. My treat,' she said firmly, because Charles had refused all her offers to go half on petrol money. 'What do you fancy?'

They decided on pizza, debated the various toppings, then, when it arrived – chicken and pesto for Sophy, truffle and goat's cheese for Charles – they all but inhaled it while they watched a true crime documentary on Netflix. Just when Sophy thought that she might have Charles figured out, he always managed to surprise her. He had layers. So many layers and she wanted to unpeel them all.

But that wasn't going to happen, especially not tonight when it was half past ten and she kept yawning so hard it was a wonder that she didn't dislocate her jaw each time.

She followed Charles, who insisted on carrying her holdall too, up a narrow and very steep staircase, past the first floor and up into the converted attic. 'I thought you'd be more comfortable up here and you get your own en suite,' he said, opening the door to a pretty room in the eaves, papered in the most extravagantly flowered manner so it was like stepping into a spring meadow.

'But you've been driving so you deserve the most comfy room,' Sophy said.

'I also deserve a room that I can stand up in,' he demurred, pointing at the sloping ceilings. 'I'd get some sleep if I were you. We have a really early start tomorrow.'

Sophy stiffened all her facial muscles so she wouldn't scowl. Her Sunday morning lie-ins were sacrosanct. Egan had always gone to the gym on Sunday mornings, so she'd only surface in time to just make it to the local Côte before they stopped serving brunch at two o'clock. She'd also spent the last few weeks training Caroline not to disturb her before at least eleven.

God knew how she was going to manage on a sheep station when they got up before cockcrow. Though would a sheep station have cockerels? She'd ask her grandparents next time they spoke.

Now, Sophy tried to look bright and up for anything as she asked, 'How early is really early?'

'Seven,' Charles stated as if it were an absolute fact and that the early start was non-negotiable.

Sophy brushed against Charles as she navigated the narrow doorway. Just that incidental touch was enough to send a shiver through her.

She turned round to say goodnight, only to find that Charles had taken a step into the room to put her bag down and so they were suddenly standing so close to each other, only a whisper could have come between them.

Charles's eyes were dark but his mouth curved into a smile as he lifted his hand so he could run his fingers through a strand of Sophy's hair.

'You usually have it tied up,' he murmured. 'I like it loose. It suits you.'

Sophy didn't know what to say. All she knew was that if she leaned forward just a couple of centimetres, stood on her tiptoes, she'd be in the perfect position to kiss the smile right off Charles's face.

If he would give her just a sign; some indication that she was more his fancy than his fixer-upper; but Charles just blinked slowly, then stopped threading his fingers through her hair to hold it up to the light.

Then he took a very definite step back and Sophy was so relieved that she hadn't made an absolute idiot of herself.

Charles being Charles would have let her down gently, but it would have ruined their trip before it had even started.

He cleared his throat. 'So, yes, seven, tomorrow morning.'

Nothing like the reminder of their early Sunday start to cool Sophy's heated thoughts. 'Getting up at seven or leaving at seven?'

'Leaving at seven,' Charles said in the same implacable tone, then he pressed his lips together as if he were trying hard not to laugh, though there was nothing funny about having to get up way before seven on a Sunday morning.

'It better be worth it,' Sophy grumbled, all thoughts of seduction very definitely gone now. 'And it better not be church.'

Even when Charles shut the door and went back down the stairs, she could still hear him laughing.

PART THREE

Chapter Seventeen

It seemed to Sophy that as soon as her head hit the impossibly comfortable goose-feather pillow, the alarm on her phone chirped into life at a very ungodly six thirty. For the first time since she'd set it, Sophy wished she hadn't chosen 'Waltzing Matilda' as her wake-up music. It was far too jaunty for this particular morning.

She'd actually had almost eight hours' sleep, but it didn't feel like it as she blearily made her way into the en suite and wasted several precious minutes figuring out the shower.

Charles hadn't said where they were going but her fancy new cocktail frock was definitely not the right dress code for a Sunday morning. Instead she pulled on jeans and a jumper and was just doing up her trainers when there was a gentle knock at the door.

'Are you up? Are you decent?' Charles called out.

Sophy opened the door. 'Barely up, barely decent,' she said and she sighed because, of course, Charles looked box-fresh in the black suit of yesterday, this time with an impossibly crumple-free shirt the same colour as his blue eyes. 'Do you own a pair of jeans? Trainers? A casual t-shirt?'

'I have a certain standard of sartorial excellence to maintain,' Charles said loftily. It was far too early for so many multi-syllabic words.

There wasn't even time for coffee, though Charles apologised profusely as he hustled her out of the house. It was cold, the air damp, and so early that the sun was still getting ready to shine.

But it was worth taking a minute to appreciate the beauty of the sun rising and turning everything gold as it rolled along the hills and peeked out from behind white tufty clouds that looked so perfect that they could have been painted on the sky. Sophy hardly even minded having to get up so early to be rewarded with such a vision.

'It's going to be a lovely day,' Charles said, making it sound like a promise, and Sophy hoped so. Though she needed coffee really soon; as it was, her fingers fumbled with the seatbelt and, as the engine purred into life, she found it hard to keep her eyes open.

They drove out of Bath, pootling along small country roads, fields and hedgerows a green blur outside the window. Sophy snuggled down into her jumper but tried very hard to keep her eyes wide open. The last thing she wanted to do was fall asleep and have Charles hear her snore or, worse, see her dribble.

Thankfully it was only a short drive, not more than half an hour until they drove into a...

'A cattle market?' Sophy thought she might cry.

'Not on Sundays.'

'Charles, I get that you like surprises but if you don't tell me exactly where we're going, I'm going to throw myself out of the car.' Sophy's fingers were already curled round the door handle.

'Flea market,' Charles said quickly to save Sophy from an untimely death or at least a broken limb or two. 'A huge car boot-cum-flea market that only happens once a month. You're going to love it.'

Sophy wasn't sure about that and, when they pulled up at a little booth and a man in a bulky jacket with a hi-vis tabard over the top told them that the market wasn't open to buyers for another half an hour, she thought she might have a little cry.

'Oh, I know Gerry,' Charles said and they were waved through because was there a single person in England who Charles didn't know?

They parked in an almost empty car park. Sophy steeled herself for the smell of animal manure when she opened the door, but thankfully there wasn't anything to make her retch.

'Though it smells weird, doesn't it?' she remarked to Charles as she did a good impersonation of one of the Bisto kids. 'What is it?'

'I think it's what people call fresh air.' Charles took in a couple of big lungfuls too. 'When you live in London you forget that the whole time you're breathing in pollution and exhaust fumes and God knows what else.'

They stood there for several long moments inhaling the fresh air that they'd heard so much about until more urgent needs took over.

'Coffee!' Sophy cried, her eyes alighting on a food truck and a sign that said they sold the magic elixir that she craved. 'I'm going to get us coffee.'

Despite Charles knowing Gerry there were very few stalls ready to be picked over and Sophy was amused to see Charles sitting in a white plastic chair in the car park of a cattle market demolishing a bacon butty and sipping from a styrofoam cup of instant coffee. He still managed to look as elegant and refined as if he were drinking brandy and smoking a cigar at the most exclusive gentlemen's club in Mayfair.

Charles explained that while most of his stock came from dealers, he had found some absolute gems ('pun intended, Sophy') at car boot sales. Although even quite a few car boot sellers had got notions after watching too many episodes of *Antiques Roadshow*.

'I've been quoted the most outrageous prices for items whose provenance can be traced back to the local branch of Argos. Then again, haggling is all part of the fun,' Charles said, standing up and brushing his suit for crumbs. 'I hope it won't be too boring for you. Do you mind that I dragged you here at the crack of dawn?'

Now that she'd had caffeine and carbs and salty bacon, Sophy was feeling no pain. 'Are you kidding? This is just like being on *Bargain Hunt*.'

'I don't know what *Bargain Hunt* is,' Charles said, assuming a bemused air that wasn't even a little bit convincing.

'I don't believe you,' she told him as they walked over to the large paddock where they more often sold livestock rather than antiques, bric-a-brac and all manner of assorted tat.

There was a lot of tat. Sophy even recognised the Next duvet set she'd had as a kid on one stall, which claimed to sell vintage home furnishings. It was fascinating to see what was for sale and what people would buy. Old suitcases. An ancient petrol pump. An antique commode chair. So much heavy, dark furniture; wardrobes looming round every corner.

Charles made a beeline for any stall selling jewellery. He'd pore over the contents of display cabinets and brooches and rings laid out on pieces of cloth. He even rifled through the '£1 per item' baskets but, though he bought a couple of watches and a fistful of beaded necklaces, he didn't seem that excited about any of it.

Not that Charles would be the type to show excitement even if he happened across the Crown Jewels. Sophy watched his face as a stallholder, a wonderfully imperious older woman with masses of white hair scooped up in a precarious bun, harangued him at length over a pair of earrings, which she said had belonged to a famous suffragette.

'Solid gold, fourteen carats, and of course the stones in the suffragette colours of purple for loyalty, white for purity and green for hope. They belonged to Mary Richardson, who was famous for slashing the *Rokeby Venus*.' She folded her arms with a smug smile. 'So, I couldn't let them go for any less than a grand.'

A thousand pounds! Sophy wanted to scream at the top of her voice about daylight robbery. It was a car boot sale. She'd never get away with that kind of price on *Bargain Hunt*.

'Oh, do you have the provenance to link it to Mary Richardson?' Charles asked politely.

'She was a friend of my grandmother. Lovely woman.'

'It's a pity that she was such an active member of the British Union of Fascists after she left the suffrage movement.' Charles pulled out a jeweller's loupe from the inner breast pocket of his suit. 'May I?'

The woman didn't look too happy about it; she pursed her lips and muttered to herself as Charles inspected the earrings more closely. Then he straightened up. 'Far too rich for my tastes, I'm afraid, and I'm sure you know as well as I do that the majority of so-called suffragette jewellery is tribute pieces rather than pieces owned and worn by suffragettes.'

From the sour look on the woman's face, she had known that but was hoping that Charles didn't.

'I bet you're a good poker player,' Sophy said as they walked away with the woman shooting daggers into Charles's back. 'Even I could tell that she was trying to play you, but you didn't so much as twitch one eyelash.'

The market had filled up by now with people who'd paid extra for an early bird ticket, so it was perfectly natural for Charles to take Sophy's arm so that they didn't get separated by the crowd.

'If I had a pound for every time someone had tried to sell me a piece of suffragette jewellery that had been worn by one of the Pankhursts, I'd have an offshore bank account in the Cayman Islands by now,' Charles said a little mournfully. 'Oh, there's a stall that looks promising. Shall we?'

An hour later, they'd done two laps of the market and Charles had only bought a few more pieces. Sophy, on the other hand, was laden down with her purchases. She'd bought a hideous Royal Doulton figurine of Anne Boleyn for her gran, who collected them and had the five other wives of Henry VIII, but his second wife had eluded her. 'For a fiver,' Sophy marvelled. 'Though I read somewhere that she had an extra finger, so it's not anatomically correct.'

She'd also bought three lengths of vintage fabric for Cress, who had repurposed her mother's box room as a sewing workshop. What she didn't keep herself, she sold in her Etsy store. For Caroline, Sophy had found what Google insisted was a genuine Mulberry handbag for a not completely ridiculous price. Then, on a stall hiding behind all the garish eighties and nineties clothes that the stallholder described as genuine vintage pieces (though Phoebe insisted that anything made after 1975 was just second-hand), she'd unearthed three 1950s dresses.

By the time Charles came to find her, she'd haggled the stallholder down from thirty pounds for each dress to fifty quid for all three.

'You'd make quite a good poker player yourself,' he said as he stashed their spoils in the boot of the car. 'Even I thought that you were absolutely taking the piss with that lowball offer but you stayed strong. Nerves of steel.'

'Wait until I sell them to Phoebe for three times what I paid for them,' Sophy said with a swagger, though she thought it unlikely that Phoebe would want anything for the shop that Sophy had sourced. Also, if it came down to a battle of wills between the two of them, Phoebe would win every time.

'I think you should keep them.' Charles opened the passenger door for Sophy, though she was quite capable of opening it herself. But he was like that. When they were in town, he always walked on the road side of the pavement to protect Sophy from any car that might suddenly veer out of control. He held doors open for her. Took her elbow to steer her through busy crowds.

Not because he thought she was a little woman who couldn't fend for herself but because he was unfailingly polite, with manners and a innate courtesy, which sadly was as old-fashioned as his pocket squares and French cuffs.

'I couldn't wear them myself,' Sophy said once Charles was sitting next to her. 'Maybe the blue one with the white polka dots but the other two. I mean, when would I ever wear a black velvet dress?'

'Whenever you wanted to,' Charles said, but it was different for him. He had a way of carrying himself, of being comfortable in his own skin, that meant he could wear his beautiful peacock clothes. Whereas although Sophy knew that, objectively, she looked all right (though she could never really love her own hair when men, always men, felt the need to shout 'Ginger pubes' at her from the windows of their cars and vans), she only felt truly comfortable in a sack dress or a jumpsuit. Maybe it was because her hair drew so much focus?

'We'll see. But also, Lollipop moults white fluff everywhere, so black velvet, not really practical.'

Charles took the bait. 'Who's Lollipop?'

'Lollipop is my mother's Maine Coon cat and, although she denies it, her favourite child,' Sophy said, and as they drove back to Bath she kept Charles entertained with tales of Lollipop tarting around the neighbourhood and terrorising the local cat population.

It was only eleven, but felt much later. Once they got inside, Sophy put the kettle on as Charles arranged his spoils on the kitchen table. There were no tiaras but his best buy was a Victorian mourning necklace of jet beads that he'd bought from a man who'd thought they were glass.

After coffee and brownies that they'd bought from a stallholder who had a sideline in baked goods, it was time for the next item on Charles's mysterious itinerary.

'Do you need lunch or could you hold out for an early dinner?' he asked Sophy as she loaded their mugs into the dishwasher. 'I was going to make reservations at a little place I know halfway between here and Bristol?'

'I could last, but it depends what you've got planned for the afternoon. Like, are we going paintballing?'

Charles huffed in faux outrage. 'Do I look like I go paintballing?'

Sophy leaned back against the worktop and shrugged. 'You know what they say about hidden depths?'

'We're not going paintballing, but you will need to change into your fancy daytime outfit,' Charles said and immediately Sophy was intrigued and also a little trepidatious. Knowing Charles, they could be going anywhere; or he could have plans to meet some of the many people that he was acquainted with.

Her nerves gave way to something else when she saw the appreciative look on Charles's face as she clumped, rather inelegantly, down the stairs in her green brocade dress and silver wedges. She'd tried to do a fancy daytime make-up look too, which involved a lot of mascara and a lipstick that was a daring three shades deeper than her actual lips. For once, she'd left her hair loose, though there would be no driving with the top down.

'You look enchanting,' Charles said as Sophy did a clumsy twirl in the hall, and Sophy knew he was just being polite, his version of friendly, but it was very hard to be friendly with a man you were secretly crushing on. Especially when he was so far out of Sophy's league, like Charles was Premier League and Sophy was EFL League Two and hoping not to be demoted.

'Whatever!' Sophy wondered why she'd even bothered with blusher when her cheeks were doing a good job without it. She'd also forgotten that she might need some fancy daytime outerwear, but her denim jacket would have to do.

'God, woman, learn to take a compliment,' Charles said, shaking his head as he ushered her out the front door.

'I'm not wired that way,' Sophy explained, though the way she tripped over her own wedged feet and would have gone sprawling if Charles hadn't been there to grab hold of her explained it far better than she could.

Chapter Eighteen

Of course, Charles couldn't simply tell Sophy where they were going, so she decided to just sit back in the Mercedes' very comfortable passenger seat and enjoy the ride.

England in spring was so pretty and this part of England was prettier still. Sophy was a Londoner born and bred who could find beauty in the most prosaic of sights: the London Underground roundel, the sun glinting on the slightly murky waters of the Thames; there was even poetry in the brutalist architecture of Centrepoint as it loomed over the northern tip of Oxford Street.

But green fields studded with wild flowers, tiny lambs skipping on unsteady legs, twisty country lanes canopied by trees showing off their new green leaves and village after village of those buttery-stoned houses with thatched roofs was a different kind of beauty. A bucolic sort of beauty that Sophy could appreciate, especially when she was seeing it from the window of a car and didn't have to be at one with nature, which was sure to lead to nothing good but the stench of manure, and mud. Sophy didn't do mud. She did wonder, yet again, how she might fare on her grandparents' sheep farm, but that would only be for a few weeks. Plus, she might well get to bottle-feed some lambs, so that was an added bonus.

Eventually the country lanes became even narrower and twistier, until they took a left onto a long drive bordered by lime trees, according to Charles. The drive seemed to go on for ever until it suddenly opened out onto a circular area in front of a large house. Not even a house. It was a *Downton Abbey* sort of stately home. Sophy's fancy daytime wear didn't seem quite fancy enough now.

Sophy eyed the ornate fountain and, beyond that, formal gardens that looked as if they'd been imported straight from the set of a Sunday-night period drama. If she looked hard enough, she might even see a young Colin Firth emerge from a lake, with a white flouncy shirt clinging damply to his chest.

'What?' she grunted when she realised that Charles was saying something to her. 'Sorry, I was miles away. God, are these people friends of yours? Are they titled? Will I have to curtsey?'

Charles placed his cool hand on Sophy's, which she'd clenched into a nervous fist. 'We're here for an estate sale. We're not having afternoon tea with the local aristocracy.'

'I'm very grateful for that,' Sophy said as the car crunched over the gravel to the car park at the back of the house and, now that she wasn't having fevered fantasies about a young Colin Firth and freaking out, she could see that there were actually large signs advertising an estate sale, though she wasn't entirely sure what that was.

Once they were out of the car they followed more signs, which led them through a pair of huge French windows into a long, wood-panelled gallery, and Sophy quickly worked out that an estate sale was like a very posh jumble sale, one with catalogues and items with numbered tags hanging off them. This was *Bargain Hunt* on steroids.

'We're not here for any of that,' Charles said, hurrying Sophy past a series of portraits, which mostly consisted of stern-faced men and even more stern-faced women. 'Besides, they sold off all the good paintings years ago to pay death duties.'

It went on and on. A heck of a lot of silver plate and cutlery. A gilt-heavy dinner service, which ran the entire length of a very, very long table. A pair of guns, though they looked so old, Sophy supposed that they were actually called muskets or blunderbusses or some such. Tapestries, their colours dimmed over the years. Eventually they came to a corner that had been allocated for clothes.

There was an entire rail of fur coats, which Sophy wanted nothing to do with. Also, some very droopy, long dresses yellowed with age.

'Not for us,' she said as firmly as she could, because she didn't want to travel back in the car with them and she doubted that even Cress's magic touch would be able to perform miracles.

Charles beamed. 'The pupil has become the master. Yup, absolutely not for us.' Then he went very still as he stared at another long table, this one full of large, flat garment boxes.

Sophy knew that Charles hadn't come here to play when he reached into his pocket and pulled out two pairs of white gloves, like the ones Cress used when she was working on something very old or very delicate or very expensive, or more usually the whole trifecta.

The first item that Charles very gently uncovered, under layers of tissue paper that crumbled to dust, was a long dress, made of a beautiful plum velvet and chiffon, with a lace bodice and undersleeves.

Charles moaned in much the same way that Sophy did when she bit into a Twirl after a two-day self-imposed chocolate detox. But when Charles did it, it made Sophy a little light-headed with lust.

'A Worth gown, late 1890s,' he breathed. 'Slightly torn at the neckline and the trim on the sleeves is a little damaged but on first sight, it's in pretty good nick.'

It was a lovely dress. Even Sophy could see that. But... 'For the shop?'

Charles shot her a look that was part indulgent, part exasperated. 'For a museum, my darling.' He looked over the heads of browsers, caught someone's eye and nodded. 'No wonder I've just spotted a curator from the costume department of the V&A and two people from Christie's. Now, let's see what else we can find.'

Although Sophy wouldn't have minded lingering, Charles said they were on a clock and ignored anything that he dated later than 1920. There were still plenty of dresses, which he paused over, then rejected, although Sophy now recognised the names that he recited in much the same way that he'd recited the names of all those precious stones; like they were sonnets, like they were poetry.

Lucien Lelong. Pierre Balmain. Balenciaga. Digby Morton. Marcelle Chaumont. Jeanne Lafaurie. Jacques Heim. Jacques Griffe. Lachasse. Michael Donnellan. Victor Stiebel. Ronald Paterson. Michael Sherard.

There were even a couple of dresses that he said he was going to bid on for the shop, but with a very strict budget in mind that he wasn't allowed to go over by even a penny or 'Freddy will have my guts for garters.'

'Phoebe, more like,' Sophy scoffed.

'If Phoebe really set her heart on a dress then she'd be quite happy to bankrupt us all,' Charles scoffed right back. 'Besides, haven't you figured it out yet?'

'Figured out what?'

'That Freddy is the real power behind the throne,' Charles said, very wrongly because it was clear to anyone with half a brain and a pair of eyes that Phoebe was at the very top of the shop hierarchy, Coco Chanel was second and everyone else, including Freddy and Johnno, languished at the bottom.

'I don't think so—' Sophy started to say, but she stopped when Charles gripped her arm.

'Oh my goodness, I think we've died and gone to heaven,' he said. Sophy followed his gaze to a royal purple dress, the one dress that had been put on a mannequin. Probably because its impeccably constructed, heart-stoppingly beautiful draping wouldn't have been done justice if it had been left in its box or wherever it had been hiding for the last few decades.

'Is that... Charles, is that a Madame Grès?' Sophy asked because they'd seen a couple of similar dresses by the French designer in the V&A and that painstaking pleated draping really couldn't be anything else.

'Sophy, I could kiss you for that.' Sophy really wished that Charles wouldn't say things like that; it gave a girl ideas that she had no right to be having. 'It *is* a Madame Grès. Mid-1940s...' Charles glanced down at the catalogue. 'Silk jersey. The V&A have a lot of Madame Grès dresses, but I don't think they have anything earlier than the 1950s and one of them is a replica.'

Sophy drifted closer. It seemed to be made from just one piece of material, but surely that couldn't be possible? The tiny, infinitesimal pleats of fabric, gathered at the bust, cascaded down the form like an elegant waterfall. She couldn't stop looking, marvelling, probably because she knew that not many people got to see this sort of dress, this sort of craftsmanship, so up close and personal and not behind glass at a museum.

'There's no way that you could wear a dress like that and not feel beautiful,' she said to Charles, who seemed similarly starstruck. 'I'm guessing this is a bankruptcy dress.'

Charles blinked and seemed to come out of his trance. 'Afraid so. Come on, let's move on.'

The dresses petered out and they came to an assortment of clothes that hadn't been lovingly stored away for future generations. There were five open suitcases with clothes spilling out of them, each one with a low starting bid of fifteen pounds.

'Now *this* we can work with.' Charles sifted through the first suitcase with ruthless efficiency. 'Most of this is from the thirties. Look! M&S beach pyjamas! And these cotton frocks. We can never get enough summer dresses. These slips aren't silk but they are good-quality rayon...'

'Lovely,' Sophy said flatly with a backwards longing glance at the purple silk jersey Madame Grès dress of dreams.

Charles laughed and nudged her with his elbow. 'You're repulsed by them, I can tell.'

'I'm not,' Sophy said even though she absolutely was. No way would she ever want to wear some other woman's (a long-dead other woman's) underwear. Slips totally counted as underwear. 'Except they are kind of whiffy. I can smell them from here.'

'Nothing your stepsister can't sort out,' Charles said undaunted and they moved on to accessories, which was much less controversial as they agreed to bid on some evening bags, before Charles's attention was taken by the jewellery laid out in its cases and overseen by a burly security guard.

When it came to the actual auction, it was equal parts thrilling and terrifying. Exactly like it was on telly, there was a posh man in a blazer on a podium with a gavel, describing the lots, while when possible, a uniformed flunky held them up for view. The bidders were arranged in rows on hardback chairs and Sophy sat on her hands and tried to hold her face very still so that she didn't accidentally end up buying a dreary painting of a horse for hundreds of thousands of pounds.

Charles, on the other hand, was excellent at auctioneering. He bid and won several pieces of jewellery by raising one authoritative finger and got a couple of evening bags and three of the job lots of whiffy clothes, though he was going to have to stash them in the boot.

The real excitement wasn't even the Madame Grès dress (which, along with several of the other dresses and a landscape, were withdrawn from the sale. Probably to be sold by one of the big auction houses like Sotheby's or Christie's, Charles said), but a small, insignificant Chinese vase made of celadon jade, though it wasn't green but a greyish-white colour.

It was in the catalogue with a list price of between £800 and £1,200, though Sophy wouldn't have paid more than a tenner for it, but ended up being the target of a ferocious bidding war between someone on a mobile phone and an impassive-looking woman sitting at the back.

The atmosphere in the room became so tense and charged that Sophy didn't even care that she might accidentally put a bid in herself as her head whipped from one bidder to the other. Even Charles was shamelessly rubbernecking.

'Sold to the lady at the back for one point three million pounds,' the auctioneer finally announced with great relish, banging his gavel so hard that it was a wonder it didn't smash into smithereens as the spectators burst into wild applause.

As they waited to pay and to collect their items, Sophy fell into conversation with a middle-aged woman in twinset and pearls, her greying hair held back by an Alice band.

'All that fuss over that fugly vase,' Sophy exclaimed. 'I wouldn't have paid more than five quid and a fish supper for it.'

'That's what I said to hubby but luckily he didn't listen to me and had it listed in the auction anyway,' she said in a voice so posh it sounded like she had several plums in her mouth.

'Oh my God, I'm so sorry.' Sophy pulled a suitably contrite face. 'I had no idea that you lived here...'

'My dear, one doesn't live in a house like this,' the woman – some Hon or Lady or Marchioness, according to the details in the catalogue – sighed. 'One is merely a custodian, looking after it on behalf of future generations. To be quite frank with you, I'd much rather live in a nice centrally heated flat with wall-to-wall carpets so we wouldn't have just sold the family silver to pay for a new roof and windows.'

'I suppose that is one way of looking at it. I bet you're not even allowed to stick up a satellite dish,' Sophy said without thinking, while next to her she could *feel* Charles shaking with laughter.

He was still laughing when they drove off, whiffy second-hand clothes in the boot because Sophy had been very firm about that.

'It was just like something out of *Antiques Roadshow*,' Sophy said. 'The only thing that would have been better was if that lady with the Alice band had confessed that they used to use the vase as a doorstop.'

'I love it when that happens,' Charles said. 'We did pick a good afternoon to attend an auction. I've rarely seen a sale like that even at the big London houses, so you've really got something to dine out on.'

Right on cue, Sophy's stomach let out an almighty rumble. 'You can't take me anywhere.'

'On the contrary, you can hobnob with anyone, even viscountesses.'

'I thought she was a marchioness!' Sophy peered at the clock on the Mercedes' dashboard. It was coming up for five. 'What time did you book the restaurant for?'

Charles had booked them in for six. It was only a short drive away, but they decided that if their table wasn't ready they could get a drink at the bar and eke out some peanuts.

On a weekend full of beautiful sights and stunning scenery, the restaurant was picture-perfect too, repurposed from an old watermill, with thatched roof and a wishing well out front. The late-afternoon sun glinted off the ripples of the pond and, despite the early start, it was a perfect end to a perfect day.

They were seated almost immediately. Though Charles said that he was only going to have one drink because he was driving, he ordered a bottle of Sancerre because Sophy couldn't drink red after an incident with a bottle of Pinot Noir and a dodgy Thai takeaway. Not that she went into details with Charles.

Even though they'd spent a whole twenty-four hours with each other, bar sleeping, they hadn't run out of things to say. Despite the edge of nerves that Sophy got around him, even after so many outings together, Charles was still so easy to talk to and so easy to be around.

She couldn't tell him how she felt – what would be the use? but in the pause between the shared vegetarian char-cuterie plate they'd had as a starter and their mains arriving, Sophy had to say something.

'I'll miss this... you... hanging out with you when I go to Australia,' she said a little sadly and with what she felt was great daring.

Charles's face was turned to the side so she couldn't read his expression. 'What was your departure date again?' he asked in a voice that was equally expressionless.

'According to my countdown, it's exactly four and a half months today that it's my grandparents' golden anniver-sary,' Sophy announced and, as she did, she felt the familiar fizz in her stomach that was split evenly into thirds: excite-ment, anticipation and terror. 'Do you know what? I really haven't saved up as much money as I planned to.'

'Four and a half months isn't a very long time,' Charles pointed out, turning to face her so she could see that he looked faintly disapproving at her lack of organisational skills.

'It's ages away. Eighteen weeks. A third of a year...'

'And do you have to get a visa? How long does that take?' Charles still looked like he thought Sophy was being very flighty on the whole topic of emigration, savings, long-term planning.

'I don't need a visa. I'm eligible for dual citizenship but I'm waiting on Johnno to sort out some paperwork. Hopefully they can process my application quite quickly, once he's managed to unearth his birth certificate. I was texting him reminders every other day but I think I might have to start doing that daily,' she added. Sophy wasn't looking forward to putting the pressure on Johnno, who'd probably do one of his famous disappearing acts. Also she'd have saved up a lot more if she didn't keep taking so many Ubers and being persuaded to buy dresses with her staff discount.

'So you are planning to stay in Australia for ever?' Charles asked as the server arrived with their Sunday roasts.

Sophy didn't answer at first, grateful that there was a flurry of activity as their side dishes, from roast potatoes to cauliflower cheese and braised red cabbage, were placed on the table. Once their feast was laid out before them, Charles made no move to pick up his knife and fork and start eating.

'I was just asking… so the move to Australia is a permanent one then?'

'For ever… permanent,' Sophy echoed. 'They're such big, final words, aren't they?'

She didn't know why she was prevaricating when she was one hundred per cent excited about making such a huge change in her life. Shake herself out of a rut. Explore new places, new things, connect with the family that she'd never met. Eventually settle down in Sydney, where she'd already know Radha, and welcome all the opportunities that might come her way.

'Do you still want to go to Australia?' Charles persevered, though Sophy wished that he'd drop it because they were having such a nice time and she'd much rather live in the moment with him than discuss her forever, permanent plans, which absolutely didn't include him. She only had another four and a half months with Charles; this funny, handsome man who'd taken her under his wing and had become her friend. Though hopefully he didn't know that Sophy's feelings were more lustful than platonic.

'Of course I do, but there's a lot of logistics involved and I don't want to be thinking of filling in citizenship forms and how many thousands of pounds I'm meant to have saved up. Let's talk about more cheery things,' she said with an edge of desperation to her voice. 'Tell me a funny story about a client. Your most demanding client. I bet you've had a few.'

Charles took the hint that Sophy was drawing a line under all talk of Australia and launched into an amusing anecdote about a businessman who wanted a ring for his mistress and, although Charles had told him 'repeatedly' that he didn't deal in precious stones, the man insisted on biting every ring that Charles showed him to test the authenticity of the stone.

'I didn't have the heart or the energy to tell him that the reason why people bite jewellery is to see if it's real gold. It's a soft metal so tradition states that you can leave teeth marks in it, but I much prefer going by the hallmark.' Charles arched his eyebrow. 'Far more hygienic.'

He had many more stories all ready to go and Sophy countered with tales about the absolutely unbelievable things that people did in shop changing rooms. Though not at The Vintage Dress Shop, she was happy to note.

The conversation was light-hearted, but it seemed to Sophy that the atmosphere between them had been strained ever since the topic of Australia came up and their usual effortless banter was now taking a lot of work.

It also took a lot of wine. Charles had been true to his word and the law, and only had one glass of Sancerre, but

Sophy had finished off the rest of the bottle without breaking a sweat. When it was time to leave, after a bit of argy-bargy over who was paying the bill before they unwillingly agreed to split it, she realised that she wasn't altogether sober as she wobbled her way through the restaurant and nearly sent a heavily laden server flying because she wasn't looking where she was going.

She hoped that the cold night air might sober her up, but when she was back in the Mercedes the world was still in soft focus and her limbs felt heavy. 'I've had such a lovely time, Charles,' she said, her words slurring ever so slightly. 'Not just this evening, but this whole weekend. I don't suppose you fancy coming to Australia with me?'

Charles didn't say anything at first because he was negotiating those twisty, unlit country lanes, but then he came to a straight stretch of road. 'It's a tempting offer, but my whole life, my business, it's here,' he said softly.

'You could come and visit,' Sophy said and then cringed at herself because she'd only known Charles a few weeks and yet she was acting as if she expected him to travel halfway across the world to see her. 'Or, you know, we could FaceTime.'

'Well, let's cross that bridge when we come to it,' he said non-committally and then neither of them talked until they were pulling up outside their little house for the weekend.

It was still early. Not even eight o'clock. Ordinarily, Sophy would be looking forward to spending an evening with Charles, but everything felt scratchy and weird and, once they were inside with their spoils from the day's sales, she didn't know what to suggest to make things unscratchy and unweird again.

'Did you maybe want to watch television?' Charles asked doubtfully as if he didn't know what to do with himself, with them, either.

'We could,' Sophy said without much enthusiasm. She dumped her packages on the stairs. 'But I think I really need to drink some water.'

She hurried downstairs to the kitchen/lounge, so she could drink her bodyweight in water and stave off a hangover before she went to bed but mostly because she didn't even know how to be around Charles right now.

Sophy was halfway down her second glass of water when she heard Charles's tread on the stair. She looked up to see that he was carrying her bag of dresses from the car boot sale.

'Do you want to try these on?' he asked, dangling the carrier from his long fingers. 'I think you might have lucked out with the black velvet. It's not quite designer but it's not far off.'

Of course, as if Sophy needed reminding, Charles was only interested in what she looked like when she was wearing a vintage dress or adorned with his semi-precious stones, and that was in a purely professional manner as he schooled her in the way of vintage fashion so Phoebe didn't end up garrotting her with a 1960s Pucci scarf.

'Sure,' she agreed, taking the bag from him and heading for the little shower room that had been carved out of the side return.

Sophy's face was flushed, her hair full of static, as she swapped one vintage dress for another. She had a good sniff of the black velvet before she put it on and it didn't smell of dead people or mothballs.

It wasn't the kind of dress that nipped in then swooshed out. It was tight, the velvet draped, not like anything that Madame Grès could create, but still clinging to every millimetre of Sophy. She tugged it past her hips and then, no cunning side zip, contorted herself round to try to do up the back. It was a futile exercise. She wasn't bendy enough, her arms not long enough.

Sophy twisted round again to see her back view in the mirror. Her skin looked even whiter than normal against the stark black of the dress and the strap of her functional black bra.

There was a gentle knock on the door. 'Everything all right in there?'

'I can't do it up.' Sophy flailed her arms again.

'Can I help?'

Charles was a man of the world. He was comfortable in the presence of women. It wasn't like the sight of Sophy bulging out of a black velvet dress was going to bring him to his knees. Not when his type of woman was elegant, sophisticated and definitely didn't get their underwear from good old M&S.

She opened the door, back to him. 'If you could get the zip up, but I think it's going to be too tight.'

She felt Charles's breath ghost over the nape of her neck, enough to make her shiver, then one hand gathered the material at the base of her spine and the other pulled up the zip with no muss, no fuss.

'There you go,' he said in a voice that was a little unsteady. 'It looks... you look good.'

'I doubt that very much,' Sophy grumbled, taking a couple of steps forward so she could assess the damage in the long mirror that was fixed to the far wall. 'Ugh... Oh! Maybe not ugh...'

The pleated bodice, the sweetheart neckline, the figure-hugging skirt, the exquisite cut of the dress, were giving Sophy the kind of figure she'd always dreamed about. She stared transfixed at her reflection in the mirror. Then Charles came into the bathroom, his eyes locked with Mirror Sophy's eyes.

What was it that Egan used to say whenever he saw a Dua Lipa video or, worse, an attractive girl in a bar, while Sophy was in earshot? 'She's an absolute weapon!'

Sophy felt like an absolute weapon in that moment. A bombshell. A siren. She'd never looked like this before and no one had ever looked at her the way Charles was looking at her before.

'It's the artistry in vintage clothes,' he said in a low, purry sort of voice. 'You could argue that each one is a piece of art, but really they're the frame that showcases the art to its best advantage.'

'Like the Madame Grès dress,' Sophy whispered though she didn't know why she was suddenly whispering.

'You can tell that she understands the female form, respects it, uses it as her inspiration, not like some of the designers today who design clothes that require women to whittle their bodies down to nothing.' Their eyes were still caught in the mirror so Sophy saw Charles's hands gently come to rest on either side of her waist a nanosecond before she felt the warmth of his long fingers through the silk velvet. 'Madame Grès and whichever genius made this dress knew how to make women look their best, which also meant that they knew how to make women feel their best.'

His hands smoothed down her waist to settle on the curve of her hips, stroking the fabric and stroking Sophy by proxy, so she was swooning and light-headed in a way that had nothing to do with the best part of a bottle of Sancerre.

But the magical, wonderful spell was broken when she gave in to the urge to lean back against Charles, and also because her legs didn't really want to hold her up any more. He felt so strong and hard against her back and goodness! Sophy gave a choked giggle because she was ridiculous and Charles was so out of bounds, which was why he suddenly snatched his hands away from her as if she were leaking radiation.

'Oh my God, I'm so sorry,' he muttered, turning his face away from the mirror as he obviously couldn't bear to look at

Sophy. If he had then he'd have been able to see the puppy-like adoration on her face and recognise it for what it was. He was retreating back to the safety of the doorway. 'You must think… That I'm some awful pervert.'

Without Charles behind her, Sophy felt untethered, adrift. Also, like a prize idiot. 'Oh no, I don't think that,' she quickly assured him. 'I know you're not interested in me in that way.'

He shot her a curious look, eyes narrowed, lips thinned, which she couldn't read. 'In what way wouldn't I be interested?' he asked.

'What?' Sophy shook her head, confused. 'Look, I need to get out of this.'

Of course then Charles had to come back into the bathroom to unfasten the dress and Sophy had to try not to shudder, but didn't do a very good job of it, when his fingers accidentally brushed against her bare, *naked* skin.

'I think you can manage the rest on your own,' Charles said, further compounding Sophy's misery by giving her a little push away from him.

Chapter Nineteen

Sophy didn't want to leave the relative safety of the little shower room. If things had been a bit scratchy and weird before, now they were so bloody awkward that she wished that she could jemmy open the window and flee into the night.

However, that wasn't really an option. So, with her silver wedges in her hand and back in the green glittery brocade dress, which was actually quite itchy, she emerged from her hideout.

For one glorious moment she thought that Charles had gone upstairs even though it would have been because he couldn't bear to face her; the woman who was taking advantage of their friendship to lust after him.

But then his long legs were coming down the stairs followed by the rest of him, a bottle in his hand. 'Brandy. Fancy a nightcap?'

Drinking was what had got her into this mess in the first place. 'I wouldn't say no.'

Although Sophy had had a vague idea that she'd escape to the sanctuary of her attic room and stay there until morning, when she'd pretend that nothing untoward had happened, instead she found herself sitting side by side with Charles on the sofa.

He'd taken off his suit jacket and she could feel the heat emanating from his body. His lean, surprisingly muscular body. She'd asked for ice in her brandy, which had made

Charles wince, and now she held the glass to her burning cheeks.

'So, I still don't get it, Sophy,' Charles suddenly said, angling his body so she had nowhere to hide. 'Why do you think I wouldn't be interested? You don't still think I'm gay, do you?'

'No! We've been through this before, I don't think you're gay. But we both know that... that... I'm not your type,' she finished sadly, and also, she'd thought the whole chat they'd had in his office about him not being gay had been embarrassing. But it turned out that had just been a dress rehearsal for this chat, where Charles would gently explain all the reasons why he wasn't attracted to Sophy.

And right on cue: 'Why do you think you're not my type?' Charles asked.

She threw him a hurt, reproachful look. 'Don't make me say it. Look, I know you like to flirt...'

'But I don't flirt with just anyone...'

'...and I know it doesn't mean anything...'

'Because I'm an indiscriminate flirter?'

'Because...' She was just going to have to come out with it and then die of humiliation at some later date. 'Because I'm not a *Vogue* editor or French. I'm not sophisticated. I'm nothing special. I currently live with my mum and I'm not much to look at so—'

'No, Sophy!' Charles said sharply enough to pierce her pity party and, when she dared to glance up at him from her slumped position, he was frowning, lips tight, like he was quite cross. 'I don't want to hear another self-defeating word. I can't even recognise the person you're describing, though she's clearly been gossiping with someone about my love life. Possibly Phoebe?'

His voice had softened so that teasing edge was back, and his mouth wasn't set in quite such a tight, thin line any more.

'Phoebe was actually quite discreet,' Sophy muttered. She was so confused. Had it not just been indiscriminate flirting? Had it meant something? And the compliments and the hip-stroking; what did they mean? Then again, hadn't she already been humiliated enough for one evening, so a little more couldn't hurt. 'You've been showing me the ropes of the vintage clothing business. Which has been very kind of you, but I know you see me more as a project. Like, um, your very own Eliza Doolittle,' she finished.

'You do know that Henry Higgins was interested in more than just Eliza's phonetics?' Charles was using his dark, purry voice again, which made Sophy's cheeks fire up but also gave her hope.

'So, theoretically, are you saying... do you... you're interested in *me*?' She just couldn't spit out a fully formed sentence.

'So, theoretically, yes I am very interested in you,' Charles said, taking pity on Sophy and flinging her from the depths despair to higher, happier ground. 'But you're emigrating to Australia as soon as you've saved up all those thousands of pounds, so I don't want to start something only to have my heart broken when you disappear off into the sunset.'

Oh! He kept throwing these curveballs at her and Sophy didn't know if she should try to catch them or duck her head. She was disappointed, but also insanely flattered. 'I'm not really the sort of person who's capable of breaking someone's heart,' she said wistfully. Not that she wanted to run around causing that kind of havoc but it would be nice to know that, for once, just once, someone was pining for her.

Charles took her hand and threaded his fingers through hers and, like it was a reflex action, Sophy immediately raised her head again so she was looking into his eyes. His face, soft and tender, as he looked back at her. 'I know that

I shouldn't flirt with you as much as I do but I just can't help myself. You're funny and you're kind and you're open to new experiences, to welcoming new people into your life. Also, indulging those new people when they're banging on about semi-precious stones and oxidisation. And you're very beautiful, Sophy, you must know that.'

Sophy scrunched up her all-right-but-certainly-no-oil-painting face because she didn't know that. On a good day, she thought she was pretty. On a not-good day, she hoped she was passable but, compared to Cress's effortless, ethereal beauty or Phoebe's traffic-stopping, striking looks, then no, she didn't know that. Not at all. Then there was a lifetime of having the word 'ginger' hurled at her as an all-purpose term of abuse.

As if he could read her mind, Charles put down his brandy on the coffee table in front of them so he could run his fingers through her hair, hold it up to the light. 'There are colours here that I don't even think we have words for,' he said softly. 'Your hair is as extraordinary and vibrant and beautiful as you are.'

'Oh, stop it,' Sophy whispered. 'If you keep saying things like that then it's my heart that will get broken when I have to leave.'

Charles kept stroking the same strand of hair as if he was entranced. 'Also, talking of breaking things, Johnno would smash my legs if I did anything to hurt his little princess.'

That was a mood-killer if ever there was one. Sophy freed herself from Charles's soothing touch so she could loll back on the sofa and laugh. 'As if I'm Johnno's little princess. He's always been the most hands-off father and he would never resort to physical violence in the unlikely event that I was suffering.'

'Really?' As ever, Charles quirked one eyebrow to devastating effect.

'Yes! Really!' But then Sophy remembered that Johnno had threatened to pay Egan a visit after their split and that he'd even threatened to call in to the official receivers to get back her outstanding wages. Then there'd been the time when she'd worked in that awful pub and the manager had kept sexually harassing her and then sacked Sophy when she'd told him to cut it out. Johnno had paid him a visit and put the fear of God into him. 'Well, maybe not your legs,' she conceded. 'Maybe just a couple of fingers.'

Charles lifted his hand and waggled the fingers in question. 'I do like having fully operational digits,' he said. Then he stopped smiling and looked at Sophy in the same way that he'd looked at Mirror Sophy wearing the black velvet dress. It was a rapt, hungry, even a little desperate, look. 'But I think I'd like kissing you even more.'

After that, kissing was inevitable. Sophy couldn't even tell who kissed who first. They leaned into each other, like magnets unable to resist the rules of physics.

There was some face-stroking. Sophy realised that she'd wanted to trace the beautiful angle of Charles's cheekbones with one fingertip ever since she'd first met him, and his hands were back in her hair. But only to cup the back of her head and draw her closer; not that Sophy needed to be drawn – she was already there, eyes fluttering shut for that first shocking brush of her lips against his.

They were sweet, soft kisses like butterfly wings. Kisses just for the sheer glorious sake of them. Kisses because why the hell not?

Sophy found herself sliding backwards until she was lying on the sofa, which worked out very well because it meant that Charles slid too so he was lying on her, hard and lean where she was soft and yielding. The kisses became fiercer, more passionate, tasting of brandy and expectation, but, though they kissed for what felt like hours (because it was hours), it was just kissing. Hands touched and caressed only the non-erogenous bits (although it seemed to Sophy that her entire body had transformed into one gigantic erogenous zone), clothes stayed very much on and, like a hero and heroine in an old Hollywood film, they both kept one foot on the floor at all times.

When it was so late that they heard a church clock somewhere strike the midnight hour, Charles took Sophy by the hand up the stairs and walked her to her bedroom door, and, with one last gentle, gentlemanly kiss, wished her a good night.

Chapter Twenty

The next morning Sophy felt as shy as a debutante at her first cotillion as she came down the stairs to the smell of coffee brewing. Charles was waiting for her at the foot of the stairs and he looked so pleased to see her, as if he didn't have any regrets about what had happened the night before, that Sophy decided that there was nothing to feel shy about.

He even kissed her hand but didn't make any move to kiss her lips again. That was for the best. Sophy had spent a sleepless night replaying a greatest hits of the night's kisses but, as dawn had started to streak through the dark sky outside her window, she came to the sober realisation that the kisses were a one-off.

You couldn't keep kissing someone like that, even with a foot on the floor at all times, if you were going to be emigrating quite soon.

'Last night, it was wonderful, more than I could ever have hoped for, more than I dared dream,' Charles finally said, when they'd had a cup of coffee each and were fortified enough for the difficult conversation ahead. 'But it's not that I don't want to, because I do…'

'But I'm going to Australia in a few months and to keep on kissing… well, it wouldn't be fair on either of us, would it?' Sophy finished for him.

Charles threw her a grateful look. 'It sucks though.'

It was such an unCharles thing to say but Sophy was in complete agreement. 'It really does.' And then she thought about the night before and how Charles had kissed and nibbled and yes, sucked a tiny patch of skin behind her left ear and Sophy wasn't capable of saying anything else until the toaster popped out four slices of toast and she could ask him if he wanted jam and butter or just jam on his.

Packing their bags into the boot of the Mercedes and then driving out of Bath felt to Sophy as if she was leaving a world that only existed in dreams and was now heading back to grim reality. Never had a Monday felt so Mondayish.

But then Charles lightly brushed her leg as he changed gears, and shot her a smile that was much sweeter than the two pieces of toast and jam she'd just had, and Sophy decided that everything was going to be all right.

They stopped outside of Reading to call on a vintage dealer Charles knew, who met them at his lock-up, a garage in a breaker's yard that was full of clothes and accessories, but everything reeked of petrol so they made their excuses and left.

It was after three when Charles pulled in to the kerb, outside the neat little three-bedroom semi in Hendon that Sophy currently called home.

'This is me,' she said unnecessarily, making no move to unclip her seatbelt and get out of the car because then the spell really would be broken.

'This is you,' Charles echoed and, as if he couldn't help himself, he stroked a hand through her hair one last time.

'I should get going... I have so much to do.' Again, Sophy made no move to get going or do anything other than sit and stare at Charles, who seemed hypnotised at the feel of her hair against his fingers.

'You should go but... Look, I just wanted to be sure,' he began hesitantly. 'Neither of us want to start something that will end in tears, unless... are you definitely absolutely moving to Australia?'

'I am. I really am.' Sophy hoped that she sounded firm, but for the first time doubt was clouding her mind. Could she stay? Was that a thing that she could do? She hadn't actually shelled out any of her hard-earned cash yet, hadn't signed any legally binding documents.

Then again, she really wanted to spend time with her grandparents, Bob and Jean, who shared approximately twenty-five per cent of Sophy's DNA and yet she'd never met them. Then there were aunts and uncles and cousins. All her life, Sophy had felt like she barely had enough family to go round, but there was this whole other family waiting for her on the other side of the world. And then there were the places that she wanted to go. The adventures she wanted to have.

More than anything, she wanted a do-over. Ever since she'd left school, she'd felt as if she'd been drifting. Into the relationship with Egan. Into every job that she'd ever had. It had been a small life. An OK life, but maybe you couldn't have a bigger, better life without making some huge decisions.

When Sophy was an old lady looking back on her life, she didn't want to be full of regrets about all the things she hadn't done. All the chances she hadn't taken. Always opting for the easy way out of a situation.

What a boring life to look back on. Everything black and white. No light, no shade. No glorious technicolour.

And what was it that Charles had once said? You can't make an omelette without breaking a few eggs.

So, she pushed the doubt away because yes, it would be the easiest thing in the world to not go to Australia and disrupt her safe, boring little life. Especially when there was all the promise and potential of starting something with Charles. But Sophy didn't want to be one of those women who was only defined by their relationships or let their relationships define their life.

Even if there had been some stellar, life-changing kissing.

'I am going to Australia,' she said again, slowly this time so that the words would sink into her own head as well as Charles's. She didn't want to give him false hope. That would just be cruel. But… 'The kissing. I get that it's not the right time for us to jump into something but we could still kiss, right? If we both agreed that it was commitment-free kissing.'

'It's something to think about.' Charles wasn't stroking Sophy's hair any more but cupping the back of her head and, when she did finally unclip her seatbelt, it was only so she could wriggle in her seat to get closer to him.

'It seems a waste when we both like each other and we're not kissing anyone else…' Sophy frowned. 'Are you kissing anyone else?'

'I am not.' Charles sounded quite affronted at the very idea. He pressed his thumb to the pout of Sophy's bottom lip as if he was staking a claim on it.

'Well, if we're not kissing anyone else and we're both clear-headed about the future, then there's no reason why we couldn't kiss,' Sophy whispered against Charles's mouth because he was so close now that she could see that the blue of his eyes had darkened to the colour of the sea in winter.

'We could take the kissing under advisement,' he whispered back but there wasn't time to take it under advisement because his mouth was on hers. In the old car there was no console, just a gap between the passenger seat and the driver's seat, so it was easy for Sophy to slide nearer, the gear knob jabbing into her thigh, so she could grip Charles's shoulders and kiss him back with a fervour that she couldn't quite believe she was capable of.

Despite the cramped and confined location, once again, when they started kissing and Charles did that thing with his teeth and Sophy did that thing with her tongue, time seemed to slip away. It only came back when Charles tried to pull Sophy even closer and his elbow knocked the horn, which sounded out loud enough to wake the dead.

Or loud enough for them to spring apart.

Sophy smoothed down her hair, which was feeling very bird's-nesty, and got out of the car. Charles got out too to open the boot and then, with one last kiss, a respectable peck on the cheek this time, he said goodbye.

'I'll see you soon,' he said. 'Very soon.'

'Can't wait.'

As Charles got back in the car, Sophy saw a movement at the living room window. It was no surprise that the front door opened before she'd even got her keys out of her handbag and there was Caroline craning her neck as Charles drove off.

Sophy should have known. Her mother was a curtain-twitcher from way back.

'Why aren't you at work?' she asked, having to fight her way past the immoveable object that was Caroline, who was still staring after Charles's car.

Caroline was a receptionist at a dental surgery round the corner. 'Oh, we had to close early. Suspected gas leak in a house a few doors down,' she said vaguely, then hurried after Sophy, who was already halfway up the stairs. 'Not so fast! Who was that? Is that the famous Charles? I thought you were just friends. My goodness, I hope you don't kiss all your friends like that! So, is it serious? Is this why you didn't want to get back with Egan? Does this mean that you're not going to Australia after all?'

'Oh my God, just listen to you!' Sophy sat down heavily on a stair because otherwise Caroline would follow her to her room and continue the haranguing.

'Yes, that's Charles. And he's just a friend… But a kissing friend,' she said unwillingly because Caroline already knew that much.

'What's a kissing friend then?'

'Friends who kiss but it's not serious. It's just *kissing*.'

'Really? Just kissing is it?' Scepticism oozed from every single syllable and Sophy was pinged back to being fifteen years old and in trouble for staying out after her curfew.

Except she wasn't fifteen years old. She was a proper grown-up. An autonomous being who could kiss whomever she liked without getting her mother's approval first.

'Just kissing,' she repeated airily, her eyes boring into Caroline, whose eyes bored right back. 'Can't be anything else because yes, of course I'm still going to Australia. Australia is happening! Australia is a done deal! I wish people would stop asking me about it.'

Chapter Twenty-One

To show that she was fully committed to Australia, Sophy decided to look the devil in the face and check out what flights currently cost. Not even on her phone on the tube going home, but on the big computer at home. She was even toying with the idea of a spreadsheet. Though she could have done without Mike's naysaying about the cookies on the family computer and that once they knew that Sophy was set on flying to Australia ('Yes! For the millionth time, I'm set on going to Australia'), the algorithm would never ever show her a cheap flight again.

'You'll need to clear out the cache,' he said, hovering behind Sophy and sucking in a breath every time she so much as touched the space bar. 'I wouldn't hit the keys so hard. It's a very delicate instrument, Soph.'

'Go away, boomer! I'm a digital native,' Sophy gritted but Mike wouldn't leave her alone until she promised that she'd let him clear the cache once she made a comprehensive list of the cheapest flights to Adelaide.

Caroline was hovering too, not out of concern for Sophy's unnaturally hard fingertips damaging the keyboard but because she still couldn't believe that her baby bird was planning on leaving the nest.

'It's not actually that expensive,' Sophy reported in surprise. 'I mean, it's expensive. It's over a thousand pounds for an economy seat but if I only get a one-way ticket, then it's five hundred quid or so. By the time I've added in taxes and baggage allowance then it's about…'

'One way! You can't get a one-way ticket,' Caroline all but shrieked. 'What if you hate it? What if you need to come home suddenly? What…?'

'Mum, please, not with the hundred questions again.' Sophy turned to see Caroline actually wringing her hands. 'If I need to come back in a hurry, I can get another cheapo one-way ticket. It will be fine. I'll only ever be a day away.'

'It's not as simple as you being a day away and you know it…'

They both sighed. 'I can't stay here, stuck in this rut while everyone I know moves on with their lives. Gets married, has babies, settles down outside London.' Sophy felt like she'd pointed out these facts time and time again. 'And I want to spend proper time with Bob and Jean and that side of my family. Not a snatched couple of months.'

'Yes, but…'

'Mum!' Sophy turned a full one-eighty in the swivel chair, which made Mike suck in his teeth again, so she could take Caroline's hand. 'I love you. You are my absolute favourite and no one will ever take your place. I'm not going to Australia so I can lose you; I'm going so I can find myself. Please will you be OK with this?'

Caroline patted her on the shoulder. 'Well, I'll *try*,' she said but, before Sophy could even finish sighing in relief, she was off again. 'But look at what happened with your friend Radha. She was only going out for a gap year and that was five years ago! What if you meet someone out there and you get married and then have children and I won't even know them apart from FaceTime and you know we can never get the screen in the right position so we can see all of someone's head—'

'I told you that we need to check the resolution on the monitor…' Mike interrupted.

'Well, why haven't you?' Caroline demanded and Sophy had been also planning to check, once again, how long it would take to process her citizenship once she had the documentations from Johnno, but she decided to quit while she was ahead. She carefully slid out of the chair and tiptoed out of the room while Caroline and Mike had a very fierce argument about the computer, which Sophy couldn't help but feel she was responsible for.

Still, five hundred quid and change for a ticket wasn't a lot of money. Despite her extravagant lifestyle, Sophy had saved up that much already. All she needed now was enough funds in her bank account to keep her going for a while. And when she did need a top-up, it couldn't be too hard to find work, even if she had to waitress or barmaid again, until she found her feet.

If only her citizenship were sorted, then potentially, theoretically, Sophy could be in Australia in a month. It was just as well though that she'd set herself a deadline of mid-August, because there were still a lot of moving parts that needed to be, er, moved about. Would she need any vaccinations? Should she sell some of her stuff? And what if, even with all the correct documentation, her citizenship was declined because the Australian Powers That Be thought Sophy was a wrong 'un?

It took a lot of deep breathing and a bag of Maltesers before Sophy calmed down and reminded herself that it was only the second week of April and she had almost four months to get things in order for her new Antipodean life.

Once she had decided that almost four months was a good, not very panicky timeframe, she felt sure she'd be able to tie up any loose ends. Especially as some of those loose ends did involve kissing Charles a lot.

A week passed with no sign of him since that Monday afternoon when he'd driven off after kissing her senseless, but he'd sent her a text to say that he'd see her soon and finished the message with xxx, instead of his usual x.

It was the first time that the sight of an 'xxx' had made Sophy a little misty-eyed. Of all the things she'd miss most about London, even though she'd known him only a short amount of time, Charles would be one of them.

And as spring finally sprang after a soggy start to April, London was also determined to show Sophy what she'd be missing. The days were longer. The sky was bluer. The sun was brighter.

At work, they all took their tea breaks outside on the terrace to soak up all the glorious vitamin D and gaze out at the boats floating past on the canal, as the trees dipped their green leaves in greeting.

Sophy was even able to coax Cress out for a proper lunch hour, so they could stroll up Primrose Hill and be in nature. They were both certified cat people, but they couldn't help but admire the many dogs of Primrose Hill, which almost outnumbered their human counterparts. Their favourite was a sturdy Staffy called Blossom. As soon as anyone made eye contact with her, she'd come scampering over, immediately roll onto her back and demand a belly rub.

'Much more friendly than Coco Chanel,' Sophy said every time, and Cress agreed.

'The only reason Phoebe burns those expensive scented candles up in the atelier is to mask the stench of Coco Chanel's farts,' she'd recently confessed because the honeymoon was over. She and Phoebe were still on very cordial terms, but Cress no longer started every other sentence with 'Phoebe says…' or 'Phoebe thinks…'

On rare occasions, Phoebe actually allowed them to take Coco Chanel herself for a lunchtime perambulation. Not that either of them wanted to, but it was very hard to say no to Phoebe.

Not surprisingly, Coco Chanel was very much her own hound and didn't take kindly to other dogs smelling her bottom or play-bowing. She preferred to keep herself to herself, occasionally barking at a small child wobbling past on a balance bike.

But mostly they would find a bench where they could eat their sandwiches (Sophy was on a major economy drive now – no more ten-pound baguettes from the swank Primrose Hill deli) and tip their SPF-ed faces back to worship the sun. They didn't even talk that much. When you worked in retail or, in Cress's case, were naturally reticent, it was quite lovely to have an hour off from talking. Cress was the best person Sophy knew to be quiet with.

Cress was another thing that Sophy was going to miss desperately.

She wasn't going to miss The Vintage Dress Shop, not one little bit. Despite Charles's expert tutelage, she still missed the fast world of high street fashion. Of new lines dropping every day and a steady stream of customers so the hours just flew by.

The fashion and the pace were much slower in Primrose Hill. Plus, Phoebe. Plus, brides, mothers of brides and bridal parties, each lot worse than the last. But now that it was April, business had really picked up and, to Sophy's delight, after four on weekdays and all day on Saturday, the shop was full of teenagers shopping for prom dresses and students looking for the perfect Leavers' Ball frocks.

They lounged about on the sofas, phones glued to their hands, waiting for one of the changing rooms to become available. Or, much to Phoebe's annoyance, sometimes they'd cram into one cubicle all together or wriggle into dresses over their cut-off jeans and crop tops on the shop floor.

They were loud and excitable and some of them definitely hadn't washed their hands before handling the merchandise, but Sophy loved their energy and enthusiasm. Now that she knew the stock as well as she knew the contents of her own wardrobe, she was happy to keep suggesting other dresses to try on when the first or second choice wouldn't do.

Maybe that was where vintage fashion had the advantage over the high street. It would be very rare or very unlucky to buy a prom look from The Vintage Dress Shop and then come face to face with someone wearing an identical outfit. Besides, buying that special-occasion dress should be a fun experience and if they wanted to take selfies in the shop then post them on Instagram, Sophy wasn't going to stop them. She just asked them to tag the shop in the post too. She didn't even mind when four girls did a synchronised dance in their new prom dresses so they could post it on TikTok later.

It was a point of honour with Sophy (even though she wasn't on commission – but she did wonder if that was something to discuss with Freddy) that she wasn't going to let any girl, or the devastatingly handsome boy from one of the local schools who was determined to do a Harry Styles on the cover of *Vogue* and turn up for prom in a ballgown, leave the shop with anything less than their soul dress.

Even if it took an extra hour, Sophy loved seeing customers walk out a little taller, their shoulders a little straighter, and a lot, lot happier than when they walked in.

On Friday afternoon, with the promise of the pub beckoning, Sophy was still smiling valiantly as Persephone, a limpid-eyed seventeen-year-old, dithered over two dresses; a classic seafoam 1950s prom dress with a poufy skirt consisting of layer upon layer of tulle and an almost identical dress but in a more sophisticated black.

'I just don't know,' she sighed for the tenth time while her three friends, who were collapsed on the sofas, groaned.

'Come on, Seph. Losing the will to live here!'

'In your heart of hearts, do you feel like you're more seafoam or more black?' Sophy asked.

Persephone shrugged. 'It's hard to say.'

She really was one of the drippiest girls that Sophy had ever encountered, so the seafoam would have been the perfect choice. But she could hardly tell Persephone that. She changed tack.

'OK, would you say that you're more the Little Mermaid or more, um, Wednesday Addams?'

Another shrug. 'It depends. Maybe I should try them on again?' Persephone suggested, while behind her Beatrice, who was waiting to cash up, put her hands round her neck and pretended that she was dying.

Sophy looked at Persephone, who was wilting on the spot. Then she looked at Persephone's schoolbag, which was actually new season Louis Vuitton, which went perfectly with her Gucci trainers, a steal at four hundred and sixty quid, and, she'd need Charles to verify but she was pretty sure those were real diamonds on the watch that circled Persephone's delicate wrist.

'Maybe you shouldn't make a decision,' Sophy said. 'You obviously love both dresses so, you know, why not buy both of them?'

Persephone blinked slowly. Over the sound of her friends moaning at her to get a move on and Chloe ramming discarded dresses back on the rails in a very noisy, very passive-aggressive manner, Sophy was convinced she could hear the cogs of the girl's brain slowly turning.

'Why not both?' she murmured. Sophy held up the dresses and shook them tantalisingly. 'OK, yeah, I'll get both. Yeah! Do you take Amex?'

'Absolutely!' Sophy gestured at Beatrice, who was now smiling encouragingly. 'My lovely colleague here will pack those dresses up for you. You're going to look amazing.'

There was a collective hiss from the sofas. Sophy turned to Persephone's long-suffering friends. 'You're *all* going to look amazing. Don't forget to tag us when you post your prom pics online.'

She jumped when an arm suddenly slung itself round her shoulders. 'Bloody hell, kiddo!' said an unmistakeable Australian-accented voice. 'You could sell ice to an Eskimo. What a chip off the old block.'

'You're not meant to say Eskimo, you're meant to say Inuit now,' Sophy said, but she couldn't help but feel pleased that Johnno had been there to see her mad selling skills. She even allowed herself to rest her head on his shoulder for one brief moment, until she remembered that she and Johnno didn't do moments like that. 'But I think I get half my sales skills from Mum. She's an absolute menace on Facebook Marketplace.'

Johnno looked at Sophy thoughtfully. 'You know, I've got a whole load of stock that Phoebe won't have in here because she says it won't sell, but I reckon you could shift it if—'

'Over my dead body, Johnno,' snapped Phoebe as she came down the stairs with her last bridal party of the day, Coco Chanel tucked under one arm. 'That job lot of *crushed velvet* from the seventies that reeked of patchouli oil. What were you thinking?'

He held up his hands in defeat. 'What I'm thinking is pub. You're all coming to the pub, right?'

Minus Persephone and friends and the bridal party, they were all coming to the pub, including Cress, which was a rare occurrence; usually she saw Colin on Friday nights, but this week Colin had actually stirred himself out of his usual, unyielding routine to attend a pop quiz in Streatham. 'All the questions are on B-sides,' Cress had told her.

'What's a B-side?' Sophy asked, though if it was something that Colin was into, then it was bound to be quite boring.

'So, like, vinyl singles have an A-side, which is the song they're releasing to get into the charts, and then it has a B-side, which is a song that isn't going to make it into the charts and didn't make it onto an album either.' Cress must have realised that she wasn't really selling the quiz night – or Colin. He was an obsessive music nerd who only listened to music on vinyl, and most of the music he listened to was recorded during the previous millennium. Sophy was sure that one of the reasons why he and Cress still weren't cohabiting was because Colin couldn't bear (or couldn't afford to) move his massive, massive record collection. 'Anyway,' Cress soldiered on, 'there are quite a lot of good B-sides. Like, did you know that Queen's "We Will Rock You" was originally a B-side?'

'No, I did not know that.' Sophy had never been so pleased to step inside a pub. If she'd needed a drink before, after all this chat of B-sides she was now gasping for a gin and tonic. Light on the tonic, heavy on the gin.

'It's good that Colin has a passion, just like I have my passion for vintage clothes and dressmaking,' Cress said a little defensively. 'Neither one is hurting anybody else and it's good to have interests outside of your relationship.'

'Of course it is,' Sophy said quickly as she flung her bag down on an empty corner banquette before it could be claimed. 'And you're lucky. Not all of us have passions…'

'You have passions,' Cress said. She'd left the shop without taking off her work smock. Today's was another 1940s novelty print, which featured apples and oranges cascading on a black background. Knowing Cress, she'd probably knocked it up in less than thirty minutes and could tell you to the exact year when the fabric was made and who had originally sold it.

Sophy didn't have anything close to that kind of passion in her life. If pressed, she could still remember all the Spice

Girls lyrics and word for word every argument she and Egan had ever had. But those were hardly ruling passions. Another reason why Australia beckoned. Maybe her passion would be unlocked there. God, it might even be bush-walking.

'Well, I'm very passionate about having a g & t in the next five minutes,' she said as Johnno made his way to them with a tray full of drinks. 'I'm also very passionate about having a bowl of chips about an hour from now.'

'Here you are, ladies,' Johnno said. Sophy expected him to leave them to it while he commandeered the pool table as he usually did but, this evening, he sat down, picked up his pint glass and took an appreciative sip. 'You can't beat a beer after a hard week's graft, can you?'

Which raised the question, 'What do you do when you're not in the shop?'

Johnno took another long pull on his pint. 'Good question, Soph. I duck and dive. I wheel and deal. I go to see men—'

'About a dog,' Sophy finished for him. 'Johnno's always going to see a man about a dog,' she explained to Cress. 'When I was little, I was absolutely gutted every time he didn't show up with a puppy.'

'I always wanted a puppy too but now I spend all day in such close proximity to Coco Chanel' – they both looked over to the next table, where the doggo in question was taking up a whole chair all to herself and drooling as Beatrice ripped open a bag of cheese and onion crisps – 'I can see why I ended up as a cat person.'

Johnno had been listening to this exchange with a half-smile but now he put down his pint and looked at Cress. 'You and Soph are so close and you're on the payroll... I feel like we should get to know each other better.'

'OK.' Cress smiled nervously, because although their lives were so entwined, their families so blended, Johnno was always on the outside. 'The spectre at the feast,' Caroline would call him when he was a no-show for yet another Christmas lunch, although he always swore blind that he'd be there on the dot of one. 'What would you like to know?'

'Well, we could talk about where you went to school and how you got into the whole sewing malarkey but that would turn it into a job interview,' Johnno mused. 'How about you tell me your top three chocolate bars? But if you like plain chocolate, then you and I can't be mates. Bloody abomination!'

'I hate dark chocolate,' Cress exclaimed with great feeling. 'When people say that, to lose weight, you should just have one square of plain chocolate to satisfy your cravings? How does that satisfy your need for a Twix? It doesn't. Not that a Twix would make my top three...'

Cress was almost as passionate about chocolate as she was about vintage clothes and haberdashery and it warmed Sophy's heart to listen to her and Johnno debate their favourite chocolate bars. Cress was such a huge part of her life and it touched her that Johnno realised that and wanted to understand Cress better. But once they were done bonding over Cadbury's Giant Chocolate Buttons, which apparently tasted much better than the normal-sized buttons, Sophy was going to pin Johnno down (maybe even literally) about the paperwork he still hadn't sorted out

Then, through the open door, in walked the sunshine: Charles in a cream suit and a brilliant smile. Just seeing him, backlit by the glorious early-evening light, scanning the crowded pub until he found her and his smile became even more radiant, was enough to make Sophy ride out a delicious shiver.

Next to her Johnno and Cress were still talking about chocolate and hardly noticed when Sophy murmured something about going to powder her nose. Only Phoebe looked up as Sophy squeezed through the gap in their two tables, but that might have been because Freddy had come in behind Charles.

'Oh God, he's all I need,' Phoebe muttered, rolling her eyes. 'I'd love another drink if you're going to the bar, Soph.'

'Not right away. In a bit,' Sophy said vaguely, then she hurried through the throng at the bar and into the tiny corridor where the loos were. It wasn't the most salubrious of settings but there was Charles, leaning against the wall even though there was every chance he'd get dirt on his pristine suit.

'And there she is,' he said, in his purry, prelude-to-a-kiss voice.

'Here I am,' Sophy agreed. She was eager to kiss Charles; her memories of their previous kisses were already worn thin. But… 'Not here.'

'No, not here,' Charles said, looking around. 'It reeks of disinfectant and desperation.'

'I am a little desperate.' It really was like being a teenager again, with nowhere to go to get up to no good. 'Outside?'

They slipped through a side door, which conveniently led out to a little mews.

'Ah, this is interesting! This must be where the brewery carts would unload and send the barrels down through that hatch into the cellar,' Charles said, pointing at a metal grille over the cobblestones. 'Also probably where they stabled the horses…'

'Charles, I don't care about the historical antecedents of this alley,' Sophy said, placing a hand on his chest so she could push him back into a little alcove between the pub and the small row of mews houses that had replaced the original stables.

He arched his eyebrow, of course he did. 'Really? What do you care about, then?'

Sophy pressed up against him so not even the gossamer whisper of a single piece of chiffon could have come between them. 'You kissing me. Me kissing you. Mutual kissing.'

'Well, in that case,' he said, his hands already spanning her waist.

She thought she'd memorised Charles's kisses, but it turned out that memories weren't any substitute for the real thing; for the touch and feel and taste of Charles's mouth on hers. Sophy wanted to sink into him but had to settle for leaning hard so she could feel every inch of him pressed up against her.

It was the first time they'd kissed standing up, which was a novelty but, in reality, a little awkward. Sophy had never minded the disparity in their heights – she liked it that Charles was quite a bit taller than she was – but now she was having to stand on her tippiest of toes and stretch her neck in a position that it didn't want to go, even though Charles was leaning down.

Eventually, reluctantly, he stole one last, devastating kiss, then stopped. 'I love kissing you but this is agony,' he drawled in her ear, which made Sophy shudder with lust.

'I know,' she whispered. 'But we agreed that we'd only kiss. I'm *aching* for us to do more than that and I can only imagine that you're aching even more but...'

'No, no.' Charles shushed her with a tiny kiss. Sophy could feel his lips curve in a smile. 'I mean, yes. I am hurting in a rather basic part of my anatomy but what I meant was that kissing standing up like this is doing something to my neck that I don't think my osteopath will be able to put right.'

'Oh? Oh!' The thought of Charles wanting her so badly... Sophy was suddenly seized with the urge to fling herself down on the cobbles and beg him to take her, though she wasn't the type of person to ever find herself seized with those kinds of urges. 'So, do you want to stop kissing then?'

Charles looked left then right but they were alone. 'I'm sure we can find a way around this ergonomic problem. We're both very practical people.'

'Maybe there's something I can stand on so I wouldn't have to stretch and you wouldn't have to bend.'

There were a couple of stone flower pots outside one of the houses further down but then they'd be out in the open, and also Sophy was wearing her fancy trainers in expectation of seeing Charles and much as she loved kissing him she didn't want to get earth on them.

Perhaps this was God's way of saying that they should just get in a cab and go back to Charles's place and if they ended up doing more than kissing, then so be it.

'We could always—'

'Let's try this,' Charles interrupted, eyeing Sophy in a speculative fashion that made her knees tremble. 'If I just...'

'Oh, goodness!' Sophy squeaked as he lifted her up – he must work out – turned her round so she now had her back against the wall and settled himself into the cradle of her hips.

'You'd probably be more comfortable if you wrapped your legs round me,' he suggested helpfully.

'I probably would,' Sophy agreed breathily as if she'd just run up Primrose Hill without stopping once. 'I'm not too heavy?'

'Not at all.' Charles had one arm wrapped under Sophy's thighs, which was doing nothing to alleviate her ache, and with his other hand he tipped up her chin. 'In actual fact, you feel delightful. Shall we?'

He kissed her again. And again. And again. Though this time there was a lot more wriggling and even some grinding and Sophy couldn't...

'Ahem!'

She wanted to do more than kissing. A lot more and if she could just get her hand...

'Ahem!'

...in between their frantically straining bodies and...

'Oh my God, Sophy! What are you doing?'

Never had the voice of her conscience sounded so loud or so like Cress.

Sophy slowly drifted back into orbit to realise that Charles had stopped kissing her because Cress was standing not even two metres away from them and, even though it was dusky verging on dark now, Sophy could see very clearly the shocked expression on her face.

It was an ungraceful scramble to unlock her legs from round Charles's hips and put her two unsteady feet back on the ground.

'Hey Cress,' she said weakly.

Charles looked heavenwards, grimaced at Sophy, then turned round to face the music and the judgement of her stepsister.

'We're both consenting adults,' he said.

'And we're just kissing. Only kissing,' Sophy added.

'I don't need to know the details.' Cress did some anguished jazz hands. 'Everyone was wondering where you'd got to. You nipped to the loo over an hour ago.'

'Not an hour…'

'Over an hour,' Cress clarified as Charles squeezed Sophy's hand, then freed her.

'You go in. I'll follow in a minute,' he said, sounding and looking far more ruffled than Sophy had ever thought possible.

'I'm waiting, Sophy.' She'd also never heard or seen her stepsister looking so stern. She wouldn't have been surprised if Cress had started tapping a foot impatiently or looking pointedly at her watch.

She did neither but linked arms with Sophy at the earliest opportunity and all but frogmarched her back into the pub.

'It's only kissing,' Sophy said again.

'I'm not even going to talk to you, Soph, until I have a large drink in my hands.'

Chapter Twenty-Two

Five minutes later, when Cress had a large glass of wine, even though generally she only allowed herself one cocktail in a can on a Sunday evening and that was it for her alcohol consumption, Sophy waited for her to begin the interrogation.

But then Charles ventured back into the pub. He'd been able to restore himself back to his former neat-as-a-bandbox status except his hair was going in all directions because Sophy had been running her fingers through it. She dimly remembered at one point *tugging* on it.

'You haven't been listening to a single word I've been saying, have you?'

With some difficulty, Sophy tore her eyes away from Charles, who was also doing a pretty bad job of pretending not to look at Sophy as he talked to Freddy at the bar.

'Sorry. What?'

Cress sighed. 'I said that you've clearly found your passion in life.'

'You know I didn't mean it like that,' Sophy said and then she giggled and Cress couldn't be too cross with her because she giggled too. 'I do really like kissing him though.'

'But you're going to Australia,' Cress reminded her, not that she needed any reminding.

'I know I am,' she said, hoping that her uninterested tone would mean they changed the subject because, for this evening, she just wanted to live in the here and now. And hopefully, get a few more kisses in with Charles while they were waiting for her Uber.

'It's just if you're starting a new relationship...'

'It's not a new relationship,' Sophy said. 'It's so far from that. It's just a thing. A kissing thing solely, because I *am* going to Australia.'

'It's not just, you know, you *kissing* Charles, who's a major upgrade by the way.' Cress paused as they both giggled again. 'Is he even the same species as Egan? They're like matter and antimatter.'

'There was a time though when I thought that Egan was really good-looking. Textbook good-looking.' Sophy tried to defend not just her ex-boyfriend but her own taste.

'Maybe, when you were younger but not now,' Cress said, though Colin had been a music nerd in a Beatles t-shirt at the age of fifteen and he was still a music nerd with the same Beatles t-shirt in his weekly t-shirt rotation. 'Anyway, it's not just you kissing incredibly handsome and well-dressed men. You seem really happy at work.'

'It is just a temporary job.' She looked around, not for Charles this time but to check who might be in earshot, then she lowered her voice. 'Which is why I can put up with Phoebe in the short term. And yes, it is a lot more fulfilling and interesting than I thought it would be...'

'Plus you're not contributing to landfill any more...'

Sophy raised her gin and tonic in a toast that she was actually part of the solution rather than part of the problem '...But it's a means to an end and that end is my ticket to Adelaide and some spending money.' She frowned. 'I really need to check the ticket prices again, see if there's any special offers, but I need to use Mike's big computer for that and, well, you know the rest.'

Cress nodded. 'Dad stands over you, making really annoying panicky huffing noises every time you make contact with the keyboard. Plus, you get a lecture every time you accept all cookies without reading the small print first.'

'So annoying.'

'Beyond annoying.'

'I actually want to murder him a little bit,' Sophy admitted. 'But anyway, that's why I haven't ironed out the particulars yet. And Johnno *still* hasn't sorted out his papers... Is he around? I should have it out with him.'

'He left while you were busy snogging Charles,' Cress said slyly. Then her expression grew hopeful. 'So, if Johnno doesn't sort out his papers, then you won't be able to go?'

'Oh, I'm going to Australia. Fact. Even if I have to go round to Johnno's place myself and hunt through every drawer, every cupboard... Oh no, please don't.' Her stepsister's eyes had suddenly become glassy as if she were about to start shedding tears. 'Cress, it's ages away. Four months.'

'That's sixteen weeks. Sixteen weeks is no time at all.' For someone who hardly drank, Cress took a huge gulp of wine. 'I still don't think you'll really go through with it. How could you emigrate and just leave me here on my own?'

'But you're not on your own. You have Colin,' Sophy reminded her gently, though Cress's relationship with Colin wasn't that much different to being single. 'And you have a vocation; a job that you love that gives you interests and friends outside of work too, like your stitch 'n' bitch group. You'll manage just fine without me.'

'I don't want to be just fine.' Cress reached across the table to clutch Sophy's hand like she wasn't ever going to let go. 'I want a life that has you in it. Not thousands upon thousands of miles away in a different continent and on a different time zone.'

'Look, I have to do this and I could well be back in a couple of years...'

Cress shook her head. 'But what if you aren't? Radha was only going to Australia for six months, then she met some rippling surfer dude and now she's never coming back.'

'You could come out too. For Radha's wedding and then see what happens after that,' Sophy said in what she hoped was a tempting fashion. 'They do have a thriving fashion industry in Australia, you know. You'd be snapped up immediately.'

'I couldn't leave my mum and I know I haven't worked at the shop very long, but I love my job. I'm not like you, I don't want to have adventures. The closest I come to adventure is cutting out cloth without measuring twice.'

'And Colin.' Sophy rolled her eyes.

'What about Colin?'

This time Sophy rolled her eyes so hard, she was sure that she'd detached one of her retinas. 'You don't want to leave Colin.'

Cress glared at her. 'Obviously that goes without saying.'

'Oh, that must be why you didn't say it.' Sophy smiled round the rim of her glass and had to admit that she deserved the kick that Cress gave her under the table.

Chapter Twenty-Three

Sophy was home much quicker and much more sober than she'd intended.

Two glasses of wine was too much for Cress, used as she was to only one weak, weekly mojito in a can. By ten o'clock, she was absolutely paralytic; quite incapable of coherent speech or walking in even a vaguely straight line. It wasn't a case of putting her in a cab, there was no way Sophy would let Cress out of her sight when she was in a state like that. So she got in the cab with Cress and, though Charles waited with them, there was no opportunity for anything other than a chaste peck on the cheek and promises to see each other soon.

'You can kiss if you like. I won't look,' Cress had slurred but they'd both ignored her.

It was harder to ignore Cress once it was just the two of them in the back of an Uber, Cress crying and begging Sophy not to 'emigrate to the back of beyond', and, though Sophy knew it was just the alcohol and that Cress would be mortified in the morning, it was like a thousand tiny paper cuts right to the heart.

That was nothing compared to the cost of a car to Finchley, then taking that same car to Hendon just as Friday-night price surging kicked in. Maybe that was Cress's masterplan: to make sure that Sophy declared bankruptcy and could never accumulate the funds she needed.

Still, it meant that Sophy was home at a very respectable ten forty-five. Caroline, and more importantly Mike, were tucked up in bed and so Sophy could take a mug of camomile tea up to the office and fire up the computer. (If Mike knew that she had liquid, hot liquid, anywhere near his precious computer, there would be hell to pay.)

He also thought that Sophy didn't know the passcode to turn the computer on, but he was wrong. It was Caroline's date of birth, which was both touching and also very predictable.

She sent a quick WhatsApp to check all was well on the other side and, when she got an answer back in the affirmative, she clicked on the camera icon.

Then, in a miracle of modern technology that Sophy would never take for granted, her screen was filled up with her grandfather Bob's beaming face, as he sat on the veranda of the farmhouse. Though it wasn't like any rustic farmhouse that Sophy had seen in her rare forays into the countryside; ramshackle houses that had been there for centuries. This was a ranch-style one-level house with its wraparound veranda, a swimming pool and a back garden that eventually became farmland. Bob and Jean even had kangaroos venture into their garden; one of them was a local Lothario who'd bring his new family to see them every year.

'G'day kiddo!'

Sophy still couldn't believe that people in Australia really said, 'G'day,' just like on *Neighbours*.

'More like goodnight,' she said, returning Bob's cheery wave. 'It's eleven o'clock here.'

'Seven thirty in the morning round these parts,' Bob said. It always made Sophy double-take, just how much he looked like Johnno – minus the peacock-coloured hair. Bob was 'bald as a coot', as he described it, his face weatherbeaten and wrinkled, but it was Johnno's brilliant blue eyes, crinkling at the corners, the same irrepressible, slightly crooked grin. 'Already been up for a couple of hours.'

Sophy tried hard not to pull a horrified face. 'That sounds very early.'

'Best part of the day,' Bob said. 'And Saturday's change-over day so there's always a lot to do.'

As well as the sheep, there were several guesthouses on the property.

'We were late to finish the shearing this year, remember we're an autumn shear, but we managed just over seven hundred bales of the best merino wool so can't complain,' Bob continued as Sophy nodded, slightly confused and slightly relieved that she wouldn't have to learn how to shear a sheep as soon as she got there.

'Doesn't stop you from complaining though.' The screen was suddenly filled up by a white t-shirt that proclaimed *Holy Sheep Balls*. Then Sophy's grandmother, Jean, stepped back and came into shot. 'Hello, darling girl.'

Jean was holding two mugs of tea, which she placed on a low table in front of their two chairs, then sat down, grimacing as she did so.

'Oh Gran, is your hip playing up again?' Sophy asked in concern as Jean was clearly struggling to get comfortable. 'Any news on when they're going to book you in for your hip replacement?'

It was odd that although they'd never met, after several years of calls, which had started on Bob's seventieth birthday and then become more frequent over the subsequent five years, Sophy and her grandparents knew the minutiae of each other's lives.

They hadn't been surprised when she'd split up with Egan, because they'd seen it on the cards long before Sophy had had her epiphany. 'The only time we ever heard him was when he was asking you where something was,' Jean had said the first time that Sophy had called them from Mike's office rather than from her bedroom in the flat in Deptford. 'You don't want a man who doesn't know where half his possessions have got to. You're not there to pick up after him, Soph.'

So, Sophy knew all about the saga of Jean's troublesome hips, exacerbated by a fall a few months ago when she'd been changing a lightbulb in one of those guest cottages though 'Bob said not to do it but I thought it will take two seconds to scramble up a ladder and next thing I know I'm lying on the floor for an hour until he comes to find me.'

If Johnno had inherited his father's looks then he'd definitely inherited his mother's garrulous ways. Now, Bob and Jean shared a worried look at each other.

'Well, we heard from the hospital this week and they've had a cancellation, so they wanted to move me up the list,' Jean said, though she didn't sound too happy about it.

'But that's good, isn't it?'

'It will be mid-July and generally that's when we've got a lot of maintenance work on. We're having real trouble finding casual staff at the moment, so I'm not sure it's a great time to have the op… they do both hips at once, so that's going to take a bit of recovery time—'

'At least it's before your wedding anniversary,' Sophy said because she'd learned that it was fine to interrupt Jean when she got going, otherwise she'd never have a chance to get a word in. 'You wouldn't want to be in hospital for that, would you? Do you think a month is long enough to recover in time for your big party?'

Bob and Jean had no idea that Sophy was planning to come out to celebrate their anniversary with them. They'd talked about her coming for Radha's wedding in October, then swinging by the sheep station after that. Maybe staying for Christmas and how Sophy was looking forward to swerving a cold, damp British winter in favour of a warm Australian summer.

'It will sort itself out,' Jean said airily.

'I could come earlier maybe. There's nothing keeping me here. Not really,' Sophy said.

'Have you heard about your citizenship application then?' Bob asked.

Sophy couldn't help but roll her eyes. 'I'm *still* waiting on Johnno to get me his paperwork and then I'm hoping it won't take long after that.' But if she changed her plans and did go out a month early, then chances were she might not have her citizenship by then. The Australian immigration department's methods were strange and mysterious and also kind of cruel. Once your application was in you weren't allowed to chase them up and, if you did, they sent you right to the back of the queue again. It sounded even worse than trying to get visitor's parking permits from the local council, which was saying something.

'Now listen, kiddo, we can't wait for you to come out and when I get my hands on you, I'm going to hug you half to death, but we're not expecting you to act like some kind of skivvy when you get here,' Jean said, hands on her dicky hips.

'But it would be useful to have some extra help, especially once you've had your operation,' Sophy pointed out. 'I can clean, cook, though my speciality tends to be microwaved ready meals, and I can do admin, all sorts of stuff. Probably won't be any good at sheep-shearing or dealing with manure, ha ha!'

'You say that, but I reckon you'll be a pro at shovelling shit and as to the sheep-shearing, there's nothing to it,' Bob said jovially. Or rather, Sophy hoped he meant it jovially and wasn't being serious. 'Yeah, we had a fella one time who took his finger off, but you're a sensible girl.'

Sophy's smile felt a little strained. 'That *was* a joke, right?'

Both Bob and Jean laughed uproariously but didn't actually confirm or deny that one of their erstwhile sheep-shearers had lost a finger.

No wonder that when Sophy did finally manage to get to sleep that night, after a lot of circular thoughts about visas and plane tickets, she dreamed about shearing a sheep.

There was blood *everywhere*.

Chapter Twenty-Four

Waking up was much better than Sophy's nightmares of a blook-soaked shearing pen. For one thing, there was a message from Charles waiting on her phone.

Dinner tonight? I could meet you after work. C x

Yes! Sophy texted back immediately. Then she wondered if it was appropriate for Charles to meet her from work if people didn't know they were friends with kissing benefits. Apart from Cress, that was.

Charles was that rare thing. The man who messaged back immediately, without playing silly games or insisting that two hours between messages was industry standard. He was also very considerate.

I'll meet you the Camden end of Gloucester Crescent at 7. I thought we could walk through Regent's Park if you could bear to after being on your feet all day. Cx

Because she had a date for after work, Sophy decided to ditch her usual sack dress in favour of one of the fifties ones she'd bought at the car boot sale the weekend before. She chose a pale blue shirt dress with tiny white flowers scattered over the print and with the ubiquitous nipped-in waist, three-quarter-length sleeves and shawl collar. Worn with her fancy trainers, which were now looking a little less fancy due to the fact that Sophy wore them pretty much every day.

Still, she had a spring in her step as she came out of Chalk Farm station to find a very pale, very trembly Cress waiting for her, eyes obscured by a massive pair of sunglasses that were almost identical to the ones that Audrey Hepburn wore in the opening sequence of *Breakfast at Tiffany's*. Even hungover, Cress couldn't be faulted for her choice of accessories.

'Good morning, sister-friend!'

'Please keep it down,' Cress whispered. 'My head is pounding. My hands are shaking. I'm not sure I should operate heavy machinery today.'

'Does a sewing machine count as heavy machinery?' Sophy wondered aloud, but then decided it was best to shut up when Cress threw her a reproachful look that circumvented even the gigantic sunglasses.

Because Sophy felt at least fifty per cent responsible for Cress's hangover, she treated her to a large coffee and a fried egg sandwich even though Cress said that she couldn't manage solid food. Still, she managed to horse it down in three bites and decided that she was feeling a lot better.

'We'll talk at lunchtime,' she said ominously before heading up the spiral staircase, even though Sophy had been sure they were done talking about Charles. And Australia. She couldn't think of any other subjects that would necessitate Cress's ominous voice.

Sophy unlocked the door and turned the shop sign over to *Open*. Because it was Saturday, they didn't have to wait long for their first customer, and soon the shop was so busy that she didn't have time to think about anything other than dresses and if they had anything in a size fourteen in a red that would go with a pair of Manolo Blahnik Mary Janes that a customer had brought in with her.

Sophy didn't have a chance to take a lunch break, and it wasn't until gone three that she even had a moment to sit down in one of the office chairs while she waited for the kettle to boil. Then, because it had been on her mind, she opened the YouTube app on her phone and searched for sheep-shearing videos.

She watched in horror as an Irish farmer positioned a sheep between his legs, tucked one of its front legs out of the way and started shearing off its fleece like it was no big deal at all.

Sophy would never be able to do that. She always, but always, cut herself when she was shaving her legs. Who even knew what damage she could do with a pair of scary sheep-shearing clipper things? What if it hadn't been a nightmare that had made her sit bolt upright in bed but a prophetic dream of things to come—

'Bloody hell, kiddo!' Sophy dragged her attention away from the Irishman and the admittedly quite chill sheep to see Johnno standing behind her.

'We don't normally see you on a Saturday,' she said, though it was only her seventh Saturday in the shop so it wasn't like she was an authority on how often Johnno appeared over the weekend.

'I was passing and Chloe said that you were boiling a kettle and I'm gasping for a cup of tea,' he said, eyes fixed on Sophy's phone screen. 'What the hell is that?'

Sophy put her phone face down on the counter and turned the kettle on again. It had boiled minutes ago. 'Actually, now that you're here, I need some advice.'

Johnno puffed out his chest, which strained the buttons on his very tropical Hawaiian shirt (Sophy could only hope that he didn't plan on going upstairs because there was no way that Cress would be able to cope with that kind of garishness in her fragile state). 'You want advice from your old man?' he clarified with a strange note of pride to his voice. 'Well, isn't that a turn-up for the books.'

'I've asked for advice before,' Sophy said a little defensively, because she had. Though, admittedly, not in recent years. Anyway, they were getting off-message. 'How hard is it on a scale of one to ten, with one being easy-peasy and ten being so impossible that I shouldn't even attempt it, to shear a sheep?'

Johnno's mouth hung open. 'Bloody hell!' he said again but this time it was a lot louder and with a lot more feeling.

'So, it is very hard then?'

'There's nothing to it,' Johnno said but he didn't sound that convincing. 'So, you're going to shear sheep when you get to Australia? I reckon Mum and Dad would have something to say about that.'

'Well, they did say they'd had a chap who lost a finger…'

'They wouldn't make you shear a sheep, love, not unless you really wanted to.' Johnno hooked the nearest swivel chair and sat on it the wrong way round so he could rest his chin on top of the backrest. 'Anyway, they shear in autumn, so they should be done with all that now. Why? You're not going now until next autumn? That sounds like a more sensible plan.'

'No, no, no.' Sophy shook her head. 'I'm going soon. In fact, I'm glad you're here because you've saved me a phone call…'

The kettle clicked off and so she could turn away from Johnno, who was looking like the very disapproving father that he'd never actually been. She busied herself making tea. Then she had to ask Johnno how he took it because although he was her father, she didn't even know that he liked a lot of milk and four sugars.

'You were saying you were going to phone me,' he prompted once he'd taken a sip of his milky abomination.

'I'm probably going to Australia at least a month earlier than I planned. It's practically mid-April now— Oh my God, it might take much longer than that to get my citizenship,' Sophy said, the panic rising in her voice. 'I've been asking you for *weeks* for your paperwork. Have you found it all yet?'

'So you really are emigrating rather than just visiting?' Johnno asked mildly.

'I plan to spend at least a couple of years there, so maybe I'm emi-visiting,' Sophy said, as she chucked the used tea-bags in the bin.

'The thing is... I'm not sure I know where my pass-port is.' This bombshell was punctuated by an enthusiastic slurping of tea.

Sophy turned round. 'What? What do you mean?' She put her hands on her hips. 'Why are you only telling me this now?' She narrowed her eyes. 'Have you looked for it properly?'

'I might have to apply for another one,' Johnno said, a little too vaguely for Sophy's liking. Also, he'd only decided to tell her this *now* when her deadline had suddenly become urgent? 'Don't know how long that might be. In fact, it takes the Australian muckety-mucks ages to get their arses into gear when it comes to bureaucracy.'

'Maybe you haven't *permanently* lost your passport. Maybe you just need to look harder for it...'

'It's one of the reasons why I left, Soph. Australia is far too parochial a place for a free spirit like myself.' Johnno shrugged in a free and spirited way. 'I'll get Freddy on the case. I suppose I might have given him my passport for safe keeping.'

'It would have been *very* helpful if you'd thought to ask Freddy earlier. I really need to get a move on with applying for my dual citizenship and, yeah, the Australian authori-ties, they do get a bit narky if you try to rush them.' Sophy took a sip of her own tea. She hoped that you could get Yorkshire teabags in Australia.

Another shrug from Johnno. 'Don't be fooled by the easy grin and the tattoos; Freddy's not to be messed with.' His expression grew more serious, which never suited him. 'There's no rush though. You could go later in the year.'

'There have been new developments.' Sophy put down her mug so she could fold her arms and give Johnno a look that she'd inherited from her mother and which always made him squirm. 'When was the last time you spoke to your parents?'

'Christmas?'

'Are you asking me or are you telling me?' Sophy enquired tartly. 'You haven't spoken to them in ages, have you? No judgement. I'm just trying to get the facts here.'

'You sound bloody judgemental,' Johnno said, then subsided after another look from Sophy.

She sighed, because she didn't want to be the bearer of bad news, then launched into the story of Jean's dicky hips and how it was best to have them replaced sooner rather than later, especially if Sophy was there to lend a hand.

'What about Barbara? Or Barbara's girls, what are their names?' Johnno asked after the nieces he'd never met.

'Jessica's having a baby in September and Jules has a job. She teaches high school, she can't just drop everything. Besides, they all live in Melbourne.' Sophy wriggled her shoulders. 'How can you not know this? They're your family!'

'Don't be like that, Soph.'

'I'm not being like anything. Honestly, I don't ask you for much, but this one important thing that I've asked you to do, *weeks ago*, and you haven't done it! You know how much this means to me and you can't even tell me, definitively, whether your passport is dead or alive.'

Sophy hadn't even realised that her relationship with Johnno had shifted over the last few weeks. Had become more familiar, more light-hearted. She could see that now because she was back to being frustrated and angry with him.

'I'll get Freddy to sort out my documentation and OK, stop pouting, princess, I'll phone the old folks.' Johnno frowned. 'What's the time difference again?'

'Oh my God! For someone who has at least one successful business that I know about, I sometimes wonder how you even manage to get dressed in the morning,' Sophy snapped, though looking at Johnno's Hawaiian shirt and pink jeans made her wonder if he got dressed in the dark. 'I'm so disappointed in you.'

They both glared at each other, then, thankfully, Beatrice was sticking her head round the door.

'How long does it take to make a cup of tea?' she asked cheerfully. 'Did you have to milk the cow yourself? We are so busy out here!'

Johnno left soon after that, his shoulders slumped, his face on the hangdog setting, and Sophy wondered if she'd been too harsh with him, as if she was the parent and he was the child.

'Do you think this dress will fit a size ten?' A silver lurex minidress was suddenly thrust in her face by a customer and Sophy was forced to get back to the job that Johnno was paying her to do, even though she'd insisted shrilly that she'd never asked him for anything. He'd given her a job that she was really grateful for and she'd just thrown it back in his face.

By the time they shut up the shop at six thirty, the new Saturday summer-hours closing time, she was still racked with remorse and also fading fast, energy wise. Not even the promise of a few hours in Charles's company could buck her up as she reapplied her make-up in the mirror over the sink in the tiny bathroom.

There hadn't been a chance to have the ominous chat with Cress either, so Sophy was sure to get a lecture as they walked to Camden together. But when Cress came down the stairs, if anything she looked even more fragile than she'd done that morning.

'I'm exhausted,' she croaked. 'That pounding headache has upgraded to a splitting headache.'

'Poor Cress has been having to sew white on white,' Phoebe cooed sympathetically. 'Then sew on the tiniest paillettes. I'm not surprised that you've got a headache.'

Nothing to do with the two massive glasses of wine that Cress had downed the night before. But it would have been unsisterly and unfriendly to point that out. As it was, Sophy was cringing as they started walking along Princess Road. 'I'm not going home. I'm meeting a friend at the top of Gloucester Avenue.'

Cress was back in her dark glasses but Sophy would have bet money on her eyes having narrowed. 'A friend, eh?'

'Charles. I'm meeting Charles. Charles is my friend,' Sophy said.

'And what exactly are you going to be doing with your friend Charles?'

'We're walking across Regent's Park and then we're going out for dinner.' Sophy could feel herself puffing up with indignation. 'Do you have a problem with that?'

'My goodness, can you dial down the attitude, please?' Cress sniffed. 'Have I said anything untoward about you meeting your *friend*, Charles, for dinner?'

'Technically, no, but it's the way you keep saying friend, like it should have quote marks.'

That was the thing with sisters and even sister-*friends*: they knew how to wind each other up without even trying.

'I'm sure I don't know what you mean.' Cress was the picture of innocence, her lower lip trembling, so that Sophy felt guilty for giving her attitude.

'Sorry,' she mumbled. 'Long day. Lots on my mind.'

'That's all right,' Cress said magnanimously, as they both caught sight of Charles waiting at the top of the road. He waved. Sophy waved back. 'What are you and Charles going to have for dinner? Each other's mouths if last night was anything to go by.'

Chapter Twenty-Five

Sophy was footsore and weary, and had been quite sure that she was going to beg Charles to let them take the bus to wherever this restaurant was, but he looked so pleased to see her, swooping down to kiss both her cheeks despite Cress's harrumph, that the butterfly flutter of her stomach at seeing him was all she needed to agree to walk through Regent's Park.

It was a gorgeous spring evening, still warm, still cotton-wool clouds drifting lazily across a blue sky. They weren't the only people lingering in the park. There were the ubiquitous joggers huffing and puffing their way round the Outer Circle, sprawling groups of youngsters on the grass surrounded by picnic debris. Then there were the dogwalkers, children still on the swings as they passed the playground, and lots of couples like them, walking slowly because their real destination was each other.

When they left the park to cut through the many tiny streets of Fitzrovia, they passed crowds spilling out of pubs clutching drinks and people making the most of each drop of sunshine by dining al fresco, though Sophy always thought that it was too congested to eat outside. She wouldn't really fancy a side order of pollution with her spaghetti carbonara.

She mentioned this to Charles, who looked slightly crest-fallen.

'That's a pity,' he said in what was probably meant to be a light voice but sounded very strained. 'Maybe I can see if they have a table inside.'

'I didn't mean to ruin everything,' Sophy said, the flutter replaced by a leaden feeling. The time she had with Charles was on a clock, not just this evening, but all the other evenings they might spend together before she left, and she wanted every single one – every hour, every minute, every second – to be perfect.

'You haven't ruined anything,' Charles said firmly. Then he took her hand so they could walk like that, when before Sophy had had to make do with their arms occasionally brushing. 'That's not possible.'

'I'm not perfect, Charles. Far from it. I've been ruining stuff since for ever.' Her argument with Johnno was still fresh in her mind. Her ingratitude. That piercing top note she got to her voice.

Charles shook his head. 'I refuse to believe it.'

It turned out that the evening wasn't ruined. It improved immediately when they got to their destination: a little Italian tapas place tucked into a little mews, which in turn was hidden away down a small cobbled street. On the other side of the mews was a large bookshop, or rather what looked like a series of little shops all joined together in a higgledy-piggledy fashion. The shop was called Happy Ever After and, although Sophy couldn't say that she was a very romantic person, seeing the shop sign and those three words in a cursive script made her sigh a little.

She definitely didn't want to sit inside when in this mews it felt as if they'd left the hustle, bustle and pollution of London behind. They couldn't even hear the rumble of traffic any more as they sat down at a table for two and admired the fairy lights strung across the yard. There were candles on each table and soft fleece blankets in case they felt cold and, like everything that Charles planned, it was exactly what Sophy wanted without her even knowing that she'd wanted it.

Just as not going with Radha all those years before had been Sophy's big 'what if' moment, she knew that going to Australia now and leaving Charles behind would be another. One that she suspected would haunt her for the rest of her life. If she wasn't going to Australia, if this thing could be more than snatched evenings and heated kisses, then Sophy also suspected that Charles would be the god of boyfriends and who knew what else beyond that?

She couldn't tell Charles any of this, especially as he was gloating enough at her obvious delight with his choice of restaurant. They knocked knees under the table as the servers brought out a selection of tiny plates of delicious things: stuffed olives, courgette and ricotta arancini, a four-cheese crostini, meatballs in a delicious tomato sauce and fritto misto.

Usually they could talk about everything and nothing, without gaps, without any desperate searching for a topic of conversation, but tonight there was silence, apart from appreciative comments about the food and what they were going to order for pudding and was it too late for fully caffeinated coffee?

The silences grew longer but, instead of being awkward, they were charged with a tension that made Sophy feel both on edge and quite languorous. By the time their pudding had arrived, their knees weren't knocking any longer, because their legs were pressed together as they leaned forward, elbows on the table. Which was bad manners but how else could they keep locking eyes or Sophy reach across the table to wipe a stray crumb from the corner of Charles's mouth or he feed her tiny spoonfuls of tiramisu?

By the time they asked for the bill, Charles's eyes were as dark as the night sky and Sophy's leg was trapped between his. Not that she wanted to get free.

There was a slight tussle over who was going to pay, which Sophy won by simply thrusting her debit card at the server and saying in a tone of voice that even worked on Phoebe, 'I'm getting this.'

'So fierce,' Charles murmured, but he sounded as if he didn't mind her fierceness, whereas Egan had been always telling her not to get 'so aggy, babe'. Egan had also never helped Sophy on with her jacket, though it was wrong to keep comparing them, especially when Charles was a complete one-off.

He tucked her arm in his as they left the little mews. 'I should probably go home,' Sophy said, not bothering to hide her reluctance at the thought of heading back to boring, unromantic Hendon.

'You probably should,' Charles agreed. 'I would ask you to come back to mine for a nightcap but, well, I think we both know that it wouldn't really be for a nightcap.'

The unspoken question hovered between them.

'Where do you live anyway?' she asked, which wasn't a yes but it wasn't a no.

It was getting chilly now, which was at least part of the reason why she curved her body into his. He wrapped a long arm round her shoulders. 'Not far from here. A little garret round the corner from the British Museum.'

'Of course you do,' Sophy said with a little laugh, because that was so quintessentially Charles. 'I bet it's not at all garret-like. You'd keep banging your head on those sloping, leaking ceilings for one thing.'

'It's the top floor of an old house, so it probably was the servants' quarters at one point,' Charles insisted. 'But I've done wonders with the place, if you did want to...'

'I do want to.' Sophy came to a halt in the middle of Theobald's Road. 'I want to more than anything.'

'But you're not going to,' Charles finished for her, regret curled around every syllable. 'Because at least one of us should be sensible about this.'

'I hate being sensible,' Sophy said with great feeling and, even though she shouldn't, wouldn't, couldn't go back to Charles's not-garret for a not-nightcap, she could still pull him, unresisting, into a darkened shop doorway for a kiss.

As ever, their kisses made Sophy come undone. She stood on tiptoe, her arms round Charles's neck so she could lightly scratch his scalp in a way that made him groan while he fed her kisses that were sweeter than all the desserts in all the restaurants in London.

'Oh my days, get a room!'

They broke apart as they were catcalled by a gang of shrieky, giggly girls heading into town.

'We *have* to stop,' Charles whispered throatily, his breath tickling Sophy's ear in a way that made her squirm a little. 'Remind me again why we have to stop. Why all we can do is kiss and even though kissing you is my new favourite thing to do, I'm sure that there are other things we could do that would surpass it.'

For a moment Sophy couldn't think of one good reason why they could only kiss and not move off first base, like well-behaved teenagers who'd signed a purity pledge.

Then she remembered.

'Because we agreed, didn't we? That I'm going to Australia and anything more serious would just complicate everything,' she said, though the dates, these kisses, already felt serious and complicated.

'How long have we got left?' Charles asked.

'Long enough,' Sophy said because she couldn't bear to think about the change in plans. If she did fly out a month earlier, then they only had three months. A quarter of a year. Twelve-ish weeks, which felt like hardly any time at all. It would fly by in an instant. Rather than being something she was equally excited and nervous about, Sophy's plans to emigrate, even emi-visit, now seemed imbued with all kinds of doom and gloom. Like she was pencilled in for major surgery without an anaesthetic.

'About four months, isn't it?' Charles asked heavily. 'It's mid-April now and you wanted to be there for mid-August.' He lifted Sophy's chin with his thumb and forefinger so he could stare at her face as if he wanted to spend the rest of those supposed four months memorising every millimetre, every freckle, even that one stray eyebrow hair that would never lie completely flat.

'I haven't got an exact date set. It might be a little sooner than mid-August but then again, my citizenship might not come through in time.' Sophy said a little desperately. She knew she should tell Charles about the new developments. But talking about Jean's dicky hips while they were having such a romantic evening would really kill the mood and also... plans changed. Maybe her plans were still subject to even more change. 'Even if my citizenship does arrive soon, I may just go for a long holiday. A few months. Come home after Christmas. Hardly anyone would even notice that I was gone.'

'I'd notice,' Charles said. 'But I'm a great believer in seizing any opportunities that come along with both hands. You should go to Australia with an open mind, with an open heart,' he finished a little wistfully as if he knew that Sophy's heart was full of him. 'Now, what time is your mother expecting you home?'

Sophy snorted at that. 'I'm thirty! I can go home any time I want. It's not like I have a curfew and she's going to take away my TV privileges if I break it.' She paused. 'Though she does wait up for me, which is really annoying.'

Charles tucked a strand of hair behind Sophy's ear, his fingers caressing a spot that made her want to squirm all over again. 'Well, in that case I'm going to walk you to Goodge Street station and then, like the teenagers that we've regressed to due to circumstance, I'm going to snog your face off before you get the tube home.'

Though Sophy loved spending a few more minutes with Charles, his arm round her as they walked to the station, and she especially loved the kisses goodbye, she was reminded of why she'd hated being a teenager and couldn't wait until she was grown up and could do what the hell she liked.

What she hadn't realised was that when you did become a grown-up it was even more impossible to do what the hell you liked and stuff the consequences.

The consequences arrived the following Monday morning. Or rather, Sophy woke up to an email from Freddy telling her that Johnno had finally found his passport, along with his birth certificate, and he was getting them notarised and signed that morning.

> *The silly sod gave them to me ages ago for safe keeping. They've been sitting in my safe all this time.*
>
> *Now I realise that time is of the essence so if you give me all your bumf, I'll put in the application for you. Hopefully they can rubber-stamp and process it a bit sharpish. I have a mate who's an immigration lawyer who's going to have a word in the right ear, so fingers crossed. We'll get you emigrated ASAP.*
>
> *But, to be on the safe side, I wouldn't get that plane ticket just yet.*
>
> *Regards, Freddy*

PART FOUR

Chapter Twenty-Six

Just rereading Freddy's email for the umpteenth time made Sophy cross with Johnno all over again. All this prevaricating and procrastinating, when his passport and birth certificate had been safe and sound in Freddy's safe the whole time. She could already have her dual citizenship, if only Johnno wasn't so disorganised.

Now, she was going to have to put all her faith into Freddy, Freddy's lawyer mate and hopefully a kindly official at the Australian immigration office who'd take pity on her and put her application through as a matter of utmost urgency.

Sophy didn't want to get her hopes up. She also wasn't quite as excited about the prospect of Australia as she had been. Though maybe that was because after the last two months, she wasn't the same woman who felt as if she had nothing left to lose. Now she had a job that she actively enjoyed about forty per cent of the time, and she got to work with Cress. When she wasn't really annoyed with Johnno, it had been lovely to have this opportunity to see more of him, to feel their distant, stilted relationship move forward in a way that she'd never expected. They were definitely closer now.

And of course, two months ago there'd been no Charles…

Now, Australia was imminent. In a few weeks her morning commute would look very different. There'd be a lot more sheep for one thing. On the train to work that morning, Sophy realised that she needed to start making plans, making lists. She'd thought that she'd only spend a week or so on the sheep station for all the anniversary goings-on, then head to Sydney, possibly by way of Melbourne. Now it looked like she'd be spending a couple of months there at the least, while Jean recovered from her operation. Sophy had already pored over the sheep station's website for hours and hours but this morning she looked up the nearest town, which Bob and Jean said was only a fifteen-minute drive away.

Queensville was small. Very small. It had a population of only 1,648 people, which made it more of a village as far as Sophy was concerned, but it had its own Australian Rules football team and a mascot called Larry, a gigantic shrimp sculpture at the entrance to the town. It was exactly one hundred and eighty-nine miles from Adelaide, which seemed like a very long way away to Sophy: the equivalent of driving from London to Wales; but she supposed Australia was like America and everything was a long way away, unlike Britain, where you could drive most places in a day if you really put your mind to it.

As well as farming, the area was known for its winemaking – Sophy *loved* white wine – and it also had a healthy tourism industry as it was on the coast. Not that Sophy was going to be working on her tan; she'd be quite busy looking after some of those tourists who'd be staying at the guest cottages on the station.

Of course, Australia was all upside down. So, even though she was going out in early July, it would be winter. According to Wikipedia, the area had a 'warm summer Mediterranean climate;' which according to a quick search on Google meant that Sophy would be staying in a place where it rained half the month and temperatures didn't get much higher than fourteen degrees.

But the glass was half full, Sophy decided as she made her way to street level in the Chalk Farm station lift. As a pale-skinned redhead, she didn't do too well in the heat. Even the average temperature for summer in that so-called warm Mediterranean climate was a very manageable twenty-five degrees.

'It's not the part of Australia that gets super-hot and has those terrible bush fires,' she told Cress as they walked to the shop. 'And the town is famous for its shrimp. I don't think I've ever had shrimp. Do you like shrimp?'

'Shrimp, sheep, what is this place?' Cress scowled. 'Has your citizenship come through then?'

'Johnno suddenly found the missing passport, so they have all the paperwork now.' Sophy turned her attention back to her phone screen. 'There are two, like, massive national parks nearby so when you come to visit me we can go on hikes.'

Cress put a hand on Sophy's arm to still her. 'You know that I love you,' she said, her face troubled. 'You really are my family...'

'I feel like there's a but coming.' Sophy cringed in dread at another lecture about running off to Australia, kissing Charles or, who knew? Once, Cress had spent ten minutes lecturing Sophy about the optimum conditions for washing vintage dresses in a washing machine.

'But Australia is a long way away and plane tickets are very expensive and I hate flying and the jet lag will be mortal and to make it worth anyone's while, it would have to be at least a six-week trip. At least!'

'You sound like you've thought about it a lot,' Sophy said, still waiting for Cress to get to the big but that she was obviously leading up to.

'I've thought about little else ever since you announced that you were emigrating or staying there indefinitely or taking a sabbatical.' Cress shook her head as they started to walk again. 'The long and short of it is that nobody knows how long you'll be there, including you, but I can't just take six weeks off work and fork out thousands of pounds on a long holiday. Colin and I are saving up for a deposit.'

Now was not the time to point out that Cress and Colin had been saving up for a deposit for so long that they could probably afford one of the grand three-storey houses they were walking past.

'Not thousands. Not if you shopped around for a cheap flight—'

'I hate hiking and I hate seafood!' Cress shouted in a very unCress-like way. 'I'm sorry. This has affected me more than I actually realised. It's just I'm going to miss you.'

'Oh, sister-friend, I'm going to miss you too. So much,' Sophy croaked because now the tears weren't far off.

'Not as much as I'm going to miss you.' The tears were much nearer for Cress. They were already streaming down her face. 'Without you here, I'll be half a person.'

'I might not be gone that long. It depends if and when my citizenship comes through. There are a *lot* of moving parts involved,' Sophy insisted. 'I might go out earlier and come back sooner. Who knows?'

By now they'd reached The Vintage Dress Shop, coming a halt because it was quite hard to walk and cry at the same time.

It was much easier to hug and cry. Even if she did go out in mid-July, Australia was still weeks away. Months really. By that time Sophy was sure that her tear ducts would have broken from overuse.

Their touching embrace was rudely interrupted by the door of the shop opening and Phoebe standing on the door-step looking very unimpressed at such unseemly displays of emotion. 'It's far too early for... whatever it is you two are bawling about,' she said witheringly, including even her darling Cress in her condemnation. 'Anyway, get a move on. Shop meeting! It is Monday morning, after all.'

It was Sophy's eighth, maybe ninth Monday morning at the shop and in all that time they'd never had a Monday-morning meeting. Then she thought that maybe the meeting included Charles and she all but fell over her feet in her efforts to get inside.

There was no Charles. Just a full house of Chloe, Beatrice and Anita arranged on the pink sofas, all three of them looking quite put-upon as Phoebe stood on the bottom step of the spiral staircase so she could address the masses like Eva Perón on the balcony of the Casa Rosada. A couple of steps above her sat her faithful consigliere, Coco Chanel, who was wearing a new rose pink velvet collar.

Sophy leaned against the desk as Phoebe brought them all up to speed on wedding dress bookings, a consignment of dresses from a dealer in Palm Springs that had been held up at Customs and some beef she was having with the interior design shop a couple of doors down, who'd been trying to put their recycling bags outside The Vintage Dress Shop. 'I said to that horrible Jodie who works there that we pay a fortune to the council for our recycling collections and if she tries it on again, then I'm going to report her.'

Chloe and Beatrice nudged each other. 'That sounds more like Freddy's remit,' Chloe piped up with a smirk, though Sophy didn't know what there was to smirk about. Jodie from two doors down was a very unpleasant woman who'd once come out of her shop to scream at Sophy for the audacity of standing in front of her window while she was on her phone.

Phoebe drew herself up. 'I don't need Freddy to fight my battles for me,' she said grandly. 'Ha! Freddy!'

Sophy still didn't know what the deal was with Phoebe and Freddy but they clearly hated each other. She added a pair of sensible hiking boots to her mental shopping list for

Australia. She would have to check that they were sturdy enough to protect her from a snakebite. Then, not for the first or last time, Sophy wondered how she was going to cope in a place where snakebites were an actual deadly occurrence and not a pint of half lager and half cider.

Meanwhile Phoebe droned on and on. Something about an Ossie Clark dress that hadn't even been bought from The Vintage Dress Shop but the owner was a loyal customer and was bringing it in for alterations. Not that Phoebe was happy about it.

'Finally, as you know, it's the vintage spring ball next Saturday,' Phoebe said, and Sophy had never been so pleased to hear the word 'finally'. 'I persuaded so-called Freddy to fork out for hair and make-up, so my friends Vivienne and Roy are going to set up in the back office after lunch. We'll sort out a rota then.'

Chloe, Beatrice and Anita had perked up at this news. Even Cress was sitting up straight and not slumping. 'Roy does the best victory rolls in London,' Chloe said enthusiastically, though she might just as well have been talking in Martian for all the sense that made.

'Of course, you'll be off the clock, but the shop paid for the tickets and you're all ambassadors for The Vintage Dress Shop so I'm going to need pictures of your outfits, including accessories, by Wednesday morning at the latest. That gives you over a week to rectify matters if your outfits aren't good enough,' Phoebe said officiously as if she'd been huffing glue instead of eating breakfast. 'Cress, you *are* coming, aren't you? With your boyfriend?'

Cress slumped again. 'We're not really ball-type people.'

'Nonsense, it will be fun,' Phoebe said grimly.

'It really will be fun,' Beatrice added. 'There's a fantastic big band orchestra and if you get there early, then you can have a quick jive lesson.'

It did sound fun. It also sounded like everyone knew about this vintage ball except Sophy. Including Cress and probably even Charles and neither of them had told her! It stung like a thousand wasps.

'What vintage spring ball?' Sophy asked in injured tones, shooting Cress a reproachful look.

'I thought you knew,' Cress mouthed back while Phoebe, if you looked at her really hard, did seem to shift a little uncomfortably.

'I thought I'd told you,' she said with very little effort to sound at all convincing. 'Anyway, I didn't think you'd *still* be here after all these weeks.'

'Oh my God, do you actually think before you open your mouth?' Sophy demanded, too hurt at being left out to bother being diplomatic.

'Whatever, I'm sorry. You can come,' Phoebe said with a huff and an eye-roll. And then a smirk. 'Charles is already on the list, so you don't need to have to ask for a ticket for him too.'

Sophy went hot, then a little clammy. 'Charles?' She made it sound like she'd never heard his name before.

'Yes, Charles,' Chloe piped up. 'The Charles whose face you were eating outside the pub on Friday night.'

'I'm not… we weren't… No.' Try as she might, Sophy couldn't manage a full sentence.

'The same Charles who took you away for a dirty week-end.' Beatrice was practically rubbing her hands with glee. 'Been dying to ask you about it but figured there must be a reason why you were keeping the worst-kept secret ever.'

'The weekend wasn't at all dirty,' Sophy muttered, her hands on her burning cheeks.

'But isn't Charles gay?' Anita asked, which at least meant that Sophy wasn't the only one in the shop with a wonky gaydar.

267

Phoebe put her head back so she could scoff more effectively. 'Charles is so very clearly *not* gay.' She fixed Sophy with her most malevolent look, which was really saying something. 'But why you'd start something when you're heading off to Australia very soon, I don't know. Poor Charles.'

'Poor Sophy,' Cress said loyally. 'But the heart wants what the heart wants.'

Currently, Sophy's heart wanted Antipodean adventure *and* Charles.

'You are *still* going to Australia, aren't you?' Phoebe asked suspiciously and all Sophy could do was nod. 'Well, thank God for that.'

Chapter Twenty-Seven

Sophy had imagined that her boss would be delighted that her travel plans were still very much ongoing and that Phoebe wouldn't have to put up with her for much longer, but over the next few days it was as if the other woman had found a whole other level of crackpot dictatorship.

It didn't help that there was an unseasonable spring heat-wave, the weather humid and muggy. It meant that Phoebe redoubled her efforts to make sure that no one with sweaty hands was going anywhere near the dresses, and mostly that meant Sophy. She was washing her hands so often that they were red raw and when she wasn't at work she had to slather them in a hand cream that had been developed with Norwegian fishermen in mind.

Phoebe was also an absolute martinet when it came to outfits for the ball. She'd originally wanted everyone to wear gowns, until Beatrice pointed out that it would be quite hard to jive in a gown and Cress had flat-out refused to come if wearing one was mandatory.

Sophy had decided to wear the black velvet draped dress she'd found at the car boot sale. Especially as she wanted to see Charles look at her again the way he'd looked at her when she'd tried it on that fateful evening in a bathroom in Bath.

She'd dutifully shown Phoebe a picture of it, along with some gold Mary Jane shoes with a not-ridiculous heel, which she'd bought ages ago for a wedding, but Phoebe had nixed it. 'It doesn't look very special,' she'd ruled.

'It does when you see it in real life. It's actually very similar to a Madame Grès dress.' Ooof! That had made Phoebe's eyes flash.

'It's just an ordinary day dress. I can't have you wearing that.'

One of the best things about going to Australia was never having to see Phoebe again. Not talk to her. Not reason with her. Not have to deal with her on a day-to-day basis. When Sophy thought about it like that then Australia couldn't come soon enough. 'You know what, Pheebs?' Sophy heard herself say, even though she knew that being called Pheebs was another thing that made Phoebe's eyes flash. 'I'm thirty years old. I have been dressing myself for the last twenty-five years and what I wear on my own time has got absolutely nothing to do with you. OK?'

'You'll have to pay for your own ball ticket,' Phoebe hissed and, not for the first time, Sophy wondered why she was such a bad-tempered, prickly individual.

'Fine, I'll email Freddy and ask how much I owe him for the ticket, shall I?' Which were the magic words to get Phoebe's eyes to flash for a third time. If she'd been a fruit machine, her mouth would have fallen open and a cascade of gold coins would have come tumbling out.

'Fine!'

'I know it's fine!' Phoebe was one of those people who always made Sophy want to get the last word in.

'At least get a bra that fits you properly,' was Phoebe's parting shot because she was the undisputed champion of getting the last word in. 'You're a 34B, not whatever it is you're wearing.'

The next few days weren't much better. The weather had made the customers crotchety too, so that no dress was ever right for them. One woman had come in and tried on over twenty dresses and hadn't bought a single one. Coco Chanel had managed to get hold of a rancid piece of pizza during one of their lunchtime jaunts and had thrown up through the open steps of the spiral staircase, narrowly avoiding Chloe's head. And even though Sophy checked her email on an hourly basis, there was still nothing from the Australian Immigration Service. Worst of all, the weekend before the ball Charles went to Scotland on a buying trip, so that was five precious evenings of the time Sophy had left in which she didn't get to see him. Though, of course, he didn't know that her travel plans had changed and that she might be going to Australia in July, rather than August. He didn't know because Sophy *still* hadn't told him. Hadn't told anyone. What was the point until she knew what was happening with her citizenship? It wasn't as if the date of Jean's hip replacements had been definitely confirmed.

'But I'll see you at the ball,' he reminded her via the very boring medium of text message, because he couldn't get a decent enough signal in the wilds of Aberdeenshire to call her. 'By the way, I just assumed you knew about it, which was why I didn't say anything. Do you dance? I can only shuffle but will be heavenly to shuffle together, cheek to cheek.'

It was a relief when there was a tremendous thunder-storm on the Thursday night before the ball; the sky lit up with cracks of lightning, the streets shaking from the bel-ly-deep rumble of thunder. Sophy had lain awake, listening to the sound of rain lashing against the windows, Lollipop sitting on her chest because although he liked to think he was the neighbourhood tough guy he hated getting wet.

Friday was fresher. Sophy even had to wear a cardigan on the way to work and when she said good morning to Phoebe she got a very pleasant good morning and a smile back. Sophy wondered what the catch was but there didn't seem to be one. 'Oh, Hege and Ingrid are coming in to pick up their dresses,'

Phoebe said as she checked the appointments book. 'I'll buzz you to come up so you can see the dresses one final time.'

'And see *them*,' Sophy gently said, because she didn't want to ruin their current *entente cordiale*.

'Yeah, that's what I meant.' Phoebe sighed, her face suddenly soft and wistful. 'But the dresses do really look wonderful.'

Hege and Ingrid arrived mid-afternoon when Sophy was engaged in round two with the woman who'd tried on over twenty different dresses the week before. This time she made it to thirty-four before she decided to buy a blue velvet Bus Stop dress from the seventies with a cut-out back, which was the least flattering garment of all the things she'd trialled.

By the time Sophy had put back the discarded dresses, there was a message from Phoebe summoning her upstairs. Considering what had happened last time Hege and Ingrid had visited the shop with the bridal party from hell, and considering that she wanted to give Phoebe a wide berth, it was with heavy heart and heavy tread that Sophy climbed the stairs.

She was greeted by a sight guaranteed to lift her spirits; both Hege and Ingrid were on the dais wearing their wedding outfits. Hege looked impossibly chic in her grey 1930s dress and coat, and a black velvet pillbox hat with the tiniest of veils.

While Ingrid looked as beautiful as any bride could want to look on her wedding day. Cress had done a miraculous job with the oyster satin, bias-cut dress, which had been at least ten centimetres too long and big everywhere else; it now looked as if it had been made for Ingrid. Her hair had been swept back and pinned as Phoebe advised. 'I wouldn't go for a veil. You're so tiny, Inge, it would just swamp you and pull the eye away from the clean lines of your dress. I suggest that you get your florist to make you a flower headdress; just a little baby's-breath. Keep your jewellery simple. Gold is best with the oyster, not silver. You are going to be a simply stunning bride. What am I saying? You already are!'

It was like the Phoebe of the last two weeks had been replaced with a much-improved model, Sophy thought as Phoebe brought her hands together and sighed rapturously at the bridal vision that was Ingrid.

'You both look amazing,' Sophy said and hoped it sounded sincere in the face of Phoebe's extreme gushiness. 'I'm actually getting a bit teary.'

It was no word of a lie. Sophy could already feel the tell-tale prickle of her tear ducts getting ready to unload. 'Dare I even ask where the rest of the gang are?'

Hege shuddered. 'Please don't,' she said.

Ingrid grinned. She was a world away from the stressed-out bride-to-be of a few weeks ago. Phoebe did always say that once the dress was sorted, everything else fell into place. 'What's more important on your wedding day than your wedding dress?' she was fond of asking, though Sophy thought that maybe the person you were actually marrying might come higher in the pecking order than the dress. But in Ingrid's case, certainly, now that she wasn't stressing about the frock she looked a lot happier.

'They're getting ready for my hen weekend,' she said with a theatrical shudder. 'I've been instructed to arrive at St Pancras this evening with my passport so I'm hoping we're going to Paris and it's going to be tasteful. No penis straws or stripper policeman.'

Having met three of the hens, Sophy decided that was a case of hope over experience. 'You really do both look gorgeous. Do you want me to take some pictures of you?' she asked, holding up her phone.

They did, though in the end Sophy let Phoebe take over because she had very strong ideas about how the pictures should look. She even got Ingrid to agree that they could post one of them on the shop's Instagram as long as it was after the wedding.

'And don't forget to tag us in any wedding photos you post on social media too,' Phoebe added brightly but with a subtle threat that said, 'I know where you both live and I will hunt you down if you don't.'

There wasn't much left to do but to help Hege and Ingrid disrobe and pack their dresses in the special boxes they used for the high-ticket items. Cress popped out of her garret to tie the boxes with baby blue ribbon in a way that only Cress could.

'Well, I should be getting back downstairs,' Sophy said.

'Yes, you really should,' Phoebe agreed but Hege put her hand out.

'Not so fast. We just wanted to thank you, Sophy, well all three of you, really,' she said, delving into her handbag. 'This is just a small and entirely inadequate token for the way you've gone above and beyond.'

'And really, I'm so sorry about what happened last time,' Ingrid added. 'I'm still mortified every time I think about that slut-drop.'

'I think you'll be seeing a lot more slut-drops this weekend,' Sophy blurted out and she deserved the glare that Phoebe gave her at the same time that Ingrid slipped an envelope into her hand.

'That's very kind of you,' Phoebe said as she was given her own envelope. 'But really unnecessary. You can't even guess what it means to me to match a bride with her perfect dress. It's my favourite part of the job.'

Cress just smiled because, although she loved her job, Sophy knew full well that she didn't love having to hand-sew a hem that measured several metres.

It wasn't until Hege and Ingrid had left and the last customer was seen out of the door with a cheery and slightly

274

manic, 'Thank you for visiting us. Hope to see you soon!' that Sophy had a chance to look in her envelope and there tucked into a thank-you card was a John Lewis gift card for one hundred pounds.

She waited until Chloe and Beatrice had left before checking with Phoebe and Cress to see if they'd received the same level of riches.

'It happens all the time,' Phoebe said, though she looked pleased that it did. 'Once, a grateful bride gifted me a mini-break at Soho Farmhouse for telling her the hard truth that if she got married in plunging red lamé she'd regret it.' Phoebe looked misty-eyed at the memory. 'Then I sold her a darling white lace column dress for the ceremony and she wore the red lamé for the evening do. One of my finest moments, even if I do say so myself.'

Cress had also got a hundred-quid gift card and she was all ready to spend it.

'Let's go to John Lewis tonight,' she suggested to Sophy. 'I need to get some haberdashery.'

Cress *always* needed haberdashery and Sophy had been on her feet all day. 'Can we take a raincheck?'

'When you're far away in Australia never knowing when you'll see me again then you'll wish that you'd taken two hours out of your life to go to John Lewis with me,' Cress said because behind her mild exterior lay a woman who wasn't above a little emotional blackmail. 'Don't you need to buy some snake repellent, anyway?'

Wikipedia that morning had informed Sophy that snakes were indigenous to all areas of Australia and quite a few of them were venomous.

'Well, I suppose...' she said without much enthusiasm.

'If you are going to John Lewis, I'm *begging* you to detour via bras,' Phoebe called out from the back office. 'You're a 34B, Soph. No need to thank me.'

There was no way, no bloody way, that Sophy was detouring via bras to try on a 34B when she'd been a 34C all her adult life, but somehow she found herself in a changing room after some gentle chiding from Cress. ('What harm can it do? If Phoebe's wrong, then you have the satisfaction of knowing that she was wrong, and if she is right then at least you'll be in the correct-size bra.')

The bra fitter was obviously in cahoots with Phoebe; she didn't even whip out her tape measure but looked at Sophy in her trusty 34C bra and said firmly, 'Well, you *clearly* need to go down a cup size.'

Half an hour later, Sophy was trailing Cress through the haberdashery department with three new size 34B bras in her bag. On the inside she was fuming. On the outside she was fuming too. But also a tiny bit pleased at how her breasts looked in the right-size bra.

Still, as Cress said, Phoebe never had to find out. It was a secret they'd take to the grave with them.

Chapter Twenty-Eight

'Hallelujah! You're wearing the right-size bra,' Phoebe crowed the next day when Sophy emerged from the changing room in her black velvet draped dress, all ready for the vintage summer ball. 'I *knew* you were a 34B. Though if I were you, I'd have gone for a rigid rather than soft cup; looks so much better under vintage.'

Sophy cast a jaundiced eye over Phoebe's admittedly very perky bosom in the black lace Biba dress Johnno had brought in a few weeks ago and which Phoebe had immediately claimed for herself. Then she looked down at her own chest, which was a lot more perky now that she was in the right, no, a *different* cup size.

'My breasts aren't for discussion,' she said, folding her arms and scowling.

'Then I won't say how good they look in that dress, which admittedly does seem much better in real life than in a photo.' Phoebe allowed herself a small smile. 'See, I can admit when I'm wrong. Now, what on earth are we going to do about your hair?'

As promised, Phoebe's friends, Vivienne and Roy, a very glamorous couple both of them in head-to-foot leopard print, had set up a beauty and hair salon in the back office, and they only had Sophy left to do. Chloe, Anita and Beatrice had emerged with the famous 'victory rolls', their long hair pinned and curled into voluminous rolls. Their brows were arched, their lips a vivid carmine red; the three of them looked like 1940s pin-up girls. Sophy wouldn't have been at all surprised to see their pictures on the side of a Spitfire.

Cress's long, wavy hair had been braided and pinned and wound round her head like a coronet and her make-up was a lot softer but was a perfect complement to her navy blue lace dress in a New Look silhouette. Although she loved vintage clothes and collected vintage dress patterns the same way that small children collected Pokémon cards, it was very rare to see Cress in a dress.

Only Phoebe had refused Vivienne and Roy's services. Roy, a six foot five rockabilly with a towering quiff, had said gallantly, 'Well, it's not like we can improve on perfection.' Sophy hated to admit that he was right but Phoebe's sleek black, precision-cut bob and her equally precise liquid eyeliner wings and red lipstick couldn't be improved upon.

Unfortunately, the same couldn't be said for Sophy. Her hair, newly washed that morning, was so straight and shiny that it didn't want to be victory rolled. Even spending most of the afternoon in heated rollers hadn't helped. The curls fell out as soon as Roy put a comb through her hair. They settled with braiding it like Cress's and coiling it into a bun, which Roy threaded through with black ribbon in the vain hope that it might actually stay in place.

Though Sophy never bothered with much make-up, just some light bronzer so she didn't look too pale and mascara because her eyelashes tended to disappear, she gave Vivienne free rein and couldn't quite believe the results.

After half an hour, her eyes were lined in kohl and looked positively Bambi-like; and she now had cheekbones and also the poutiest, reddest lips. 'I never thought I could get away with red lipstick, not with my hair,' Sophy said when she was turned round to see herself in the mirror.

She hadn't been sure how she felt about this summer ball, other than being excited to see Charles after a week apart.

But something lovely happened to Phoebe after six thirty, when the day's takings had been stashed in the safe and the last dress put back on its hanger. Phoebe actually became fun. Who knew she had it in her?

She emerged from the back office with two bottles of Prosecco and some paper cups wedged under her arm and said, without any discernible irony, 'Come on, ladies, let's get this party started.'

It had been so long since Sophy had got ready for a big night out with friends. Beatrice hooked up her phone so they could listen to big band tunes as they drank and put the finishing touches to their outfits, spritzing perfume, dispensing heel pads and blister plasters because, as Chloe said, 'Prevention is better than cure.'

Even Coco Chanel was in a party mood and wearing a diamanté collar because apparently she was coming too. 'She gets separation anxiety,' Phoebe explained as they left the shop, all of them a bit giggly and shrieky as they climbed into the people carrier waiting for them. 'I couldn't leave her on her own for hours. Poor love. She'd never forgive me. I'd never forgive myself!'

'If I held a gun to your head and you had to choose, what do you love more, vintage dresses or Coco Chanel?' Beatrice dared to ask Phoebe once they were threading their way around Regent's Park.

Sophy tensed because Phoebe had been in such a good mood and now Beatrice had ruined it, but Phoebe simply laughed. 'It's impossible to choose, isn't it, my princess?' She nuzzled the top of Coco Chanel's head with no thought for her lipstick. 'I think I'd just have to take the bullet, Bea.'

All too soon they were pulling up outside what looked like quite a run-down venue in Bloomsbury, not far from the little mews where Charles had taken Sophy to dinner the week before.

Sophy couldn't hide her disappointment at the shabby exterior. 'I thought it would look, well, more ballroomy,' she said.

'It's much better inside,' Phoebe promised, tucking her arm through Sophy's. 'This is one of the only two intact 1950s ballrooms left in London. Every time I come here, I feel like I'm stepping into another world.'

Sophy wasn't convinced but she still had her Prosecco buzz on and Phoebe was acting like a real, live human being so she resolved not to be a party pooper. And once they stepped through the double doors into the foyer, she couldn't help but gasp in wonder at the plush red and gold interior.

It really did feel as if they'd travelled back in time seventy years.

'Just you wait until you see the ballroom,' Phoebe promised.

It was another five minutes of queuing for the cloakroom and last-minute primping before Sophy and Cress walked through another set of double doors into one of the most beautiful rooms Sophy had ever seen.

It was like finding herself inside a jewellery box. The walls were lined with red velvet heavy with gold embellishments. Huge crystal chandeliers and red silk Chinese lanterns hung from the ceiling, the light reflecting off the edges of the little gilt tables and chairs set up around the sprung ballroom floor. On a stage was the famed big band; there had to be at least forty musicians, all wearing shiny gold suits and dresses, and a conductor, dapper in white tie and tails.

Then there were the people. The men in dinner jackets, hair slicked back like they'd just walked off the set of *West Side Story*, and the women in dresses of every colour imaginable, full skirts swishing over stiff tulle petticoats, their hair arranged in pin curls and waves, faces straight from the silver screen.

But the best sight of all was the tall man lifting his hand in an elegant wave when he caught sight of Sophy. As fast as her heels would allow, she hurried over to the cluster of tables that had been commandeered by Freddy, who was wearing a suit though Freddy never wore suits, and Charles, who did wear suits but tonight had absolutely outdone himself.

'Look at you!' Sophy exclaimed, eyes running up and down trying to take it all in as Charles struck a pose. He just needed a cane and a top hat to complete the perfection that was him in black tie and tails and… 'Are those spats?'

'Too much?' Charles asked and Sophy knew that he wouldn't even care if she did think it was too much because he followed the beat of his own drum. It was one of the things she liked most about him.

'I wouldn't change a thing,' she said, leaning in for a kiss and to whisper in his ear, 'It turns out that everyone knows about us, so we don't need to sneak off any more.'

'I quite liked the sneaking off,' Charles said, taking Sophy's hand so he could twirl her round. 'You look beautiful. That dress. You in that dress. Though I'm sad that I won't be able to run my fingers through your hair.'

'Maybe later,' Sophy suggested hopefully, but their small intimate moment was rudely interrupted by Chloe and Anita barging past them to greet friends on the other side of the cavernous ballroom. 'Shall we dance?'

Charles raised his glass of champagne. 'Haven't had quite enough of this to brave the dancefloor.'

Sophy sat down next to him, Cress on her other side, to watch the couples dancing, jiving mostly. But a sedate jive; no one was being thrown in the air or sliding between anyone's legs.

Freddy, with Coco Chanel on his lap though he complained bitterly that he'd get dog hairs on his one and only suit, ordered more champagne. It was all too perfect – except there was one person missing.

It wasn't until Charles got up to see someone he knew, and Cress was talking to Phoebe about a woman who was wearing a dress that was an impeccable copy of Marilyn Monroe's white one from *The Seven Year Itch*, that Sophy could inch her chair closer to Freddy's.

'Is Johnno coming? He's probably going to be late. He's usually late,' she said, more to convince herself that that was the reason for his no-show.

'It's not really his thing,' Freddy said lightly, as he tickled Coco Chanel behind her huge bat-like ears.

'Is it because of me?' Sophy winced. 'I was really cross with him about the missing passport. We had words. Or actually I had words, and they weren't the kindest of words.'

'I'm sure he deserved them. All that fuss and delay over his passport and birth certificate. He's allergic to admin.' Freddy shook his head and Sophy was sure that whatever Johnno paid him, it wasn't enough to have to deal with his affairs on a daily basis.

'It's just as well that Johnno is really charming as well as being really infuriating,' she said. 'But still, I said some things that I'm not proud about.'

Freddy patted her hand so she could see the tattoos that snaked round his wrist and fingers. 'Soph, we both know that Johnno has heard a lot worse than whatever came out of your mouth. I bet you didn't even drop a single f-bomb.'

Sophy was appalled. 'Of course I didn't.'

'Well, then.' Freddy gave her one of his lazy grins, which always seemed to send Phoebe into a huffing fury, though she was still all smiles tonight.

The band struck up a new number, something faster and brassier this time so Sophy had to raise her voice. 'But if I'm the reason Johnno decided to bail—'

'Oh, Johnno never comes to these things,' Phoebe butted in, leaning against Freddy to adjust Coco Chanel's collar.

'Not since the time they wouldn't let him in wearing yellow dungarees – he refuses to ever wear a suit. He'd much rather be down the pub.'

'Besides, he said he had to go and see a man—'

'About a dog,' Sophy finished for Freddy with a roll of her eyes and a relieved smile. One day Johnno would be hoist by his own petard and actually end up coming home with a dog.

Then there was a touch on her shoulder and she turned round, a smile ready for Charles, but it was a man she didn't know, in a midnight blue velvet jacket, with quiff and sideburns, dark, soulful eyes and a chiselled jawline that in the ordinary way would have had Sophy giggling and blushing.

But not this time, because he wasn't Charles.

'Can I help you with something?' she asked with a smile, though she couldn't think what he wanted with her. He'd probably mistaken her for someone else.

'I hope so,' he said smoothly with a smooth smile to match. 'Would you dance with me?'

Sophy gave a little start at that. 'Oh...' She looked past him to see where Charles was but he'd disappeared and the band had upped the tempo again to something fast and swingy and...

'Go on, Soph.' Cress nudged her. 'I bet it's like riding a bike.'

It was just a dance and Sophy really wanted a dance. 'Thank you, I'd love to,' she said, taking the man's offered hand. 'I'm Sophy.'

'Christian,' he said, pulling Sophy to her feet and into his arms and then swinging her round before she'd even had a moment to catch her breath.

Cress was right. She hadn't danced in someone's arms on a sprung ballroom floor for years, but her muscle memory kicked in and she matched Christian step for step in a fast jive, and even added in some new moves of her own.

There was something so freeing, so liberating about dancing, being governed by the beat, the melody and the rhythm. Sophy danced another jive with Christian until someone cut in and for a second she thought, hoped, it might be Charles, but it was an ageing rockabilly who danced a mean foxtrot. Then the bandleader announced that he expected everyone to join in with the 'Lambeth Walk' and she found herself bookended by Chloe and Anita for a very frenetic version of the old music hall favourite.

Sophy was hot, breathless and desperate for a drink as she returned to their table, where Phoebe was looking at her as if she'd sprouted three heads. Charles was back too and as Sophy approached he gave her a round of applause and a proud smile.

'Such hidden depths, Sophy,' he said, pouring her a glass of champagne. 'You suddenly turned into Ginger Rogers.'

'Hardly,' Sophy said, ducking her head to hide her pleased smile. 'Though me and my partner, Steve Maltby, were placed second in the Greater London under-16s Ballroom Dancing Championship for three years running.'

'You decided not to pursue it professionally?' Charles asked, which was very sweet of him but there was a reason why Sophy and Steve had always been second place rather than champions. Besides…

'Sophy discovered boys and Steve tore his meniscus playing football right about the same time,' Cress recalled. 'Which was a bit of a relief because every weekend was another dance competition.'

'Cress made my dresses,' Sophy explained. 'Also, at right about the same time she discovered boys too. Or rather, she started going out with Colin.'

As if Sophy had acquired some freaky magical ability to summon up demons, at the mention of his name Colin appeared.

Unlike Johnno, he was wearing a suit. A very ill-fitting suit with a Bob Dylan t-shirt instead of a beautifully crisp shirt and tie. His long hair was greased back from his pale, uneasy face but Cress, who'd been sitting there pretending to be having a good time (because Sophy knew the difference between Cress pretending to have a good time and Cress actually, genuinely enjoying herself), lit up like Bonfire Night fireworks.

'You came!' she said.

'Said I would, didn't I,' he muttered, looking round for a chair. There wasn't one and so Colin stood awkwardly behind Cress, arms hanging limply, and now Cress was frowning...

'You can have my chair, Col,' Sophy said, jumping up because much as she didn't really like Colin – even though she'd known him for half her lifetime he hadn't improved with time – Cress liked him and Sophy loved Cress, who now shot her a grateful look.

'And you can sit here,' Charles said and before Sophy could ask where he pulled her down onto his lap.

Even though everyone knew about them, though evidently not Colin because he hissed to Cress, 'I thought she was emigrating; why has she got a new bloke?', it still felt a tiny bit wrong to be sitting on Charles's lap in public surrounded by her colleagues.

Then Sophy realised that they were perfectly placed to kiss without her having to stretch up and Charles having to lean down. She wound her arms round his neck and pressed her forehead against his.

'Are you trying to take advantage of me?' Charles said in an affronted voice, which was at odds with the twinkle in his eye.

'Of course I am,' Sophy said and then she didn't say anything at all because she was too busy kissing Charles.

They were fairly innocent kisses as far as their kisses went. No hands straying, tongues delving, but Sophy still got the heart-thumping, head-swooning, stomach-dipping rush that she always got from Charles's kisses. She was quite happy to kiss him for the rest of the evening. Phoebe had other ideas though and soon prodded Sophy between her shoulder blades.

'Your hair's coming undone,' she said, though, quite frankly, it wasn't the only thing of Sophy's that was coming undone. 'Here, I'll pin it for you.'

The thought of Phoebe shoving sharp, pointy things at her head really was a mood-killer even as the band played Glenn Miller's 'In the Mood', and Sophy supposed that she couldn't spend the *entire* evening kissing Charles.

Not when she could spend a happy fifteen minutes in the Ladies in a glorious scrum of women, swapping hairpins and tampons, complimenting each other's outfits and dispensing relationship advice.

Then there was the time spent on the dancefloor in Charles's arms and though he'd been right when he said that he didn't really dance, only shuffled, it was lovely to slow-waltz with him. He only trod on Sophy's foot once and promised that he'd make it up to her.

The rest of the night passed in a series of moments that Sophy wished she could store on her phone along with the photos she took so she'd remember how she felt. Even Freddy and Phoebe were spotted waltzing with Coco Chanel wedged between them, her paws on Freddy's shoulders. Next to them, Chloe and Anita danced together (because there was a distinct shortage of men). A sprightly middle-aged couple doing a frenetic jitterbug that would have got them all tens on *Strictly Come Dancing*. Not so pleasing was the sight of Cress sitting every dance out while Colin sat next to her and glowered; but even Colin perked up when, once the music had stopped and the lights had come on, they eventually tumbled out of the ballroom.

They ran through Bloomsbury Square, tipsy and giggly, until they found a chippy still open. While Sophy waited for her battered sausage and chips, Charles took her in his arms again and they swayed, cheek to cheek, in the middle of the queue to catcalls and applause.

But maybe the best part of the night was later, when the crowds had dispersed and Sophy's friends and colleagues had caught nightbuses and minicabs back home and it was just her and Charles walking through the dark Bloomsbury streets to the garret that he'd done wonders with.

'For a nightcap,' Sophy said, though she wouldn't have minded at all if it had been more, much more, than a nightcap.

There *was* a nightcap: the expensive brandy that Charles poured into proper brandy glasses. But that wasn't all there was. Charles had only turned on one lamp, so his lounge was more shadow than light and there was no one able to see Sophy sitting on his lap again as they kissed and kissed until the sun streaked through the dark and made it morning.

Chapter Twenty-Nine

On the Sunday morning when she woke up, stiff-limbed and parched, but still in Charles's arms on his mid-century Eames sofa, Sophy couldn't remember the last time she'd felt so content. That she was in the place, both physically and emotionally, where she was meant to be.

'No, don't wake up,' Charles murmured into her neck as he felt her stir. 'You make the most comfortable blanket.'

'My phone,' she groaned, because in some still shadowy and distant corner of the room was where she'd flung her bag the night before, and it was currently ringing.

'Who on earth would be ringing you at...' – he wriggled to get his arm free and peer at his watch – '...at not even eight on a Sunday morning?'

Sophy didn't know who would be so rude and unfeeling as to call her that early on the day of rest, and then she sat up with a start, digging her elbow into Charles's chest so he 'oof'ed on impact.

'It'll be my grandparents,' she said, her voice croaky because she had drunk a lot of champagne the night before and it felt as if something had crawled into her mouth while she was asleep and died there. 'We all get a bit confused about the time difference and daylight savings.'

Sophy didn't get off the sofa so much as slide to the floor, and then crawled towards the corner where her bag had been silent but was now chirping again. She plunged her hand into its depths and pulled out her phone.

'Please make it stop, Sophy. I beg of you,' Charles implored from the sofa, where he was still curled up.

She staggered to her feet, groped for a door handle and found herself in a small hall, its walls covered in a vibrant tropical wallpaper, which made her close her eyes, because her retinas weren't ready for lush green vegetation, bright pink hibiscus flowers and was that a lemur or a monkey?

Sophy stumbled her way to the bathroom, the cream and mint green subway tiles much kinder to her eyes, and called her grandparents, who had given up on reaching her after three missed calls.

She sat on the edge of the roll-top bath with her phone held out in front of her and at last! There were Bob and Jean, their faces wreathed in smiles until they peered at their own screen to take a closer look at their granddaughter.

'Strewth love, you look like you've had a rough night,' Bob exclaimed. 'Have you even been to bed?'

'I've slept,' Sophy said, because she kind of had and they didn't need to know that it hadn't been in her own bed. Then she squinted past her phone screen to Charles's shaving mirror and realised that she had a false eyelash stuck to her cheek, the eye make-up of the night before had smudged so she resembled a raccoon that had been in a fight and one of her plaits had made a successful bid for freedom. 'I must have forgotten to do my skincare regime last night.'

'You still look gorgeous, love,' Jean said, which was a complete lie but one that Sophy appreciated. 'I hope it's not going to be too quiet for you stuck here with us old-timers.'

'I'm looking forward to it,' Sophy said, though the sheep station and the nearby town of Queensville wouldn't begin to compare with the London of last night. 'I'm getting too old for big nights out.'

'Well, you'll want a few big nights out when you pop down to Melbourne.' Bob stroked his chin ruminatively. 'Barbara and the girls can't wait to meet you. And if you manage to come out before Christmas this year, then the whole tribe descends on us.'

'I'll be there long before Christmas,' Sophy said. It would be a very different Christmas though. No delicious nip to the air, the scent of chestnuts roasting as Sophy tried to cram all her Christmas shopping into one blood-pressure-escalating afternoon. No fighting with Cress over the green triangles in the Quality Street tin. No being halfway down a bottle of Bailey's by Boxing Day as she and Caroline did their traditional Boxing Day jigsaw. But different could be good. 'I grew up on *Neighbours*. I know all about Christmas on the beach and shrimp on the barbie.'

'Well, we can't wait to see you and now that Johnno's sorted everything out, there's no need to worry about dates and whatnot,' Jean said, which was very confusing to Sophy in her fragile state. How did they know that Johnno had sorted everything out and also, since when had Johnno *ever* sorted everything out?

'Well, yes, he finally found his passport and everything's been sent off but it could still take a while before I get my dual citizenship. If I get it. I had to prove that I was of good character and I'm a bit iffy about one of my references. My old headmistress, she never liked me.' Sophy realised she was getting off-message. 'So, have you spoken to Johnno, then?'

They both nodded. 'He rang the other day. Silly sod forgot about the time difference, didn't he? Rang us in the middle of the night.'

'I told him to call. He didn't know about Jean's hips and the operation…'

Sophy frowned through the warning tinges of what was likely to be a memorable headache. 'Have you got a date yet?'

Jean brushed the question away with one hand. 'Now don't you worry about that, sweetheart. Like I said, Johnno's going to sort it all out.'

Their faith in their only, exceedingly feckless son was touching but also very misguided. 'But I can't get my ticket until I get my citizenship, which could take months, and I've left it too late to apply for...'

'Sophy, sweetheart, you worry too much,' Bob said. Sophy was starting to understand where Johnno's carefree attitude to life came from. Whereas it had skipped Sophy and she'd got a full dose of Caroline's genes, which meant no problem couldn't be made worse by worrying about it for weeks.

She rang off after another five minutes because she was fading fast and also because Bob and Jean didn't seem to appreciate the urgency of the situation; that they, Sophy, and Jean's new hips were stuck in a holding pattern, until her citizenship came through and then she'd probably have to fork out thousands of pounds on airfare because her dates weren't flexible.

Even though she was at least four floors up – Sophy had a distant memory of having to climb a lot of stairs last night – from behind the bathroom door she could hear the rumble of traffic and other signs of life.

She wasn't hiding from Charles, not exactly. But it took long moments to repair some of the damage of the night before. Charles being Charles had a full range of skincare products, which Sophy took full advantage of. Though she didn't like to rifle through his bathroom cabinet to see if he had a spare toothbrush, so she used her finger and toothpaste to get rid of the dead rodent taste in her mouth.

Only then did she emerge to follow her nose and the scent of coffee back to the living room, which turned out to have a tiny little kitchenette off it. Charles had pulled back the heavy aubergine velvet drapes so the room was flooded with sunlight. Two walls were lined with floor-to-ceiling bookshelves, the colourful spines a design feature in their own right. Above an ornate art nouveau fireplace hung a black and white photographic portrait of an impossibly slender woman in a black dress posing between two elephants in what looked like the wild.

'It's a Richard Avedon shot from 1955, taken at the Cirque d'Hiver in Paris,' Charles said from where he was pouring coffee from a moka pot into two tiny espresso cups. 'She was a very famous American model who went by the name of Dovima. The original sold for over a million dollars ten years ago. Coffee?'

'God, yes, please,' Sophy said gratefully. She couldn't quite face sitting on the sofa again, not after spending the whole night on it, but sank down into a white leather cube-shaped armchair. 'I had to pinch some of your Clarins products. I hope you don't mind.'

'Of course not. Did you find the spare toothbrush in the bathroom cabinet?' He was walking towards her, still in last night's trousers and waistcoat, but he had discarded his tail-coat and bow tie. Though Sophy was pretty sure that she'd tugged on the bow tie last night, to get his mouth closer and closer to her.

'Charles, I wasn't raised by wolves, there was no way I was going through your cabinet,' Sophy said and she felt inexplicably shy and awkward this morning, even though they really hadn't done anything more than kiss before falling asleep in each other's arms. 'Thank you.'

She took the espresso cup from him, wishing it was five times the size, then he rested the warm weight of his palm against her cheek for a second before retreating to the sofa. 'Everything all right with the grandparents?'

'Johnno finally called them and now they seem to think he's going to perform some kind of administrative miracle and fast-track my citizenship, then maybe tackle world peace and climate change after that.' Sophy shrugged her aching shoulders. 'Sorry, I'm being very grumpy, aren't I?'

'If your head feels anything like mine does then you're allowed to be grumpy,' Charles said. He was reclining full-length on the sofa, head thrown back as he pinched the bridge of his nose. Even though he claimed to be as hungover as Sophy, he still managed to look effortlessly elegant. 'So, how long have we got, then?'

Sophy was excited about Australia. She really was. Though lately she had to keep reminding herself that she was excited about Australia. 'It's hard to say.'

Charles turned his head to look at her, the movement making him wince. 'I was thinking it must be about what? Fourteen weeks now?'

'My departure date isn't set in stone.' Sophy tried to shrug casually. She should tell him that her departure date might get moved up so it was more like ten weeks, but what was the point when she didn't know for sure herself? And it wasn't a conversation that Sophy wanted to have with a hangover. Or at any other time really. She just wanted to stay in the lovely bubble that only had space in it for Charles and herself. 'It could be earlier. It could be later. Still not sure how long I might actually stay for? Have I mentioned that Jean, my grandmother, is having her hips—'

'I also meant how long have you got for today? I could find you something more comfortable to wear, and I'll even let you have the sofa all to yourself if you did want to stay,' he added plaintively. It was a tempting thought. Especially as the prospect of having to squeeze her aching feet back into last night's shoes made Sophy want to cry. Her beautiful velvet dress was drooping now and all she wanted to do was slip into something more comfortable. More than that, she wanted to slip into Charles's arms again.

'I could maybe spare you a small corner of sofa and could we get Deliveroo to deliver some paracetamol? Actually, hold that thought,' she said, as her phone, which she'd wedged down the side of the chair, beeped with an incoming message.

Sophy! Where are you? Why didn't you come home last night? Are you dead in a ditch? I couldn't sleep a wink for worrying about you! Also, FYI, this is not a hotel and Mike's mum and dad are coming round for lunch. You promised you'd make a prawn cocktail and peel potatoes. WHERE ARE YOU????? Lots of love, Mum x

'My mother has plans for me,' Sophy said sadly, attempting to hoist herself to her feet. 'I don't want to but I have to go home and make a prawn cocktail.'

'A cruel and unusual punishment.' Charles sighed. 'You are thirty, Sophy, you are allowed to live your own life.'

Sophy was on her very own wobbly feet again, so she could walk over to the sofa and stroke Charles's forehead in what she hoped was a soothing manner. 'She's not dealing well with only having me around for an indefinite amount of time,' she said softly.

'That makes two of us then.' With a groan, Charles sat up so he could clutch his head in his hands. 'But I'll see you in the week.' It was a statement, not a question. 'There's the opening night of a new fashion exhibit at the V&A. With a champagne bar.'

A champagne bar was not the incentive it normally would be. In fact, Sophy nearly retched at the mention of champagne. But an evening with Charles would be wonderful because even though she was still here in his flat, his hand resting gently on her hipbone, she was already missing him.

'Then I could come back here?' she suggested, because Charles was right. She was allowed to live her own life. Also, she could just tell Caroline that she was sleeping over with one of the girls from the shop. She and Charles only had an indefinite amount of time too and Sophy wanted more than just memories of those devastating kisses that always left her hungry for what might happen next. 'For one of your famous nightcaps.'

Charles sucked in an unsteady breath. 'I'd like that very much. A nightcap or do you mean a nightcap that isn't really a nightcap?'

For once, it was Sophy who had to crouch down to kiss Charles and not the other way round. 'Oh, I think you know exactly what I mean.'

Chapter Thirty

Something seemed to have changed at The Vintage Dress Shop.

Now that they'd gone out, danced and got drunk together, Sophy was no longer an interloper; Johnno's daughter who'd been found a job though she wasn't really needed.

Once you'd given your last tampon to a colleague and also not cared that they'd seen you demolish a battered sausage in three hungry bites, you were part of the gang.

Chloe, Anita and Beatrice had always been polite, cordial even, but never really actively friendly. But when Sophy arrived at The Vintage Dress Shop on Monday morning, still quite fragile because she'd decided that the best way to cure her hangover was to drink most of a bottle of Chardonnay over a late Sunday lunch, she was greeted like she'd just got back from a six-month deployment to some war-torn country.

'*Such* a good time on Saturday night,' Beatrice said, as Sophy fetched a stool from the office because it was Monday morning, which was always quiet, and she could just sit behind the desk and hope there wouldn't be any loud noises. 'I think we should make it a regular thing.'

'And, girl, you have got serious moves,' Chloe said, as she pretended to waltz with the Pucci-inspired minidress she was meant to be hanging up. 'You'll have to teach me how to do the foxtrot.'

'We can definitely fit in a few foxtrot lessons before I go to Australia,' Sophy said, even though the next however many weeks were going to be crammed. Caroline had all sorts of plans for the two of them, from a spa day in an actual spa to getting Sophy to help her clear out the understairs cupboard.

She also wanted to spend as much time with Cress as possible, really work on implanting the idea that there was nothing stopping her from coming out to Australia for a long holiday. And she wasn't averse to going out dancing with the girls either.

But she'd also be happy to spend every day, and every night, of those however many weeks with Charles. They'd barely scratched the surface and there was so much more that Sophy wanted to know about him, do with him—

'Sophy! You look rough!' cried Phoebe as she came down the stairs. Maybe some things hadn't changed. 'Are you one of those people who have two-day hangovers?'

'This is my hangover from yesterday. My hangover from Saturday night was completely different,' Sophy admitted, because when you had pale skin it was very hard to hide exactly how ropey you felt. 'That was more headachey. This is more like I might keel over at any moment.'

Phoebe paused in caressing a pastel blue, silky evening shift like she wanted to go to second base with it. 'Well, if your hands are clean…'

'Always!' With great effort Sophy managed to waggle her clean fingers.

'Then I don't mind if you want to sit on the sofa and sort through a box of evening gloves we've just had come in,' Phoebe said crisply but also quite kindly. 'Can you arrange them by colour, light to dark? Though it might be an idea to remove your sunglasses first.'

If Sophy needed any further sign that she'd now been accepted into The Vintage Dress Shop Official Club, then it happened about thirty minutes into her glove sorting as she was pondering where to put the three pairs of green gloves, after or before blue?

There was the sound of nails skittering on the wrought-iron treads of the spiral staircase, and much huffing as Coco Chanel descended. Then she waddled over to where Sophy was sitting and headbutted her shins until Sophy got the message and hefted her up (Coco Chanel was as dense and heavy as a bowling ball) so the dog could turn in a circle three times before collapsing into a bagel shape, resting her chin on Sophy's thighs. She immediately went to sleep. Sophy couldn't help but envy her.

It was a slow, quiet day in the shop and Sophy spent most of it in the basement checking the inventory. There were rails of plastic-shrouded garments and cardboard boxes of accessories that she suspected everyone had forgotten about – and she was right. When Phoebe came down the basement stairs to offer Sophy an unprecedented cup of tea, her eyes widened at the pile of dresses Sophy was checking for the dreaded signs of moths.

'Is that...? Are those...?' Phoebe put one hand on the banister to steady herself. 'Is that the 1960s Chelsea Girl deadstock that I decided I must have dreamed about because I've been looking for it for months?'

'I hate that term, deadstock.' Sophy held up a lime green minidress. 'But yes, they've still got their tags on. They were in two bin bags that had fallen behind one of the clothes rails.'

'I could kiss you,' Phoebe announced, then thought better of it. 'But I won't. I might ask Beatrice though to pop out and get you a cupcake.'

'I would much rather have a cupcake than a kiss from you, no offence.'

'None taken!' Phoebe called out; she was already halfway up the basement stairs. If Phoebe had turned over a new leaf, a very friendly, personable leaf, it almost made Sophy wish she were staying at the shop. Almost.

Though Sophy no longer felt like she wanted to die or go to sleep for a very long time as she had done that morning, she was hitting her mid-afternoon energy slump and was in need of caffeine and sugar.

She took her cupcake and her mug of tea out onto the terrace and marvelled, not for the first time, that she was only two miles away from Oxford Circus. Yet out here she could hear gentle birdsong, the distant chug of a boat coming towards her. The sun cast beams of light on the water, interrupted only by the shadow of the leaves of the overhanging trees.

It was a sight worth sighing over. Sophy sipped her tea, determined to take her time. And as she did whenever she had a break, she slipped her hand into the pocket of her sack dress to reach for her phone and see if she had a message from Charles.

There wasn't a message from Charles but there was an email from someone called E. Harper at the Australian Department of Home Affairs. The subject line was just Sophy's reference number, so no clues there.

Her hands were actually shaking as she opened up the email, the words swimming in front of her eyes. She blinked and tried to focus.

Dear Ms Stevens

I am delighted to confirm your Australian citizenship by descent.

That was the headline. Sophy blinked again.

Your Australian citizenship certificate is now available from the Australian High Commission in London. Please arrange a time and date for collection, contact details below.

It really was true what people said about carrying the weight of the world on your shoulders, because immediately Sophy felt a lightening as if that weight had been taken away.

Now she could just go to Australia. Didn't need a visa. Didn't need thousands of pounds in a bank account. She could just go, like she was getting on a train to go to Manchester. Though actually, going to Manchester didn't cost huge sums of money, take over twenty-four hours and necessitate stopping en route in Bangkok, but still, same vibe.

There was so much to sort out; Sophy still didn't know if she was going to emigrate, emi-visit or just have a super-long holiday. There were so many people she needed to tell, but one person she wanted to speak to more than any other.

Sophy expected it to roll to voicemail because he was incapable of answering a ringing phone, but he picked up on the third ring, his voice wary. 'Sophy?'

She took a deep breath. 'G'day mate, are you having a ripper afternoon?'

'Are you on drugs?'

It was a reasonable question. 'No, I'm talking Australian because I'm an Australian citizen, officially.' Making her Australian heritage official had just been a means to an end; but now that she was on the books, Sophy was surprised at how emotional she felt. Her voice was seizing up and she brushed away a tear with an impatient hand. 'I wanted you to be the first to know.'

'Oh, kiddo…' Johnno sounded as if it were an emotional moment for him too. 'I tell you what, Australia's bloody lucky to have you. Look, I'm sorry that it took me so long to dig out—'

'No! I'm sorry. I shouldn't have said those things last time I saw you,' Sophy assured him. 'I kind of got the feeling that you've been avoiding me.'

'I had to go and see a man…'

'…about a dog, Yeah, yeah!' Sophy gave a choked little laugh.

'Maybe I've been avoiding you a little,' Johnno admitted. 'You had every right to be angry with me but things have been different between us these last few weeks and then we were right back to being in a not so great place and it was all my fault.'

It wasn't like Johnno to be so introspective or offer up something approaching an apology and Sophy was touched. 'I've seen more of you these last few weeks than I have done in years and I've loved it,' she said simply.

'Yeah, me too, kiddo. I think… Freddy said that was why I dragged my heels over finding my passport, because when you got your citizenship, I'd be losing you all over again.' He grunted. 'I don't know. There might be some truth in that.'

'You won't be losing me. I'm going to meet your parents. See where you grew up. Find out if the sheep-shearing gene is actually hard-wired into my DNA,' Sophy added because she knew it would make Johnno laugh. 'Even if we won't actually be physically close, we'll still be close, right?'

'I guess so.' There was the sound of a door shutting, then the background noise cleared. 'So, nothing keeping you here. You can just get on a plane soon as.'

'It's not as simple as that.' The thought of getting on a plane soon made Sophy's palms sweat and her heart start thudding frantically. 'There's still a lot to sort out. Loose ends to tie up. People I need to say goodbye to. You're not the only person I've grown close to…'

'I'll phone Ma and tell her that she can book in for the op. They've had another cancellation, so they can move up right up the queue,' Johnno said, and Sophy's heart rate easily doubled. 'What time is it now in Australia?'

'Don't call them now!' she begged him frantically. 'Anyway, it's the middle of the night. There's no rush. I need to leave it a little while before I get my ticket, otherwise I'll get charged through the nose for a last-minute airfare. I need to know exactly when Jean's operation is.'

'She reckoned middle of June if she could move up the queue.'

'The middle of June!' Sophy all but shrieked. It was the end of April now, which would mean she had just over six weeks. Six weeks was no time at all to pack up her life and eke out every last hour that she could spend with Charles. Charles! He was still under the illusion that Sophy wasn't leaving for another three months. At least. She hadn't even told him about Jean's scheduled hip replacement and how it kept getting earlier and earlier. 'Six weeks. Wow.'

'But you don't need to wait that long,' Johnno said. 'If you're worried about money, then I'd be happy to pay your airfare.'

It was a lovely gesture. Sophy could feel herself getting choked up all over again. 'You don't need to do that,' she said firmly. 'I've got the money saved up. Almost saved up.'

'But if you go sooner then you get to spend some time with Mum and Dad before she has her op.'

'Oh my God, it sounds like you're trying to get rid of me.' It was meant to be a joke but Sophy felt like she was about to cry again. Properly cry. Big ugly cry.

'Of course I'm not. I don't want you to think that I'm standing in your way and it makes me proud, Soph, that you want to explore your Australian heritage. You're going to have to start drinking beer, love.'

'Never!' There was still panic shooting through her body. She wondered if she should stick her head between her knees, because there was a real possibility that she might faint. 'I'll see you soon, right?'

'I'll be in in the next day or so,' Johnno promised. 'Are you sure it's too early to call home?'

'Yes, I'm sure,' Sophy said and, as she rung off, she was also sure that Johnno hadn't really listened to a single word she'd said.

She could picture it now. He'd rock up to the shop for Friday-night drinks and look surprised to see Sophy vacuuming or cashing up. 'You still here?' he'd say. 'I thought you'd be in Australia by now.'

Even so, Johnno took the news of Sophy's dual citizenship a lot better than some of the other people in her life. When she trailed up the stairs to the atelier, where Cress was painstakingly mending the rip on the Ossie Clark dress ('not even on the seam but right across the bodice!'), she wasn't sure of what the reaction might be. She'd only got as far as saying, 'So I just heard that I got my dual citizenship,' when Cress burst into tears.

'I'm not going right away,' Sophy protested, knowing that she was going to end up bursting into tears herself before the day was out.

'I can't talk about this right now,' Cress sobbed, holding her head at a weird angle. 'I don't want to get tear stains on this dress.'

They didn't talk about it on the way to the station either. Instead of coming down the stairs at six sharp, Cress sent Phoebe down to deliver the message that she was staying on to finish the Ossie Clark dress and that they'd talk tomorrow.

'She's very upset,' Phoebe reported, not with relish but with bemusement that Sophy's imminent (though not *that* imminent) departure from Cress's life could cause so much upset. 'So, were you wanting to give in your notice early?'

'Oh my God, I still don't know exactly when I'm going,' Sophy exclaimed as she headed towards the stairs so she could go up to Cress and allay her fears. 'Sorry, Phoebe, you're stuck with me for a bit longer.'

Phoebe stood on the bottom step, effectively blocking Sophy's passage. 'Well, we've rubbed along all right in the end, but I don't think vintage fashion is your true calling.'

'But I love working here!'

'And we've *liked* having you here, but it will probably turn out that you're more into herding sheep or whatever.' Phoebe made a shooing motion as Sophy tried to squeeze past her. 'No, Sophy, I can't let you go up there when Cress's working on that Ossie Clark dress. She's already got two tear stains on it and her invisible mending is looking a bit wonky.'

When Sophy got home and delivered the good news to Caroline and Mike, it was another case of please, don't shoot the messenger. No, please, really!

Caroline took Sophy's phone so she could read the email from the Australian PTB, then quickly handed it back like it was radioactive. 'Well, that's that then,' she said flatly.

'I'm not going right away,' Sophy said for the umpteenth time in three short hours. 'You still have to put up with me for a bit longer.'

'You're definitely going then?' Mike asked, his back to Sophy as he chopped vegetables for dinner, but also because he hated confrontation so there was no way he was going to make eye contact. 'Even though your mum says you've started seeing someone.'

Sophy shot Caroline a look, but Caroline was quite unrepentant. 'Staying out all night,' she said, as she'd said quite a lot since Sophy had come home last Sunday morning. 'I thought that if you were starting something with someone, that Charles, then it meant that you weren't going to Australia.'

'I was always going to Australia,' Sophy said a little desperately.

'Then why have you started something with that Charles?' Caroline put her hands on her hips. ''Cause I know that's where you're planning on staying Wednesday night too, young lady. Never mind all that nonsense about you sleeping over with one of the girls you work with.'

God, it was *just* like being a teenager again. 'I only said that because—'

'You didn't say, Sophy, you *lied*.'

'Because I knew you'd give me a hard time, much like you're giving me a hard time right now,' Sophy pointed out. 'Charles knows about Australia and we both know that we're just hanging out, nothing serious, enjoying each other's company.'

Caroline snorted. 'How's that working out for you?'

'It's *fine*. Everything's *fine*.'

Sophy's original mid-August deadline had meant that Australia had been this very exciting but also not-very-real thing in the near future. Now she was going to go upstairs, count down the moments until she could call Jean and then log into Mike's computer and definitely maybe actually buy her plane ticket.

She'd miss her loved ones. Cress, her mum, Mike, even Johnno. And even though he wasn't officially her loved one, she wasn't going to just miss Charles; she was going to miss what they could have been, what they could have had. Also, she wasn't looking forward to telling him that they might only have five weeks left before she flew halfway across the world from him.

'Doesn't sound very fine,' Mike muttered, still not turning round in case the exasperated look on Sophy's face turned him into a pillar of salt.

'What time's dinner?' Sophy asked, hoping that the change of topic would be a welcome one.

It wasn't.

'What time's dinner? *What time's dinner?*' Caroline repeated, her voice rising. 'At least you won't be around to treat this house like a hotel!'

Sophy knew that her mother was being entirely impossible because she was sad that her only daughter was moving ten and a half thousand miles away for an indefinite, maybe permanent, amount of time. She knew that but Sophy still stomped up the stairs like the angry, seething teenager she used to be. But even over the sound of her stomping, she could hear Caroline say to Mike, 'I wish I hadn't put that bloody sunbed on Facebook Marketplace now!'

Chapter Thirty-One

A very pale, very subdued Cress was waiting for Sophy when she exited Chalk Farm station the next morning.

'I tried to call you last night,' Sophy began, but Cress held up her hand.

'I don't want to talk about *it* – Australia,' she clarified. 'I can't talk about it. I *will* cry.'

'We have to talk about it some time.'

'I don't see why,' Cress said with a sniff and, much as it was annoying, especially when Sophy wanted to talk about her rising panic at the thought of Australia, she also knew that this was Cress's usual MO when confronted by something she really didn't want to be confronted by. Whether it was a tricky bit of invisible mending or a letter from the doctors saying she was due for a smear test, it took Cress time to face up to her fears.

Sophy could only hope that it wouldn't take what time she had left for Cress to face up to them because she really needed to talk to someone about it.

Charles. She could talk to Charles when as they partied at the V&A because Charles, better than anyone, would understand why Sophy was both excited and completely dreading going to Australia. How odd it was to hold two opposing points of view, though both of them were valid.

'Did Phoebe tell you I found a whole lot of Chelsea Girl deadstock yesterday?' she asked, more to change the subject than anything.

Phoebe had and for the rest of the short journey Cress rhapsodised about a pink check maxiskirt that had been part of the haul but that they couldn't sell because technically it wasn't a vintage dress. 'She said I could have it but I don't really know if I'm the sort of person who can get away with a pink check maxiskirt,' Cress said, and Sophy knew that she'd take the skirt because she couldn't bear not to but would never wear it because Cress believed she was the sort of person who never did anything daring or audacious.

But Sophy wasn't like that. Or rather she wasn't like that any more. She could be daring. She could have adventures. She could take a flying leap of faith without worrying where she would land.

It strengthened her resolve so by the time they arrived at the shop she was calmer, more resolute.

She was *definitely* going to buy her plane tickets that evening. Although maybe she should wait until she had the Australian citizenship certificate clutched in her hand. And she still hadn't managed to talk to Jean.

It was a case of the universe deciding to come through for Sophy when it had spent the last few months treating her like the proverbial red-headed stepchild. Where had the universe's good vibes been when she was getting locked out of the shop she'd worked at for the last ten years, then breaking up with Egan and losing the roof over her head?

The universe had a very strange sense of priorities because Phoebe was nothing but understanding about Sophy needing to visit the Australian High Commission during work hours. 'No need for you to use your day off. I don't mind you skipping a morning or afternoon to go and sort it out,' she cooed when Sophy explained matters. She was practically vibrating with glee at the prospect of Sophy never darkening her door again, Chelsea Girl deadstock notwithstanding.

She stood over Sophy while she phoned the number on the email and made enthusiastic thumbs-up gestures when Sophy said, 'Oh? So you have some slots tomorrow morning? And I just need to bring my passport, two other forms of ID, and a copy of the email from the Department of Home Affairs. Great. I'll see you then.'

The Australian High Commission was on the Strand. It was hard to miss it, what with the serried ranks of Australian flags fluttering in the May breeze. Sophy wasn't sure what she was expecting but, when she finally gained admittance after showing her paperwork and having her bag and her person searched, it was very grand. Beautiful marble work on the floor and the walls, ornate pillars marking her way as she followed the directions she was given, impossibly grand chandeliers lighting her footsteps.

There was a short wait in a not so grand corridor and then, with little ceremony, Sophy reached the head of a queue, stepped into an office, showed her documentation and was handed her certificate of Australian citizenship.

She hadn't expected the moment to be so emotional; she'd been fretting about getting back to work, about buying her plane tickets, about what she was going to say to Charles tomorrow. Now all that noise quietened as Sophy stared down at the fancy piece of paper. It was less paper and more parchment, with a crest featuring a kangaroo and an emu; at the bottom was an official wax stamp.

There had been a time, not so long ago, when Sophy's life had been safe and small. But with this one piece of paper, a whole new life full of possibilities was hers.

'Congratulations on receiving your citizenship,' said the middle-aged man who'd handed Sophy her certificate. Probably to hurry her along because she was standing there, mouth hanging open, slightly bewildered by events.

'Wow, thank you,' Sophy said. 'I'm going to spend time with my grandparents. They have a sheep station a couple of hundred miles outside of Adelaide. On the coast.'

She must have bored the poor man rigid as she launched into a garbled speech about the wonders of Queensville, the fibreglass shrimp at the entrance to the town and how she was pleased that it wasn't going to be too hot: 'Because one of my school friends lived in Brisbane for a couple of months and she says it reached forty degrees plus in summer. I couldn't deal with that.'

'Well, you're going to a lovely part of the country,' the man said, his eyes drifting past Sophy to the impatient queue behind her. 'Good luck and safe travels.'

'I haven't even got my plane ticket...'

'You'll need to follow the signs to the exit, instead of going back the way you came,' he said a little desperately and Sophy finally took the hint.

Tucking her documents carefully into the plastic wallet, she walked down a back staircase, which wasn't as grand as the one she'd gone up. It seemed like a metaphor, though she wasn't sure what for, but then she was back on the Strand and stepping straight into Johnno's arms.

'Oh my God, what are you doing here?' she asked and, though they didn't usually hug, it felt like the most familiar and comforting sensation when he folded her up in his embrace.

'It's a special occasion, Soph. I wanted to make sure that we celebrated it,' Johnno croaked. They were practically the same height and, when she drew back to get a good look at him, she could see the tears running down his cheeks. 'I'm such an old sook.'

'I didn't realise this would mean so much to you,' she said, going in for another hug. 'You've lived outside Australia twice as long as you were ever there.'

'It's stirred up a lot of stuff,' Johnno said in the same rusty voice and, when Sophy pulled free from this second hug, she saw that he was clutching a small Australian flag, also wearing a t-shirt with the Australian flag on it; and, third time was the charm, he also had a carrier bag bearing the national flag.

'I feel underdressed,' she said, nudging Johnno to tease a smile out of him. 'Shall we head back to the shop?'

'I thought… there's a little park, nearer to the river. It's a nice day. Shall we take a moment?' Johnno was talking in disjointed sentences and seemed so unsure of himself that Sophy couldn't help but be a bit worried.

'Are you all right?'

'Never better,' Johnno assured her, but it lacked ninety-five per cent of his usual swagger.

They crossed over the Strand and walked towards Victoria Embankment Gardens, the River Thames glinting in the far distance. Because it was early, not even eleven o'clock, the park was still quite empty, just the occasional cluster of tourists walking through.

They found a bench to sit on, shaded by a canopy of trees, and, after Sophy had reapplied her SPF 50, Johnno handed her the carrier bag.

'Happy Become An Australian Day,' he said.

Technically, Sophy was half Australian and half British, but it seemed churlish to point that out. She peered into the bag and pulled out her very own t-shirt adorned with the flag.

'You're going to make me wear this right now, aren't you?' she asked and Johnno nodded happily as she pulled it on over her dress. It was a snug fit but it was the thought that counted. 'Now, what else is in here?'

There was a jar of Vegemite that Sophy would not be eating, because she didn't like Marmite either, but there was also something called a TimTam, a chocolate biscuit a bit like a

Penguin, that she would very definitely be scarfing, along with a bar of Cadbury's Caramilk and a strawberry Freddo.

'Those Freddos are like the Australian national dish,' Johnno said, as Sophy tore open the wrapper. 'And that pawpaw cream is a miracle worker. Sort you out if any nasties bites you.'

'Even snakes?' Sophy asked as she squeezed a little of the balm onto the tip of her finger.

'Maybe not a snakebite but everything else,' Johnno insisted. 'OK, maybe not a spider bite either but it's really good on mozzie bites.'

There was a bottle opener in the shape of a crocodile and a passport holder with the Australian flag on it and Sophy could hardly keep exclaiming in delight past the lump in her throat, because this assorted collection of goods from the Australian Shop in Covent Garden was Johnno forging a connection with her. A connection that they'd never really had before.

There was just one last thing left in the bag. A buff-coloured A4 envelope.

'What's in here?' Sophy wondered aloud and, next to her, she felt Johnno go quite still, so it was with some trepidation that she opened the envelope and pulled out a plastic wallet with the Qantas logo on it.

She could hear the blood rushing in her head, fingers turned to fat sausages as she opened the wallet to find… 'You haven't!' She turned to Johnno, the tears suddenly pouring down her face a perfect match for his own waterworks. 'You didn't!'

'Yeah, I did, Soph,' Johnno said as she pulled out a plane ticket. 'An open-ended return, so if you really hate it you don't have to stay.'

'But that's too expensive and these are business class…' Sophy looked at the price printed on the ticket and gasped. 'It's too much. I can't—'

'Yeah, you can,' Johnno said forcefully, pushing her hand away as she tried to thrust the tickets at him. 'I've been a crap dad, Soph, I do know that.'

'You haven't,' Sophy insisted, but it was true and they both knew it. Still, Sophy had had thirty years to get used to Johnno's benign neglect. She didn't take it personally. It was just how he was.

'I wasn't there when I should have been, not because I didn't love you,' Johnno said, taking Sophy's hand and squeezing it. 'You know what I'm like, full of good intentions but I never manage to act on them.'

'But I do love you too, I hope you know that,' Sophy said, her voice so thick with tears she was amazed that she could get the words out. 'Even when I'm really mad at you.'

'And this...' Johnno flicked the edge of the tickets. 'Well, it's to make up for all the birthdays and Christmases I missed.'

'You didn't miss *all* of them.'

'I missed enough,' Johnno said, bracing himself as Sophy flung herself into his arms again and cried hard enough to make the shoulder of his t-shirt soggy. 'Come on now, Soph. You can't be crying all the time when you're in Oz. Folks will think you're a whinging Pom.'

'I am such a whinging Pom,' Sophy mumbled, because she might be half Australian but she certainly didn't have much pioneering spirit. She levered herself off Johnno and clasped the tickets to her chest. 'Thank you for these.'

'Though I don't know why I'm giving you the means to leave the country when we've only just started getting to know each other,' Johnno said, gently cuffing Sophy's chin.

'You could come out too. Maybe for Bob and Jean's anniversary or Christmas?' Sophy suggested and Johnno nodded.

'Yeah, definitely I'm overdue a visit back to the mother-land,' he said without much enthusiasm, and Sophy knew that he wasn't going to follow through on it. 'You should probably get back to work now.'

'You coming?' Sophy asked as she gathered all the gifts he'd given her and put them back in the bag.

Johnno shook his head. 'I've got to go and see a man about a dog.'

He was impossible. Sophy grinned. 'Yeah, of course you do.'

There was time for one last hug and another fervent thank-you, then Sophy headed back to Aldwych to catch the 168 to Chalk Farm while Johnno was going in the opposite direction, across the river to whatever he had planned next.

Once she was on the bus, Sophy knew a moment of blind panic until she checked to make sure that she still had her passport and her certificate. And she couldn't cart those plane tickets around in a carrier bag. She dug them out to transfer them to the plastic folder, but she couldn't resist looking at them again. Just to make sure that she hadn't imagined them.

No, they were real. Very expensive. But also very real. She'd be flying out from Heathrow, stopping for a few hours in Kuala Lumpur, then on to Adelaide.

It was then, and only then, that Sophy noticed the date on the outward-bound ticket.

Which was why she promptly burst into tears again.

Somehow Sophy got through the working day on autopilot, waiting for Freddy to call her back after she'd left him several messages, each one more urgent than the last.

He finally called back when she was walking home from Hendon station, to where she'd have to deliver the news to her mother. It felt like she was walking the green mile to the electric chair.

'Freddy, did you know about these tickets?' Sophy didn't even waste time with hellos and how are yous? 'It's not that

314

I'm *not* grateful, because I am. I'm so grateful that I cried. But is there any way I can defer the departure date?'

'Oh, mate…' She could hear Freddy tapping on his keyboard. 'The thing is, Sophy, he was so proud of himself for organising the ticket and it's a valid ticket, fully legit, but Johnno knows a bloke at the airline…'

'Of course he does,' Sophy sighed.

'…who did him a deal on the understanding that the date for the outward-bound flight is set in stone.' Freddy sucked in a breath. 'He thought you'd be pleased.'

'I am pleased but this is much sooner than I was planning to go. Originally it was mid-August, then my gran's hip operation got moved to mid-July and I thought I might fly out then. And then we thought it might get bumped up to the middle of June but I hadn't had a chance to talk to her.' Sophy didn't think it was possible but she was close to tears again. 'I didn't have a definite date.'

'Johnno said that you'd love to go out earlier, to spend time with your grandparents before the op. If it's about giving notice at the shop…'

'It's not,' Sophy said because Phoebe would be delighted at Sophy giving early notice. She'd probably offer to come round and help her pack. 'It's just I have other commitments. Things I need to do. People I need to spend time with…'

She didn't need to say anything more because Freddy said it for her. 'Charles.'

'What do you know about me and Charles?' Sophy demanded, but then she remembered how Freddy had had a ringside seat to see Sophy sitting on Charles's lap, the two of them kissing.

Freddy sighed like, once again, he didn't get paid enough for this. 'Mate,' he said reproachfully. 'Everyone knows about you and Charles.'

Everyone but Johnno, that was.

315

Chapter Thirty-Two

It was one of the worst twenty-four-hour periods in Sophy's recent memory, as she delivered the news to her nearest and dearest.

Caroline was white-hot furious. There were several breakages as she took out her anger, while loading the dishwasher, on defenceless glasses and plates, jamming them into places they weren't meant to go while Mike whimpered in the background.

'Typical of your bloody father!' she snapped when she was capable of words. 'He's all about the big, grand gesture that always ends up being more of a hindrance than a help.'

'He was trying to do a nice thing,' Sophy said, wincing as her favourite mug was hurled into the dishwasher. 'It *is* a nice thing. And he's spent thousands of pounds on the tickets so I can't exactly throw it back in his face.'

'Instead of spending thousands of pounds on a plane ticket that robs me of all the quality time that we were meant to have before I never see you again...'

'Mum!'

'...it would have been better if he'd stumped up for new school shoes or money for some of your dance costumes,' had been Caroline's savage summing-up and she was right; Sophy knew that she was right, which didn't make her feel any better.

Especially as, when she finally managed to escape up the stairs, Caroline called after her, 'I hope you're about to make a list of all the things you need to take with you. They don't have M&S in Australia, or Boots, so don't forget to write down knickers and tampons.'

The next day wasn't much better. Sophy delivered her news to Cress on the way to work, despite Cress's protests that she didn't want to know because she would cry. Cress was as good as her word. She sobbed so hard that she couldn't even drink her coffee and, when they got to the shop, she immediately raced up the stairs still hiccupping and gasping for breath.

It was a little bit validating that Beatrice and Chloe were aghast at the new departure date and said all the right things about how much they were going to miss Sophy.

Of course, the only person who was truly happy at this latest development was Phoebe. 'No problem,' she said airily, when Sophy explained things. 'I'm sure we'll be able to manage without you again.'

Yet still Sophy's misery wasn't over, because she was seeing Charles that evening for the V&A opening-night party and then going back to his place for a nightcap that wasn't really a nightcap. She'd been so excited about both events, but especially about being with Charles again and becoming the Sophy that he believed her to be, the Sophy that she was starting to think that she might actually be too: smart, funny, sexy.

She debated telling him her news by text message, but it really was the kind of news that she had to deliver in person. So, despite the fact that she'd been crying almost as much as Cress, Sophy wanted her person to look as good as possible.

After work, she changed into the 1960s forest green metallic brocade dress that she'd worn for that magical day in Bath when she and Charles had confessed that they both fancied the pants off each other. Even the prospect of literally fancying the pants off each other later that night couldn't cheer Sophy up as she freshened up her make-up in the little shop bathroom.

Then she wiggled into her silver wedge sandals, gave her hair one last brush and stepped out into the shop, which was empty apart from Phoebe, who was waiting with Coco Chanel to lock up.

'You look nice,' she said, sounding faintly surprised. 'Going somewhere fancy?'

'There's an opening-night party at the V&A,' Sophy muttered as she grabbed her overnight bag and handbag.

Phoebe's eyes missed nothing. Not the shadows under Sophy's own eyes or the fact that she was taking an overnight bag with her to a party.

'You haven't told Charles yet?' she asked.

Sophy shook her head. 'It's on the agenda for tonight.'

Phoebe opened the door to usher Sophy through it, her face sympathetic for once. 'Poor, poor Charles,' she said. 'I knew that it would end in tears.'

Sophy was sure that the moment she saw Charles she'd immediately start weeping all over again.

But when he caught sight of her crossing the road, he stopped lounging elegantly on one of the benches outside the V&A in favour of jumping to his feet, his lovely, angular face transformed by his brilliant smile. He looked so pleased to see her that Sophy couldn't help but smile back.

'It feels like ages, *years*, since I last saw you,' he said when Sophy reached his side.

'It was only last week,' Sophy said, trying for light but actually sounding very heavy.

'Well, last week seems like a lifetime ago.'

His words were horribly prophetic but Sophy wasn't able to dwell on them, because Charles's hand was gently cupping her cheek and his kiss was light but lingered in a promise of what was to come.

He took her overnight bag from her and they joined the queue of people waiting to gain admittance to the party; a cross-section of ages, the women in brightly coloured summer dresses, the men in suits, an air of anticipation hanging in the air along with the traffic fumes.

Sophy didn't want to blurt out her awful news right away, though she was desperate to get it off her chest. But she knew it would cast a dampener over the evening, and the evening was set to be quite special.

Once Sophy's bag was in the cloakroom, they walked past the closed gift shop, across the long sculpture gallery and through the open doors into the John Madejski Garden, a beautiful open space bordered by the red-brick splendour of the museum, its green lawns dominated by an oval pool where, in summer, small children (and big children too and even adults) paddled.

Tonight, no one was paddling. They were mostly crowded around the champagne bar that had been set up in one corner. In the opposite corner was a seafood bar where people were guzzling oysters and beyond that was a dessert station, but Charles guided Sophy forward, only pausing to take two delicate flutes of champagne from a passing waiter.

He didn't stop until they'd reached a cluster of white wicker sofas and chairs on the far side of the garden, which was a lot less populated than the high-traffic areas around the food and drink.

Sophy sat down on a sofa, Charles sitting next to her so his thigh brushed against hers. 'Don't you have people you should be schmoozing?' she asked, gazing around at the other partygoers, who all looked impossibly glossy and glamorous.

Charles took Sophy's hand so he could press a kiss to her knuckles. 'I have a theory that if you stay in one place at a party, eventually everyone you want to talk to will find you. Besides, the only person I want to schmooze is you.' It was such a lovely thing to say and was going to make Sophy's own speech that much harder.

'You don't need to schmooze me,' she told him, entwining his fingers through hers. 'I've already fallen for your charms.'

'You haven't *quite* fallen,' Charles pointed out and that was a reminder of what they'd planned for when this party was over and they left to go to their own party, just the two of them on the guest list.

Sophy didn't know how it was that Charles could just look at her, his blue eyes dark, his voice dark too and full of intent, and it had the same effect on her as if he'd just kissed her.

She hoped that he'd still look at her the same way when she told him that—

'Charles! What are you doing hiding over here? Keeping the most beautiful woman all to yourself, are you?'

Sophy looked up into the weatherbeaten face yet twinkling eyes of an ageing roué in a crumpled white suit who was the first person in a never-ending stream of people who drifted by to say hello to Charles so it didn't feel as if they'd have a moment to themselves.

Of course Charles introduced Sophy to every single one of his many acquaintances (it was no surprise that Charles seemed to know pretty much everyone in attendance) and made sure she was included in the conversation. He even kept hold of her hand, his thumb brushing over the same spot again and again, which was doing everything to keep Sophy keyed up and impatient for what came next.

Except she really had to have A Serious Conversation with him first.

At last there was a small lull in the procession and Sophy turned to Charles. She took a deep, anticipatory breath.

'I don't like the look of those clouds,' Charles said and she tore her gaze away from his face to look up at the skies.

It was just gone eight thirty, not quite dark, so that Sophy could see the banks of clouds rolling ominously above them. Now, she also noticed the sudden chill in the air.

'Do you think it might rain?' she asked, but her words were drowned out by a huge, belly-deep rumble of thunder. The dusk lit up with a jagged streak of lightning at the same time as the first fat drops of rain began to fall.

'I hope you can run in those things,' Charles laughed, pulling Sophy to her feet. He tugged off the jacket of his cream suit to hold it over their heads as they dashed across the lawn, Sophy giggling as she clung on to Charles because no, she really couldn't run in her silver wedge platforms.

They made it through the open doors back into the sculpture gallery just as there was another crack of thunder. They weren't the only shelterers from the storm. More and more people were piling in behind them and creating a bottleneck.

Sophy took hold of Charles's hand again so she could pull him further into the long, long gallery full of statues from hundreds and hundreds of years ago. At the end just before the fashion galleries, she tugged him into one of the arched alcoves that ran the length of the space, so they were hidden from view by the Three Graces.

'There's something I have to say to you.'

'I know,' Charles said and for one moment Sophy knew sweet relief. Somebody, probably Freddy, maybe Phoebe, had already told him. Which made it a little bit easier. 'I've been desperate to get you on your own all evening too.'

That wasn't what she wanted to hear, but also it was exactly what she wanted to hear. Almost as much as she wanted Charles's arms to close around her, as he backed her up against the wall, and then his mouth was on hers and it was impossible to form a coherent thought.

All Sophy could think about was the firm pressure of Charles's beautiful lips, his tongue darting out to touch, to taste, one of his hands tangled in her hair, the other at her waist to pull her closer so she wouldn't have cared if they'd sunk to the floor and made love to each other right there and turned the other guests into stone so they matched the statues.

Then Charles's thigh was between hers and he kissed her so hard that everything in Sophy quivered and she couldn't bear it any longer.

She tore herself out of his arms, a hand on his chest where his heart was thundering away to hold him back. 'We have to stop... I have to tell you...'

Charles tried to reach for her again. 'What's so important that it can't wait? Sophy...'

Sophy shut her eyes so she wouldn't have to look at the tender, exasperated expression on his face. She could only say it if she didn't have to look in his eyes. 'Everything's changed. Johnno bought me a plane ticket... I'm flying to Australia in ten days.'

Chapter Thirty-Three

There wasn't just a storm raging outside. There was a storm rolling across Charles's face. His soft gaze changed into something darker, harder.

'Ten days?'

Sophy nodded. 'I only found out yesterday. I thought we still had at least two months together.'

'But you said... I thought we had about three and a half months,' he said with a slightly accusatory tone.

'Jean, my grandmother, she needs a hip replacement operation and it got moved forward...'

Charles stepped away from her. 'You never said.'

'Well, I didn't have an exact date and everything was up in the air; I didn't even know if I'd get my citizenship through in time,' she said, her voice soft and pleading. 'Then everything happened so fast. They processed my citizenship application in record time once Johnno supplied his paperwork and then he surprised me yesterday with plane tickets. He thought that it would be great if I could spend some time with my grandparents, just getting to know them, before Jean has her double hip replacement.'

She was gabbling but Charles nodded just the once. 'I see.'

'It was a nice thing that Johnno did. So generous. I'm not mad at him.' It was the truth. Sophy had wasted so much time being mad at Johnno and it achieved nothing. He was what he was. Yes, annoying and careless, but also so charming and kind. 'He just doesn't listen to the details sometimes.'

Charles shifted his weight so his face wasn't in shadow and Sophy saw hope lighten his expression. 'If it's money, then I don't mind paying to change the dates,' he said, which was very sweet of him but Sophy couldn't take his money and she'd tried to do the exact same thing last night when she called the airline.

'It's a special ticket.' She shrugged helplessly. 'Johnno knows a bloke who did him a deal.'

No further explanation was needed. Charles's sigh was one of defeat. 'Ten days.'

'I fly out next Friday.'

He stepped out from behind the Three Graces so Sophy had no choice but to follow him as he strode down the length of the sculpture gallery. Outside the windows, the rain was still lashing down, the evening ruined.

Then again, it wasn't even nine o'clock. The night was still young.

Sophy had to scurry to catch up with Charles's long-legged stride. 'Come on, Charles, don't be like this,' she said, trying to take hold of his hand, but he evaded her grasp. 'It just means that we have to make the most of what time we have left.'

'We have no time,' he said flatly, making short work of the small flight of stairs that led to the gift shop and the entrance hall beyond. 'Ten days. Actually nine days. No, eight days because you're flying out on Friday.'

'Will you stop and talk to me!' Sophy grabbed hold of his arm so Charles was forced to come to a halt. 'This is not my fault. Why are you cross with me?'

Charles reached out to take a strand of her hair and hold it up to the light as he loved to do. 'I'm not cross with you. I'm not, but you didn't even tell me that you'd moved up your departure date by a month.'

324

'I was going to tell you but only when there was something definite to tell,' Sophy said as Charles shrugged his shoulders. 'You know, you do seem cross with me.'

'I'm cross at the situation. Cross with bloody Johnno but not with you, Sophy.'

'Then let's go back to yours like we planned, like we wanted to,' she said, but he shook his head.

'It's not a good idea,' he said resolutely, even though he'd made that decision without even consulting Sophy first.

'It is! It's an excellent idea,' Sophy said, stepping aside to let two rain-soaked partygoers pass.

'It *was* when there was three months and change but I'm not going to…' Charles grimaced as if he were in pain as more people pushed past them. 'Let's find somewhere quieter.'

Sophy tailed after him as he walked back to the foyer, where there was a stone bench that they could sit on.

They sat there in silence for a moment. Everything that Sophy wanted to say boiled down to her begging Charles to take her home and make love to her. And it had to be worth a try…

'Charles—'

'I'm not the sort of man who'd sleep with a woman when I know that I might never see her again,' Charles said harshly, as if Sophy had already begged and he was shocked at her audacity.

'But you will see me again. I'm not going for another week,' Sophy pointed out. 'Over a week!'

'We both know that you must have a to-do list that probably runs to at least ten pages.' It was as if Charles had been speaking to her mother, whose to-do list that she'd seen fit to start on Sophy's behalf had already hit five pages that morning. 'At best, we'll grab a moment here and a moment there and it's just no way to say goodbye.'

'It's still better than nothing.'

'I had so many plans for the next three months,' Charles said sadly. 'I wanted to take you away for the weekend, no boot fairs, no estate sales, just the two of us being together. I thought I had time and you'd change— Well, what's the point of going into all that now?'

'You thought I'd change my mind.' Sophy could fill in the blanks for herself.

'Hoped…'

'But you knew I was going to Australia,' Sophy said. She could feel her voice and her temper rising. 'That was always the case.'

'Yes, but lately you haven't been that excited at the prospect of Australia. Not like when we first met, then you were definitely emigrating, but lately you've been talking about not emigrating, just visiting,' Charles said, which was true because until she'd met Charles, carved a little niche for herself in the shop, there hadn't been anything good in her life apart from the thought of going to Australia and having a do-over. 'We should never have started this.'

'But we did and I'm glad that we did even though I'm pretty annoyed with you right now.' In case Charles thought she was joking, Sophy folded her arms and huffed like a furious little piggy all ready to blow the house down.

'I'm flattered that you want to have sex with me that badly,' Charles drawled and even though that wasn't what Sophy meant and he was twisting her words, just hearing him say that made her want him to take her to his little garret and do things to her that she'd still remember when she was a little old lady.

'Oh, and you don't want to have sex with me, is that it?'

Before he could lie and say that he didn't, Sophy turned and kissed him.

It was her turn to cup the back of his head, to hold him still, while she plundered his mouth. Charles stayed as still as one of the statues that had witnessed their other kisses, until Sophy pressed herself against him and drove her tongue into his mouth.

Then he groaned and kissed her back with just as much passion.

They were angry kisses, both of them taking, both of them demanding, but then Charles stroked his hand along Sophy's flushed face and it shifted the mood, changed the tenor of their kisses. Softer, sweeter, full of regret.

Then Charles was gently pushing Sophy away. 'I can't,' he whispered. 'I wish I could but I can't.'

'I might not be gone for ever,' she whispered too. 'I might come back.'

Charles stood up. He touched her face again tenderly, fleetingly. 'Then again, you might not,' he said before he walked away.

Chapter Thirty-Four

Eight days.
It was still raining the next day, which matched Sophy's mood perfectly.

Seven days.
It seemed to Sophy as if time had sped up. The days going by in a flash, though she wanted to cherish every hour, every minute.

The shop was hideously busy. Every woman in London seemed to want a vintage dress for a special occasion and she was run ragged in work hours as much as she was after work on what Caroline referred to as 'Ozmin' and a to-do list that never seemed to get any shorter.

Yet she still had time to think about Charles, a messy mix of emotions: sadness, anger and then, on Friday evening, hope.

Their regular Friday drinks at The Hat and Fan had turned into an impromptu leaving party. Sophy was touched that these people she'd only known for a few weeks seemed genuinely upset that she was going. They'd had a whip-round and bought Sophy a bottle of her favourite Chanel No. 19, plus the bath oil and the body cream. 'To mask the smell of the sheep,' Chloe said with a serious face like she wasn't even joking.

Then Phoebe produced a gift-wrapped parcel 'from me & Coco Chanel', which could only have been a dress and it was. A 1950s sun dress featuring kangaroos and koalas frolicking over white lawn cotton. 'The queen toured Australia in 1954 just after her coronation, so everyone went Australia mad,' Phoebe explained. Sophy would never figure that woman out. How she could flip from loathsome to lovely in the space of a minute.

But however touched she was by the presents and the sentiments, her attention was elsewhere. Every time someone stepped through the open door of the pub, she lifted her head even as her heart lifted, but it was never Charles. There was no Johnno either, but Sophy felt as if she'd already said goodbye to Johnno on that park bench with that carrier bag of gifts. Also, Johnno knew exactly where Sophy was. If he wanted to come, if he was able to come, then he'd be there. And she was fine with that.

But she wasn't fine if her last sight of Charles was him walking away from her.

'You could text him,' Cress suggested, because she'd heard all about Charles's stinging rejection in great detail. 'He's probably had time to get used to the news now. I have. I've only cried twice today.'

'Well, I've cried three times so I think I've taken your crown,' Sophy said as she pulled out her phone because Cress was right: there was no reason why she couldn't message Charles.

It took fifteen minutes to craft two short sentences: 'We're in the Hat & Fan. Would be great to see you.'

Even though Sophy sat it out until Henry called last orders, there was no reply from Charles, no show.

Six days.
The last Saturday Sophy would work in the shop, though she had to keep hurrying to the back office to have a little cry and field phone calls from Caroline, who wasn't happy

329

about Sophy's plans to relocate to 'the middle of the bloody outback'. Still, there was nothing Caroline loved more than a project.

There was another impromptu leaving party that evening for the few old colleagues and friends that Sophy had managed to scrounge up and/or who could get a babysitter. It was just about enough people for one of the big tables at Wagamama and, once Sophy had talked about her impending move and they'd discussed how none of them had heard a dicky bird from the official receivers and her old school friend, Emily, had treated them to a monologue on baby-led weaning, the conversation petered out.

It was a timely reminder of why Sophy had wanted to shake up her life, but all she could think about was that she was in Holborn, just a ten-minute walk away from Charles's flat. It would be easy enough to head over there instead of catching the tube home. But would he even be in? Would he buzz her to come up when she rang the intercom?

After saying goodbye to her friends, making fervent promises to WhatsApp and FaceTime, Sophy even started heading in that direction. But then she remembered how Charles had turned her away, turned her down, even when she'd kissed him, and she decided that she wasn't brave enough or strong enough to handle any more rejection.

Five days.
Sunday was spent at Brent Cross shopping centre with The List and Her Mother: a fatal combination.

Two hours in they had a very heated debate outside John Lewis when Sophy insisted that she'd just bought three new bras, she didn't need any more bras and, 'Newsflash! They have shops in Australia! Strange but true!'

'They don't have John Lewis. Oh, and we still need to go to Boots. You need to get compression stockings for the flight so you don't develop deep vein thrombosis. Sophy! Come back! Come back right this minute!'

Four days.

Three days.

Two days.
And then it was the last day in the shop. There was cake from the Primrose Hill Bakery, though Phoebe wouldn't let anyone eat it in shop hours.

Freddy dropped by with Sophy's last pay packet and a hug. There were hugs from all the girls, even Phoebe, who said brightly, 'Well, if you're ever in the area, do drop by and say hello.'

'It all feels very anticlimactic,' Sophy said to Cress as they walked to Chalk Farm tube station together for the very last time. 'The shop has been such a huge part of my life these last few weeks and now… it's over. Just like that.'

'It doesn't have to be just like that. If you changed your mind at the last minute, no one would think any less of you. I'm sure Phoebe would give you your job back,' Cress said because God loved a trier and, also, she was the worst judge of character.

'I think Phoebe would rather burn the shop to the ground than ever give me my job back,' Sophy said and Cress's head, which had been sunk down, Eeyore fashion, lifted.

'So, have you changed your mind then?' she asked hopefully.

'My mind is still unchanged,' Sophy told her. 'But if there are any new developments, you'll be the first to know.'

Then it was home to Caroline, who didn't just have A List now. Mike had got in on the act too and made A Spreadsheet. That evening was blocked out for a trial run

331

at the packing, despite Sophy's protests that packing wasn't the sort of thing that required a dress rehearsal.

One day.
There were no more days. Tomorrow Sophy would be at Heathrow to check in at ten a.m. 'Though I do like to check in early, so we should aim to get there for eight thirty at the latest,' Caroline said. 'Who knows what the traffic will be like at that time in the morning?'

'Look, I really appreciate Mike wanting to give me a lift, but I think it would just be quicker to go to Paddington and get the Heathrow Express train,' Sophy said, as she had said several times before.

As a fitting goodbye, they were having a last supper at Sophy's favourite Italian restaurant, Cress invited along too.

'Because who even knows if they have Italian restaurants in Australia,' Caroline wondered aloud since she'd now decided that Australia was pretty much a third world country.

'They do, love,' Mike ventured as Sophy twirled her spaghetti round and round on her fork but couldn't face actually eating any. 'There are very big Italian communities in Sydney and Melbourne.'

It was just the kind of fascinating fact that Mike always had ready to go. Cress kicked Sophy under the table and they shared their first smile of the evening.

What with the packing, the prospect of the long flight, all the goodbyes, it was hard to look forward to what was to come when Sophy was so painfully aware of everything that she was leaving behind.

Including her mother, who had now produced a sheaf of papers from her handbag. 'I almost forgot,' she said, thrusting them across the table at Sophy. 'I printed these out for you. What to do if you get bitten by a snake. They have

332

eastern brown snakes where you're going. They're the most venomous,' she added grimly.

'Good to know,' Sophy sighed as she took the papers and glanced at the top sheet to show willing.

'Also huntsman spiders, they're nasty little buggers,' Mike chimed in.

'And if you do see a koala bear, I know they look cute…'

'They're *so* cute, I'd love to cuddle one,' Cress agreed, then wilted when Caroline fixed her with a look. 'Sorry.'

'You would be sorry Cress, because most of them are *riddled* with chlamydia,' Caroline revealed with some relish and, although she'd promised herself that she wouldn't, Sophy delved into her bag to retrieve her phone just to see if anyone had been trying to contact her.

She didn't know why she was even bothering, until she saw that she had five missed calls, four WhatsApps and three texts. All from Charles.

She could hardly get her fingers to work and open her message app to read the first line of the first text, 'Sophy, I've been a fool…' when her phone rang; Charles's name flashed up.

'I have to take this,' Sophy said, standing up and not even caring that she managed to splatter arrabbiata sauce down her top. 'I won't be long.'

'Is it the airline? Maybe your flight's been cancelled,' Caroline called after her, hope ringing through every syllable.

Sophy hurled herself through the street door that a waiter was holding open for her as she answered the call. 'Charles!' Then she didn't know what else to say.

'I'm sorry, so sorry.' Charles said it for her. 'Sorry about how I left things, sorry that I didn't come to the pub, sorry that I've left it so late and now I won't be able to see you.'

'It's not too late,' Sophy burst out. 'There's still time.'

'But you're flying tomorrow morning,' Charles pointed out, which really seemed like an unnecessary detail.

'It's not tomorrow morning yet. It's the evening before. It's not even eight o'clock!' Caroline had insisted that they were home by eight thirty so that they could do the packing for real, even though the packing was all but done. 'I'd love to see you.'

When you really wanted to be with someone, there was no point in playing games or prevaricating. You had to be real.

'I could come to you. Now.' Charles obviously felt the same way and Sophy was about to tell him to jump in an Uber when she saw Caroline peering out of the steamed-up window of the restaurant, then making an impatient beckoning motion at Sophy.

'No, I'll come to you,' Sophy said, thanking whatever foresight had made her bring her handbag out with her. 'I'm ordering an Uber now.'

'But don't stop talking to me,' Charles said throatily. 'Just to hear your voice. Sophy, I really am sorry.'

'You've already said that. Look, I have to go but I'll be with you soon.'

The universe was going to do Sophy one last solid – there was a car a minute away and already doing a U-turn to get to her. Sophy made shooing motions at Caroline, who was still at the window and was going to be furious with Sophy, quite rightly too, but Sophy was flying across the world tomorrow and she was thirty so it wasn't like she could be grounded or have her allowance docked for jumping in a car that was headed to Holborn when she should have been going home to do her packing for real.

She sent Caroline an apologetic message from the cab, then another message to Cress, even more apologetic, because Cress would have to bear witness to Caroline's fury. Then, in an act of sheer defiance, Sophy switched off her phone and sat on her hands and willed the Thursday-night traffic to melt away.

It took thirty-five minutes to get from Hendon to Blooms-bury, then Sophy was tumbling out of the car to find Charles waiting for her in the open doorway of his building.

He was in his lilac tweed trousers, his shirt still snowy white, but his sleeves were rolled up so she could take a second to appreciate his forearms as he raised a hand to brush it through his hair.

All of a sudden, she felt inexplicably shy. Just a girl stand-ing in front of a boy and... 'Oh God, I look a state,' she blurted out, looking down and remembering that she was in her third-tier jeans, the ones that sagged at the knee and did unspeakably awful things to her bum. 'And I have spaghetti sauce down my top.'

It wasn't even a nice top but a t-shirt she'd borrowed from Caroline, because all of hers were packed away, that said, *I save my carbs for wine.*

'You don't.' Charles stepped forward. 'You look beauti-ful. You always look beautiful.'

Sophy didn't. Also on the agenda for tonight had been a hair-wash, face mask and the eradication of every superflu-ous hair on her body, but it was nice of Charles to think that.

'You look beautiful too,' she said gravely, because both Charles and his cheekbones really were exquisite.

'I'd settle for ruggedly handsome rather than beautiful.'

Then there was nothing to say, or rather there was so much to say, but they just stood there, gazing at each other and grinning like idiots.

'Do you want to come in?' Charles asked at last, but he was already taking Sophy's hand to lead her inside.

'For a nightcap?'

'For anything you want,' Charles promised and they hadn't even reached the first-floor landing yet somehow they were in each other's arms, balancing precariously on one stair, kissing like it was the end of the world.

Sophy couldn't think straight when Charles was kissing a path from the sensitive spot behind her left ear back to her mouth, but she managed to gasp, 'I love this, love kissing you, but I don't want either of us to plunge to our deaths.'

'Neither do I. No kissing until we've reached the top,' Charles said and then it was a breathless scramble to get to the fourth floor.

He'd left the door to his flat open and walking through it seemed significant, life-changing, especially when he shut the door behind Sophy and said, 'We need to talk.'

Sophy nodded and turned to face him. 'I know we do.'

'There's so much that needs to be said.'

'We could literally spend the whole night talking to each other.'

'The whole night?'

'Maybe not the whole night.'

'Because even though I said that I wasn't going to be the sort of man who'd sleep with a woman even if I knew...'

'I'm not here for sleeping...'

'Did you still want to...'

'If you do...'

'Then why aren't you kissing me?' Charles demanded, holding out his arms.

They didn't stop kissing all the way down the hall to Charles's bedroom. Sophy had a vague glimpse of black walls, white floorboards, an elegantly shabby Persian rug, as Charles lowered her onto his bed, and followed her down.

They were still kissing as they undressed each other with impatient hands, then caressed each millimetre of skin uncovered as if they had all the time in the world.

They only stopped kissing for long enough for Charles to murmur against Sophy's mouth, 'Are you sure about this?'

'Never been more sure of anything,' Sophy said and it was the absolute truth.

She'd agonised over and tried to swerve every life-changing decision she'd ever made but this here, now, felt so right.

Sophy had always thought of sex as an act. Something that usually lasted half an hour, tops. But this, with Charles, was making love. There was no beginning, no end, and Sophy couldn't help but wonder why she was leaving the next day because now that she was in Charles's arms, she felt like she'd come home.

Chapter Thirty-Five

Sophy only closed her eyes for a second. Just a second. But she must have fallen asleep. They both must have done, because when she sat bolt upright, adrenalin suddenly coursing through her, Charles woke up with a start too.

'Go back to sleep,' he said, reaching out to stroke Sophy's shoulder. Just that one touch was enough to ignite all those delicious nerve endings, which had been slumbering. Sophy leaned in closer just for a moment, then wrenched herself away.

'Oh my God! What time is it? Where's my phone? Is it morning?' Every thought was worse than the last. She yanked the duvet off the bed to wrap round her as she retraced her steps to the hall, where she'd flung her handbag the night before.

'It's all right. It's not even six,' Charles said, following her out into the hall. He was in just his boxer shorts, all lean limbs, not that Sophy had a spare second to appreciate the view.

'It's not all right. Mum had this crazy notion that I needed to check in at eight thirty—'

'You can check in online.' Charles was at her side, his hands on Sophy's shoulders. 'Take deep breaths. It's going to be fine. It really is.'

'I can't check in online,' Sophy all but wailed. 'All my stuff is at home. I need to get back to Hendon and I still haven't finished my final packing...'

'But they have shops in Australia...'

'And I need to wash my hair!'

'Your hair's perfect,' Charles insisted, which was a lie because it currently looked as if it had dropped on Sophy's head from a great height. 'You need coffee.'

'I haven't got time for coffee,' Sophy said but she followed him to the kitchen, clutching her phone, which, when she switched it back, lit up and flashed and vibrated. 'My mum is going to kill me.'

'I think she'll probably give you a pass,' Charles said as he spooned ground coffee into his moka pot.

Sophy wasn't sure about that. Caroline answered her phone before the first ring had even ended. 'You've really gone and done it, young lady,' she screeched.

'I'm so sorry, Mum. Time just got away with me.' Sophy pulled a face and Charles, on his way past so she could have some privacy, patted her on the shoulder.

'Where are you?' Caroline demanded. 'Are you on your way home?'

'I'm in Bloomsbury.'

'What the *hell* are you doing in Bloomsbury?' Caroline hissed through her teeth. 'Really? Doing things with your fancy man was more important than coming home and packing?'

'He's not my fancy man,' Sophy said and the situation was so awful that she actually felt like giggling because Charles was a man and he was very fancy.

'You were thinking of just going to Australia in the clothes that you're standing up in? You don't even have your passport, Sophy! Have you taken complete leave of your senses?'

'I really think I have. I don't know what's wrong with me,' Sophy admitted, but there was no reply, just a muttered exchange, then her mother was replaced with Mike.

'OK, here's what we're going to do,' he said calmly because Mike was absolutely who you wanted in a crisis.

339

'You're going to go to Heathrow, I'll send you the details of which terminal, and we'll meet you there with your luggage.'

'I'm so sorry, Mike…'

'Well, if you ever come back from Australia, you're totally grounded,' he deadpanned. 'And if anyone asks you who packed your suitcase, then you're going to have to lie and pretend that you did it all by yourself. It's fine. Just as well that we did so many practice packing dry runs.'

'No need to thank me!' Caroline shouted in the background.

'I am very thankful,' Sophy said. She arranged to meet them at nine, then hung up to see Charles standing in the doorway just as the moka pot started bubbling on the stovetop. 'It's all sorted. I'm going to meet them at the airport.'

'I could come with you if you like,' Charles said casually.

Sophy did like but she didn't want their last goodbye to be hurried and harried and with Caroline glowering in the background. She didn't want to say goodbye at all.

'If you tell me not to go, then I won't,' she heard herself say as Charles turned to look at her as if she'd just spewed ectoplasm from her ears. 'If you want me to, I'll stay.'

Charles sighed. Then he stopped fiddling with his tiny espresso cups so he could pull out the stool next to Sophy's and sit down. 'I do want you to stay,' he said. 'I want it more than anything.'

Relief and disappointment, equal measures of both, washed over Sophy. 'So that's that then.'

'But you're going to Australia, Sophy,' he said, taking her hand in his. 'You're going to have adventures, you're going to fall in love with the family that you've never met, you might even end up shearing a sheep…'

'I don't want to shear a sheep,' she mumbled, trying to bite back the sobs. 'I want to go, but I want to stay. I don't know what I want.'

'Then I'm deciding for you because we both know that it's better to regret something that you did do than something you didn't do,' Charles said, his gaze fixed unwaveringly on her face.

Sophy squeezed his fingers. 'What if I regret *not* staying?'

He rolled his eyes. 'You'd still regret *not* going. And if you come back, and you're under no obligation to do so, then I'll be here. I have no plans to be anywhere else.'

'Then I am going?'

Charles pressed a kiss to her forehead, then got up to fix the coffee. 'Are you asking me or are you telling me?'

'I'm going,' Sophy muttered, more to herself to see how the words sounded. To get used to the idea. 'Yeah, I am. I'm going.'

'Good,' Charles said, because he really was the best; the fanciest of men. 'Right, so here's coffee. Is there anything else I can get you?'

'No, nothing. This is just perfect,' Sophy said because she had coffee and she had Charles sitting next to her again and she couldn't think of anything else she wanted for the next fifteen minutes.

Except... 'Actually, I need shampoo and conditioner. And Charles, you don't have a single open pore so I know that you must have a highly effective face mask around here somewhere.'

Chapter Thirty-Six

Charles came with Sophy as far as Paddington. Her hair was still wet and she was wearing one of his t-shirts (though Sophy was amazed that Charles had anything as run-of-the-mill as a t-shirt) because she didn't want to check in wearing a t-shirt with pasta sauce splattered on it that looked a little like blood and get put on a no-fly list.

She was also grateful that Caroline had texted to say,

I've put clean knickers in your hand luggage, you dirty stop-out!

Plus several of the lady-holding-up-her-hands-in-despair emoji, so Sophy guessed she was almost forgiven.

'I will see you again,' Sophy told Charles as they waited for the next Heathrow Express train to be announced. It wasn't just to make him feel better; it was also a promise to herself. 'And until then we'll FaceTime and WhatsApp and Zoom. Even Skype.'

'We will.' Charles nodded gravely. 'But not too much, because I want you to have adventures and new experiences without worrying that we agreed to FaceTime while you're currently mid-bungee jump.'

'I'm absolutely open to new adventures but not bungee jumping. Never bungee jumping,' Sophy said, as she eyed the departure boards to see that the Heathrow Express was now waiting for people to board. 'But we'll keep in touch, unless you fall in love with some impossibly elegant French fashion editor who dresses exclusively in Dior. Then I won't stand in your way.'

Sophy was only half joking, or, more accurately, a quarter joking. If Charles fell in love with anyone, she'd be devastated. He seemed to understand that because he pulled her close again and kissed the top of her head.

'And if you fall in love with a ranch-hand or an actor from *Neighbours* then absolutely go for it,' Charles said so Sophy was still half laughing, half crying as she leaned in for one final kiss before she boarded her train.

She got to Heathrow at eight twenty but of course, of course! Caroline and Mike were already waiting for her and had already checked her in online, so they could all have slept a bit more and got there for ten.

Not that Sophy was going to point that out. She suffered a ten-minute tongue-lashing from her mother, which she absolutely deserved, then it was time for one last breakfast together.

'You are the most annoying girl,' Caroline said as they were lingering over coffee. 'It's a wonder that I'm not completely grey.'

'I've said that I'm sorry. I am *really* sorry,' Sophy said again.

'But I adore you and I'm going to miss you, and Soph, please, don't fall in love with an Australian,' Caroline said, clutching hold of Sophy's hand and putting it on her heart. 'I know they're very tanned and strapping, those surfers, but strapping isn't everything. Look at Mike.'

Sophy looked at long-suffering Mike, who wasn't strapping but was steadfast and kind and considerate as long as you didn't want to use his computer. 'You're going to look after Mum for me, aren't you?' she ordered him. 'Though without me around, you're going to be the one she gets aggy with.'

'What's that meant to mean, young lady?'

Mike smiled. 'I'm counting on it.'

It was Mike who stepped in at passport control and finally led a weeping Caroline away so that Sophy could go through to the other side.

The point of no return.

Stepping through the security barrier to pick up her hand-bag and put her shoes back on felt weighed down with significance. Sophy couldn't help but feel sad. But she decided that she was allowed to feel sad. Then, when she got to Kuala Lumpur for the changeover, she'd allow herself to start feeling excited. Also a bit panicked about the final leg of her journey. A five-hour two-bus ride from Adelaide to that small coastal town with the fibreglass shrimp. Then a taxi to take her to the sheep station and hope that Bob and Jean would be delighted to see her. But Sophy would worry about all that on the plane from Kuala Lumpur to Adelaide.

Normally she loved the downtime in an airport before her gate was called. Loved stocking up on magazines and spritzing herself with perfume she couldn't afford in the duty free, but this morning she was happy to find somewhere quiet to sit so she could go through every message on her phone that Charles had ever sent her. Including the very last one, which had arrived five minutes earlier.

Missing you already. Now go off and have some fun! x

It wasn't long before her gate was called. There was just time for one last wee on British soil, then Sophy was making her way along the motorised walkways, jittery with nerves and stopping every now and again to make sure that her passport and her boarding pass hadn't mysteriously disappeared since the last time she checked them.

When she got to the gate, she could see the sleek nose of the plane that would carry her away. There was already a queue of people waiting to board but Sophy sat down and it couldn't do any harm to make sure that her passport and her boarding—

'Fancy some company, love?'

With a deep inward sigh, Sophy looked up, all ready to tell whoever it was to hop it and hope that they weren't assigned the seat next to her—

'Johnno! What the actual hell? Am I seeing things?'

She blinked but he was still here. Johnno, with a massive backpack that he must have sweet-talked someone into letting him have as hand luggage, grinning down at her.

'Surprise!'

Sophy stared at him. 'Again. What the hell?'

'You know I've been talking to the folks.' Johnno shrugged off his backpack, which was almost the same size as he was. 'Decided that I'd go over to help too.' He puffed out his chest. 'I used to be able to shear a sheep in less than two minutes. You don't lose a talent like that, Soph.'

'But it's not even shearing season and the idea of *you* on a sheep farm…'

'It's more of a station than a farm, love,' Johnno reminded her as he sat down and stretched out his legs.

Sophy prodded him with one finger, just to check he was real. 'What are you going to do with the shop?'

Johnno shrugged again. 'That's what Freddy's there for and you'll be back in a few months, won't you?'

'But I might be emigrating. I just don't know. What if Jean's new hips don't work?'

'Let's see where you are after six months,' Johnno advised. 'A lot can happen in six months. Look what's happened in the last six months.'

Sophy rested her head on his shoulder and certainly six months ago she hadn't felt this rush of affection for her dad. 'We found each other, that's been a real highlight.'

Then again, she hadn't been in love this time six months ago.

'Better than meeting Charles?' Johnno asked slyly as if he could read her mind. Then he yelped when Sophy smacked him.

'I thought you didn't know about me and Charles.'

'Soph, love, *everyone* knows about you and Charles.' Johnno put an arm round Sophy's shoulders. 'He's a good bloke, you won't find a better one.'

Sophy sniffed even though she'd promised herself she wouldn't cry today. 'I know.'

'So you'll come to Oz long enough to help out, take in some sights, spend time with the fam and then decide if you want to stay on or come home.' It was Johnno's turn to prod Sophy. 'Why do you think I got you an open-ended return?'

'You are *so* annoying,' Sophy said, straightening up so she could fold her arms. 'An absolute pain in the arse.'

'Ah, you wouldn't have me any other way,' Johnno said and he was right. 'Now, do you reckon they'll have the new James Bond film on the plane? I can never sleep on planes. There's never enough room and it's not like I'm the tallest bloke in the world either but...'

It was then that Sophy realised what she was in for. They weren't even on the plane yet and Johnno was already manspreading. 'You're going to talk all the way to Adelaide, aren't you?'

Johnno grinned. 'You can count on it, love.'

Sophy grinned back. 'I'm going to go and see if I can change seats,' she said, though she made no move to get up and fling herself on the mercy of the boarding staff.

'So, Soph, do you want the window or the aisle seat?' Johnno asked, stretching out his legs just a little bit more. 'I prefer the aisle seat but don't you worry about your old man. I'll let you choose.'

Epilogue

One year later

It was almost a year to the day and Sophy was back at Heathrow Airport, about to walk through the nothing-to-declare channel this time.

What a twelve months it had been!

Sophy had a suntan for the first time in her life because it turned out that a warm Mediterranean climate was quite different to a cold British summer when it was only properly hot for a week. First she'd freckled. Then her freckles had joined up. Then she had a tan.

She'd tried shrimp and kangaroo meat but much preferred the shrimp. She was addicted to double-chocolate TimTams. And she'd been devastated to discover how hard it was to find pork sausage or a proper rasher of bacon in the whole of South Australia.

She'd done things that she'd never dreamed that she'd be capable of. Been bush-walking, even if only for a couple of hours. Had come face to face with a snake and hadn't got bitten or, more importantly, wet herself. And, even though it hadn't quite been shearing season, Sophy had only gone and bloody well sheared a sheep. Neither sheep nor Sophy had shed a single drop of blood.

While Jean was recovering from her operation, Sophy had taken over the guest cottage side of the business and cooked Sunday dinner for thirty people. She'd even learned to do hospital corners when she made up the beds because Jean used to be a nurse and she had quite exacting standards.

Maybe the best thing about Australia had been meeting Bob and Jean. After a couple of days to acclimatise and get over the jet lag, Sophy had felt as if she'd known both of them her whole life, and wished that she really had. The three of them had instantly fallen into an affectionate, gently teasing rapport that helped with her homesickness.

After Jean had got used to having two working hips again, she and Bob had celebrated their golden wedding anniversary and Sophy had met more family than she'd ever imagined. A gazillion cousins and first cousins once removed and second cousins that she didn't even know she had.

Then she'd flown to Sydney to be reunited with Radha, a week before her friend's wedding. The other bridesmaids had welcomed Sophy with open arms, her dress, thank goodness, had fitted, and she'd cried her make-up off as she'd watched Radha and Patrick's choreographed first dance to ABBA's 'Fernando'.

Sophy had planned to travel to Melbourne to meet up with the gazillion new cousins, but while she was in Sydney a room had come up in a houseshare with two of the other bridesmaids, Kate and Jedda. Then she'd found a job in, of all places, a vintage shop called Clive's Closet. The owner, Clive, had treated Sophy as if she was some kind of vintage fashion oracle, which had made a very nice change from the way Phoebe had used to treat her.

Then it was back to the sheep station for Sophy's longed-for Christmas on the beach with shrimp on the barbie and most of her Melbourne cousins flying in again to celebrate with her. Then back to Sydney and the life that she'd somehow created for herself.

It had been a glorious twelve months full of adventure and new experiences, laughter and some serious hard work.

Lots of spectacular Sydney sunrises and sunsets, though Sophy's hair had never settled into tousled beachy waves. She'd even met a really nice guy called Rob in a bar in Bondi, though everyone called him Robbo, but really nice just didn't cut it any more. Not when she thought about Charles, which she did all the time, or saw his beautiful but tired face filling up her phone screen. Because of the time difference, one of them was always getting ready to go to work when the other one was getting ready to go to bed.

As time went on and it was summer even though it was meant to be winter, Sophy's homesickness returned full force. How she yearned for those grey colourless London skies. And drizzle. She missed drizzle! Sophy thought a lot about staring out over the Regent's Canal as she drank her morning coffee because, strangely, she was even missing The Vintage Dress Shop. She'd cleared South Australia out of all its vintage dresses, which were now in a packing crate making its slow way to Primrose Hill although Phoebe had emailed to say that they probably wouldn't be up to snuff but she'd do Sophy a favour and at least have a look at them.

Sophy had decided to leave it to Freddy to break the news to Phoebe that she was coming back to work in The Vintage Dress Shop. Just until she found something else.

While Sophy might not miss Phoebe, not even a little bit, there were plenty of other people she missed. Cress, of course. Not having Cress with her was like not having a full set of fingers and toes. She missed her mum and Mike, she even missed them telling her off because Bob and Jean had been so delighted with Sophy that they never told her off. Not even when she'd driven straight into a gatepost the first time she'd borrowed their car.

Then there was Charles. Every night she slept in the t-shirt he'd lent her, though it didn't smell like him and she'd never even seen him in a t-shirt. She missed his suits.

His Liberty print shirts. The way he made the names of precious stones and fashion designers sound like poetry. Missed the soft, tender expression on his face after they kissed. She missed the very essence of him.

But mostly, she just missed everything that she'd been so desperate to escape.

'It's time for you to go home now, Soph,' Johnno had decided when he'd come to visit her in Sydney and found her watching an old episode of *EastEnders* one evening and crying. She didn't have it in her to make even a token protest.

A month later, after one final stay at the sheep station, Bob and Jean drove her to Adelaide airport and Sophy cried again when it was time to go through passport control.

'You've turned us all into whinging Poms,' Jean said, her own voice thick with tears, as she hugged Sophy one last time. 'We'll see you soon, love. The world's not that big.'

Bob said, 'Are you sure that you don't want to take Johnno back with you?' and looked genuinely devastated when Sophy said that they were stuck with him.

Australia had been a once-in-a-lifetime experience and Sophy was forever changed, but when the woman who stamped her passport at Heathrow Airport said, 'Welcome home', it was the truth.

It was so good to be back in London. When Sophy had checked the weather there on the second leg of her flight, even though it was May she was promised grey, colourless skies and a persistent drizzle.

Mike and Caroline had said they'd pick her up. A kind and simple enough task though of course it had involved timings, factoring in the possible late arrival of her plane, the cost of the short-stay car park and whether Sophy would need sandwiches and a cup of tea immediately or could she wait until they got home? Sophy was pretty sure that A Spreadsheet had been created.

As she wheeled her trolley into the arrivals lounge, she couldn't wait to see Caroline's worried face. Of course, the worry would melt away as soon as Sophy was in her arms while Mike muttered about how many minutes they had left on their parking.

Sophy scanned the throng of people waiting for their loved ones to emerge. She couldn't see Caroline and Mike anywhere, even though it wasn't like them to be late.

No, she couldn't see her mother – but she could see a tall man in a beautiful tweed suit with a pink fleck and a pink shirt to match.

Sophy knew it was Charles even though she couldn't see his face because it was obscured by a large sign that read, *The Most Beautiful Woman In The World*. As she wheeled her trolley closer, her heart was pounding away like the cannons in 'The 1812 Overture'. Charles lowered the sign. No one had ever looked so pleased to see her.

She headed straight for him, not caring who she mowed down in the process, until she was standing right in front of him. He was all she could see.

'Ah, there you are!' Charles said, as if it had been no time at all since they last saw each other.

'How did you know?' Sophy asked, blinking rapidly because she wasn't sure if he was an apparition or if she was about to burst into tears. 'I wanted to surprise you.'

Charles shrugged. 'Johnno,' he said and didn't have to say any more, other than, 'God, I've missed you.'

Sophy had planned this moment the whole year that she'd been away. In all the different scenarios she'd imagined, she'd been wearing a becoming vintage dress and red lipstick and had had a decent night's sleep.

Never had Sophy considered that she might be wearing baggy trackie bottoms, a t-shirt that said *Sheep happens* and one of Bob's ancient, holey cardigans. Her hair was

351

a static mess and she was sure she reeked of eau de aeroplane.

'I missed you too,' she said, her voice catching. 'Missed you so much, but I wanted this to be perfect.'

'You're finally standing in front of me again.' Charles cupped her cheek with a gentle touch. 'It doesn't get more perfect than that.'

Then he kissed her.

And that was perfect too.

Acknowledgements

A thousand and one thank yous to Rebecca Ritchie, Euan Thorneycroft, Alexandra McNicoll, Tabatha Leggett, Jack Sargeant and all at A.M.Heath. Olivia Barber, Kimberley Atkins, Katy Blott, Emily Goulding, Rachel Southey, Sarah Christie and the team at Hodder & Stoughton, I am very lucky to have them.

An invitation from the publisher

Join us at www.hodder.co.uk, or follow us
on Twitter @hodderbooks to be a part of
our community of people who love the very
best in books and reading.

Whether you want to discover more about a book
or an author, watch trailers and interviews, have the
chance to win early limited editions, or simply browse
our expert readers' selection of the very best books,
we think you'll find what you're looking for.

And if you don't, that's the place to tell us what's missing.

We love what we do, and we'd love you to be a part of it.

www.hodder.co.uk

@hodderbooks

HodderBooks

HodderBooks